THE ENEMY OF MY ENEMY

THE ENEMY OF MY ENEMY

Brainrush 2

RICHARD BARD

Text copyright © 2011 Richard Bard
All rights reserved.
Printed in the United States of America.

Published by Thomas & Mercer
P.O. Box 400818
Las Vegas, NV 89140

ISBN-13: 9781611098037
ISBN-10: 1611098033

Library of Congress Control Number: 2012916521

For my sister, who uses a smile to

push through adversity.

Part I

Chapter 1

J AKE SUSPECTED HE WAS ABOUT TO SIGN HIS OWN DEATH warrant.

"You want to run that by me again?" he said, hoping to buy a few precious minutes. He edged back on the stick to put the open-cockpit Pitts Special aerobatic biplane into a shallow climb. Their altitude needed to be at least three thousand feet AGL—above ground level—if he was to have any chance of surviving the desperate maneuver. Using one of the rearview mirrors mounted on the side of the cowling, Jake watched the passenger seated behind him. The man's image vibrated in harmony with the engine's RPM.

"You heard me, Mr. Bronson." The first-time student held up a cigarette-pack-size transmitter that had two protruding toggle switches and a short antenna. He peeled open his jacket to reveal a vest lined with thin panels of plastic explosives.

"I throw the switch and"—he paused, his eyes vacant—"paradise." His lips curved up in a smile. "I'm ready to meet Allah. Are you?"

The vintage leather helmet that was Jake's trademark style statement blunted the sound of the wind rushing up and over the windscreen, but the menace in the guy's tone came through loud and clear on his headset. Jake inched the throttle forward, steepening the climb, passing through twelve hundred feet.

The hawk-faced man in the backseat was in his early twenties. He'd ambled into the flight training school like a young cowboy walking into a Texas bar, wearing boots, hat, and a drawl to match. When he insisted on "the wildest ride ever," the head flight instructor had turned to Jake with a smile and said, "He's all yours." The newbie had been filled with a wide-eyed enthusiasm that Jake found infectious. It reminded him of his own excitement over a decade ago when he'd gone on his first acro flight in a T-37 during air force pilot training.

But the endearing Southern drawl was gone now and the man allowed his natural Dari accent to accompany his words.

"I'm not a fool, Mr. Bronson," he said, apparently looking at the altimeter in the rear cockpit. "Regardless of how high you take us, we shall both die. Your fate was sealed four months ago when you blew up my village. Ninety men from my tribe died in the blast. My friends, my brothers."

Jake grimaced at the reminder. His actions had sparked the explosion that brought the mountain down on the terrorist village. He deeply regretted the loss of life, but given the choices he faced at the time, there'd been no alternative.

The man sat taller in the seat and a tinge of pride crept into his voice. "I am Mir Tariq Rahman, and it is profoundly fitting that the enhancements to the brain implant I received—largely as a result of what our scientists learned studying *you*—shall become your undoing. My newfound talents made it so very simple for me to get past airport security and immigration. I've walked freely through your malls and amusement parks, attended baseball games, and eaten popcorn at the movies. I purchased a car and rented an apartment. I infiltrated your decadent society and remained above suspicion while I watched you and those close to you. Planning…dreaming of this moment."

The revelation jolted Jake. The last of the implant subjects was supposed to be dead. News reports had confirmed it. There had been a desperate shootout with US immigration officials as the three jihadists attempted to enter the country through Canada. The evidence had been compelling, right down to the implants found in their skulls. The news had come as a blessing since each of those men had deep-seated reasons for wanting to see Jake and his friends dead. At the time, Jake had discounted a gut feeling that it had all seemed too good to be true.

If he lived through the next few minutes, he swore he'd never make that mistake again.

As if reading Jake's mind, the man said, "You believed we were all dead, yes?"

"I read the reports."

"Of course." He sounded amused. "The sheikh's final three subjects, killed at the border. One careless mistake and they are gone. At least that's what authorities were led to believe." His tone turned contemplative. "The three martyrs chosen for the deception died with honor. They served a divine purpose under Allah's plan. As do we all."

Jake centered the man's face in the small mirror. It was difficult to judge the expression behind the helmet and goggles, but there was no mistaking the determined clench of the jaw or the satisfied smile. This was a man not just ready to die; he was anxious to die. Thank God it's happening up here, Jake thought, away from my friends. He banked the wings westward to angle the plane past the crowded beaches eighteen hundred feet below.

"I wouldn't turn just yet," the man said with an unnerving calmness. "There's something you're going to want to see first."

Anxious to keep the guy talking, Jake switched to Dari. "Why should I even listen to you?" He spoke in a dialect that matched that of his assailant's tribe. He'd learned to speak the difficult language in less than a week following the freak accident that had transformed his brain into an information sponge. "If I'm going to die anyway, it's going to be on my terms." He steepened the bank westward toward the ocean.

"You are more predictable than you are observant, Mr. Bronson." Tariq held up the device, pointing at the switches. "Aren't you the least bit interested to learn why there are two toggles?"

Jake tensed. His mind raced through a myriad of possibilities, none of them good. He leveled the wings and edged the throttles forward. He needed to gather as much speed as possible as he continued their steady climb.

"That's better," Tariq said. "Steer a heading of zero-one-zero."

Jake checked his instruments. The new heading would take them over the Palos Verdes Peninsula.

Ocean on three sides. That would work.

He complied, adjusting their heading, passing through 2,200 feet.

"Okay," Jake said. "Tell me about the second switch." He watched as his passenger leaned over the port edge of the cockpit, as if looking for something down below.

"There!" Tariq pointed to a bend in the shoreline ahead.

Jake banked the aircraft to get a look. It took him only a second to realize he was over Malaga Cove.

Francesca's school.

Tariq held up the transmitter, his thumb hovering over the second button. "Now it's your turn to pay."

Instinct took over.

Though Jake knew he was still too low for the maneuver, he didn't hesitate. Slamming forward the throttle, he dumped the nose and yanked the Pitts into an eighty-degree power spiral.

Chapter 2

Hathaway Middle School
Malaga Cove, California

FRANCESCA KNEW HOW IMPORTANT ROUTINE AND STRUC-
ture were to her autistic students. Children who understand
the behavior expected of them are less anxious, especially when
they're given schedules and visual reminders as they need to
move on to the next task or activity.

It was story time. She read aloud from *The Adventures of
Tom Sawyer*—the chapter where young Tom and Becky found
themselves hopelessly lost in the caves. She sat on the floor with
her legs tucked to one side under the spread of her full-length
knit skirt, her thick auburn hair spilling onto an olive cashmere
sweater. The book was in her lap. Her soft Italian accent caressed
each word of the story, punctuating the growing sense of danger
in the scene.

*"Under the roof vast knots of bats had packed themselves
together, thousands in a bunch; the lights disturbed the creatures
and they came flocking down by hundreds, squeaking and darting
furiously at the candles..."*

Ranging between the ages of seven and ten, the children
were captivated by her words. They sat in a semicircle within the
designated "imagination zone" at the back of the classroom, each
on a different-colored pillow. A Mickey Mouse clock on a stool

7

next to Francesca allowed them to count down the time until the session was over.

Francesca glanced up to absorb their reaction to the story. She cherished her time with these marvelous children. Her graduate education in child psychology and a natural empathic ability helped her guide them through the challenges they faced.

Unlike most children suffering from autism or other spectral disorders, these children had joined Francesca's unique class because they were exceptionally gifted in some way. Nature had provided a unique balance in each of them, replacing their lost interactive social skills with a genius-level talent. Three of the children were amazing artists, two with oil and the other with pen and ink. The images they created were astoundingly lifelike. Another had a remarkable affinity for memory and numbers, able to perform complex mathematical calculations in his head in a matter of seconds. Two of the children were natural musicians, including seven-year-old Sarafina, who could simultaneously compose and play masterful music on the piano, each score reflective of her mood at the time.

Francesca loved each for his or her indomitable spirit.

A nine-year-old boy seated on a plush green pillow raised his hand. He wore an Indiana Jones T-shirt over baggy jeans and sneakers. An unruly mop of blond hair and oversize dark sunglasses covered much of his cherubic face, but twin dimples at the corners of his generous lips hinted of mischief. A golden retriever with a guide-dog harness was sprawled on the floor next to him. As the boy's hand came up, the dog immediately raised his head.

Francesca glanced at the clock. She smiled when she confirmed that story time had ended exactly when Josh put up his hand. Though he was blind, his internal clock was every bit as accurate as any expensive timepiece. "Yes, Josh?"

"Miss Fellini, why can't Tom and Becky just walk out of the caves the same way they came in?"

"That's a good question," Francesca said. "Apparently they couldn't remember all the turns they made."

Josh's face screwed up into a question mark.

Francesca shared a knowing smile with the teaching assistant seated behind the group. "Well, Josh," the man said. The children turned his way as he spoke. "Not everyone has a memory like yours. Most people would find it very difficult to keep track of *every* turn."

Bradley Springfield dwarfed the tiny wooden desk chair he sat on. He was in his late twenties, two inches over six feet tall, and had the trim body of an avid cyclist. The rich tan of his skin and a jaguarlike grace reminded Francesca of the star soccer players from her home in Italy. He wore light Dockers, a button-down white shirt with rolled-up sleeves, and an Ohio State baseball cap he never took off. The children adored him.

Josh scratched his chin as he considered Bradley's comment. Finally he said, "Then they shouldn't have gone in the cave in the first place."

"I can't argue with that, big guy."

"Well, I can!" Sarafina said in a voice that came out much louder than she intended. When everyone turned her way, she immediately dipped her head forward so that her dark shoulder-length hair hid most of her face. The fingers of one hand danced unconsciously on her lap, playing an unheard melody on an imaginary keyboard. She wore a pink sundress and sandals sprinkled with sparkles.

She peeked up tentatively with a pleading expression that accented her big brown eyes. "I...I mean, sometimes when you're on an adventure, you have to take chances, right? Otherwise it wouldn't be a real adventure."

Francesca knew Sarafina was drawing on memories of her own recent escapades—the painful portions of which she'd learned to bury in the past few months. She'd met the girl three years ago at the Institute for Advanced Brain Studies in Venice,

Italy, after Sarafina's parents had been killed in a car accident. Francesca had been a teacher at the institute, specializing in children with mental and emotional challenges. She'd cherished the position—until she discovered that the institute was a cover for an international terrorist organization.

When she and Sarafina were taken hostage and held in the caves of the Hindu Kush mountains, it was the courage of Jake and his friends that helped them narrowly escape with their lives. After the institute was closed down, the child was alone, and Francesca was determined to protect her. But Italian law prohibited adoption by a single parent, so she acquired the help of a local magistrate—a long-term family friend—and was appointed Sarafina's guardian. The friend helped Francesca secure the documents necessary to allow them to travel to the United States.

"You make a good point, *cara*," she said. "But you shouldn't take risks that could end up getting you into—"

Francesca stopped when she heard the buzz of an aircraft outside.

It sounded like Jake's plane.

Chapter 3

WITH A FLOOD OF CONCENTRATION, JAKE SWEPT THE plane into a spiraling dive, thankful for the Pitts's exceptional control response and maneuvering abilities. The move loaded the airframe with over eight g's—a multiple of the force of gravity exerted on the body—pushing him and his passenger deep into their seats. After the first rotation, he held the turn steady at five g's.

Everyone had a different tolerance for how much his body could handle before losing consciousness. As a trained fighter pilot, Jake had developed a high tolerance, a factor he was gambling on now. The wannabe martyr in the backseat was great at mimicking a Texas cowboy, but his brain implant wasn't going to help him now.

Jake let out controlled grunts as he tightened the muscles in his torso and legs. This inhibited the pooling of blood in his lower extremities and delayed the loss of blood to his brain. In the end he knew it would be a losing battle. He'd have to ease off on the stick before he blacked out. He just needed to last longer than the man behind him.

Jake's eyes darted from the rapidly falling altimeter to the rearview mirror. Tariq's eyes bulged under his goggles. His facial skin sagged into his chin. His hands and arms were out of view.

They'd feel as if they each had hundred-pound weights attached to them. Jake hoped that the force would keep the man pinned down long enough.

He tightened the spiral. The ground spun more rapidly in the windscreen. Francesca's school was dead center beneath him. He didn't alter course. To do so meant reducing g's.

Passing through seven hundred feet.

The ground rushing up fast.

Jake's vision began to tunnel. He focused his mind on the school below and screamed a mental warning to Francesca.

There's a bomb at the school. Get out now!

* * *

Francesca wondered why Jake was flying so close to the school today. His regular flight-training area was on the other side of the peninsula.

There was a commotion outside. The distinctive sound of the buzzing Pitts grew louder, more urgent. Francesca felt a growing sense of alarm. She rushed to the open window. Josh's dog, Max, was at her side. Sarafina and several others scurried to join them. Josh beelined to his "safe place"—a large cardboard box on its side in a corner of the room. He curled up in the box's shadows and pressed his hands to his ears. Bradley moved to comfort him.

Outside, children scattered on the playground. A teacher shouted and pointed at the sky. Max barked. Francesca shielded her eyes from the sun with her palm and looked up. Jake's plane spiraled toward the ground at an incredible speed. Before the scream could escape her throat, Jake's urgent voice invaded her thoughts:

There's a bomb at the school.

She saw from the shocked expression on Sarafina's face that she'd heard it, too.

* * *

Jake sensed he wasn't going to make it. The ground was too close. Tariq's eyes had glazed over but he wasn't out yet. Jake needed another second or two. But time had run out.

Two hundred feet. No choice.

In one quick movement, Jake pushed the nose at the ground, leveled the wings, and yanked back on the stick. The accelerometer snapped to ten g's and the Pitts broke out of the dive barely thirty feet over the schoolyard. Jake caught a brief glimpse of children running across the playground before a welcome blue sky filled his windscreen.

In the mirror, Tariq's face paled, his eyes lolled, and his head slumped forward in his seat.

Jake pushed the throttles to the max. He put the Pitts into a high-speed climb toward the Pacific Ocean. He had to move fast. Tariq would regain consciousness in less than thirty seconds. He'd be disoriented for a minute or so, but that wouldn't prevent him from detonating the explosives strapped to his chest.

Or those he'd placed at the school.

At two thousand feet, Jake reduced power and trimmed the nose into a shallow dive toward the water. He unfastened his safety harness and headset, flipped a middle finger to the unconscious man in the backseat, and jumped out of the plane.

Chapter 4

Malaga Cove, California

THE ROUND CANOPY OF THE EMERGENCY CHUTE SNAPPED
open above him, jerking Jake from his tumbling free fall
into a controlled eighteen-feet-per-second descent. His pounding heart felt like it wanted to break out of his chest. For just a
moment, he felt a slight tingling in his left hand. His breath was
short. He sucked in deep lungfuls of air to calm himself. The
sensation passed.

The altimeter on his watch read fifteen hundred feet.
He was over the water but the breeze was pushing him back
toward the shore. In ninety seconds he'd be on the ground,
or at least in the breakers. Craning his neck over his shoulder, Jake watched as the Pitts descended toward the dark blue
water. The starboard wings of the biplane began a slow dip
as it lost trim. In another few seconds, the double wingtips
would strike the water and the plane would cartwheel to a gut-wrenching end.

Jake reached for the smart phone he usually kept in his
breast pocket. He came up empty-handed. The phone was still in
its cockpit holster on the plane. Too bad, he thought. The crash
would've made a great YouTube video. In any case, the violent
scene he was about to witness would be forever ingrained in his
brain. Like so many others.

Jake watched in fascination, counting down the seconds to impact. A small part of him would die with the loss of the Pitts, but *every* part of him was glad to say good riddance to the suicide bomber in the backseat—and the detonator that threatened to blow up the people he loved. He prayed that Francesca had heard his warning.

The Pitts was at eighty feet and dropping fast. The wings dipped farther.

Right...about...n—

The biplane's altitude shifted abruptly. The lower wingtips jerked upward. The whine of the three-bladed prop surged. The plane leveled off just above the undulating water. Every nerve in Jake's body seemed to fire off simultaneously. He jerked his head toward the approaching shore, willing himself to fall faster. Five hundred feet above the water. The school was nearly a mile away.

The drone of the plane behind him increased in pitch. Jake twisted in his harness to get a better look. The Pitts accelerated as it skimmed over the water. It was headed straight for him. It didn't take a genius to calculate that the plane would be on him before he completed his descent. He pulled down on the starboard riser, twisting to face the approaching plane. With both hands on the risers, he fought to maintain his position against the offshore wind.

At three seconds before impact, Jake was sixty feet over the water. The Pitts streaked straight at him.

Two seconds.

Now!

Jake dropped his hands and snapped open the chute's quick-release levers. He slipped out of the harness and fell like a stone.

Before he hit the water, Jake saw the Pitts veer sharply away from the collapsing chute. It headed directly toward Francesca's school.

* * *

Francesca knew better than to hesitate when she received Jake's mental warning. "Bradley," she said as she raced over and pulled the red fire alarm handle on the wall. "Get the kids out of the building now!" She grabbed her cell phone from the desk, punched in 9-1-1, and rushed into the hallway. Sarafina was at her side.

With the phone clasped to her ear, Francesca shoved open the door to the next classroom. The startled teacher and children were lined up at the window. "Quickly," Francesca shouted, her voice controlled but urgent. "Outside. *Now*. This is not a drill."

Before she could elaborate, the emergency operator came on the line. "Nine-one-one. State the nature of your emergency."

Francesca turned her back to the class. She cupped her hand over the phone. "I'm calling from the Hathaway Middle School. There's a bomb in the building. This is real. Get here fast!" She snapped the phone closed, took Sarafina by the hand, and ran to the next classroom.

* * *

Jake's head broke the surface of the water. He took a huge gasp of air, ripped off his leather helmet, kicked off his flight boots, and broke for the shoreline fifty yards away. He saw the Pitts circle toward the school.

Jake's brain kicked his muscles into afterburner. The crests of the breaking waves in front of him seemed to suddenly move in slow motion. Licks of foam reached upward like rising oil in a lava lamp. A pair of surfers sat on their boards, their mouths agape as Jake sliced through the water. It must have looked to them like a fast-forward video of Michael Phelps at the 2008 Summer Olympics.

Jake embraced the changes that had occurred to his brain. A freak accident during an earthquake had caused the MRI scanner he was in to go haywire and send him into a seizure, giving him incredible mental and physical capabilities afterward. One of the most shocking changes was the ability to move very fast for short periods of time, like the burst of strength a parent might find to lift a car to save their child; it seemed Jake was able to call upon that ability at will. The accident had also sent his terminal cancer into what he prayed was a permanent remission.

As soon as Jake's knees scraped the sand, he peeled off his soggy socks and charged toward the rocky escarpment that hugged the coastline. The incline was steep. He scrambled upward on all fours as sharp-edged rocks cut into his feet. He ignored the pain, but the swim to shore had sapped his reserves. His heart raced like a machine gun. He couldn't seem to draw enough air into his lungs to keep up with the demand for oxygen. A wave of dizziness assaulted him.

But he refused to slow. The ridgeline was just ahead. Jake pulled himself over the edge and pushed to his feet. He was at the edge of the hillside neighborhood that fronted the school. A quarter mile to go. He looked up at the plane circling over the school. Jake knew in his gut that Tariq was watching him. Taunting him.

He sprinted toward the road, his bleeding feet slapping painfully against the concrete. The wings of the Pitts wagged in the universal sign of acknowledgment.

Then it dipped from view.

A moment later there was a huge explosion over the ridge. From his vantage point, Jake could see only the top edge of the fireball that rose over the rooftops in front of him. Chunks of debris spewed into the sky.

"Noooo!" Jake screamed.

Chapter 5

Hathaway Middle School
Malaga Cove, California

THE CHILDREN HAD PRACTICED THE FIRE DRILL MANY times. By the time Francesca and Sarafina reached the third classroom, the rest of the doorways had opened. Children filed out just as they had been taught.

Once outside, Francesca urged the principal to escort the children into the street across from the school yard. Jake still circled the school above them in the Pitts. She dialed his number for the third time, wondering why he wouldn't pick up.

It was then that she noticed Josh was missing.

Per l'amor di Dio!

She took off running toward the school. Bradley caught up to her, grabbing her arm. "Where the hell are you going?"

"It's Josh. He's still inside!"

Bradley scanned the crowd of children across the street. Josh was not among them. A dog barked. Bradley turned to see Max rushing toward them from the school. The leather handle of his guide harness flopped against his back.

"Stay here!" Bradley shouted to Francesca. Once Max neared, Bradley grabbed Max's harness and handed it to Francesca. "Hold him."

Francesca knelt on the grass, her arm around Max's neck, and pulled him close. They were both shaking as they watched Bradley run across the school yard and disappear into the building.

Thirty seconds later, the building exploded. The blast wave knocked her on her back, sucking the wind from her lungs. She shielded her face as small bits of debris rained down around her. Max whimpered at her side and licked her face. She struggled to her feet, her ears ringing. The world was a blur. Max pressed against her, urging her away from the heat of the burning building. She staggered back toward the street and the crowd of stunned children and teachers.

Sarafina ran to her side. She wrapped her arms around Francesca's waist and Francesca could feel her little body trembling.

Francesca looked up at Jake's plane. It was lower now. She appealed to him with her mind: *We need you.* She hoped he could sense her thoughts. He'd been able to do that sometimes since the accident.

As if in response, the plane descended toward them. It appeared as if it was going to land. Children and teachers scattered to either side of the street.

When the plane touched down, Francesca and Sarafina ran toward it. The rest of the class followed.

* * *

Jake sped up the street toward the school. His brain screamed warnings. His body would give out any second. He ignored it by allowing images of Francesca to fill his mind. A wave of despair assaulted him. He had worried from the outset that a romantic relationship with her would put a target on her back. But in a moment of weakness—after their impossible escape from death at the hands of the terrorist Battista—he'd given in to his heart, to the joy in her eyes when she discovered he was alive, to the softness of her touch, her lips…He had woken the next morning steeped in guilt. Not because he didn't care about her, but because he realized she had become the lever that his enemies could use to cut him the deepest. Though she'd returned with Jake and his friends to California— needing desperately to leave the memories and potential threats of Venice behind her—Jake had kept her and Sarafina close enough to watch over. But not so close as to place them in danger.

Or so he had hoped.

Houses rushed past him. Startled neighbors came out of their homes and pointed to the smoke up ahead. He faltered when he saw the Pitts descend toward the school. He would have expected Tariq to use the opportunity to flee…

Unless something had gone wrong with Tariq's plan.

Unless the explosion had failed to kill Francesca and the children.

Jake pushed harder.

He was 150 yards away when he saw the plane touch down on the cliffside road abutting the school. Children scattered to clear a path as the plane slowed to a stop. Jake saw Francesca and her students pressing toward it. They were led by the barking golden retriever that he knew was Max.

They think it's me.

Everything seemed to slow. External sounds faded. Jake's aural senses filled with the solid thumps of his heart, each one stretched in time. His vision tunneled to the scene now one hundred yards before him. And getting closer.

Using the pop-out step on the side of the Pitts closest to the cliff, Tariq climbed down from the cockpit. He made his way toward the tail of the plane, his helmet still on. The detonator was in his hand.

Jake saw Max rush toward the terrorist, his tail wagging wildly in greeting. Francesca, Sarafina, and the rest of the children were less than twenty yards behind.

Jake tried to send a warning thought toward Francesca, but his brain wouldn't cooperate over the repeated alarms it received from his screaming heart.

Fifty yards to go.

Tariq rounded the tail of the plane.

Faster.

Max slid to a halt ten feet in front of the terrorist. His head cocked to one side, ears forward, and his tail straight back.

Tariq hesitated.

Max inched backward, body lowered, ears flat, hackles up. A low growl escaped his bared teeth. Francesca stopped abruptly behind him, her arms stretched to either side to prevent the children from running past.

Thirty yards.

Tariq's gaze fixed on Francesca and the children. He slowly raised his hand. The aluminum detonator glinted in the sun. His mouth stretched in a grin.

Jake leaped through the air, his inhuman speed eating up the final few yards in an instant. The tackle pushed Tariq off his feet. The detonator flew from his hand and skittered across the pavement. Shocked recognition spread across Tariq's face just before his lower back impacted the guardrail. His arms flailed, then he tumbled backward over the barrier and down the rocky slope.

Jake's shoulder hit the rail, and shock waves of pain radiated through his system. He collapsed to his knees on the pavement, his head spinning. His chest heaved as he gasped to gather oxygen into his lungs. He wanted to collapse, but there was one last thing he had to do. He crawled several feet, grabbed the detonator, and threw the switch.

The explosion echoed from the canyon below. Jake's sigh of relief was stifled by a sharp, agonizing pain in his chest.

The last thing he remembered was the odd sensation of a tongue licking his face.

Then nothing.

Chapter 6

THE MIDSIZE WAREHOUSE WAS INDISTINGUISHABLE FROM the dozens of others in the industrial zone between Alaska and Maple Avenues in Torrance. Situated just two blocks from the city center and police headquarters, the well-kept industrial district was home to high-tech manufacturing and service firms willing to pay a premium for the convenient low-crime location.

It had been a fairly simple matter for Abbas to acquire the stand-alone facility. The location at the end of a quiet dead-end street made it perfect for his needs. It had been all too easy to make the deal. As soon as the seller discovered it was an all-cash offer, he'd risen from the bargaining table and shaken the hand of the well-dressed businessman across from him.

These Americans have much to learn, thought Abbas. It will be my pleasure to teach them. He was perched on the second-floor balcony fronting his office that overlooked the factory floor. With his gray Brooks Brothers suit, groomed dark hair, and soft-spoken manner, he'd perfected his role as an educated owner of this high-tech start-up. He'd learned that appearances and mannerisms could be easily adopted to fool the most astute observer, even when the polished image belied the true nature of the man behind it.

He was proud of who he was beneath the disguise. His men had nicknamed him "The Lion" when he was a young man growing up in his mountain village in Afghanistan. The speed and agility of his wiry frame had earned him a reputation as a vicious and undefeated fighter, one both feared and admired. In those moments when he lowered his current facade, his eyes had been likened to those of a cobra ready to strike.

The short, sallow-faced man who stood beside him now didn't seem affected by Abbas's reputation, even as Abbas's knuckles whitened around the balcony rail. "Tariq was a fool!"

"Of that, there can be no doubt," the sixty-year-old Iraqi said with an irritating calmness. Kadir was no stranger to Abbas's outbursts. He wore a white lab coat over gray slacks and a collared blue shirt. Thick-framed glasses perched on a bulbous nose. His thinning silver hair was slicked back behind a high forehead, and his bifocal lenses made his seemingly lifeless eyes bulge to triple their size.

"I imagine, however, that you can relate to his motivations," Kadir said. He spoke like an American, with no trace of the guttural accent that had previously clouded his voice, a fact that Abbas resented. The sheikh had selected Kadir over him to receive one of the final brain implants, hoping to fuel the doctor's creative genius. The device had lived up to its promise, increasing Kadir's mental capacity by a factor of ten. In retrospect, Abbas could see that Kadir had been the logical choice for the implant, especially in light of the imaginative weapon the man had concocted since then. That he had also been able to perfect the colloquial language and mannerisms of an American was astounding. Abbas couldn't help but wonder what such a tool would have done for him.

"Damn Tariq's motivations," Abbas said, pounding his fists on the rail. "Had he killed the American, he could have jeopardized everything." Abbas narrowed his eyes at the older man. "And I would advise you to steer clear of further comments regarding my own motivations."

Kadir shrugged.

No one wanted to see Jake Bronson dead more than he did, Abbas thought. His hatred had intensified to a barely restrained fury following the death of his younger brother at the hands of the accursed infidel. That Carlo had died in a knife fight with the man had shocked Abbas. He'd mentored his brother in the way of the blade for years, passing on his own unequaled expertise. Only a trick of fate could have enabled Carlo to be defeated. The American would not be so lucky once his role in the sheikh's current plans was complete.

"The time will come," Kadir said. "Soon."

Kadir had a singular knack for cutting to the quick. The man seemed utterly devoid of emotion, whether he was eating his favorite food or devising another in a long string of bioweapons, the training for which he received as a young scientist under Saddam Hussein's former regime. Abbas imagined that Kadir would have appreciated the opportunity to set up a personal laboratory in one of the Nazi death camps seventy years ago. Bodies for testing his concoctions would have been so much easier to come by back then.

It came as no surprise to Abbas that their leader had placed them together on this latest project—Kadir to perfect the weapon and delivery system, and Abbas to provide leadership and security.

Abbas's English was good as well, though it came after years of training rather than a brain implant. He'd learned Spanish, too, as had most of the men who had trained for insertion into the infidels' nest. For all its claims as being one of the most secure nations in the world, the United States had yet to learn how to protect its borders from the masses of illegal immigrants slipping in from its southern border with Mexico. It had been easy to slip in among them.

Abbas disliked being here, surrounded by nonbelievers. He abhorred the decadence. He missed the easy rhythm of his homeland and the muezzin calling the faithful to prayer. But he would endure, as was his duty. From their second-floor perch, they watched as another batch of chemicals was wheeled into the freestanding clean room in the center of the warehouse. The men wore full protective garb, including white jumpsuits, hairnets, shoe covers, and masks.

The windows of the clean room were obscured, though Abbas could see the silhouettes of the men as they moved inside. A sign on the door read AUTHORIZED PERSONNEL ONLY. A visitor would never suspect that the policy was enforced by two men with AK-47s just inside the second set of doors. Others were stationed elsewhere in and around the building.

Abbas's encrypted cell phone chimed. He checked the caller ID and exchanged a glance with Kadir. The two men stepped into the privacy of Abbas's sparse office and closed the door. He pressed the SPEAKER button and set the phone on the desk between them. In Dari he said, "We are both here."

The voice on the line was stern, with a rasp that hinted at damaged vocal cords. "How did you let this happen?"

"It was Tariq," Abbas said. "I knew noth—"

"Excuses are beneath you. It was your duty to know."

There was a long pause. Abbas paced the room. He had absently pulled his switchblade from his pocket and was caressing its pearl handle in his palm. Kadir was steady, his face devoid of expression. Both men remained quiet.

"And Tariq?" the voice asked. "He is dead?"

"Yes," Abbas said. He flicked open the blade and flipped it in the air, catching it first in one hand and then the other. His eyes remained fixed on the phone. He waited as the man on the other end considered his options.

After a long moment, the raspy voice said, "Move up the timetable. Make immediate preparations. I'll be there tomorrow."

The line went dead.

Abbas's smile was feral. In a blur of movement, he hurled the knife at a scarred target on the wall of his office. The blade impacted with the force of a hammer. The loud crack caused Kadir to flinch. It sank deep into the underlying plywood backing, directly through the eyeball in the pitted photograph of Jake Bronson.

"At long last," Abbas said.

Chapter 7

Hathaway Middle School
Malaga Cove, California

FRANCESCA CRADLED JAKE'S LIMP HEAD IN HER LAP. HE LAY sprawled on the pavement beside the Pitts. "Please, God," she prayed as she rocked him back and forth. "Don't take him."

The stunned crowd of students and teachers stood in a semi-circle around her. Children sobbed in fear and confusion, clinging to the adults. Some of them nursed cuts and bruises. Sarafina knelt next to Francesca, her arms around Max's neck, her face buried in his golden coat.

The school burned in the distance behind them. Nearly two-thirds of it had been destroyed by the blast; flames licked at the remaining structure. Thick columns of smoke rose from the tangled mass, pushed away from the crowd by the offshore breeze. Debris littered the playground.

Emergency sirens echoed in the distance, still several minutes away from the remote location.

There was a commotion among the children. Bradley staggered through the crowd, holding Josh in his arms. Both of them were coated with a blotchy layer of dust and soot but appeared uninjured. Josh's hands were pressed to his ears. A shock of relief swept over Francesca.

"We went out the rear exit and slid down the ravine," Bradley said. "Josh handled it like a champ."

When Max saw his master, he swiveled from Sarafina's grasp and scurried to greet Josh. His tail beat rapidly against Bradley's pant leg, and the teaching assistant slid Josh down to the grass beside Max. He then rushed over to Francesca and placed his fingers against Jake's neck. With an authority that Francesca had never seen in him before, Bradley said, "Out of the way."

Francesca scooted clear, setting Jake's head on a rolled-up jacket.

Ripping open Jake's flight vest, Bradley immediately commenced CPR chest compressions. He looked over his shoulder and located the school principal. "Sandra," he shouted, "the portable defib—is it still in your car?"

The woman's eyes widened in understanding. "On my way!" She turned and ran for the parking lot.

"How long has he been out?" he asked Francesca.

"Two, maybe three minutes."

Continuing the compressions, Bradley muttered, "Brain damage begins at three or four minutes."

* * *

The sensation was pleasant, thought Jake, like floating on a cloud. There was activity around him, but for some reason his body refused to respond to any signals from his brain. His eyes wouldn't open and his limbs were nothing but a distant numbness. He realized he wasn't breathing. How odd. There was a repetitive irritation at his chest, but that was fading, too. There was no pain. External sounds were dissolving…

I'm dying.

A flush of sadness as images of those he cared about danced across his final thoughts. Francesca—I should have married her. Sarafina—so young, so innocent. His best friends Marshall, Tony, and L—

A jolt sent a burst of pins and needles through his consciousness.

"Clear!"

Jake's brain was still trying to compute what he'd just heard when a second jolt shot through his body. Pain enveloped his senses. His chest convulsed into a cough.

His eyes twitched open.

Bradley hovered above him, a defibrillator paddle in each hand. "We couldn't let you die just yet, Jake, now could we?"

Francesca leaned into view, her relief palpable. "*Dio mio*, I thought I lost you." She caressed his face.

Jake's mind cleared, and his body ached all over. Sarafina lunged and squeezed her arms around his waist. "Daddy!" she cried. Her real father was dead, and she'd started calling Jake her dad after the events in Venice and Afghanistan. He embraced it.

"My girls," Jake said, looking at them, knowing they'd been targeted because of him. "Don't worry," he said. "Everything's going to be okay."

The lie tasted bitter on his tongue.

Chapter 8

The mountains of Northern Nevada

THE TOP-SECRET UNDERGROUND FACILITY WAS SITUATED in a remote location in the mountains of Northern Nevada. It had been carved out of the remains of an abandoned gold mine nearly sixty years ago when fear of nuclear attack prompted the government to build blast shelters across the country. Several of the sites had been maintained and updated over the years, including this one. In a flurry of recent activity, the normally quiet site had been converted to a research facility. The few drab structures aboveground belied the fifty-five-thousand-square-foot space that existed one hundred feet below the surface.

Sole access to its depths was through a secured forty-foot-wide blast door, carved into the side of a rocky escarpment at the end of a natural canyon. The facility was home to two dozen scientists and technicians, each of whom had undergone extensive background checks. An elite US Air Force security team guarded the site.

"You're missing the point, Fester," the chief scientist, known as Doc, quipped to the USAF lieutenant colonel. "Area 51 is two hundred fifty miles south of here. It's received so much publicity over the past half century that no agency in its right mind would ever conduct serious research there. Conspiracy quacks have even established tent cities in the hills around the place, just hoping to catch a glimpse of the next alien encounter."

The sixty-year-old scientist scratched the salt-and-pepper beard that covered his face. His wavy silver hair spilled to just above the collar of his shirt. Beneath frameless spectacles, his light blue eyes twinkled as he ribbed his military counterpart.

"So, when the government set us up here, we decided to call it Area 52. Get it?"

"I don't like it," the new arrival announced. Lieutenant Colonel Patrick Brown stood ramrod straight on his five-foot-six frame, as if by doing so he might appear taller. For a man in his late forties, his muscles bulged impressively under his USAF dress uniform. He had a bald pate that shimmered under the banks of fluorescent lights. A pronounced brow shaded a pair of deep-set brown eyes that were permanently ringed by dark circles.

With tight lips, the lieutenant colonel added, "And if you ever call me Fester again, I'm gonna take that silly-lookin' pipe right outta your mouth and shove it—" He caught himself when he heard a muffled chuckle from one of the civilians seated at a high-tech computer console beside the two men. The lieutenant colonel threw the man a shriveling glare.

The offending young scientist snapped his attention back to his console. There were a dozen such stations in the cavernous space, six in each of two semicircular rows. They surrounded a ten-foot-wide, bell-jar-shaped steel enclosure that had been lowered from ceiling cables and electronically locked to thick fittings embedded in the concrete floor. The shroud encased the object of the research.

An intricate array of remote-controlled sensors and equipment within the housing allowed the scientists to study the object with what they hoped was a reduced risk of exposure. Blast-hardened windows embedded within the enclosure permitted direct viewing. An electronic polarizing shield sandwiched within the glass rendered it opaque for the moment. When necessary, the security "jar" could be raised by a select few authorized personnel using the proper authentication code. Without the code, the enclosure was impregnable.

"Sorry, Colonel," Doc said. "Just joshing you. Sort of a *welcome to the family*, that's all."

The lieutenant colonel mumbled something under his breath. He turned on his heel and made for the exit.

Men and women looked up from their stations as the lieutenant colonel departed. With a gleam in his eye, Doc pointed the stem of his pipe at the man's back, holding his other palm up in a mock attempt at hiding the gesture. To his audience of scientists and technicians, he silently mouthed, "Uncle Fester." There was a chorus of muffled laughter, as everyone present acknowledged Brown's uncanny resemblance to the character from *The Addams Family*.

Doc felt a tinge of guilt about ribbing his new head of security, but it wasn't ill intended. After years of experience, he'd learned not to take the military hard cases too seriously. Sure, they'd been trained to maintain their crusty exterior in the face of underlings and the enemy, but Doc believed that subjecting a group of research scientists to such an attitude was unproductive. It stifled the creative process. As far as he was concerned, his military counterparts needed to either lighten up or leave the room.

With a satisfied smile, he slid his favorite meerschaum pipe—with a hand-carved face of the wizard Gandalf the Grey— into the front pocket of his sweatshirt. Although Doc was never without it, no one had ever seen him smoke it.

Dr. Albert Finnegan had earned his PhD in astrophysics at Princeton by the unprecedented age of twenty-one. He'd risen quickly through the ranks of scientists in the nation's space program. Though his quirky manner had kept him out of a leadership role in the many renowned projects he'd participated in, those in the know credited his genius with the success of nearly every significant space exploration and discovery project funded by the US government in the past three decades.

Throughout his career, in the face of considerable criticism, Doc had steadfastly maintained his position that life existed on other planets. After the recent incident in Afghanistan, his long-time friend Alexander Jackson, who happened to be the president of the United States, had reluctantly agreed with him. Quirks or not, Jackson had asked Doc to take charge of what was known as the Obsidian Project.

Doc had jumped at the opportunity. He had told his family he'd be "gone quite awhile." He knew he'd be working on nothing less than the most important discovery in the planet's history.

Chapter 9

Hermosa Beach, California

Sam's Cyber Bar and Restaurant in Hermosa Beach had been Jake's favorite hangout ever since it opened. The eclectic gathering hole was known for its wide selection of beers on tap, good food, and touch screens at each table. The high-speed terminals allowed patrons to interact in real time with sports websites during games, ping other tables for a chat session, and win free drinks and T-shirts by participating in trivia contests after each sporting event. It was during one of those contests that Jake had discovered the magnitude of his new talents.

He now sat with his friends in a secluded second-floor booth overlooking the main bar. He leaned his arm over the balcony, losing himself in the crowd below. The family dinner patrons had thinned out, replaced by soccer fans anxious to see USA versus England in the FIFA World Cup. Baby back ribs and Caesar salads gave way to chips, salsa, and pitchers of beer. Jake caught a whiff of chili cheese fries as they floated past on a server's tray. Large flat-screen TVs positioned throughout the space were tuned to the pregame show. The twenty-five-foot bar was packed two deep. Classic rock and roll played beneath the din of laughter and boisterous conversation.

Francesca nudged closer to him. She looped her arm through his and squeezed his hand. He squeezed back and returned his attention to the group.

Tony sat across from Jake. The spread of his shoulders took up two spaces in the six-person booth. He wore a Yankees baseball cap turned backward over closely cropped hair. He was a member of the LAPD SWAT team, but Jake knew that underneath the crusty exterior, Tony was a dedicated family man who would do anything to help a buddy. Tony had used his experience as a former Special Forces sergeant to help rescue Jake after terrorists kidnapped him.

"So how're ya *really* feelin'?" Tony asked, his dark eyes trained on Jake. His New York accent peeked through as it usually did when he was concerned or agitated.

Jake's best friend Marshall sat next to Tony. His fingers froze in front of the table's touch screen as he looked up, waiting for Jake's reply.

Jake blew out a long sigh. He'd already told them he felt fine, and in most respects, that was true. The dizziness was gone, the cuts and bruises on his feet had been treated, and the son-of-a-bitch terrorist was dead. Yes, he'd had a minor heart attack, but it could happen to anybody, right? "Look, guys. The doctor gave me a clean bill of health. I just need to take it easy for a couple days, that's all."

"According to WebMD, you're anything but okay," Marshall said, swinging the display around so everyone could see it. Though there was never a lack of women who showed an interest in his boyish features, Marshall's genius was with computers, not the opposite sex—a point that Jake and Tony often ribbed him about. Marshall tapped the computer screen. "There's no such thing as a minor heart attack."

Jake smiled to himself. Leave it to Marshall to cut to the chase. But Jake had prepared himself for this line of questioning. Within an hour of leaving the emergency room, he'd memorized volumes of medical information regarding myocardial infarctions and coronary heart disease.

"You're right," Jake said, "and I'm not trying to shrug it off. But mine was caused by a coronary artery spasm rather than coronary artery disease. The doctors ran me through it all—EKG, treadmill, stress echocardiography—you name it." He rubbed at the bandage covering the entry wound on his neck where the doctor had inserted a catheter. "I even had an angiogram. All clear."

"A spasm, huh?" Tony asked.

"Yeah, kind of a freak thing."

"So what's to keep it from happenin' again?"

"Simple." Jake's crooked smile was back in place. "A good first step would be to keep terrorists away from my plane." He clinked his near-empty mug against Tony's and downed the rest of his beer.

Jake could tell from the expression on Tony's face that he wasn't buying it, but after a glance at Francesca, Tony dropped it. At least for now. He pasted a grin on his face, returned the toast, and chugged his drink.

Thanks, buddy.

"I just need to slow down a bit. That's all," Jake said, thinking there was more truth in that statement than they'd ever know. The doctor had been dumbfounded by the test results. In the simplest of terms, the doctor had explained that Jake had the heart of a ninety-year-old. Apparently, the repeated use of his super fast reflexes had taken a toll on Jake's heart. The doctor said if he pushed himself again, his heart would fail.

Jake noticed Lacey snaking her way from the bar below toward the staircase. He was surprised to see her expertly balancing a tray full of drinks over one shoulder. People at the tables on either side of her path seemed to stop talking as she glided past. Besides her shoulder-length blond hair, golden tan, and sparkling blue-green eyes, she also had a smile that could turn most men into blithering idiots. All except Marshall, that is, which is one of the reasons they'd become inseparable.

"I see you haven't lost your touch," Jake said as Lacey distributed the drinks around the table.

"Yeah, it's like riding a bike," Lacey said. She slid into the booth next to Francesca. "Two of Sammy's servers showed up late, so I thought I'd lend a hand with our drinks."

"Afraid the acting gig won't last?" Marshall quipped from across the table.

Jake looked at Lacey, waiting for the barrage he was sure she'd unleash.

Instead, her shoulders collapsed and her hands dropped to her lap. She tilted her head and her hair spilled forward to hide the sides of her face. Her lower lip quivered and a lone tear ran down her cheek.

Marshall reached both hands across the table. "Hey, I'm sorry."

Lacey wouldn't meet his eyes. A soft sob escaped.

Marshall slid out of the booth, knelt beside her, and wrapped an arm around her in a gentle embrace. "Lace, I'm really sorry. I didn't mean it. I was just messing around."

She peeked over Marshall's shoulder at the group. Her eyes twinkled as she smiled.

Tony burst out in a laugh. Jake and Francesca joined him.

Marshall pulled away. "You—"

"Don't say it, dude," Lacey said. "You deserved it. Still think I might have trouble keeping my acting gig?"

Jake admired the performance. After a constant string of auditions over the past three years while waiting tables to make ends meet, she'd finally landed a major role in a studio movie last month. It being an action flick came as no surprise to Jake. Not only had she played the role of her life when she and Jake's friends infiltrated the terrorists' cover organization in Venice, Italy, but in the desperate firefight that followed, her martial arts experience had saved Marshall's life.

"Okay, Jake," Tony said as Marshall made his way back to his side of the booth. "We're all here. Let's talk about what happened."

"What about Becker?" Jake asked.

"He's keeping an eye out downstairs."

Jake nodded. After rethinking the details of his encounter yesterday, he felt pretty sure that the risk had finally passed. The terrorist had been working alone, now he's dead, end of story. Nevertheless, a small part of Jake felt good knowing that the Australian was down below watching their back.

Jake recounted the event to his friends and left nothing out. Because of the dangers they faced as a result of their involvement in rescuing him from Luciano Battista and his followers, they deserved the entire truth.

When Jake finished, Tony said, "So d'ya really think it's over?"

"If there were more of them, wouldn't he have bragged about it, knowing he was about to die?"

"Who the hell knows?" Tony said. "The man was a suicide bomber. They live by a separate set of rules."

The comment fueled the spark of doubt that had taken residence in Jake's gut. He glanced downstairs. Becker was seated in the far corner.

Under wavy blond hair, the Aussie's blue eyes glimmered in stark contrast to his chocolate skin, darkened as much from the sun as his heritage. He'd served as Tony's right-hand man during the assault in Afghanistan. He was a demolition and specialized weapons expert, but it was his upbringing in the outback under the tutelage of his aboriginal grandfather that had taught him to sense beyond what was visible to the naked eye.

* * *

Becker's sixth sense told him something was off about the bloke seated at the far end of the bar. The Latino had barely touched the beer sitting in front of him. Though he was wearing a USA World Cup team jersey, he didn't pay much attention to any of the monitors. Instead, he was focused on the telephone conversation he was apparently having through the Bluetooth device attached to his ear.

Perhaps it was nothing, thought Becker. But he'd keep his eye on him.

The Latino nodded in response to the person on the phone. He swiveled and aimed the back of his cell at the balcony. Becker tensed.

He quickly pulled out his own phone and hit Tony's number on speed dial. "Sorry to spoil the party, mate. But we've got a bleedin' problem."

Chapter 10

Hermosa Beach, California

J AKE FORCED HIMSELF TO APPEAR CASUAL AS HE WALKED out of the bar's swinging front door at 11:00 p.m. Fog had rolled in from the ocean, moving across the street in wispy currents. It diffused the light from the streetlamps. He flinched when a parked Jeep across the street chirped and its lights flashed briefly. A young couple climbed in and pulled away from the curb. Jake blew out a sigh, then glanced left and right. The street was deserted for a couple blocks in either direction. He zipped up his windbreaker against the chill and started down the sidewalk, maintaining a steady but unhurried pace.

His nerves were stretched tighter than a bowstring. Francesca, Tony, Marshall, and Lacey should be making their way out the back entrance. If everything went according to plan, he'd see them later at the lodge. By then he hoped he'd have some answers.

After the first block, a glance at a reflection in a store window revealed the silhouette of the man who had stepped out of Sam's to follow him. Jake prayed that Becker was close at hand, though he knew he'd never spot him.

It didn't take long for the stranger to halve the distance behind Jake.

Jake crossed the boulevard and headed toward the deserted beach strand. The narrow block ended at the sand, with cars parked on both sides of the street. He readied himself when he sensed his follower closing on him.

The fog thickened, and the single streetlamp ahead was out. The meager light from the drawn windows of condos and apartments along the street did little to push away the shadows. Heavy footsteps behind him alerted Jake that the moment had arrived.

Reminding himself that he couldn't kick into super high gear if he expected his heart to survive the confrontation, Jake ran. He was less than ten strides from the strand when an engine roared and a van lurched in front of him from a side street. A man's head jutted out the window. In heavily accented English, he growled, "Get in."

The scene flashed through Jake's brain in slow motion: the yellow-toothed smile of the driver, thudding footsteps a few yards behind him, the van's side door cracking open, the barrel of an AK-47 peeking out of its dark interior.

"Flat!" Becker's shout boomed down the street.

Jake dove to the pavement just as the muffled spits of two silenced assault rifles opened up on the van. It was riddled with dozens of high-powered slugs. A double line of smoking pockmarks stitched the van's side panels from front to back. The head in the front window disappeared in an explosion of bloody grit that coated the interior of the windshield. The AK-47 toppled from the van's interior to clatter to the pavement in front of Jake's face, the stock dripping with blood. No one inside could have survived the onslaught.

Jake turned to the grunts of a struggle behind him. Becker had tackled the man following Jake. They rolled and twisted on the pavement, arms and legs punching and flailing as each man searched for an advantage. Though small in stature, Becker was strongly built, with corded muscles that flowed under the ebony skin on his forearms. In a deft blur of movement, he rolled onto one knee and spun behind the man. One hand twisted the man's arm to the breaking point behind his back, the other pressed the blade of Becker's combat knife across the man's neck.

Beads of sweat rolled down the captive's forehead. His wide nostrils expanded and contracted with each strained breath. He stared at Jake, his eyes filled with hate.

As Jake pushed himself up from the walkway, two men appeared from the shadows of a side alley. They moved quickly, with military precision, their Heckler & Koch MP5 assault rifles pressed into their shoulders as the still-smoking barrels swept the area for remaining targets. Pedro "Papa" Martinez and his taller partner Snake had been on the fire team that had saved Jake's butt in Afghanistan. Papa had a round shaved head, a dark goatee, and eyes that constantly scanned for threats. Snake was clean shaven and built like a featherweight boxer—fast and agile. Both Latinos' arms were sleeved with tattoos that marked them as former LA gang members.

"Clear," Snake whispered after a quick check inside the van.

Papa nodded. He moved toward Becker's captive and trained his weapon at the man's head.

"Wait," Jake said. "We need him alive."

The grimace on the attacker's face faded, replaced by a defiant glare that bore into Jake. He stopped struggling against Becker's hold, but his free hand remained fixed on Becker's knife-wielding wrist. Something suddenly changed in the captive's countenance. His eyelids relaxed to half-mast. He whispered, "*Allahu Akbar.*"

Jake caught the determined spark in the man's eyes a second too late.

In a flash of movement, the man pulled Becker's knife hand inward, forcing the razor-sharp edge deeply into his neck. At the same time he jerked his head forward, twisting from side to side to ensure that the blade severed his jugular. His eyes went wide as a cascade of blood rushed from the wound.

Becker jerked the knife away. Jake lunged and pressed both hands around the wound, trying in vain to staunch the flow.

"Too late, jefe," Papa said. "The shit-head will be dead in less than two minutes."

Jake screamed at himself. He lifted the dying man's head, his lifeblood seeping through Jake's fingers. "What do you want?" Jake shouted. "Who the hell do you work for?"

The man's head lolled. He coughed twice, spitting up blood. His eyes glazed over, but the corners of his blood-soaked lips lifted into a smile. In a faint gurgle, he said, "Allah's wrath is upon you." The man's eyes rolled back and his body went limp. Jake released his grip and the body slumped to the pavement.

Snake's voice was urgent. "We gotta move, holmes." He pointed up the strand. "People coming."

Chapter 11

THE KEY TO EXTERMINATION IS PATIENCE," LUCIANO Battista said in a throaty rasp.

He was sitting behind the executive desk that took up much of the second-floor office above the Torrance warehouse space. His conservative blue pin-striped suit and neatly trimmed Van Dyke beard were all part of his disguise as a wealthy Italian businessman traveling to America to interview plastic surgeons.

Abbas seemed to relax slightly with the conversation's change in direction away from the bungled attempt to capture the American the previous night. He sat across from Battista in one of two chairs that fronted the desk. "If it works," he said, "Kadir's plan is genius. The Western world will cease to exist."

"Yes," Battista said, imagining a world exclusively governed by the teachings of Muhammad. "By the time the Americans realize what has happened, they will be powerless to reverse it." He managed a slight smile, but his seemingly calm exterior belied the anger that roiled within him. Tariq's actions made it necessary to advance the timetable. As a result, the cornerstone of their ancillary mission—Jake Bronson—had slipped from his grasp. Not to mention the fact that three of Battista's followers had been killed in the process. Make that four, if he included the traitor Tariq. Despite all the benefits the brain implant had given

Tariq, it had done little to help him control his emotions. The fool could have ruined everything.

Battista understood Tariq's desire for vengeance, if not his timing. He slid his hand unconsciously across the blisters and craters that scarred the left side of his neck and lower face, remnants of a fragmentation grenade that the American had dropped in his lap in Afghanistan. Had one of Battista's loyal followers not sacrificed himself by grabbing the grenade and falling on it, Battista would have been killed.

Yes, he would make certain the American suffered a hundred deaths before he left this world.

But not yet.

Abbas pulled around his chair from the front of the desk and sat beside his leader. Both men focused on the image of Kadir on the video monitor on the desk.

He was downstairs in the clean-room laboratory, carefully pouring the phosphorescent liquid from a tall beaker into a mixing vat. The automated stirring paddles slowly churned through the syrupy mixture, the bright yellow additive disappearing in gentle swirls.

Battista clicked a button on the keyboard and spoke into the monitor's microphone. "How much longer?" he asked.

"Forty-eight hours," Kadir said. His focus never wavered from the half-empty beaker.

"Well done," Battista said.

"But we won't have enough for all of the targets."

"We shall make do," Battista said before he flicked off the monitor. They had two days, perhaps three, to get the job done. Bronson and his friends still had no idea what was going on. They knew someone was after him; that was all. They had their own reasons for hesitating in bringing in the authorities, at least for the moment. Battista had learned that they'd all kept their lips sealed following their illegal attack in Afghanistan. Military authorities were still unaware of exactly what occurred there and the parties involved. Battista worried that the group's reticence to dredge up such questions might fall by the wayside now that they'd uncovered a threat in their own backyard. But Battista intended to round them up before they could do anything about it.

"Prepare the teams," he said.

"Right away," Abbas said, rising.

Battista sensed his eagerness. "We need him alive."

"Yes, sheikh." Abbas hurried from the room.

Battista clenched his jaw, embracing the spasm of pain it sent down the length of his wound. His frustrations mounted over the seemingly endless complications caused by the American. He gazed at the scene outside the window.

There was a beehive of activity along the row of warehouses and office buildings that lined the street. Cars filled the parking lots and much of the street. He heard the warning beeps of a tractor-trailer rig as it backed up to a loading dock. Forklifts moved into view in practiced formation as they arranged heavy pallets of boxed goods for transport. Two well-dressed businessmen finished their outdoor conversation with a handshake before moving to their respective Mercedes sedans.

"Americans," Battista said to himself. "An anathema to Islam. Their decadence blocks the path to the sacred purity of the life we are commanded to follow by Allah."

A trio of women walked briskly up the sidewalk across the street, apparently taking advantage of their lunch break to get a little exercise. One of the women was pregnant. The corners of Battista's lips lifted slightly. The genius of his plan brought a flush of pride to his callused face. "The key to extermination is patience," he repeated.

Soon enough, Americans would no longer need diapers.

Chapter 12

Redondo Beach, California

JAKE HAD NEVER BEEN INSIDE THE REDONDO BEACH ELKS Lodge. Neither had any of his friends. That's why he chose it as their default rally point.

The lodge's exalted ruler had befriended Jake ten years ago when they met in the West Los Angeles VA hospital. They'd bonded over what they jokingly referred to as chemo-cocktail hour. They'd sat next to each other every day while they received their daily dose of intravenous chemicals that would help them in their battles against cancer, knowing that each toxic drop would also send their bodies into nauseous convulsions so severe that death might have been welcome. They had kept in touch ever since, and his friend had been more than happy to allow Jake to use the lodge's private back room. Though the aging one-story building was located on a main thoroughfare next to the popular Redondo Beach Pier, no one would think to look for them there. At least that's what Jake hoped.

He paced beside the long conference table in the center of the room, while Tony, Becker, and Papa sat at one end with several pistols and assault rifles spread out before them. The three were engrossed in cleaning the weapons and reloading spare magazines.

The midmorning sunlight peeked through the slits in the vertical blinds, laying a pattern of thin stripes across an assortment of half-empty soda cans and water bottles that littered the table. Two pizza boxes lay open as the table's centerpiece. A lone wedge of Hawaiian-style was all that remained of their overnight meal.

Francesca was curled in a leather lounge chair in a corner of the room, a throw pillow held tightly against her chest. She flinched as Tony rammed home a magazine in one of the MP5 assault rifles.

Marshall hunched over his laptop at the other end of the table. His fingers danced on the keyboard while Lacey sat beside him. The glum look on her face was not an act.

Jake pulled up behind Marshall. "How much longer?" he asked.

"Almost there. This phone has three layers of encryption. Three!" The phone was linked to the laptop through the USB port. Marshall had worked through the night trying to access the phone's memory.

"Stick with it, buddy," Jake said. Frustration was getting the better of him. Becker had retrieved the phone from his pursuer's body. It was the only clue they'd found in their rushed search of the three men who had attacked Jake last night. None of them had ID. Marshall had traced the van and found it was a rental under a phony name.

Jake had obviously been wrong when he had assumed the terrorist in the Pitts was a lone fanatic. Someone *was* after him. That meant his friends were at risk as well. Hopefully the phone would provide the clue they needed to determine the extent of the threat.

He peeked through a slit in the blinds to again check the parking lot. A slight movement behind the tinted windows of a customized pickup confirmed that Snake was alert and still on watch. Jake wondered how long he would have to live like this, with armed guards watching his back.

"I'm telling you, mate," Becker said to the group, "we need to make tracks for the safe house while we still can." He holstered the pistol he'd just cleaned and started snapping 9mm slugs into an empty magazine. "This cave was fine for the night, but it's time to move on. Staying put is just going to get us killed."

Here we go again, thought Jake. The group had been arguing the point for most of the night. He remembered the fear they'd all shared when they returned home from Venice. Jake had explained that Battista and his followers at the Afghan mountain stronghold had been killed in the huge explosion. But Battista's last three implant subjects had departed the facility the day before, headed for America and, if Tariq could be believed, were now not presumed dead as the news had earlier reported. They knew all about Jake—where he lived, who his friends were—and they had surely learned he was responsible for the deaths of hundreds of their jihadist brothers. No doubt they would seek revenge.

Jake and his friends needed a place to hide until the three jihadists could be found. With the help of Papa's relatives in Mexico, they'd located a safe house in the desert. They readied for their clandestine departure the next morning.

Lacey pounded her fists on the table, bringing Jake's attention back to the group. "No way, no way, no way!" she said. "I can't leave now. We start shooting tomorrow, for Christ's sake."

"I ain't goin' nowhere without my family," Tony said. His wife and two children were visiting his mom up at Big Bear. He'd called last night to make sure they were all right, but didn't tell them anything about what had happened.

"Don't worry about it, Sarge," Papa said, reverting to the use of Tony's rank when they'd met on active duty with Special Forces. "We got time, man. It's not like anyone knows where we're at."

Jake shared Tony's concern for his family. He'd long ago moved his own mom and sister to a small village just north of Pisa, Italy, where they remained safely ensconced with distant relatives. Besides Sarafina, who should arrive any minute with

Bradley, Tony's family was the last of those in the immediate circle of risk.

"I got it!" Marshall's pronouncement electrified the room. Everyone stopped what they were doing and gathered around the laptop.

"Okay," Marshall explained, "I still haven't cracked into the list of incoming and outgoing calls. But I was able to reconstitute parts of the final deleted voice mail." He turned up the volume on the laptop speakers and hit the PLAY button.

A stream of static scratched its way out of the speakers, rising and falling with a cadence that hinted at the existence of an underlying voice.

"Hang on," Marshall said, pausing the recording. He tapped a quick series of commands and hit PLAY again.

The static dissipated, replaced by a raspy, angry voice speaking Dari. "*...don't care what you have to do. Bring him to me now. The woman, too. If his friends get in the way, kill them!*" The line went dead.

Every one of Jake's nerve endings seemed to explode at the same time. He shared a look of shock with Tony, the only other person in the room who understood the Afghan language.

Francesca gasped. She stumbled backward to get away from the voice. She looked around wildly, her chest heaving. Jake rushed to catch her before she fell and wrapped her in his arms. He knew Francesca didn't need to understand the words in order to recognize the voice of her previous mentor—the same man who had torn apart her life. The man had kidnapped her and Sarafina, giving them over to his vicious and perverted executioner, Carlo, to do with as he pleased. Her body shook.

Luciano Battista is alive.

Jake embraced the burst of adrenaline that prepared his body for action and clarified his thoughts. The scene around him moved as if it were a slow-motion video. The stunned and worried looks on the faces of his friends seemed glued in place.

Through a slit in the vertical blinds, he saw Bradley's Jeep Grand Cherokee come to a stop in the parking lot. Sarafina sat in the backseat, an anxious smile on her face. Max was next to her, his tail wagging in slo-mo. Josh sat on the other side of the dog, his arm around Max's neck. Back inside, Tony had raised his cell phone to his cheek, his teeth clenched in concern. Papa and Becker were both strapping on weapons and ammo magazines. Lacey and Marshall stared at Jake, fear etched in every line on their faces.

It felt to Jake as if a noose had just been looped around his neck and slowly tightened. He shook his head to tamp down the growing sense of rage that threatened to overwhelm him. He needed to get everyone to safety. After that, he would take care of Battista. Once and for all.

"Either we get to the safe house immediately, or we're all dead."

Chapter 13

Redondo Beach, California

WHAT'S THE MATTER, DADDY?" SARAFINA ASKED. SHE clung to Jake's neck as he hurried around the Jeep to retrieve her backpack from the rear compartment. They were in the Elks Lodge parking lot. Car doors slammed on either side of Jake as the rest of the team rushed to their vehicles. Papa and Becker squeezed in with Snake on the front bench seat of the pickup truck with their weapons within reach. Tony, Francesca, Marshall, and Lacey had piled into Tony's Highlander, leaving space in the backseat for Jake and Sarafina.

"Everything's just fine, sweetie," Jake said as he popped the lid on the rear hatch. "We're going on an unexpected vacation, that's all."

"What about me?" Josh asked. "I wanna go on vacation."

"Sorry, buddy," Jake said. Bradley stepped out of the car. Jake caught his attention and turned back to Josh. "You and Max need to stay here to keep Bradley company."

"Hey, Josh," Bradley said in a calm voice. "Let's you and I take Max to the beach today, okay? It'll be a blast." The confused expression on Bradley's face didn't match the enthusiasm of his words. Noting that Sarafina's head was turned away, and that Josh's blindness would prevent him from catching on, he silently mouthed to Jake, *What the hell is going on?*

Jake ignored the question. He slung Sarafina's backpack over his shoulder, then reached out and clasped Bradley's hand. "I'll never forget what you did for me yesterday at the school. I owe you my life."

Bradley tightened his grip on Jake's hand, preventing him from leaving. His expression left no doubt—he wanted to know what was up.

Pulling Bradley close, Jake turned his head to one side so that Sarafina wouldn't hear. "The guy in the plane yesterday?" he whispered. "He's got friends."

Before Bradley could react, Josh shouted from the backseat, "That means Sarafina's not coming back!" Jake had forgotten that the boy's sense of hearing was exceptional. From the shattered look on Josh's red face, Jake knew he was about to burst into a fit.

"No fair, no fair, no fair!" Josh screamed.

Max's tail tucked between his legs. He licked at the tears streaming down his master's cheeks. Josh's screams only got louder.

"We've gotta go," Jake said to Bradley, pulling his hand free. "I—I'm sorry."

As Jake turned to leave, there was a screech of tires. Two white vans careened around a corner a few blocks down the street, headed directly toward Jake and his friends. The rest of the team noticed the vans as well. Engines started. Becker leaped out of the pickup's cab and jumped into its rear bed. He pulled back the slide on his assault rifle to chamber a round as Tony's Highlander lurched forward. The rear passenger door, which had been left open for Jake and Sarafina, slammed shut from the momentum.

Jake didn't hesitate. Like it or not, the circle of death that surrounded him had just expanded to include Bradley and Josh. "In the car, now!" he ordered. "I'm driving!"

The two men dove into the car. Jake passed Sarafina over the console into the back. "Kids, fasten your seat belts." He started the engine, put it in Drive, and floored it. It bounced over the curb, onto the sidewalk, and fishtailed into the street. He pulled behind Tony's Highlander, heading south on Catalina. Max lost his footing and yelped. Josh and Sarafina pulled him across their laps and held him tight. Josh was no longer screaming. Sarafina buried her face in Max's fur and hummed a nameless tune.

Jake checked the rearview mirror. Snake's yellow pickup truck was immediately behind him. The two white vans were three or four cars back in the morning commute traffic. They swerved from side to side, moving fast. Jake motioned toward the cell phone gripped in a holster on the dash, and said to a scared-looking Bradley, "Get Marshall on speaker. Quick."

Jake gave him the number. Marshall answered immediately, his voice panicked. "What the hell, Jake? How did they know where we were?"

"Doesn't matter," Jake shouted. "Tell Tony to head for the hangar. Then put me on speaker and conference in Papa and Snake." While he waited, Jake sifted through their options. When they'd originally set up the safe house escape plan four months ago, Jake had used the last of their funds to purchase the aircraft that would take them there.

Papa's voice came over the phone. "I'm up, jefe. You makin' for the plane?"

"No other options," Jake said. He leaned on the horn to alert an older couple to stay clear of the crosswalk. "Becker was right, man. We've got to get to the safe house."

"My family ain't here, Jake," Tony said over the line.

"No worries, Sarge," Papa chimed in. "I'll send a couple of my crew to watch over them."

"I owe you," Tony said.

"Forget about it, compadre."

"No one can possibly know where they are right now," Jake interjected. "They need to stay put. We'll get everyone else to the safe house. You and I will come back for them tomor—"

Staccato pops from automatic weapons erupted behind Jake. He checked the mirror to see the first of the two vans swerving back and forth behind Snake's truck. Flashes of gunfire flared from the van's passenger window. Snake's pickup dodged. Becker returned fire from the rear bed as the deadly caravan sped through the quiet residential district of South Redondo.

Jake floored the accelerator to keep up with Tony's Highlander. His worst nightmare was unfolding behind him—terrorists on the tail of nearly everyone he cared about, all because of him. He knew that the man behind it all, Luciano Battista, would never rest until everyone was dead. Jake couldn't believe the terrorist leader was still alive. How the hell had he lived through the massive explosion at the mountain fortress? Or the frag grenade that Jake had dropped into the man's pocket just seconds before it detonated?

Jake's brain went into overdrive, his senses aflame. He recognized the instinctual reaction that boiled up inside him. His mind formulated the details of an escape plan even as he considered the fight-or-flight response his body was going through. His hypothalamus had fired signals, releasing adrenaline, noradrenaline, and cortisol into the bloodstream. Blood was redirected from his digestive tract to the muscles of his arms and legs to provide more energy for quick movement—in Jake's case, *super* quick movement. Respiration rate increased, fueling the blood with extra oxygen, pupils dilated to improve vision, perception of pain diminished, awareness sharpened, and the immune system mobilized, prepared for the worst.

Fight or flight?

Jake wanted to fight, but he'd choose flight for now, until he could get his friends to safety. After that, he intended to give Battista the fight of his life.

"Okay, guys," Jake said into the phone. "Here's what I want you to do."

Chapter 14

THE HOPKINS WILDERNESS PARK WAS HIDDEN WITHIN THE rolling hills of a tree-studded residential neighborhood in Redondo Beach. The eleven-acre protected site boasted four ecological habitats: forest, meadows, streams, and ponds, transporting visitors to an environment that felt more like the High Sierra than a tiny beachside community. It included a small amphitheater and three overnight campgrounds. Trees shrouded the entrance inset from a heavily traveled boulevard.

Jake sped up a steeply inclined street, hoping to beat the yellow light at its crest. He'd led the speeding caravan through every twist and turn he could find on the way to the park. Tony's Highlander was directly behind him. Snake's pickup hugged his rear bumper. The vans were fifty yards back, the gap widened because the unwieldy vehicles had been unable to keep up on the squirrelly route. The gunfire had ceased, replaced by the sound of police sirens in the distance. Not good news. Jake didn't want to get held up by the authorities any more than by the bastards chasing him. For the time being, safety could only be found by disappearing.

The one-way road intersected the boulevard that fronted the park. The entrance was on the opposite side of the four traffic lanes. As the light changed from yellow to red, Jake floored it. The Jeep's V-8 responded with a throaty rumble and the car charged forward. He tightened his grip on the steering wheel, ignoring a sign that read RIGHT TURN ONLY.

The Jeep leaped into the intersection; its front wheels hit the median strip. A gut-wrenching jolt launched the car into the air. It roared past startled drivers into the camouflaged park entrance. A quick check in the mirror confirmed that Tony and Papa were still with him.

Jake took a deep breath against the flash of memories that assaulted him as he raced through the entrance. It had been exactly 460 days since he was last there. He knew every tree, every slope, each twist and turn of the walking paths. The sweet scent of moist earth and pine needles filled his senses, reminding him of the games of hide-and-seek with his wife and five-year-old daughter.

The park office was dead ahead. He whipped the Jeep to the left but it was traveling too fast. The right fender clipped a corner of the wooden structure. The side mirror went flying and Sarafina and Josh squealed in fear.

Bradley had one hand braced against the dash and the other had a death grip on the handhold over the window. Through clenched teeth, he said, "I hope you know what you're doing."

"Me, too," Jake said as he accelerated out of the turn. He aimed the nose of the Jeep at a partially open chain-link gate. "Hang on tight!"

The force of the speeding two-ton frame smashed through the twin gates with a resounding screech of metal against metal. The left gate bent back around its support post. The other tore from its hinges and cartwheeled into a nearby copse of trees. The children's screams grew into a constant shriek.

Jake spun the Jeep into a hard right. The four-wheel drive performed as advertised as the car dug into one turn after another, dodging around trees and boulders. Its thick tires churned through the turf as they throttled down the steep hill, porpoising over the uneven slope.

Jake caught the yellow flash of Snake's truck in the rearview mirror. It swerved back and forth behind Tony's Highlander. Jake wondered how the hell Becker was holding on in the rear bed. There was still no sign of the white vans, though he expected them to show up any second. Jake couldn't help but smile at what was about to happen.

"What—the hell's—so funny?" Bradley stammered through the twists and lurches of the ride.

"The vans," Jake said as the Jeep bottomed out. He aimed it up a steep slope. The wheels kicked up rooster tails of dark soil. "They're two-wheel drive."

As the Jeep crested the hill, Jake spotted the two vans careening down the hill behind him. The initial slope helped them gain purchase. Climbing up the other side isn't going to be quite as easy, Jake thought. He refocused his attention. The trickiest part of his hastily forged plan was ahead. The park's fenced perimeter was hidden behind a thick layer of thorny bramble.

The path declined sharply and the Jeep picked up speed. Jake adjusted his aim. He knew that Barbara Street lay just beyond the thick hedge, a dead end in an older residential neighborhood. There was an eight-foot drop from the edge of the park to the street. A chain-link fence separated the two.

"Hang on!" Jake shouted. He stomped on the gas and held his breath.

The Jeep ripped through the shrubs like a charging rhino. The fence collapsed under its momentum. Jake felt a momentary weightlessness as the Jeep arced through the air trailing a dozen feet of fencing. The front bumper hit the pavement first, crumpling inward from the impact. The front light housings shattered. Bits of glass and plastic splattered outward.

Jake struggled to keep the vehicle on its path down the street. The rearview mirror had shifted downward from the jolt. He adjusted it and was relieved to see both of his friends still behind him. He spoke into the speakerphone, still gripped by the dashboard clip. "Beck, you up?"

"Quite a trek, mate," Becker said. "I think we've lost the wankers, at least for the moment."

"Time for you to switch rides," Jake said. He knew that Papa and Snake wouldn't be going with them to the safe house. They preferred their own tough neighborhood in South Central, where no one in their right mind would attempt to follow. Becker, on the other hand, wouldn't allow Jake to leave without him.

Jake stopped the Jeep in the center of the street. Snake's pickup lurched to a stop on his left. Becker jumped out and piled into the backseat with Josh and Sarafina. The Highlander pulled up on Jake's right. Francesca's face was ashen but otherwise appeared okay. Jake mouthed, *I love you*, and she forced a smile.

Jake stepped on the gas. The vans were still not in sight. He needed to get to the airport before Battista's men found their trail.

As they drove through the neighborhood, Becker focused his attention on the children. "So, how are you two ankle biters enjoying the ride?" he said with a wide grin. His Aussie accent added a kick to his words. "Quite an adventure, eh?" He mussed their hair as his customary greeting. "I haven't had this much fun since I was chased by a pack of 'roos on walkabout."

As usual, Becker's presence had an immediate effect on the children. Tension leaked from their shoulders. Max lifted his head from Josh's lap. His tail carved a tentative wag that clipped Sarafina in the chin. She wiped her eyes with her sleeve while Josh asked, "Do you mean kangaroos?"

"Right as rain, Josh. Those buggers are faster than spit and their drumsticks pack a mean wallop."

Sarafina smiled at the comment, her right hand twisting an endless curl in her dark hair.

Jake appreciated the calming influence Becker had on the kids, especially Sarafina. He'd marveled at her ability to bounce back after the terror she'd lived through, first at Battista's institute near her home in Italy, and later as his hostage in Afghanistan. Since her arrival in America, she'd adapted quickly to her new lifestyle, from the clothes she wore to the ease with which she had perfected her command of English. She embraced her new life— in spite of her spectrum disorder—as if by doing so she affirmed that she was in control of her life, a life that after three years as an orphan now included a mother in Francesca and a father in Jake. But in the face of what lay before them, Jake feared that her thin veil of armor might not survive the onslaught.

Chapter 15

Zamperini Field
Torrance, California

ZAMPERINI FIELD WAS BUILT BY THE US ARMY AIR CORPS in 1942. The airport had been an emergency landing strip for military aircraft on training flights. It had since become one of the busiest municipal airports in the state. It was home to more than five hundred based aircraft, one of which Jake had housed in a double-wide private hangar at the southeast corner of the field. He'd purchased and outfitted the 1981 ten-passenger Sabreliner 65 with the remaining money from his impromptu visit to the Casino de Monte-Carlo, where Jake had used his new talents to manipulate the roulette wheel in order to gain the funds necessary for the rescue mission in Afghanistan.

Jake swerved the Jeep onto the airport frontage road. The tires squealed in protest. Tony's Highlander and Snake's pickup were close behind. There was still no sign of the vans. Jake pulled up to the unmanned electric gate and punched in his personal code. The gate swung open and Jake gunned through.

Each of the eleven rows of hangars stretched over six hundred feet long. The rows were situated side by side with just enough space in between to allow an aircraft to taxi to and from its private garage.

The airport was alive with early morning activity. Jake saw one plane touch down, another on approach, and several more in the traffic pattern. Aircraft were parked three deep in the holding area at the south end of the runway, waiting their turn for takeoff clearance. Support vehicles moved back and forth alongside the taxiways. Jake braked as a twin-engine Beechcraft emerged from between the rows of hangars in front of him.

The Sabreliner was housed near the end of the eighth row of hangars, just two rows away. Jake had flown the plane periodically over the past few months, making sure the inspections were current, the tanks filled, and all the emergency gear stowed and ready to go. He and Tony had taken great pains to make sure everything they needed was on the plane for a quick getaway: comm gear, weapons, ammo, ready-to-eat meals, clothes, water, even a couple games for Sarafina and Tony's children. Jake had prayed they'd never have to use it.

When the Beechcraft was halfway through the intersection, Jake swerved around its tail, sped up, and made a sharp turn in between rows eight and nine. What he saw next sent a slithering eel up his spine.

He slammed the brakes. A car was parked a hundred yards ahead of him—in front of his space. The vehicle was empty. All four doors were open, as was the hangar. He spoke into the speakerphone, trying to sound calm for the children's sake. "Aah, we got company."

"Shit," Tony said over the phone as the Highlander pulled up behind Jake.

"Bad word!" Josh said. He rocked back and forth in his seat.

Jake heard the telltale click of the safety being released on Becker's assault rifle.

"Jefe." Papa's voice was tense. The pickup slid in front of the Jeep. "Me and Snake will do a little drive-by. You've got to go to plan B."

This *was* plan B, Jake thought. Part of his mind raced through alternatives while another part wondered how in the hell Battista's guys continued to be one step ahead of him. The two vans had to be nearby. If they cornered him here…

"I won't forget this, guys," Jake said. "Show 'em what's up and we'll see you on the flip side."

"Hoorah," Papa replied.

Jake saw Papa and Snake slam full magazines into their assault rifles. The pickup laid a patch of smoking rubber on its way toward the hangar door.

Jake made a U-turn and stepped on the gas.

"Now what?" Bradley asked, bracing himself as the Jeep swerved around the end of the row of hangars.

Good question, Jake thought. Without the plane, their escape route was cut off. He said, "First step, get away from the airport."

"Then?"

Jake's reply froze on his lips. The two vans careened onto the taxiway at the other end of the flight line.

"Dammit!"

"Bad word, bad word!" Josh shouted.

Jake reacted instinctively to the threat. He stomped on the accelerator and angled the Jeep directly toward the holding area at the end of the runway.

"Lock 'n' load, Tony," Jake said into the speakerphone. "We need a new ride."

* * *

Papa positioned his assault rifle outside the passenger window of Snake's speeding pickup.

Papa had met Jake when he and his four-man fire team were hired to help rescue Francesca and Sarafina from the mountains of Afghanistan. His three younger Latino partners, Snake, Juice, and Ripper, had been part of his crew since they all ran together on the streets of South Central in LA. When they'd joined the US Marines eight years ago, as an alternative to prison after a major gang bust, there'd been seven of them. Three tours in Iraq and Afghanistan had whittled them down to five. They tried going back to LA, but when one of the boys got drilled in a drive-by, Papa pulled Snake and two others together and they went to work for an international private security company. That had been four years ago.

"Keep your speed up," Papa said to Snake. "I don't want to trade lead with these fools unless we have to. Ruining their ride will keep them out of the game long enough to let Jake get away."

"Got it," Snake said. He tightened his grip on the wheel. "But I wouldn't mind giving these salamis the big picture."

Papa couldn't agree more, but now was not the time. Snake raced forward and Papa focused the sights of his assault rifle on the other car's wheels. At twenty yards he opened fire on full auto. The back tires exploded and the rear end slammed into the pavement. As Snake sped past, Papa puckered the front grill with a half-dozen smoking holes.

Snake put the pedal to the floor. The customized pickup answered with a throaty roar.

"Let's fly," Papa said, craning his neck over his shoulder to see four men rush out of the hangar. Their automatic weapons spit fire.

Snake whipped the pickup around the far end of the hangar just as three hammer blows impacted the side of the truck's rear bed.

"Not even close, eh, holmes?" Snake said.

The two men shared an adrenaline-charged grin.

Chapter 16

WHICH PLANE?" TONY ASKED OVER THE SPEAKERPHONE. His Highlander sped alongside the Jeep.

"The P-750," Jake said. "It's second in line for takeoff."

"Skydiving written across the fuselage?"

"Yep."

Jake hoped the specialty aircraft was fully fueled. It wasn't an ideal choice. The cruising speed and range was well below what he would have liked. But it did have one crucial thing going for it—an extremely short takeoff capability. Jake glanced back and forth between the plane and the two vans speeding toward the hangar area. Battista's men apparently still hadn't noticed them. That might give them just enough time—

The vans suddenly steered off the taxiway and headed directly toward him.

"They're onto us," Jake said.

"Bloody crawlers," Becker mumbled from the backseat.

"I'll head 'em off," Tony said over the speakerphone, steering the Highlander toward the vans.

"No!" shouted Jake, frightened for Francesca, who was in Tony's vehicle.

"*Hola,* compadres!" Papa's voice chimed in over the speaker. "The Mexican cavalry is on it. But hurry up and get off the ground because we're gettin' pretty goddamn tired of pulling your asses out of the fire."

"Bad words!" Josh shouted. "Bad, bad, bad!"

Tony responded immediately, swerving the Highlander back toward the plane. In the rearview mirror, Jake saw Snake's pickup kicking up dust as it tore across a grassy sleeve between the taxiways, homing in on the lead van.

Becker reached through the console and offered Jake a 9mm semiautomatic.

"Keep it. If I need that, it'll be too late," Jake said. His eyes focused on the plane ahead. "Bradley, as soon as we stop, I want you to get the children and Max out of the car and ready to board."

Becker holstered the pistol and readied his rifle.

Jake spun the Jeep around the front of the plane. The wide-eyed pilot stared openmouthed from the cockpit. Jake braked hard to stop the Jeep in front of the port jump door, which was open. Becker rushed out and got into a defensive position behind the Jeep, his rifle trained on the approaching vans.

Jake abandoned any concerns for his heart condition. He was out of the Jeep and inside the cabin of the plane so fast that its ten occupants, geared up for a group jump, had barely enough time to register their shock.

Jake shouted over the muted roar of the plane's props, "Drop your chutes, helmets, and goggles, and get out of the plane immediately."

The men and women looked at one another with expressions leaving little doubt that they thought Jake was crazy. One of them—apparently the jumpmaster—started to speak. "Listen here—"

"You heard the man!" Tony interrupted, his bulk filling the doorway. His MP5 was pressed into his shoulder; its muzzle tracked the line of skydivers that filled the inward-facing row of seats. "Now!"

The divers jumped to attention. Hands scrambled. Gear spilled to the floor. When the first of them dropped to the tarmac, he beelined toward the terminal, away from the approaching vans. The others rushed after him.

The pilot watched over his shoulder from the cockpit and spoke rapidly into his boom mike. Jake stepped forward and yanked the headset off him. "You too, pal. Sorry." As the man hurried to leave, Jake added, "Keep your head down and steer clear of the hangars."

Jake slid into the pilot's seat and fastened the shoulder harness. He scanned the instruments and placed a hand on the throttle. Outside, Snake's pickup shot directly at the speeding vans. The Mexicans were challenging the terrorists to a deadly game of chicken. Jake knew Snake. He'd die before he budged from his path.

Hoorah.

At the last possible instant, the vans swerved away in either direction. Snake's pickup shot between them like a cruise missile. Jake saw flashes from both windows as Snake and Papa let loose with their assault rifles. Jake could imagine their death-defying cries of victory.

One of the vans veered away too sharply. Its top-heavy profile caused it to lift onto its outer wheels. For a fraction of a second it just hung there, speeding at sixty or seventy miles an hour into the turn. But then the startled driver apparently slammed on the brakes—the last thing he should have done. The front wheel locked and the momentum whipped the vehicle onto its side. It left a trail of sparks as it slid across the pavement.

"Go!" shouted Becker as he launched himself into the rear of the plane. He cradled the dog in his arms.

Jake slammed the throttle and released the brakes. The plane jerked forward in response. He angled for the runway, accelerating quickly.

Marshall slipped into the copilot's seat, out of breath. "You ever flown one of these?" he asked.

"Uh-uh," Jake said. "You better strap in." He focused on his takeoff roll.

The remaining van hadn't given up yet. It was approaching fast from the plane's starboard front quarter, bouncing across the grass that abutted the runway. Jake watched in frustration as he calculated speeds, angles, and distance. There was no way he could reach takeoff speed in time to avoid the suicide collision.

"Crap!" Marshall shouted. "They're going to ram us!"

"The hell they are," Jake said. Instead of steering away from the van, he turned the nose directly at them. The plane shuddered as the wheels left the pavement and spun onto the grass.

"Oh, no," Marshall muttered. He swept the harness over his shoulders and cinched it tight.

"Hang on tight, everybody!" Jake shouted. He glanced at the instruments.

Fifty feet...

Twenty...

He jerked back on the stick. The plane vaulted over the van. The bottom of the starboard landing gear clipped the van's windshield. Jake jerked the stick hard to the left, smashing his foot on the rudder to keep the right wingtip from dipping into the ground and cartwheeling the plane.

The van passed beneath them; the plane dropped back to the ground and accelerated. The parking area was less than a hundred feet ahead, filled with tied-down aircraft. Jake slapped his palm against the throttle, making sure the powerful engine had every ounce of fuel it could handle. Though he'd never piloted a P-750, he knew it was touted for its abilities to perform where other planes cannot.

Sweat dripped down his brow. Rows of aircraft filled the windscreen. The speed indicator inched upward. At the last possible moment, Jake yanked the stick to his chest and the plane leaped into the air, clearing the vertical stabilizers of the parked aircraft with only inches to spare. He banked the plane starboard to avoid the double-tall hangars behind the lot. The stall-warning buzzer filled the cockpit. Jake lightened the load on the stick and the warning lights flickered out. The plane swept abreast of the control tower's bank of windows. The controller behind the glass was screaming into his microphone as he shook his fist above his head.

It took a moment for Jake to realize that Marshall had wailed through the entire event. Jake sucked in a long breath and gawked out the side window at the receding van.

"What the hell are we going to do now?" Marshall shouted over the roar of the engine.

Jake worked the controls to keep the plane above stall speed while they climbed.

"Shit!" Marshall gasped, his palm pressed against the Plexiglas window. "Flashes from the van!"

Jake jinked the plane from side to side, thankful for the responsive controls. A staccato of metallic plunks signaled a few lucky strikes from the ground fire.

Francesca screamed.

God, no!

"Sweet Jesus," Marshall said. He unstrapped and rushed to the back.

Jake dove the plane behind a row of commercial buildings skirting the east end of the airport—beneath the van's sight line. The aircraft picked up speed as drivers on the street below swerved and braked at the sight of an airplane screaming toward them less than a hundred feet off the ground. In the distance Jake saw a column of police cars and first-response vehicles racing up the boulevard. Their emergency lights flashed as they carved a serpentine line through traffic.

With miles of congested traffic to his left, and the Palos Verdes mountain range to his right, Jake didn't hesitate. He pulled the P-750 into a turn up a ravine that led into the mountains. He allowed his training to take over as he banked back and forth up a twisting network of forested ravines and high-end horse properties. He turned off the transponder and flew the aircraft as close to the ground as possible. Radar was their enemy.

Another part of his brain was numb with fear for Francesca. He risked a quick glance over his shoulder. Marshall and Tony blocked the view. Wind from the open jump door swirled around them as they worked over someone on the portside seats. Jake gritted his teeth and returned his gaze forward.

Everyone would have been better off if he had just died months ago from the brain tumor, he thought. Instead, the goddamn freak accident in the MRI had cured his cancer while giving him mental and physical abilities that were the envy of one of the top terrorists in the world. His life had spiraled out of control—like an F-16 in an unrecoverable flat spin. But there was no ejection seat to save him, to pull him out of the inevitable crash that would obliterate him and everyone he loved. It seemed that no matter how desperately he tried to live a normal life, he was destined to play out a role that put him at dead center of a terrorist confrontation. And if that wasn't enough, the grim specter of the alien pyramid increased the stakes a billionfold. He'd uncovered the 25,000-year-old object in the caverns of a terrorist stronghold in Afghanistan. His enhanced abilities had allowed him to solve the riddle of its pictograms, unwittingly launching it into space, triggering events that threatened nothing less than the survival of the human species. He shook his head in disgust at the irony of it all. If he had simply died, the entire world would be a safer place.

Jake bit off his concern. He needed to fly the aircraft.

The plane crested the peak and Jake pushed the nose downward. Hovering close to the ground, he steered a route that would avoid pockets of hillside homes on the windward side of the mountainous peninsula. The vast expanse of the Pacific stretched out in the distance before him, sparkling under the morning sun.

Jake dove the plane toward the coastline. As the airspeed passed 130 knots, he felt a shimmy through the controls. The plane yawed to starboard as if it were out of trim. The sensation worsened as the speed increased.

He eased off the throttle. The shuddering disappeared as soon as the speed dropped back to 120 knots. The gear had been damaged by the impact with the van and the undercarriage was probably a twisted mess. Under different circumstances, he'd do a flyby at the tower or request the aid of another aircraft in the area to get a visual confirmation of the extent of the problem. Neither was an option. He'd have to assume the gear was toast.

A flock of geese flew in a V-formation a couple miles off the coastline, heading south. Jake turned to follow them, mentally recalculating his ETA to the safe house in the Mexican desert. He wondered how the hell he was going to land with a busted gear.

Marshall interrupted his thoughts as he reentered the cockpit. He placed a hand on Jake's shoulder.

Jake held his breath.

"It's Bradley," Marshall said. "He took a slug in the arm. Tony said it went clean through flesh. He's going to be all right."

The news brought a rush of relief that Jake felt to the bone. He allowed himself a brief smile.

"Thank God," he said.

"I need your cell phone," Marshall said. He held out a small plastic grocery bag as if he were trick-or-treating.

Jake glanced in the bag. It held several phones, a couple digital watches, and an iPod.

"What's the deal?"

"Dude, isn't it obvious? Battista and his assholes have been one step ahead of us ever since that creep tried to blow you to kingdom come yesterday. They're tracking us somehow. If I had my scanning equipment I could tell you exactly how, but in the meantime we need to ditch anything electronic." He shook the bag for emphasis. "So give it up."

Jake dropped his phone into the bag.

"Watch, too?" Jake asked, flipping his wrist so the face of his ten-year-old air-force-issued timepiece was visible.

"No," Marshall said, displaying his own Mickey Mouse watch. "Low-tech is fine."

Tony stepped up behind Marshall. He filled the narrow space between cockpit and cabin.

Marshall knotted the top of the grocery bag. Rather than attempting to maneuver around his big friend, he held up the bag.

"You want to toss these?"

Tony shook his head, his face tight. He turned sideways and Marshall squeezed past him. Tony sank into the copilot's seat.

"I tried Mel's cell one last time," he said softly. "All I got was voice mail." His voice was strained, and worry lines shadowed his features.

"Reception's never good at the lake," Jake said. "You know that."

"Yeah," Tony muttered, staring blankly out the front of the cockpit. "I left another message. Told her to sit tight until we pick her up."

Jake cringed. He knew Tony expected the two of them to make a quick turnaround after they dropped off everyone else at the safe house.

"Listen, pal. Your family's going to be okay. Papa's guys will be there soon to keep an eye on them." He hesitated before continuing. "But we're going to have a problem getting back there right away."

Tony's head snapped toward Jake. Every muscle in his body seemed to tighten at once. "What the hell you talkin' about?"

Jake told him about the damaged landing gear. Tony pressed his palms against his eyes. His chest heaved from several deep breaths. It took a moment before Tony regained his composure and his military background took over. The two men spoke in hushed voices as they crafted a plan around the only viable option left to them.

Chapter 17

Torrance, California

BATTISTA CONSIDERED THE TEN MEN BEFORE HIM. THEY knelt in a row on the cold concrete warehouse floor, their heads bowed. Twelve additional jihadists, including Kadir and the lab techs, were grouped behind the men. They looked on somberly, shifting from side to side.

The kneeling men had failed miserably in their task to capture the American. Their only saving grace lay in the fact that they had escaped the debacle at the airport and made their way back to the warehouse. Lesser men would have stayed to die in a firefight with the local authorities rather than face their leader in shame.

Though they knew the fate that awaited them, none gave any outward sign of fear.

"Up," Battista ordered. His voice echoed in the cavernous space.

The group jumped up and snapped to attention with military precision.

"Who shall I hold responsible?" Battista asked.

The line of men marched one step forward as a unit, each man signaling his readiness to accept the blame. They wore casual Western clothes, some in jeans and polo shirts, others in khakis and button-downs. Their brown skin only hinted at their

Middle Eastern roots, and some even had surgically softened features. The only thing that separated their appearance from that of other young South Bay professionals was the ceremonial *jambiya* that each man had tucked in his belt. Battista had adopted the short, crescent-shaped daggers as the bonding symbol of their cause, a reminder of their roots. He himself wore a *saifani jambiya* passed down from his ancestors. Its aged rhinoceros handle glimmered with a dim yellowish luster.

He walked along the line, studying each man, searching their eyes for signs of weakness. Abbas followed closely behind, his hand resting casually on the ivory pommel of his own double-edged *saifani*. Though Abbas much preferred the switchblade that lived in the front pocket of his slacks, Battista knew that he was every bit as skilled with the ancient tool.

Battista had personally selected each of the men before him for this mission. He knew their backgrounds, their capabilities, their loyalties. He had even insisted on meeting their families. They had demonstrated their willingness to die on behalf of their cause. The blood of martyrs is the fuel that will ultimately lead us to victory over the infidels, Battista thought, even if their death must come at the hands of one of their own in order to remind those who remained of the importance of Allah's mission.

He stopped before one man. They locked eyes. Other than a slight dilation of the pupils, the jihadist showed no fear. Instead, he seemed to expand his chest as if he were about to receive a medal from his general. Battista forced down a wave of reluctance and gave the silent order with a slight nod of his head.

Abbas moved with the speed of a cobra. The curved blade of his *jambiya* shimmered under the lights just before it left a crimson line across the man's neck. His eyes bulged. His hands went to his throat. Blood seeped from his fingers. With a gurgling cough, he slumped to the floor. His head leaned at an awkward angle against the shoe of the man beside him. The soldier held his ground, eyes forward. So did all the other men in line.

Battista felt a surge of pride. Yes, his men had failed to apprehend the American, but their dedication to the cause was resolute. Show me this level of faith in an infidel, Battista thought. He reminded himself that capturing the American was essential, but it was still secondary to their primary mission here in Los Angeles.

One that would make September 11 pale by comparison.

Chapter 18

ARE YOU SERIOUS?" FRANCESCA WHISPERED.

Jake nodded. He sat beside her in the back of the plane. Becker had relieved him at the controls. They'd passed into Mexican airspace nearly an hour ago, using the code words that Jake had established long ago with a Mexican radar control manager who was more than willing to accept the generous *mordida* from the friendly American. The initial down payment had equaled more than two years' salary for the controller. The follow-up payment he would receive for clearing the unregistered flight through his airspace would set him up for life. It was a small price to pay for their anonymity.

Jake squeezed Francesca's hand. She was staring at Josh and Sarafina, her face shadowed with worry.

He followed her gaze. "It'll be all right," he said.

The two children had settled into the adventure. That might change when they discovered what was in store. Jake listened as Sarafina described the stark desert landscape beneath the plane to Josh. She sat next to the boy, acting as his eyes during the flight. Max was sprawled across both of their laps, his body relaxed but his eyes alert. The children had removed his guide harness and were stroking his thick mane of golden hair.

Jake marveled at Sarafina. Though she still hid behind her dewy-eyed mannerisms, he knew that the frightening experiences in Venice and Afghanistan had driven some of the child out of her. In times of stress, she seemed to exhibit the situational awareness of someone three times her age. He saw it again now, as she comforted Josh in the cooing manner of her mother figure, Francesca. It seemed to work. The boy was intent on her eloquent descriptions of what was going on around them. As long as no one used any bad language around him, the kid would cope just fine.

Lacey sat beside Sarafina with Marshall's arm draped over her shoulders. Jake knew Sarafina idolized the striking young woman. Lacey's spunky spirit, as well as her physical attributes as a top-notch surfer and tae kwon do master, gave her an allure that was difficult to resist. For the children's sake, Lacey had stopped complaining about the acting gig she had been forced to abandon. But Jake still saw flits of anger flash across her face from time to time. It had been the biggest role she'd ever landed. She'd been waiting for such a break ever since she moved to LA nearly five years ago. Now that it had finally happened, it had been ripped away from her. Jake felt terrible about it, though a small part of him couldn't help but wonder at the irony of it all. She'd be seeing plenty of action very soon.

Jake glanced at his watch. In fifteen minutes they'd be over the safe house.

It was time to break the news to the rest of the team.

* * *

Francesca's knees were shaking. Tony stood behind her. He gave a final tug on the harness of the parachute strapped to her back.

"Looks good," he said. "You're all set."

She couldn't believe she was about to jump out of an airplane into the middle of the Mexican desert. When Jake had first explained his plan, she'd thought he was joking. How in heaven's name could he be serious, especially with two young children? Not to mention a dog! But here she stood, trussed up like a game hen about to go into the oven. *O Dio.*

The other adults were geared up as well. The children were next. They'd be hooked to Tony's and Becker's chests. For Josh's sake, they'd all remained subdued as they put on their gear.

Becker cinched a tandem harness around Sarafina. He sat beside her and whispered into her ear.

Tony knelt beside Josh. "Hey, pal. I'm going to slip a harness over your head."

Josh crossed his arms on his chest. "How come?"

"Uh…"

"We're going to jump, huh?"

Tony raised an eyebrow. "That's right. But I'm going to hold you the whole way."

Josh tightened his arms across his chest. He rocked back and forth.

Tony mussed his hair. "It's fun. I've done it a hundred times. It'll be just like G.I. Joe."

"I—I'm scared."

Sarafina stepped next to him. "Hey, Josh," she said. "You're supposed to be a little scared. That's what makes it fun. Besides, just wait until we tell the kids in class about it!"

The boy stopped rocking. He tilted his head, as if imagining the reaction the other kids would have to the story. After a moment, he slowly lifted his arms over his head. Tony slid the harness into place.

Francesca marveled. She wished her courage had been as easy to find.

Marshall and Becker stood in the aisle in front of her.

"Su-weeet Jesus, I hope this is over quick!" Marshall said as he tightened the straps on his own harness.

"Actually," Becker said with a wide-toothed smile, "if it's over too quick, then your chute didn't open." He patted Marshall on the shoulders and added, "No worries, mate. Get ready for the ride of your life!"

"Terrific."

Lacey had already donned her goggles. Francesca watched her calm demeanor with envy. Lacey leaned out the door, one hand on the jump rail. The wind whipped the loose strands of blond hair that leaked from the bottom of her helmet. Her grin stretched from ear to ear. She would be the first one out, trailed by Marshall, Bradley, and then Francesca. Becker would follow with Josh. Sarafina would be next, strapped to Tony. Jake had insisted on being last. The dog was going with him, trundled within a canvas stow bag.

The yellow standby light above the jump door began to flash.

"All right, missy," Becker whispered, placing his hand on Francesca's shoulder from behind. "No worries. The chute will open on its own. If not, just yank on the D ring like we rehearsed. It's going to be fine."

Francesca inched forward to get in line behind Bradley, willing her unstable legs to keep her upright. She recited a silent prayer and glanced over her shoulder for Jake. But he was still in the cockpit, making sure the plane was in position for the jump. As if hearing her thoughts, Jake's voice entered her mind.

Be brave. Love you.

She found a small modicum of peace in his words. Lies couldn't hide within the purity of one's thoughts. It was why she guarded her own mind from him now.

* * *

Jake sensed Francesca's resistance to his thoughts. He couldn't blame her. She was a psychologist and schoolteacher, not a thrill seeker. All she wanted to do was help challenged children.

Instead, her life had been turned upside down and she'd been forced to live as a target. Now, he was asking her to jump out of an airplane into the middle of nowhere. *It's a wonder she'll speak to me at all,* Jake thought.

A wide expanse of desert scrub rushed beneath the low-flying aircraft. They were over the Sonoran Desert. The distant horizon rippled under the heat of the afternoon sun. The Sea of Cortez, which separated the Baja Peninsula from the mainland, was fifteen miles off the starboard wing.

A bead of perspiration dripped down Jake's side under his shirt. He shifted in the pilot's chair, unable to get comfortable under the tightly cinched straps of the parachute harness. The dry desert air whisked into the plane from the rear hatch, smelling of sage and creosote. Jake adjusted their course to follow a flood-carved ravine that abutted the remote ranch that would be their home for the next several weeks. He double-checked the GPS on the instrument panel. *Two miles.*

Flicking a switch on the instrument panel, Jake turned on a yellow standby light in the rear cabin. He confirmed the settings he'd entered for the automatic pilot. Following the jump, the plane would continue on its programmed flight plan, making a number of course changes along the way. With any luck, it would remain aloft for about an hour before crashing into the southern reaches of the Sea of Cortez. If anyone tracked the aircraft to its final destination, it would be impossible to determine when or where Jake and his friends had vacated it.

He leveled off at the minimum safe jump altitude of sixteen hundred feet. He flicked the standby switch to the middle indent, causing the yellow light in the cabin to begin blinking. The ranch was dead ahead.

In its heyday over a hundred years ago, the expansive single-story adobe structure and its dilapidated outbuildings had served as a way station between southern Mexico and the American territories. According to Papa, whose family had lived nearby before moving to Los Angeles, the property had more recently been used as a narco ranch, a retreat where the local drug lord could reward his crew with wild parties filled with imported women from neighboring villages. Two years ago, it had been shut down in a rare drug bust by Mexican authorities. Apparently, the regional official in charge didn't feel the monthly bribe he received was enough to overlook the fact that his daughter had been among the girls coerced into attending one of the parties.

The desolate property lay above a network of underground rivers and streams that originated in Arizona and eventually dumped into the Sea of Cortez. As a result of the constantly shifting aquifer, the defile that skirted the eastern edge of the property had grown to a small gorge over the years, encroaching ever closer to the main structure. Jake saw remnants of two outbuildings strewn at the bottom of the gully.

Max whimpered at Jake's feet. He lay in an open canvas sack, his legs trussed up beneath him. A nest of parachute material lined the sack, cushioning the nervous dog. Jake reached down and scratched his head.

"Don't worry, fella. Before you know it, you'll be chasing long-eared jackrabbits across the sand."

Thirty seconds to go. Jake flipped on the autopilot, placed his finger on the jump switch, and started the silent countdown. For the second time in twenty-four hours, he was going to abandon a flyable aircraft. As a pilot, that didn't sit well with him. His only solace rested in the fact that the ploy would make it impossible for Battista and his crew to find them.

Chapter 19

Torrance, California

ABBAS FLIPPED HIS CELL PHONE CLOSED, ENDING THE CALL.
"The plane crashed in the Gulf of California," he said.
"They found no survivors."

"Of course not," Battista replied. "Mr. Bronson is smarter than that. He and his friends obviously left the plane long before it went into the water."

The two men were seated on a small couch in the office above the warehouse. An ornate ceramic teapot rested on a coffee table in front of them. Kadir sat in a chair on the opposite side of the table. He leaned forward and poured a short stream of Turkish tea into the sheikh's demitasse cup.

"They could be anywhere," Kadir said, shaking his head in disgust.

Battista shared a knowing smile with Abbas, the only other person who knew the entire scope of Battista's plans.

"Do not worry, Kadir," Battista said. "Allah shall provide."

Kadir bowed his head. "Of course, my sheikh."

Battista sipped the thick aromatic tea. The smell reminded him of times long ago, sitting before the fire with his father, listening to tales of the vast world outside his village. His father's stories always highlighted the dangers of the Western crusaders and the need for all good Muslims to fight back in the name of the one true religion.

Battista's real name was Abdul Modham Abdali. He was descended from a long line of chieftains who had led his prosperous mountain tribe for over a thousand years. At the age of ten, with his father's teachings firmly implanted in his psyche, he had been sent to live with his mother's wealthy family in Venice, Italy. It had been so different from the small village of his birth. He hated it at first. He longed for his friends, the fresh air, and the pride and furor that drove his father and the men of his tribe. But he adapted; his father demanded it. Allah demanded it.

He had excelled at the Italian schools and made new friends of a sort, friends who were never permitted to learn his true identity. In time he settled in and feigned appreciation of the comforts of the West, attending the best universities in Europe, earning his PhD in applied cultural philosophy by the age of twenty-five. His life was cocooned in a web of lies that became second nature to him.

So much had happened since then. His mother lost her battle with Alzheimer's, his father was tortured and killed in the American prison in Guantánamo, and his wife lost her life to an errant American missile. Shortly thereafter, his six-year-old son—the last of his family—suffered a seizure that left him with a severe spectrum disorder.

Battista met with top doctors in the field to see what could be done for Rajid. Though none of them could help, he'd learned of some promising research being conducted with TMS—transcranial magnetic stimulation—brain implants. He'd turned his efforts—and the considerable financial resources he'd garnered after a few "accidents" ensured that he was the sole heir to his mother's ancestral estate—to development of the technology. Not only could it provide a cure for his son, but it would also facilitate the creation of a small army of mentally enhanced super soldiers who could infiltrate the West in preparation for the final glorious battle.

Everything had been on track—until Jake Bronson entered the scene. The sheikh's blood boiled at the thought of the arrogant man who had ruined everything.

He sighed. The scales would tip in the opposite direction very soon, in spite of Bronson's temporary disappearance. The insidious nature of Battista's current plans appealed immensely to him. The residents of Los Angeles, and later all of America, would never suspect what was coming. There was but one loose end to tie up. He turned to Abbas.

"Take the jet," he said. "Meet the shock team in Mexico." He glanced at his watch. "They depart Venezuela in two hours. That will put them on the ground late tonight. By then we will know where Mr. Bronson and his friends are huddled."

"Will Kadir be joining me?" Abbas's nose wrinkled in disgust when he added, "For the procedure?"

"No, he must finish his work here. Take Muhammad."

"The scientist?" Abbas said.

"Yes. He has the medical training necessary."

"But I need him here," Kadir protested. "He has been instrumental in developing the final formulation."

"Are you telling me that at this late stage you cannot complete the task without him?"

"No...but his absence will be felt. There will be a delay."

"So be it," Battista said.

"He has no field training," Kadir added.

"It is decided," Battista said. There was an edge to his voice that ended the conversation.

Abbas stood to leave.

Battista studied the eagerness in the assassin's face. He was well aware of the man's enmity toward the American. Battista didn't question the man's loyalty, but he did worry that his desire for revenge might cloud his judgment.

"No mistakes, Abbas," Battista added.

"Of course," Abbas said through tight lips. He offered a bow of his head. "I have never failed you, my sheikh. And with Allah's blessing, I shall not fail you now."

"*Allahu Akbar*," Battista said.

Kadir and Abbas responded in unison. "*Allahu Akbar!*"

Chapter 20

Sonoran Desert, Mexico

JAKE KNEW SOMETHING WAS WRONG THE MOMENT HE opened the heavy oak door of the desert ranch house.

He stepped into an expansive great room dominated by a massive stone hearth that stretched twenty feet across the far wall. The fireplace resembled a gaping maw, its interior and trim blackened from a century of soot. Arched doorways on either side of the hearth opened to a kitchen on one side and a long bedroom hallway on the other. The gathering room reeked of age, with rough-hewn oak beams overhead and cracked terra-cotta tiles underfoot. A dozen arched windows spilled sunlight into the space, highlighting swirls of dust motes in the dry air. A chandelier hovered in the center of the room over a scatter of old sofas, end tables, and overstuffed chairs. A pitted and nicked dining table stretched along one side of the room, surrounded by sixteen high-backed chairs.

But the room's interior had changed dramatically since Jake's last visit with Papa over a month ago. A thick aroma of booze and human sweat hung like a pall over the room. Empty tequila bottles and Tecate beer cans were strewn throughout the space. A pair of women's panties hung from the yellowed shade of a table lamp.

"Pee-yoo!" Lacey said as she shouldered her way past Jake.

Jake grabbed her arm and her attention as he pressed one finger against his lips.

"This is supposed to be our safe house?" Lacey whispered.

The rest of the group piled through the door behind her. Each sported a look of disgust and dismay. Even Max was subdued. His tail was still while he sniffed the air.

"Crap," Tony mumbled, exchanging a worried look with Jake before he glanced Josh's way. Tony's arms overflowed with the parachutes he'd gathered in order to stow them out of sight of search planes.

"Everyone stay put," Tony ordered under his breath. He silently dropped the chutes on the floor and pulled his automatic from its holster. He quickly snaked his way through the room and into the dark hallway that led to the back rooms.

Becker moved toward the kitchen, his assault rifle pressed into his shoulder.

Jake pulled his own automatic and corralled the rest of the group into a corner of the room. He felt Francesca shiver beside him as they waited.

Becker returned quickly. "Kitchen's clear," he whispered. The sound of doors opening and closing echoed from the hallway. Becker followed the sounds to back up Tony.

After several long minutes, the two men returned with their weapons lowered. Tony had a long canvas bag draped over one shoulder. He dropped it onto the dining table.

"Whoever it was," he said, "didn't find our emergency stash."

Jake breathed a sigh of relief.

* * *

"It's amazing how quickly children bounce back," Jake said. He emptied the rest of the water bottle down his parched throat.

He and Francesca watched as Sarafina and Josh crouched on their haunches beside the tattered remains of a corral that fronted the ranch house. The two held hands as Sarafina acted as Josh's eyes. She shone a flashlight over a coil of shed rattlesnake skin and described its transparent texture in detail.

Bradley hovered near the children. His injured arm was in a sling. He used the other to wave a stick in the air. Max pranced at his feet, hoping for one last toss before night settled in over the Mexican desert.

"A full day of carefree exploring does wonders," Francesca replied. "They believe the danger has passed."

She sat beside Jake on a small wooden bench in front of the house. The final sliver of sun winked out as it dropped below the line of foothills that bordered the western edge of the ranch. The temperature had cooled to eighty-five degrees, encouraging a buzz of insects to venture out for the night's forage. The arid landscape stretched out before them, broken by shadowed copses of scrub oak and cactus. The diesel generator rumbled softly on the other side of the house.

Jake slid his arm around her. She rested her head against his shoulder.

"I envy them," she added, knuckling away a tear.

Frustration gnawed at Jake. He'd hoped this ranch would be a safe haven for them. Instead, he'd dropped them all in the middle of another mess. It was apparent that the ranch had once again been claimed by one of the nearby drug lords and they'd be back. Jake had read of the growing number of kidnappings and murders. He didn't want his group to be anywhere close when the drug lords returned, all hopped up for their next party.

Jake had used the satellite phone from the emergency stash early this morning to contact his air force pilot buddies, Cal and Kenny. The two men had provided air transport for their assault on Battista's mountain fortress in Afghanistan. Jake needed their help again to get out of this spot, but neither had answered his call and he'd left a voice mail. If they didn't call back by morning, Jake and his team would have to head out on foot. The closest village was ten miles away.

He didn't want to worry Francesca with the news. He'd shrugged off her concerns about the ranch's recent visitors as a onetime event. *A bunch of kids having a party,* he'd said. But he knew better, and he suspected she did as well. Fortunately, she hadn't pressed him on it. Not yet.

They planned to spend the night on the couches and floor of the great room, preferring to avoid the sweat-and-sex smell of the bedrooms. They would sleep in shifts through the night so that there were always two people on watch. They intended to use what was left of today to recharge after the adrenaline-filled events of the previous twenty-four hours.

Jake caught a glimpse of Tony and Becker not far away. They had looped their rifles over their shoulders while they dragged a bundle of tumbleweeds toward a nearby stand of trees. Becker was tapping into his aboriginal roots as the two prepared a few special surprises for any unwelcome visitors.

Tony had calmed down somewhat after finally reaching his wife on the satellite phone the night before. His family was safely ensconced in his mom's cabin. Two of Papa's crew were keeping a sharp eye on them.

Nevertheless, with Battista on the loose, they were all in danger. If he turned himself over to the terrorist, Jake wondered, would his friends be safe? Jake's mind raced through the options, running various scenarios to their logical end, weighing Battista's apparent motivations against his friends' lives. In each case, the answer was the same...

"*Non sono stupido,*" Francesca said in her native Italian, interrupting his thoughts. "I know you are hiding something from me."

Jake tensed. Her ability to look right through him was uncanny. For the most part, he'd learned how to block her empathic gift when necessary, though he hated doing it. His impulse was to share his heart and soul with her. Under different circumstances he would have done so long ago, but there was no future in the cards for them now.

"Sorry," he said, suspecting where this conversation was headed. "I've got a lot on my mind, that's all." Over the past couple weeks, something had changed in her. He knew she wanted more out of their relationship. She'd been honest about that from the beginning, but lately it seemed she was on the verge of pressing the issue.

"I'm trying to figure out our next move," he added. "I'm hoping we don't have to use the tunnel."

A flash of confusion crossed Francesca's face.

"Tunnel?" she asked.

"There's an underground river that flows just behind the main house. A trapdoor inside hides an entrance to a tunnel leading down to the caverns. According to Papa's grandfather, the original owners used it as an escape route in the event of an attack by banditos."

Francesca turned on the bench so that she was facing him. She took his hands in hers.

"Jake," she said. She took a deep breath. "There's something I need to talk to you about."

"Sure," Jake said. "In a minute. The tunnel hasn't—"

"The tunnel isn't important right now," she said, riveting him with an impassioned stare. "We need to talk."

"Yeah, but—"

"Now," she said. "It's important."

"O...kay," he said, drawing out the word as his mind grappled for an exit strategy.

Rescue came in the form of Lacey when the front door swung open and she stepped onto the porch.

"We need you inside right away," she said. "We've got big problems."

"Sorry," Jake said to Francesca. He stood and extended his hand to help her up. She drew her knees close and hugged them to her chest. The look of disappointment in her eyes sent a pang of guilt through Jake. With a sigh, he turned and followed Lacey.

* * *

"Dude," Marshall said. "This place is wired to the max!" Nervous excitement spilled from his words. He sat in front of a keyboard and three flat-screen monitors that stretched across an old credenza. The central monitor had a small camera clipped to the top edge.

"Where the hell did those come from?" Jake asked.

"You can thank me for that," Lacey interjected. "I was snooping around to see if I could find any games or maybe a deck of cards for the kids. But the credenza's front doors wouldn't open."

Marshall said, "So I—"

"We," Lacey said, hands on her hips.

"So *we* pulled away the cabinet from the wall and—"

"Power cords," Lacey said.

"It only took a few seconds to find the hidden switch that slid back the cover and lifted the workstation and monitors. It's all state-of-the-art stuff. Pretty sweet, huh?"

Jake waited for the other shoe to drop. "And…so?"

Marshall tapped the keyboard and all three monitors lit up at the same time. Each of the screens displayed four separate surveillance images. Jake recognized the kitchen, bedrooms, and the area immediately outside the hacienda. Four additional images revealed infrared captures of the perimeter. Jake saw Tony and Becker heading back toward the house. He felt a twinge of concern when another image revealed Francesca walking aimlessly in the opposite direction.

"This is not good," Jake said.

"Damn right, pal," Marshall agreed. He leaned over the keyboard and absently rolled up one of the sleeves of his shirt, revealing two fresh scars that crisscrossed up the length of his forearm. He'd gotten them in a fight in Venice while trying to rescue Jake, when Lacey's swift reaction had prevented Marshall from getting killed.

Lacey stood behind Marshall, her hands on his shoulders while he tapped the keys. The images on the central monitor were replaced by an overhead map of the ranch and the surrounding area.

"It's an integrated wireless security and monitoring system," he said. "There's gotta be a sat-dish nearby, probably on the roof." He pointed to a rotating icon on the corner of the screen. "Because this is a link to a remote server."

"Remote?" Jake said, his gut tensing.

"Yeah, but the good news is, the external link wasn't connected when I started it up." He pointed to a series of green dots that circled the land surrounding the ranch. "I figure the link is designed to juice up if one of these perimeter alarms is tripped. It's set up that way to preserve power when no one's here and the generator isn't running. The field sensors probably run on solar batteries. When one of them is tripped, it sends a signal that takes this server out of standby mode using the backup battery system. It then notifies the remote location." He turned to Jake. "God was on our side, man, because we dropped from the sky inside the perimeter sensors. The alarm never went off. We were damn lucky. I've deactivated the sensors so we don't have to worry about accidentally tripping them."

"So...we're okay?" Jake said, praying that they'd finally caught a break.

"No way, dude," Marshall said. A couple of quick keystrokes opened a new window with a list of time-stamped data. "According to this, the remote server is scheduled to automatically interrogate the system at nine tonight. And there's not a damn thing I can do at this end to stop it."

Jake checked his watch. "That's less than an hour from now. What happens when they hook up?"

"If I leave the system in standby, their query will register my intrusion into the system. If I completely shut down the local server, it will signal an alarm. Either way, you can bet they will send someone to check it out pronto."

"Shit, Marsh, can't you hack around it somehow?"

"Not without activating the link to the remote server. The instant I connect, the alarm goes off."

Apprehension clamped around Jake's chest.

"We've got to go," he said.

Marshall was already moving.

Chapter 21

Sonoran Desert, Mexico

ABBAS'S SMILE WAS FERAL. HE STARED THROUGH THE NIGHT vision binoculars from his prone position below the crest of a low foothill that fronted the ranch. He couldn't believe his good fortune. Allah was surely watching over them.

"It appears as if one of the lambs is on the loose," he said, keeping his voice low.

A helmeted officer wearing a desert camouflage uniform adorned with a full combat kit lay beside him. He had his own night vision lenses pressed to his eyes.

"Your orders?" he asked.

Abbas considered this. The woman had wandered directly toward them. She was only a couple hundred meters from their position. It appeared as though her chest was hitching with sobs. Her hands clutched her underbelly, as if she had stomach cramps. He panned the glasses again toward the structure. The big man and the dark man were heading back to the house. The children and the other man were still outside, but they posed no threat.

"I want her alive," he said. "Quickly. Silently. Her friends must not be alerted."

A twelve-man squad of elite Iranian shock commandos blended into the dark landscape behind the two men. An open-air jeep and old panel truck were parked behind them. Abbas had rented the vehicles while waiting for the team's plane to land at the distant Puerto Peñasco airport.

The officer issued an order in Dari. Two of the men snapped on night vision combat goggles before disappearing like wraiths into the darkness. A third man crawled up the rise beside the officer. He tracked his two comrades through the high-powered scope of his sniper rifle.

While he waited, Abbas marveled at his leader's ability to garner resources on the heels of the disaster at their mountain fortress. The sheikh was a master strategist whose multilayered plans contained a web of deception and ingenuity. Less than twelve hours after the American and his friends had disappeared over the vast Sonoran Desert, the sheikh had identified their exact location. Abbas swelled with pride.

He sucked in the sweet aromas of the dry desert air. They reminded him of his home in the foothills of the Hindu Kush. He thought of his younger brother who'd walked the land with him as a child, and who later fought beside him against the infidels. Carlo had idolized Abbas. When their father had been killed by an American mortar attack, Abbas had stepped up to fill the parental role. He'd taught his brother the way of the knife and the two of them struck back at the infidels at every opportunity. They had earned a lethal reputation among their peers and risen quickly in the sheikh's ranks.

Hatred surged within Abbas as he thought of the American killing Carlo by his own blade. Anger blurred his vision. He lowered the binoculars and rubbed his eyes. Though he knew he would eventually avenge his brother, he must resist doing so tonight. He would follow his orders from the sheikh to capture the American alive. Bronson would serve them well in the next few days as an integral part of the sheikh's plan, but after that, Abbas thought with a smile, he would be made to watch as the woman was slowly tortured to death before him. Afterward, the American would smell the reek of his own disembowelment.

Turning to the officer at his side, Abbas said, "We shall use the woman to lure out the American. I want them both alive."

"And the rest?"

The sheikh had asked that they be kept alive, if possible, to use as a lever against the American's cooperation. But Abbas knew in his heart that the woman would be enough.

"Kill them all."

Chapter 22

THE CHILDREN, MAX, AND BRADLEY HURRIED IN THROUGH the front door, ushered by an anxious Becker.

"I didn't see Francesca outside," Becker said. "Is she in here?"

"No," Jake said. He slid another water bottle into the backpack he was stuffing.

"I called out to her," Becker added, "but she didn't answer." He turned to go back out the door.

"Hold on. I'll take care of it," Jake said, handing the backpack to Lacey and marching toward the door. "She's a bit miffed right now. My fault."

"Stop!" Marshall shouted so loudly that it stunned everyone in the room. He stared wide-eyed at one of the computer displays.

Jake hurried to his side. The images on the screen fractured his mind. Even in night vision mode, Francesca's grayscale image was unmistakable as she struggled within the grasps of two men. They dragged her up a short rise.

Jake tried to speak, but emitted only an anguished gurgle.

Tony was beside him in a heartbeat. Several more figures suddenly appeared on the screen from over the ridge. They ran toward the house.

"Get everyone into the tunnel!" Tony shouted.

"What tunnel?" Bradley asked.

"What's happening?" Josh yelled from the couch.

"I'll explain later," Tony said, scooping up Josh in one arm and grabbing Sarafina's hand in the other. He ran toward the hallway that led to the back rooms, urging Bradley to follow. Sensing the tension in the room, Max scurried to get in front of the group. The hair on his hackles went stiff.

Jake's momentary shock was swept away under a maelstrom of fury. Somehow, Battista's men had found them. His pulse quickened, his eyes narrowed, and his brain sorted through options. He knew what must be done.

"Marsh, activate the perimeter alarms," Jake said.

"But that'll alert the narcos."

"Just do it!" Jake ordered. He turned his attention to Lacey. "Switch off all the lights. Then follow Tony and help him with the kids."

She was moving before he finished the sentence.

Becker ran from window to window, closing the shutters. They wouldn't stop a bullet, but at least they'd provide visual cover.

"The narcos have linked up with the remote server!" Marsh said, his face pale.

"Good," Jake said. He placed a protective hand over the satphone on the table so that Marshall wouldn't grab it. "Now get the hell down to the tunnel."

Marshall sprang to his feet. His chair flipped over backward. The dim light from the monitors provided the only illumination in the darkened room. He disappeared into the shadows of the hallway just as Tony returned.

"Lacey and Bradley got things under control with the kids," Tony said, moving quickly to one of the last two open windows. He closed the shutters and latched them. "What's our play?"

Jake's eyes remained glued to the monitor. He couldn't imagine more capable men than Tony and Becker in a firefight, but he needed to face this threat alone, and he knew that neither man would allow him to do so willingly.

There was a loud thud at the front door. Tony and Becker swiveled their weapons toward the opening, but the expected breach didn't occur. Becker risked a quick peek between the slats of a shuttered window.

"Bloody hell, they just dumped a satchel charge at the door!"

Another thud at a window sparked the men into action.

"Move. Now!" Jake shouted, rushing toward the hallway as he calculated how this unexpected element would affect his plan.

Tony's and Becker's rubber-soled shoes slapped the ground right behind him. The two men flicked on the LED flashlights affixed to the bottom of their weapons. The beams of light bounced off the walls.

Jake skidded into the third bedroom and ducked into the walk-in closet. A recessed panel at the back wall had been slid to one side. The thick door on the other side of the panel was open, revealing a narrow wooden staircase that led to the underground tunnel. The dank air drifting out of the opening had a rich earthen smell.

"What about Francesca?" Becker said as he shouldered his way past Jake to illuminate the staircase.

"It's handled," Jake shouted with more confidence than he felt. "No time for explanations. Let's go!"

Becker started down the stairs. Tony motioned for Jake to go next. Jake hesitated. Feigning the best surprised look he could muster, he said, "Shit, I forgot the sat-phone." Edging past his friend, he added, "I'll be back before you're halfway down the steps."

"But—"

Tapping the flow of adrenaline that surged through his system, Jake disappeared around the corner so fast that it must have seemed a blur to Tony. But instead of running back to the great room, he flattened himself against the wall in the corner, his ears tuned to the closet. He heard a brief grumble from Tony, followed by the sound of him padding down the staircase.

Jake moved back into the closet. He grabbed the staircase door and slammed it shut. He latched it so that it couldn't be opened from below.

"Hey!" Tony yelled, his voice muffled by the door. Jake heard him clamber back up the steps.

"Sorry, pal," Jake said as he moved the panel back into place. "This is something I've got to do on my own."

"Jake!" The panel vibrated as Tony's ham-size fist pounded on the door.

"Trust me," Jake said. "I know what I'm doing. But for any of this to work, I need you and Beck to get everyone else to safety."

Tony protested with his silence.

"I'm counting on you, Sarge," Jake said, and turned his back on the bedroom.

He ran down the hallway and positioned himself in front of the small camera above the computer console. He clicked on the remote-link icon. A videoconference window opened on the center screen, filled by the stern face of a well-groomed Hispanic gentleman. This wasn't what Jake expected.

"You will regret that you trespassed on my property," the man said smoothly. A tough-looking hombre with a machete appeared at his shoulder. The man in back bared his yellow teeth beneath his straggly beard. That would be the muscle, Jake thought. These were the right guys.

"Hey, shit-face," Jake said. "Me and my pals have decided to take over this little charnel house."

Before the boss man could say anything, Jake added, "We'll be throwing the parties around here from now on. Your mama's invited. Your wife, too. But you and your ugly friend? You can pound sand. And you know what? There ain't a goddamn thing your pussy ass is going to do about it. Because if I catch you or any of your greaseball pals anywhere near this place, I'll cut you into tiny pieces and feed them to any children that your shriveled excuse for a dick might have fathered." Jake cringed at the foul sentiment, but didn't let it show.

The drug lord's eyes widened, the only sign of his anger. A stream of expletives came from the man behind him, who splattered spittle on the camera lens. "You are already dead, gringo!"

Jake flipped them the bird and disconnected the link.

That ought to bring 'em.

Chapter 23

Sonoran Desert, Mexico

J AKE NEEDED TO BUY TIME.

He flinched when he heard muffled thuds outside two more windows on the opposite end of the great room. Satchel charges now surrounded the structure. One flip of a switch by the man holding Francesca and the hundred-year-old ranch house would be blasted to rubble.

Jake turned off the satellite phone and dropped it on the table. By the time Cal and Kenny retrieved his messages, it would be too late anyway. Jake was on his own.

Scanning the images from the surveillance cameras, he counted at least ten soldiers surrounding the house. They crouched well beyond the anticipated blast radius with assault rifles to their shoulders. Two men had positioned themselves behind one of the thickets of tumbleweeds that Becker and Tony had arranged earlier. The detonator was taped to Jake's thigh beneath his cargo slacks.

Twin headlights appeared over the ridgeline that fronted the property. They bounced on the uneven desert floor as the vehicle threaded its way toward the ranch. Jake could make out four shadowy figures in the open-air jeep. One of them had long, flowing hair.

Francesca.

Jake released a long-held breath. She was alive. He'd counted on that, though a part of him had feared the worst. But Battista's men wanted him, not her. He'd assumed correctly that they'd keep her alive, at least for the time being, to get Jake and his friends to surrender. He willed the approaching jeep to keep moving. He needed Francesca as close as possible to the hacienda if his plan was to have any chance of success.

* * *

Abbas held up his hand. The driver brought the jeep to a stop abreast of the line of soldiers that circled the target. The head-lights illuminated the front of the ranch house fifty meters ahead. A soldier trotted over and handed one of two remote detonators to the officer sitting behind Abbas. Each was the size of a pack of cigarettes.

"All is ready," the soldier reported. "A total of eight charges surround the structure."

The woman whimpered. She sat beside the officer in the backseat, her hands restrained in front of her with flex-cuffs.

"Well done," the officer said, flipping a switch to illuminate a green ready light on the device. The soldier saluted and returned to his station beside a tangle of brush.

Abbas approved the team's efficiency. The Iranian shock troops were well disciplined and highly trained. There were several thousands of the elite soldiers stationed throughout Venezuela, all part of the pact between the Iranian and Venezuelan presidents, an alliance spurred by their shared hatred of America. That Battista had been able to tap into that alliance was further testament to his influence.

Abbas discerned no movement within the house, though he was certain that the American and his friends were peeking through the slats of the shutters. He smiled as he imagined their fear. He stepped out of the jeep, and the officer followed. He pulled

Francesca behind him and shoved her forward. She stumbled in the sand at Abbas's feet, just in front of the vehicle's headlights.

"Up!" he ordered.

* * *

Jake checked his watch. Only ten minutes had passed since he'd spoken with the drug lord. Assuming he and his men were located in the village ten miles distant—and assuming that Jake had pissed him off enough to get him off his ass right away—it would still be another twenty minutes or more before he'd show up.

Jake wondered if the complicated scenario he'd scripted had the slightest chance of working.

The occupants of the jeep exited the vehicle. His chest tightened when Francesca stumbled. He closed his eyes and projected a single desperate thought toward her.

Stall.

* * *

The woman stared up at Abbas. Defiance flared from her eyes.

"Get up!" he repeated.

She didn't budge. Instead, her gaze shifted toward the ranch house. Her expression softened and the corners of her lips curled upward.

"He will make you pay," she said.

Her sudden calm was unexpected. A part of Abbas admired her spirit. He would enjoy breaking it later. "Is that so?"

She nodded. "You are like lambs who have invited a wolf into your midst."

"We shall see."

She studied his face with a curious expression. "You remind me of another of Battista's peons," she said. "Carlo. Did you know him?"

Abbas stiffened at the mention of his brother.

"I thought as much," she said. "He died badly, squealing like a child."

Abbas backhanded her with such force that she rolled twice across the sand.

"Whore!" he shouted, ignoring the look of surprise from the officer beside him. "Do not speak of my brother."

Francesca pushed herself to a sitting position. She wiped at a rivulet of blood that ran from a gash on her already swelling lip.

"I see you share his weakness," she slurred. "Unable to control your emotions. Did you know that he wet himself before he died?"

He instinctively drew his switchblade and snapped it open. The urge to end her worthless life was intense. But he stayed his shaking hand, wondering why she was taunting him. Did she want to die? It was then that he noticed her hands hovering unconsciously over her belly. He loosened his grip on the knife.

"Interesting," he said. "I'll not kill you yet, woman. But rest assured, the time shall come for us to share a very long and intimate conversation about my brother." Pointing the tip of the knife at her belly, he added, "We shall also discuss your unborn child."

The stunned look on the woman's face confirmed his suspicion.

"But first, why don't we ask the child's father to join us."

Abbas hauled Francesca to her feet.

Chapter 24

Sonoran Desert, Mexico

Abandoning the video monitor, Jake watched through a cracked window shutter as two men escorted Francesca to within earshot of the house. They'd left the jeep well behind them. The rising moon cast a pale glow on their faces. One of the men was dressed in full combat gear. The night vision goggles hinged to the front of his helmet were raised, since the headlights from the distant vehicle illuminated the scene. The other man was dark featured with a confident bearing that left little doubt he was in charge.

"Jake Bronson!" the man shouted.

Time was running out on Jake's plan. It would be at least another fifteen minutes before the local cartel boys showed up, assuming they took the bait. Jake remained silent.

"So that's how it's going to be?" the man said. "In that case…" With his free hand, he ripped open Francesca's blouse, exposing her bra and midriff.

"Wait!" Jake shouted.

"Too late for that," the man said, displaying the knife he held. "Listen carefully, Mr. Bronson. And don't make any sudden movements within the house."

Jake felt a swell of panic when he saw the blade pressed against Francesca's abdomen, its point sliding partially beneath her waistband. With a flick of his wrist, the man sliced through the soft material of her slacks, exposing her lower abdomen.

"Stop!" Jake yelled. "I'll come out."

"Not yet," the man said. He pressed the tip of the blade at a point midway between her belly button and crotch. "You will come outside only when I tell you to. But first I want you to fully understand the price of noncompliance with any of my instructions."

Ice rippled through the sheen of sweat on Jake's skin.

"If I plunge the blade here to a depth of five inches, it will surely kill her. It will be a slow and agonizing death." He paused to give Jake a moment to absorb the image. "However, if I limit the puncture to only two inches, then only your unborn child will die. Tell me, Mr. Bronson, do you know yet if it is a boy or a girl?"

The question stunned Jake. A part of him wanted to fling open the door and rush outside. But the man's words had taken control of his movements like a puppeteer's strings. His mind reeled. That's what she wanted to tell me, he thought. I'm going to be a father. He saw from the strained expression on Francesca's face that it was true. That he learned the news while she was in the grasp of terrorists accentuated the desolate state of affairs that had been his life since the accident in the MRI scanner. But the knowledge also strengthened his resolve, stripping away all his emotions except one—determination.

"I will assume from your silence that we understand each other," the man said. "Why don't you come outside and join us? Alone."

Comforted that the others were out of harm's way, Jake swung open the door and stepped over the satchel charge on the doorstep. He raised his hands over his head.

"Fifteen steps forward," the man ordered, the knife still pressed against Francesca. The soldier beside her leveled a semi-automatic pistol at Jake.

Jake complied, his eyes scanning the field that stretched before him. He noted the location of each soldier in the distance, measuring angles and distance against his ability to move faster than they expected. A spate of adrenaline tightened his skin.

"That's close enough," the man ordered. Jake was still ten yards from them. "Empty your pockets."

Jake dropped his wallet, keys, and loose change on the ground.

"Now remove your shirt and spin around."

Jake did as he was told, thankful that he'd left the pistol in the house.

"Ankles next."

Lifting the cuffs of his cargo pants over his sneakers, Jake felt the tug of the masking tape that he'd used to strap Becker's small triggering device to his inner thigh. It felt as if one end of the tape had lifted. Taking care not to dislodge it, he straightened slowly. But as soon as the tension in his trousers loosened, the transmitter slipped a fraction down his leg. Jake sensed that the last inch of tape would give way at any moment.

"Please don't hurt her," he said, diverting the men's attention.

The man shoved Francesca to the dirt. "Silence!" His underlying rage seemed barely contained.

Jake's muscles tightened at Francesca's whimper. She curled into a ball at the man's feet and pulled the corners of her torn blouse around her, but the glint of determination in her eyes didn't match the cowering visage she displayed.

Ten paces separated Jake from the trio. He felt the device under his pants sliding lower like a worm on his skin.

He assessed the two immediate threats in front of him. The soldier wore officer insignias on his collar. His pistol didn't waver. Clipped to his belt was a small instrument with a green light. *A detonator.* It was likely linked to the string of satchel charges. His boss still held the wicked-looking knife and it was apparent he knew how to use it.

The soldier issued a quick order over his headset. From behind him, the jeep's engine revved and the vehicle moved toward them. Jake shifted away his gaze from the headlights to preserve his night vision.

The last fraction of tape separated from Jake's skin and he felt the device lodge above his calf. He stilled. The slightest movement would drop it to the sand.

The jihadist sneered at Jake. His fingers caressed the ivory handle of his knife. "I've waited a long—"

"Hold on!" the officer interrupted in Dari. His eyes narrowed as he pressed a hand to his earpiece. "Switch to night vision immediately," he ordered into his mouthpiece. The jeep's headlights were extinguished and the officer quickly lowered his goggles into place before returning his attention to his leader. "Several vehicles approaching from the west."

Both men shifted their gaze to the horizon.

Jake tensed his ankle and the small triggering device slid to the ground. Disregarding the risk to his heart, he released an avalanche of pent-up energy into his muscles, willing his body to move at top speed—

Nothing happened.

The familiar sensation of the world around him moving in slow motion didn't transpire.

Jake panicked. He'd crafted his plan around the use of his enhanced speed, but some part of his body had overruled him. He dropped to the ground, grabbed Becker's device, and threw the switch.

Three ear-numbing explosions tore through the desert. Becker's hidden C-4 charges blasted through the six-packs of plastic bottles they'd filled with gasoline siphoned from the generator. Even from fifty yards away, Jake felt the wave of heat from the fireballs.

The officer in front of Jake yelped in pain. The glare through his night vision lenses would have seared his irises.

Pushing to his feet, Jake gauged the two men guarding Francesca ten yards ahead of him. They were backlit by a widening swath of flaming scrub brush. The officer buckled over at the waist, his pistol held awkwardly in one hand as he knuckled his eyes. His helmet and goggles lay on the ground beside him. The one with the knife had turned away from Jake, momentarily transfixed by the blasts. Francesca shifted behind the man's feet.

Jake rushed him. Two steps later the jihadist turned. A smile flickered across his face. He lowered his stance and held the switchblade in an ice-pick grip. Though Jake's enhanced speed had shut down, his brain was still on overdrive as he calculated his optimum line of approach. Francesca provided the solution—she lunged at the back of the man's legs. Jake shifted his weight and launched himself feetfirst at the fighter. The jihadist pitched forward just as Jake's heels crushed into his chest. The knife flew from his grasp and his body somersaulted backward over her. He hit the ground with a grunt.

Praying that the soldiers circling the front of the property were still distracted, Jake turned his attention to the still-blinded officer. He ripped the pistol from the man's grip and hammered it against his temple. The soldier folded to the sand.

"Back to the house!" Jake shouted to Francesca as he unclipped the satchel charge detonator from the officer's belt.

Four sets of bouncing headlights appeared over the distant ridge. The narcos had arrived. A burst of gunfire from one of the jihadist soldiers was answered by a fusillade from the fast-approaching vehicles. A cacophony of sharp cracks blistered the night. The remaining jihadists returned fire. Tracers arced into the darkness.

Francesca sprinted toward the hacienda. Her still-cuffed hands held up the front of her torn slacks. Jake was right behind her.

A half-second later the world turned white in front of them. The simultaneous blasts from the eight satchel charges blew them onto their backs on the sand.

* * *

Jake was enveloped in a heavy blanket of pure silence pierced only by a loud ringing in his ears. His limbs were dead weights rooted to the ground. He stared unblinkingly as a dust-filled cloud billowed across the night sky above him, slowly obscuring the star-studded blackness. A scorched slat of wood tumbled in slow motion from the sky, growing ever larger in his vision as it descended toward his face. It impaled the ground twelve inches from his head, its upright end quivering. A thin trail of smoke drifted from its smoldering edge. With no accompanying sounds, the entire scene felt surreal to Jake. He squeezed his eyes closed against a trailing shower of particulate matter that pelted his body like hundreds of hailstones. His hand went up to cover his face and he felt the tingle of sensation returning to his limbs.

Muffled sounds crept through the dazed membranes of his ears and the faint staccato cracks of gunfire flooded his awareness.

Francesca!

Urging his muscles to respond, he rolled over and pushed to his knees. Francesca lay curled beside him, eyes closed, a veil of dust covering her face. A dribble of blood snaked out of her ear. He crawled to her side, wincing at the stab of pain that shot through his wrenched shoulder. He blew the dust from her eyelids and brushed bits of debris from her cheeks.

"Please, Lord," he muttered.

Her eyes fluttered open. Her body tensed.

"Wh—what? Where—?" she mumbled.

"You're okay," Jake said, pulling her into his arms, relief washing over him. "Be still for a second. Give your body a chance to recover."

"I—I can't hear you," she cried out. "What are you saying?"

Jake calmed her with his mind. *Relax a moment. Your hearing will return.*

Francesca pressed into his embrace. Her fingers dug deeply into his back.

A rush of footsteps broke the silence behind him. He turned toward the sound in perfect timing with the rifle butt that smacked into his forehead. The world went dim. Strong arms yanked him from Francesca's grasp. His confused vision centered on the troughs his heels left in the desert sand as he was dragged backward.

* * *

Jake drifted in and out of consciousness in the backseat of the jeep. His hands were flex-cuffed in his lap. His head lolled against Francesca's shoulder as the driver slammed the gas pedal to escape the oncoming truck of narcos. The jihadist sat shotgun in front of him. His hands gripped the top of the windscreen as they bounced across the rough terrain. The officer beside Jake glared at him. He had a golf-ball-size lump on the side of his head from where Jake had coldcocked him. The man jabbed the muzzle of his pistol into Jake's ribs, twisting its tip to accent his anger. But the flame of pain in Jake's side was a welcome distraction as he stared at the fifty-foot-deep sinkhole that used to be the ranch house.

The massive explosion had collapsed the hacienda into the network of tunnels and caverns that hid the underground river. Before he blacked out again, Jake's last thoughts were of his friends. No one could have survived that blast.

Part II

Chapter 25

T HE MAN'S NAME IS JAKE BRONSON," LIEUTENANT COLONEL
Brown said as he paced before Doc's cluttered desk. They
were in a small office one hundred feet belowground in the Area
52 complex. "He's a former air force pilot. Lives in Redondo
Beach, California."

"One of yours, eh?" Doc said, leaning back in his chair. He
tapped the stem of his pipe against his bearded chin.

"Not anymore. He's a civvy stunt instructor at a small municipal airport."

"And you're certain this is our boy?"

"The intelligence team confirmed it. The field operative
received the tip less than an hour ago. He was one of the guys
who surveyed the scene right after the Afghan mountain explosion. The local tribesmen he interviewed weren't very helpful at
the time, but he left them his business card in case they thought
of anything else. One of them just called."

"After so long?" Doc said.

"I know. Sounds suspicious. The guy is suddenly a fountain
of intel. Something, or someone, decided it was in their best
interest to fill us in."

"So this Jake Bronson was there when the object was
launched?"

"He wasn't simply there. According to the source, he was the one who triggered it."

"You're kidding," Doc said, rising to his feet.

Brown shook his head.

Doc slid the pipe into his pants pocket. "My God, we need him—"

"I know, I know. But there's a problem."

"What?"

"Lieutenant Bronson's been involved in an incident. It seems he was in a high-speed chase and gunfight in the LA area."

"A gunfight? With the cops?"

"No. Someone else. We're not sure who yet. According to witnesses, the guys chasing him had automatic weapons. AKs, from the sound of it. In the end, Lieutenant Bronson and a group of his friends—including two young kids and a guide dog, if you can believe it—stole a plane and low-leveled it to Mexico."

"He had children with him?"

"Plus two women. A real family affair. We haven't isolated their position yet. But we will. We're getting a satellite retasked and I've sent teams to contact known associates." He glanced at the printout he'd brought with him. "There's one connection in particular that has us intrigued. It seems that ever since Lieutenant Bronson did his short stint with us, he's been buddies with one of our CV-22 pilots, a Major Springman."

"And?"

"According to the report from our new source, a USAF CV-22 was used to transport Lieutenant Bronson's team to and from the Afghan mountain stronghold."

"Jeez..."

"Exactly," Brown said. He checked his watch. "And Major Springman is just about to complete a training exercise at Miramar in San Diego. We'll be on him within the hour."

Doc swiveled the large desk monitor so Brown could see the live image of the black pyramidal object that filled the screen. "Finally," he said. "A break."

He recalled the remarkable chain of events that had brought them to this point. The ancient object had been discovered in a sunken cavern in the Grand Canyon over forty years ago. But when military scientists were unable to unlock its secrets, it had been left to gather dust in an obscure government vault—until recently, when a duplicate object was inexplicably launched into space from the mountains in Afghanistan. Tracking computers made the connection. The government had immediately moved the object to this secure facility under Doc's charge.

"Colonel," he said, "I don't have to tell you how critical this Bronson character is to what we're trying to uncover here."

"I understand. But we need to proceed with caution. Something doesn't smell right about the timing on this sudden flow of intel. The source seemed to know a lot more than he let on to the field op. At one point he even let it slip that Lieutenant Bronson was out of the country."

"And how in the hell could a tribesman from the mountains of Afghanistan possibly know that?"

"Exactly."

Chapter 26

Beneath the Sonoran Desert, Mexico

Tony swept the assault rifle back and forth. The under-barrel flashlight illuminated the narrow path ahead. The downward-sloping tunnel stretched into the darkness. The floor was uneven, and the limestone walls were pitted with cracks and fissures. Sarafina clung to his chest like a monkey, her feet lodged on his belt. Becker and the rest of the group trailed behind them.

"Watch your steps," Tony said over his shoulder as he maneuvered around a jagged outcropping. His voice sounded hollow between the rocky walls. He'd been furious that Jake had fooled him so easily, but he'd quickly buried his anger, honoring his friend's sacrifice and fixing his mind on the task at hand. It was his job to make sure the group wasn't anywhere close to the house if the satchel charges went off.

After several minutes the passageway leveled. The air grew moist and Tony heard the flow of water ahead. Ten paces farther and the tunnel exited into an airy grotto. It was so large that its walls disappeared beyond the reach of his flashlight.

Sarafina gasped.

A twenty-five-foot-wide river split the space. Its smoothly undulating surface shimmered beneath Tony's light. Gravel crunched underfoot as the rest of the group moved forward to absorb the view. Their flashlights panned the space, causing ominous shadows to dance across a forty-foot-high ceiling that bristled with colorful stalactites. Some of the larger ones had joined with stalagmites to form an endless row of crude columns on the opposite side of the emerald river. Small clusters of crystalline quartz jutted from the rock walls, twisting the beams of light and separating them into a rainbow of hues that flickered against the stone.

Max rushed to the river's edge and sniffed the water. It must have passed the nose test because he lapped it in a long drink, his tail wagging at full speed.

Tony lowered Sarafina to the ground.

"Be careful," he said. She ran over and motioned for Becker to lower Josh as well. The boy's face was filled with apprehension.

"It's really cool, Josh," she said softly. "Let me show you."

She took his hand and carefully escorted him to the river's edge. She painted the scene with her words.

Everyone paused for a moment to listen to her artful description of the ancient underground world that surrounded them. Watching the two children triggered a new round of worries in Tony about his family. He said a prayer for their safety.

When Sarafina was finished, Josh inhaled deeply.

"It smells like Pirates of the Caribbean," he said.

"You're right, pal," Tony said. It was his kids' favorite attraction, and he was relieved that Josh latched on to a happier memory in the midst of this nightmare. "And we're going for a boat ride just like at Disneyland."

Two inflatable four-man rafts were tied off on the narrow shoreline. Their ends bobbed at the river's edge. Tony and Becker had prepped the rafts just hours before, loading them with life jackets and emergency gear. Papa, Jake, and Tony had brought the gear on a previous visit and navigated down the river to the exit point. It was a quarter mile away.

Marshall picked up on the need to keep the mood light. He began singing the Pirates' theme song, *"Yo ho, yo ho, a pirate's life for me…"*

When he stumbled over the next verse, Becker took over. "*We pillage, we plunder, we rifle, and loot, drink up, me 'earties, yo ho,*" he sang, waving his free hand as though it held a mug of ale. "*We kidnap and ravage and don't give a hoot, drink up, me 'earties, yo ho.*"

Everyone joined in the chorus. "*Yo ho, yo ho, a pirate's life for me.*" Their voices echoed off the canyon walls.

Becker kept the song going. Tony grinned at the fact that the tough Aussie knew all the words. The release of tension in the group was palpable. It was just what they needed at the moment.

Tony used the distraction to get everybody outfitted for what lay ahead. He handed out life vests one by one. Caving helmets were next. Each had a fully charged LED lamp affixed to it. He added his burly voice to the chorus, "*Yo ho, yo ho…*"

Though the adults exchanged worried glances, they kept the song going for the sake of the children. Lacey and Marshall helped them with their gear.

After donning his own gear, Tony picked up the two remaining vests. Like the others, they each had a bright yellow cylinder the size of a soda can strapped to the front. The clear rubber mouthpiece on top of the can provided up to thirty breaths of emergency oxygen. He leaned them against the wall of the cavern. Whatever Jake planned to do up above, if he and Francesca made it down here, they'd need the vests to float downriver without a raft.

He hoped like hell they'd get a chance to use them.

* * *

Becker, Bradley, Josh, and Marshall piled into one of the boats. The boy clung to his teacher's side. Max jumped in and Marshall pressed him to the floor near his position at the front. As soon as he took his hand from the dog, Max sat back up. Marshall urged him down again. Max popped back up. Relenting, Marshall let

Max settle in with his front paws on his lap and his head on the bow. Lacey and Sarafina huddled together in the lead boat with Tony. The entire group stared into the blackness beyond the reach of their lights. No one was singing.

It seemed as if everyone took a collective breath when Tony and Becker pushed them from the shore. The slow current grabbed the boats and pulled them downstream. Neither raft had an outboard motor. Tony and Becker steered with paddles from their seats at the stern. Marshall and Lacey had paddles in hand, but they wouldn't be required on the short ride. Between here and the exit point, the river flowed with a gentle ripple.

"Beck," Tony called out to the raft behind him. "The river splits at the end of this cavern. We take the right fork. After that, our landing point is about three hundred yards on the right. We've posted a string of luminescent flags on the wall to mark the spot."

"Righto, Cap'n," Becker said in his best pirate drawl. After a moment, he added, "Just out of curiosity, what happens if we take the left fork?"

Tony glanced over his shoulder at Becker and gave a subtle shake of his head. With the children hanging on every word, he wasn't about to relay what Papa had told him—that the few people who had ventured down that fork had never come out the other side.

He focused his attention ahead, steering the raft along the right edge of the river. He hummed the chorus to the pirate song.

The deafening explosion behind them fractured his nerves. Tony felt a rush of air just before the shock wave hit his back like a Mack truck. The wind was knocked from his lungs, the paddle flew from his hands, and he somersaulted into the water.

The life jacket pulled him to the surface, and he bobbed alongside the spinning raft. The cavern rumbled all around him, shaking like an 8.0 quake. Stalactites split from the ceiling and speared into the water. One of them impacted not three feet from his head. Smaller pellets clattered off his helmet. A huge slab of limestone separated from the nearby cavern's edge and crashed into the water like a calving iceberg. Heavy splashes emanated from the darkness all around them.

"Tony!" Lacey shouted.

He looked up to see Lacey's face in the beam of his helmet lamp. She leaned over the edge of the boat with her hand extended. He grabbed her wrist and steadied himself against the side of the raft. Another deafening rumble and a huge wave cascaded over them, sucking Tony's head underwater. Lacey's grip tightened. Her nails dug into the flesh of his wrist. He surfaced and coughed water from his lungs. He caught a brief glimpse of Max paddling desperately past him in the sudden rage of water. Like a huge breaker rushing to shore, the wave raced onward and vanished into the blackness, taking the dog with it. Tony feared the worst for the poor animal. With a grimace, he reached up with his free hand and grabbed the rope that was looped along the top edge of the raft.

He was about to heave himself upward when the water calmed. He felt his feet drag along the river bottom and in a matter of moments both he and the raft came to a lurching halt. They rested on a sprawling bed of polished river rocks that suddenly had less than three inches of water flowing over it.

"What the hell?" Tony said as he pushed himself to his feet.

Lacey and Sarafina peered over the edge of the raft. Their eyes widened in dismay. The second raft had come to a rest ten paces away. The rest of the team was cocooned safely within its confines, huddled together under Becker's watchful gaze. A catfish flapped in a small pool of water beside them. The river was gone.

Tony looked past them upriver. "Shit," he muttered.

The entire ceiling of the cavern had collapsed under the force of the explosion above. Thousands of tons of earth and limestone had mixed with debris from the hundred-year-old structure. It filled the cavernous space from wall to wall, damming the river behind it. Pale moonlight shone through a new vent in the ceiling.

He jogged upriver to get a closer look, dodging around broken stalactites and splashing through puddles. "Get everyone out of the rafts and up to the shoreline," he shouted as he passed Becker's boat.

"What's happening?" Josh screamed. "Where's Max?"

Tony ignored him and kept moving. The beam from his helmet bounced across the riverbed. Twenty paces later the dam towered before him. Tony's worst fears were confirmed when he saw water bubbling through the mud wall. The sodden earth would soon succumb to the mountain of water pressure behind it. A chunk of debris punched outward from midway up the dam. The gurgle of water that replaced it widened to an angry, spitting stream.

Tony spun around and ran like hell. The river would not be denied. Streams could grow to torrents at any moment and blast through the makeshift dam, pulling mud, stone, and debris along with them. Anything in their path would be obliterated.

* * *

Tony and Becker scooped up the children and the group raced toward the end of the cavern.

"How much farther?" Marshall asked. The team's emergency pack bounced on his shoulder as he jumped over a boulder.

The water level in the center of the riverbed continued to rise. The previous trickle had grown to a fast-flowing creek. Running past a row of twisted limestone columns, Tony glanced up and noted that the cavern's ceiling was beginning to slope downward.

"The split's just ahead," he shouted. "From there it's a couple minutes to the exit."

Five paces later the group came to a stop. The beams from their helmet lamps panned the sight before them. Tony's heart sank. The entrance to the right fork—and safety—had collapsed during the explosion. The stream boiled and splashed against the limestone obstruction before coursing with growing force into the center of the downward-sloping left passageway.

Max's bark pierced the gloom as he safely reappeared. He bounded from the opening and spun twice around as if eager to lead the way.

No choice, Tony thought.

"Let's go," he shouted. He ignored the warning bells going off in his head and followed the dog into the darkness.

Chapter 27

THE TUNNEL STRETCHED BEYOND THE REACH OF THEIR lamps. It looked like a smaller version of the expansive cavern behind them. There was a forest of stalactites suspended thirty feet overhead. Crystalline structures jutted from the walls.

The tunnel was about double the width of a New York subway. A wide trough ran down its center, much of it already underwater. The expanding stream twisted and turned as it stretched into the darkness. The loose silt along its edges shimmered under the beam of Tony's lamp and he wondered if he was running over a fortune in gold dust. But he wasn't about to stop and check. This tunnel was a death trap that could spring at any moment.

The stream of water rose a few inches with every step. Small rooster tails began to form over some of the larger rocks in its path. The flow would soon be impossible to ford.

"Hug the right wall," Tony shouted to the group behind him. Josh pressed against his chest, supported easily by Tony's left arm as he clung to Tony's neck, humming the pirate theme song. Josh's voice caught with each of Tony's steps. Max scampered beside them, occasionally glancing up as if to ensure his master was safe.

The path sloped downward, the walls narrowed, and the stream picked up speed. Tony prayed for a path that would lead them to the safety of the right fork. He scanned for any sign of an opening. That's when he noticed the wavy line of discoloration that suddenly appeared along the base of the wall. It angled upward as the passage continued to narrow. Within ten paces the line was at chest level.

He panned his light across the other side of the cavern. He grimaced when he saw the matching delineation along the far wall. The waterline had been created when only half of the river had traveled down this course. What would happen when its entire volume was forced through these confines?

He scanned the ceiling. The longest of the stalactites hovered just fifteen feet overhead. Would the torrent rise above that when the dam burst? If so, they'd be shredded to the bone.

He picked up his pace. "Keep it moving!" he said over his shoulder. He searched the gloom ahead, but there were no ledges, no beaches, no signs of an exit. If anything, the tunnel seemed to narrow more. Whether he liked it or not, it sure as hell looked like they were going for a swim.

He stopped and turned to face the team as they caught up to him. Marshall sucked in several wheezing breaths. He seemed to need the break more than the others. The air was thick with moisture and Tony suspected it was taking its toll on his ex-smoker buddy. It didn't help that he also carried the fifty-pound emergency pack on his back.

Unfazed by the run, Lacey jogged in place for a moment before settling down. Bradley had kept up, cradling his injured arm.

Becker brought up the rear with Sarafina in his arms.

"We gotta tie up," Tony said. He moved behind Marshall and unzipped his backpack with his free hand. Josh clung tightly against his chest. Tony reached into the pack and pulled out an eighty-foot coil of climbing rope and a bundle of carabiners.

Lacey separated the carabiners and handed them out.

"Hook the clips to the waist straps on your life jackets like this," Tony said, as he snapped one to his vest and another to Josh's.

"What's this for?" Marshall asked.

Tony ignored him for the moment.

Becker lowered Sarafina to the ground. "Hang tight, darlin'. I need both hands for a spell." She edged up against his leg, her eyes vacant. Her fingers danced, as if along imaginary piano keys, playing a song only she could hear.

Becker took the coil of rope and looped a climber's knot through Josh's clip. Cinching it with a firm tug of his wrists, the two men exchanged a look. Neither of them spoke. Becker spanned three arm lengths in the rope and tied another knot on Tony's clip. He continued the process until all of them were linked together, spaced at ten-foot intervals along the rope.

The dog ambled over and nudged one of the dangling loops of rope with his nose, as if wondering why he was the only one not tethered to the leash. Lacey leaned over and scratched his head.

"What about Max?" she said.

Becker glanced at Marshall's backpack, thoughtful.

"I've got just the thing," he said. He rummaged through the pack and pulled out a pouch labeled NECK SPLINT. He unrolled the clear plastic sleeve and looped it over the dog's head and around his neck. Pressing his lips to the valve, he inflated the makeshift flotation device until it was snug.

"That'll do it, big fella," he said with a ruffle of Max's fur. The dog padded backward. He shook his head, trying to dislodge the uncomfortable collar. "You're gonna have to get used to it, pal."

Becker lifted Sarafina to his chest and nodded to Tony.

Surveying the group, Tony realized he had one more thing to do before they could proceed. He unstrapped his Spare Air canister and pressed it gently against Josh's chest.

"What's this?" Josh said, his fingers probing the rubber mouthpiece of the device.

"That's for when we go swimming," Tony said.

"Really?"

"Sure, it's fun," he said. He opened the safety valve. "You wrap your lips around it, grip this little rubber piece with your teeth to hold it in place, and suck in with your mouth, like when you use a straw. Give it a try."

Josh's eyes widened as the pressured oxygen drove into his lungs.

He pulled it free. "Cool!" he said.

Clinging to Becker's chest, Sarafina watched the exchange. Tony splashed the mouthpiece through the stream and held out the can to her.

She nodded, tightened her mouth around the dripping mouthpiece, and drew in a breath. Her eyes revealed her surprise. She smiled around the rubber.

"What about this thing?" Lacey said, fingering a bright orange tab on the front of her vest.

"It activates a transponder," Tony said. "It sends out an emergency signal."

Lacey's eyes brightened.

"Don't get your hopes up," Tony said. He pointed at the rock ceiling that stretched above them. "They're worthless down here."

He restrapped the air canister to his vest. "Okay, we're all set. The rope will keep us together when we get into the water."

"When's that going to happen?" Marshall asked. His voice cracked.

Tony glanced at the stream. In the two minutes it had taken them to tie up, it had doubled in size.

"Soon," Tony said as he stepped forward to lead his friends into the maw. "Very soon."

Chapter 28

C AL SPRINGMAN'S TANNED FACE WAS USUALLY PLASTERED with an exuberant smile. Growing up riding surfboards on the unpredictable waves of Southern California beaches had taught him to enjoy whatever life threw his way. *Enjoy the wave you're on*, he'd say, *because they may not be breakin' tomorrow.* His no-worries attitude had followed him into the not-so-friendly skies of Afghanistan, where he'd served as a decorated combat pilot in the US Air Force. His infectious smile and cocky radio techniques in the face of life-or-death situations had earned him pats on the back from his peers and the disdain of his superiors.

Cal wasn't smiling now.

On loan to a specialized fighter-attack squadron temporarily based at the Marine Corps Air Station Miramar in San Diego, the pilot was about to rush into the squadron commander's office when he overheard the man's angry discussion with his aide.

"What the hell did Springman do this time?" the colonel shouted.

Cal flattened himself against the wall just outside the office.

"Uh...I'm not sure, sir," the aide said. "The man from the agency said they wanted him and his copilot taken into custody immediately."

"Goddamn air force pukes," the colonel said. "No discipline. That's their damn problem. And Major Springman's at the top of that list. If we take him and his brainy what's-his-name sidekick into custody, what the shit are we supposed to do about the test we're smack in the middle of? Where the hell are we on that anyway?"

"The copilot is a Captain Lyons, sir. He's still technically on active duty, but he's currently on loan to Northrop as a consultant. First name, Kenneth. The minidrones are his brainchild. So far, they have definitely lived up to his promises. Our teams still haven't figured a way around their stealth and jamming capabilities. It's amazing technology, sir. We can really use it overseas." He pointed out the window to the flight ramp. "Major Springman's plane is on the flight line now. They're scheduled to take off for the next sortie in…" He checked his watch and added, "Fifteen minutes."

"Well, screw that!" the colonel said. "I'm not going to get my pecker twisted into a knot by some obscure government agency just because Springman and his pimple-faced buddy happen to know this Bronson character."

Cal tensed at the mention of Jake's name.

"Yes, sir," the aide said.

"So what are you waiting for, Lieutenant? I want them grounded. Now!"

"Sir!"

Cal split around the corner, down the hall, and out the exit to the flight line. He flipped open his cell phone and ran toward the parked CV-22 Osprey. His phone had been off all day—in accordance with the operational guidelines of the flight tests—until ten minutes ago. That's when he'd listened to the two voice mails from Jake. Cal had hoped to get the squadron commander's permission for emergency leave. That wasn't going to happen.

Considering what he'd just heard inside the colonel's office, Cal knew the timing of Jake's calls was no coincidence. He picked up the pace. Kenny was in the plane, updating Northrop on the results of the morning test. Cal speed-dialed his number.

Kenny answered on the first ring. "Hey."

"Start the engines," Cal ordered. "Ignore the checklist."

"What the—?"

"Shut up and just do it. I'm a hundred yards out with bogeys on my six. If we're not in the air in forty-five seconds, we're going to jail."

The phone went dead. Cal heard the whine of the Osprey's powerful Rolls-Royce engines power up and he knew that Kenny was assholes and elbows in the cockpit. The sixty-foot-long high-wing aircraft was a hundred yards ahead of him. The oversize wingtip-mounted engine nacelles were tilted upward in vertical lift mode. The wide rotors spun up to speed. Cal was relieved to see that Kenny's experimental minidrones were still hitched to the underside of each wing. In dark slate hues and manta-ray designs, they were like miniature stealth bombers. With any luck, their cache of electronic equipment would give Cal and Kenny the edge they needed to make a clean getaway.

The aircraft that supported the twin drones was like a second home to Cal. He'd turned down two separate opportunities to switch to fighters, preferring the hands-on feel of the tilt-rotor Osprey, given its name more for its gull-like appearance than its ability to switch from vertical to horizontal flight. The versatile performance of the CV-22 meant more diverse missions, many of which put him in the middle of the action with ground forces. That was a hell of a lot more attractive to him than splitting the high skies at Mach 2 in a fighter, waiting for that once-in-a-lifetime dogfight that would end in the blink of an eye after a computer-assisted missile launch. Where was the fun in that?

Cal raced up the rear ramp and past the inward-facing web seats to the cockpit. Kenny was strapped into Cal's pilot seat, one hand on the cyclic stick and the other on the throttles.

"Ramp is closing," Kenny said. "Ready for takeoff."

"Get off the airplane, Kenny," Cal said to his red-haired, freckle-faced friend. Though Kenny was an experienced twenty-five-year-old pilot, his childlike exuberance and resemblance to a skinny sixteen-year-old video gamer engendered an overprotective attitude in Cal.

"This is going to be a one-man show," Cal added.

"Cut the crap," Kenny said. "I don't know what the heck's going on, but I'm not about to miss it."

"This is no time to mess around, kid. I'm about to break enough laws to get me locked up forever. I'm *not* taking you down with me."

"I ain't moving 'til you tell me what's up."

"Dammit, K—" Cal stopped when he looked out the windscreen and saw the flashing lights of three security vehicles speeding toward them. They were out of time.

"Okay, listen up," he said. "Jake's in trouble in Mexico. Needs an evac, like, yesterday. And suddenly the Feds are here to take us into custody. It can't be a coincidence. I'm up for doin' the deed, but there's no sense in both of us putting our necks in a noose. So unstrap and jump off."

"No way," Kenny said. He advanced the thrust-control levers. "We're outta here."

"This is going to end your career, you know."

"Ha! The existence of the entire human race is at risk and you think I give a shit about my career? If Jake is in trouble, I'm going with you." He pulled back on the stick and the aircraft lifted into the air.

"Shit," Cal said, as he clambered into the copilot's seat and strapped himself in. "You know how much I hate it when you sit in my seat."

"Whatever. Enjoy the ride."

Cal arched an eyebrow. "The force is strong with this one," he said, imitating Darth Vader from the *Star Wars* trilogy. Kenny was a devout fan. Donning his flight helmet, Cal threw several switches beneath the avionics display and added, "Let's power up your toys and show these jarheads what's up."

* * *

As soon as they cleared Miramar's airspace, Kenny gave control of the aircraft to Cal. He knew Cal was a hell of a lot better pilot than he was—at least with manned aircraft—but he'd enjoyed the rush of taking charge during their hasty exit.

The two men had met a couple years ago when Kenny was assigned as Cal's copilot. It was an unlikely alliance. Cal was an aggressive pilot who was into surfing, girls, and any outdoor adventure that would get the adrenaline pumping. Kenny was happier sitting comfortably in one of his custom-made "action" chairs playing video games—when he wasn't at his computer tweaking the design on his latest drone. As the oldest son of a family-owned crop-dusting business in the Midwest, he'd been around airplanes his entire life. He was a decent stick, but as a wunderkind—that's what Granddad always called him—he'd always been more interested in piloting and designing remote-control aircraft.

He and Cal found common ground in their love of being in the air. Cal worked his charm to get his young copilot to loosen up, getting him out on the town on a regular basis to enjoy the sweet fruits that life offered, while Kenny opened Cal's eyes to a brave new world of unmanned aerial vehicles, or UAVs—the future of air combat.

Together they'd played a critical role in Jake's insane rescue mission in the Hindu Kush mountains of Afghanistan earlier this year, using their individual talents to get the team safely in and out of the hotbed region. It hadn't been their first combat mission together, and the way things were going, it sure as heck wasn't going to be their last. But the bond the two men shared now was much more than one formed because they'd faced death together. It was the mind-scrambling knowledge they'd gleaned from Jake's contact with the alien artifact that had made them comrades for life—what was left of it. They shared a loyalty to Jake Bronson that was absolute.

Kenny made his way to the UAV control console in the main cabin. He slid into the swivel-mounted chair and wrapped his fingers around the joysticks at the end of each padded armrest. The trio of flat-panel displays before him was already powered up. The center screen displayed the drones' status boards, and the outside panels were slaved to the UAVs' forward cameras with overlays that streamed input from their onboard sensors.

An eight-inch model of the *Millennium Falcon* from the movie *Star Wars* was affixed to the top of the center display. He gave it a customary love tap and went to work. Under his breath he muttered, "Game on."

Chapter 29

THE VAST NETWORK OF TUNNELS UNDER THE SONORAN Desert was fed by thousands of acres of aquifers. Tony imagined the tremendous amount of pressure they exerted on the dammed underground river. When the wall collapsed, its full force would be released all at once.

The stream had grown to a small river. Tony estimated it at five feet deep at the center. Its edges lapped against the cavern walls. He jogged forward, hugging the right wall. His shoulder scraped against a small outcropping of rock. Being tethered together made the going more difficult. Marshall was directly behind him, panting fiercely. Splashing footfalls resounded behind him. Helmet beams bounced off the walls.

They were nearly a half mile into the unexplored fork when the ground began shaking. A roar echoed down the passage behind them. Time had run out.

"Into the water!" he shouted. He high-stepped through the shallows toward the center of the swift-flowing river.

The rest of the team splashed after him.

"Oh, crap, oh, crap, oh, *crap!*" Marshall cried out, putting a voice to the fears everyone felt.

The current pulled harder against Tony's legs with each stride. He tightened his grip on Josh. Two steps farther, his feet slipped out from under him. He sat back as the current took him—and Josh—in its grasp. Max paddled alongside them, his head held unnaturally high in the water thanks to the inflatable neck splint. There was a brief tug on the rope behind Tony as the rest of the team lost their footing, and then they all were rushing through the oily darkness.

The current swept them forward double time. Tony welcomed the speed. There was no way they'd outpace the monster that was rushing to catch them, but the farther away from the breach, the less severe the impact. Tony squinted into the gloom ahead, scanning for signs of boulders or obstructions in their path. He struggled to keep his feet pointed downstream, using his free hand as a steering oar.

The monster was nearly upon them.

Tony pulled his hand through the water and ripped the can of Spare Air from its Velcro strap. Sensing the shift in Tony's posture, Josh dug his fingers deeper into the back of Tony's neck.

The current quickened. The roar grew louder.

"Josh," Tony yelled as he touched the rubber mouthpiece to the boy's trembling lips. "Now's the time, buddy. Remember to breathe through your mouth, not your nose!"

Josh nodded, slipping the mouthpiece in and clamping his teeth around it.

A thunderous rumble overwhelmed them. The air filled with mist.

"Hang on!" Tony shouted. He tightened his grasp around the shaking child.

A second later the wall of water slammed into them.

The frenzy impacted Tony's back with the force of an NFL linebacker. He curled himself into a protective ball around Josh. He kept one hand wrapped around the air canister to hold it in place against the boy's mouth. They twisted and tumbled through churning water. Tony's face broke the surface for an instant and he caught a brief glimpse of the tips of stalactites rushing by not two feet above his head. He grabbed a breath just before the undercurrent sucked them back down into its vortex.

Tumbling within the deluge, Tony focused on protecting Josh. He pressed him fiercely to his chest. His lungs were on fire, but he refused to risk loosening his grasp on the boy in order to grab the second can of air. Seconds felt like minutes. Something cracked hard against his helmet and wrenched his neck. Another object punched into his thigh. Violent tugs on the rope latched to his belt reminded him that his friends battled the same demons.

Tony's lungs sent desperate signals to his brain, commanding him to open his mouth. He clenched his jaw and refused the order. A growing part of him wondered if the end was near. His mind slowed.

All at once the current loosened its grip. The combined buoyancy of two life jackets blew Tony and Josh to the surface. Tony's face broke through the water and he sucked in a huge breath. The roof sloped upward and the spearlike rock formations were now a good distance above him. He panned his helmet lamp from side to side. The tunnel had expanded considerably, dissipating the pent-up forces and slowing the current to nine or ten knots. The river still stretched the full width of the cavern and there was no place to land. But for the moment at least, the violent flow had declared a truce.

"We made it, pal," he said softly to Josh.

In spite of his blindness, the boy's eyes were as wide as saucers. Tony removed the mouthpiece from his lips.

"I'm proud of you," Tony said, patting his back.

Josh buried his face in Tony's neck. His chest hitched with sobs. A rapid series of splashes brought Max to their side. His front paws clawed through the water and onto Tony's outstretched arm. The dog struggled with a feverish need to climb out of the water. Tony wrapped an arm around the dog's torso and held him firm. Max's tongue lolled out the side of his open jaw and his eyes drooped with exhaustion. The shredded neck splint hung loosely around the dog's neck.

"Attaboy," Tony said with a squeeze. "You're gonna be okay, fella."

A dog never looked more grateful.

Tony spun around in the water and confirmed that the rest of the group had made it as well. Marshall and Lacey held each other in a tight embrace. Blood trickled from a gash in Marshall's forehead. Lacey pressed her shirtsleeve against it.

"It's worse than it looks," Marshall said. "Just a scrape."

Bradley was beside them. The bandage around his wounded arm was saturated with blood.

"You okay?" Tony asked.

"Not to worry," he said. "Just a few bumps and bruises."

Becker and Sarafina floated into the light. Her arms clung to the Australian's neck. She blinked away the dripping water.

"Is Josh all right?" she asked, shivering.

She's something, Tony thought. She just got pulled out of a washing machine on full spin cycle and the first thing she wants to know is if her schoolmate is okay. Even though she wasn't related to Francesca by blood, there was no denying she shared the woman's empathy.

Josh must have heard Sarafina's question. He sniffled away a sob and nodded several times. Tony could sense that the boy wanted to hide his tears from her.

"He says he's fine," Tony said. When the dog licked Tony's hand, he added, "Max, too."

Josh stiffened suddenly in Tony's arms.

"N—noise," he said, pointing downstream.

Tony swiveled his helmet lamp just as the river made a sharp bend to the right. They entered the turn, the acoustics shifted, and the rumble of water cascading over rocks breached the silence. They rounded the turn with increasing speed. The roof of the cavern sloped sharply downward.

The rumble became a roar. The river disappeared beneath them and they were suddenly weightless amid a shower of raging water.

* * *

They plunged deep into the pool at the base of the massive waterfall. The aerated water cushioned the impact. Tony felt several sharp tugs on his belt as the rest of the group dropped beside him.

The life jacket pulled at Tony's shoulders. Aided by kicks from his powerful legs, he broke the surface well beyond the crushing wall of water. Josh was still firmly within his grasp. He coughed up water. Max paddled in a frenzied circle nearby.

One by one the others bobbed to the surface. They found themselves in a large rippling pool. The river's gripping force had disappeared. Tony imagined it plunging deep beneath them into an unseen underwater exit. The chamber they'd tumbled into was half the size of a high school gym. The ceiling rose nearly sixty feet overhead.

"Is everyone okay?" Tony shouted through the thick, swirling mist.

Nobody heard him. His voice was buried under the thunderous roar of thousands of tons of water crashing down from above. He used the universal okay hand signal and was relieved when each of the group responded in kind. Lacey and Marshall pulled a grateful Max into their embrace.

The surface current pushed them away from the cascading mass of water. As they neared the center of the circular pool, the howl of the falls seemed to double in volume, reverberating off the walls. Josh pressed his palms against his ears. The group banded together to form a single island. The beams from their helmet lamps panned and swiveled across the rocky surface of the tomb that enveloped them.

Tony studied the faces around him. It was apparent from their strained expressions that the adults understood the nature of their predicament. Becker was the only one whose expression showed no fear. The Aussie's eyes narrowed on a rock outcropping fifteen feet overhead. The area immediately above it was shrouded in shadow.

An exit?

Tony scanned the wall beneath. It was sheer, with no fissures or handholds. He was considering how to get up there when he sensed that the ledge wasn't as far away as he'd first thought. That's when he realized the water level was rising. The chamber was filling up.

A few minutes later, Becker unhooked his rope from the others, lunged up and grabbed the edge of the shelf. It was now just a few feet overhead. He pulled himself up and disappeared from view. The rest of the group held a collective breath as they bobbed in the rising pool, their eyes fixed on the shadowed recess. Lacey crossed her fingers. Tony saw Marshall's lips mouthing the word *please* over and over again.

A moment later, Becker's wide, toothy smile beamed at them. He reached his arm down and said, "This way out, mates."

Chapter 30

Tony pulled himself onto the shelf in time to see Becker and Josh disappear into the shadows of the narrow fissure. The trail of dripping water in their wake glistened under the beam of Tony's helmet lamp.

It felt good to be on dry land once again. Damn good. He unstrapped the LED torch that he'd salvaged from his abandoned assault rifle. He panned its powerful beam over the pool they'd left behind. The water continued to rise; it was less than a couple feet from the ledge. A cluster of bubbles broke the surface along the wall, as if the chamber had sprung a leak. A second string appeared a few feet away, gurgling and sputtering. He didn't know what was going on down there, but it couldn't be good. He was glad as hell to be out of there.

He turned sideways to fit his body through the narrow fissure that led to the adjoining cavern. He heard the echo of conversation in front of him. The tension had eased in his friends' voices. The dog barked, sounding playful. Maybe their luck had finally turned.

The passage widened into a high-ceilinged cavern with walls that sloped outward from its depths, like the cone of a volcano, though this one had a solid roof over it. He found himself on an elevated shelf that was about midway up the space. Wide limestone ledges and outcroppings broke up the ragged walls above and below him. They combined to make a network of natural pathways and handholds that spiraled up, down, and across the entire perimeter of the unusual cathedral. It was a natural playground. There was an unusual aroma in the air. It smelled like a mixture of household cleaner and urine.

Lacey and Sarafina had hiked halfway up the opposite wall. Lacey no longer wore her life jacket. Sarafina had chosen to keep hers on. Tony aimed his light above them and could readily identify the twisting path they could take to reach the apex twenty-five feet above his head. The unusual texture of the roof captured his attention—there wasn't a stalactite to be seen. Instead, the shadowed recesses seemed to absorb the light rather than reflect it. The girls had apparently gone to take a closer look.

A bright LED lantern sparked to life below Tony's perch, bathing the bottom half of the cavern in cool light. The rest of the team had gathered along the edge of a small pond of water. Their life vests were piled beside them. Marshall rummaged through the emergency backpack and sorted its contents onto the rocky floor beside the lantern. Tony unbuckled his life jacket and made his way down to them.

As he approached, he noticed that the gently swirling pond seemed to be fed from underground. The spillover drained into a tubelike channel the size of a large sewer main. The thin stream of water disappeared into its depths. He grimaced at the prospect of exploring the constrictive chute on hands and knees.

"Su-weeet!" Marshall said as he unpacked a midsize cooking pot, a can of Sterno fuel, and a number of vacuum-sealed packages of freeze-dried food. "I didn't realize I was hauling dinner on my back. Dude, there's even coffee and sugar in here. All we need now is a campfire."

"I—I'm hungry," Josh said, his teeth clattering. He sat on a flattop rock, his knees pulled to his chest, one arm draped over Max's neck.

Bradley sat down beside them. He smacked his soggy baseball cap against his thigh, pulled it back over his head, then wrapped an arm around the boy to keep him warm. His eyes were fixed on Marshall as he emptied the pack. "Is the satellite phone in there?"

A shadow passed across Marshall's face. He shook his head. "Jake kept it," he said.

Tony dumped his vest and helmet on the pile with the others and crouched down beside Marshall. He placed his hand on his buddy's shoulder.

"He's gonna be okay," Tony said. "Francesca, too. One way or another, Jake would've put one over on those assholes."

Marshall's eyes were hopeful. "You think?"

"Bank on it," Tony said. "And we're gonna be all right, too." He reached down and sorted through the packets spread out on the ground in front of Marshall. When he found the one he was searching for, he held it up.

"Hell, man. We've even got cocoa for the kids," he said with a grin.

Though the temperature in the cave hovered in the high sixties, their soaking clothes were taking a toll. A steaming cup of coffee or hot chocolate would feel pretty good right about now.

Using his pocket knife, Tony levered the top off the Sterno can. "You get the water," he said, unfolding the wire frame that would support the pot. "And I'll start the stove."

He unscrewed the top from a small waterproof cylinder. Pulling out one of the strike-anywhere matches, he angled its tip against the surface of a nearby boulder.

"Stop!" Becker shouted.

Tony froze.

Becker jogged out of the shadows. He held a clump of what looked like dried mud in his hand. "Whatever you do, Sarge, don't strike that match."

"What the hell, Beck?" Tony asked. He lifted the match away from the rock.

Becker squeezed his fist around the dark gray mound in his hand. It broke into dust and drifted to the floor. "Bat guano," he said. "Emits ammonia. Highly flammable. The air's full—"

The girls' ear-splitting screams echoed down from their perch near the top of the cavern. Tony's gaze snapped upward but the lantern's glow wasn't enough to penetrate the thick shadows overhead. He started climbing immediately, with Becker right behind him. Max's barks echoed from below.

Tony saw scattered flashes of light from the girls' helmet lamps. They flickered on and off as if they were in the midst of a whirlwind of flying debris. The renewed shrieks spurred the two men up the steep path. Tony flicked on his torchlight. The strong beam brought the undulating mass of blackness above them into crisp detail. The area at the top of the cavern was filled with a swirling mass of angry bats.

"Hold on!" Tony shouted as he and Becker clambered up the twisting mesh of ledges and outcroppings.

"Bloody hell," Becker said. "There're thousands of the bleedin' buggers."

As they neared the girls, the black cloud of webbed wings thinned out. Becker trained his helmet light on the ceiling. Tony saw the spiraling formation of flapping wings begin to disappear into a shadowed vent as if they were being sucked into a giant vacuum cleaner.

The screaming transitioned to sobs. Tony climbed the final ledge to find Lacey and Sarafina huddled in a tight embrace within a narrow crevice. Lacey's hands shielded the girl's face. He crouched beside them and wrapped them in his arms.

"I've got ya," he said. "You're gonna be fine."

"A-are they gone?" Lacey asked, panting. There weren't many things that shook her. Apparently bats were on the short list.

"No worries, sugar," Becker said as he walked up and watched the last of the bats vanish. "You girls scared them silly." He shone his light into the opening above them. "And in the process, you may have discovered a way out of here."

* * *

Tony and Becker stood on an eight-foot-wide ledge that curved nearly twenty feet around the crown of the cavern. They stared up at the vent.

"It's too damn narrow," Tony said. "Especially farther up." He extended the flashlight into the fourteen-inch-wide crevasse and scanned its interior. The twisting orifice stretched upward seven or eight feet through the rock.

"What about the kids?" Becker asked. "Could they squirm through?"

"I don't think so," Tony said. His gut tightened at the thought of Sarafina or Josh getting stuck halfway up. He flicked off the flashlight and saw a twinkle of starlight beyond the opening.

"Dammit," he said, pounding a fist against the rock. "We're so close!"

What a load of crap, Tony thought. Two days ago they'd all been safe at home. Now he and his friends were trapped beneath the surface of the Mexican desert, with two kids and a dog, no less. Jake and Francesca were either captured or dead, and his family was in serious danger. And to top it all off, Luciano Battista was on the loose and likely planning something monumental on Tony's home turf in LA. Man, he'd give anything to have his hands wrapped around that asshole's throat.

Becker chipped at the limestone opening with his bowie knife. Bits and pieces flaked away with each strike. "It won't be easy," he said. "But in five or six days, working in shifts—"

"Guys!" Marshall's shout reverberated from below. "You need to get down here fast."

Tony and Becker made their way to the base of the chamber. Tony noticed that the overflow from the pond had grown considerably. A steady stream of water snaked into the nearby chute. Marshall played his hand over the wall that climbed above the pool.

"It's leaking," Marshall said. He lifted the lantern above his head to illuminate more of the wall. It glistened with a thin sheen of water. "I don't think the lower section of this wall is solid rock. It's marbled with compacted dirt." He pointed to a wavy line of discoloration higher up the wall. "See how the texture changes above that line? There's no water seeping through up there. But down here?" He shrugged his shoulders. "It's as though there used to be a passage through here, but it's been blocked by centuries of silt buildup."

As Tony stepped forward to get a closer look, a man-size chunk separated itself from the sodden wall and splashed into the pond, sending a wave of water across everyone's feet.

Bradley picked up Josh. Tony and Becker backed away. Marshall rushed to rescue the food packets. He stuffed them into his backpack along with the Sterno and cooking pot. Lacey and Sarafina were relatively safe, as they sat on a ledge on the far side of the pond.

Rivulets of mud slithered down the wall.

All at once Tony realized what was happening. Pressure from the rising water in the chamber they'd left behind had reached a critical point. *If that wall bursts…*

"Everyone up to the top!" he shouted.

Another chunk of wall calved into the water. A torrent of mud flowed behind it and flooded the pond. A wash of water pushed through the fissure and swept the pile of life jackets and helmets into the exit chute. One of the helmet lamps had been left on. Its beam lit the tunnel like a car's headlights as it vanished around a corner.

Bradley and Josh scrambled up the ledges. Max bounded beside them. Marshall followed with the backpack slung over one shoulder. Becker was next.

Lacey and Sarafina hugged the wall above the chute. Tony leaped to a nearby ledge. Lacey passed Sarafina across and he lifted her to the next ledge. Her life jacket was still snug around her, and her helmet remained strapped to her chin. Lacey jumped up on her own, agile as a mountain cat.

Tony was next.

He was midstride when the river blasted through the passageway. The wave shoved him chest-first against the wall. He would have lost his footing had it not been for Lacey's sudden grip around his wrist. The initial surge of water fell from his shoulders and he heaved himself to the ledge.

"Go!" he yelled to Lacey, pointing upward. He knew the deluge would quickly return after it bounced against the opposite wall and reversed its course. Its force would be tripled by the continuing surge from the other chamber.

Lacey and Sarafina hustled up to the next shelf. Tony jumped up beside them just as the successive wave struck. His feet flew out from under him and he spilled toward the edge. He clawed blindly at the rock. His fingers found a sharp outcrop and he held on for dear life.

The swell retreated. He shoved himself to his feet and blinked water from his eyes. The next surge would impact any moment, carrying an even greater volume of water. Lacey stood beside him, her eyes wide in horror. He followed her gaze into the tempest below.

A flash of orange.

A girl's scream.

Sarafina's tiny body spun only once in the swirling vortex before it was sucked into the chute and disappeared. Lacey didn't hesitate. She dove headfirst into the abyss, just before the next surge smashed Tony against the wall.

Chapter 31

Fifteen hundred feet above the California/Mexico border

BOTH FALCONS ARE RUNNING TRUE," KENNY ANNOUNCED over the radio. "Maintain a heading of one-five-five while I set up the stealth corridor."

"Roger," Cal replied from the cockpit.

They were about to cross the border into Mexico. It had been only a few minutes since their unauthorized takeoff at Miramar. By now every radar operator on both sides of the border had their eyes on them.

It was time to disappear.

The UAVs flew a tight formation off the CV-22's starboard wing. Kenny's fingers did a rock dance on the console's keyboard. The twin birds peeled into a sharp climbing turn that would send them into high-cover slots on either side of the CV-22's route.

The genius of the drones' manta-ray design lay in its miniaturization and lightweight construction. With a wingspan of only fifteen feet, a cruising speed of 400 knots, and an engine buried deep within its body, the sleek craft had a virtually undetectable radar and infrared signature. The drones were outfitted with a sophisticated array of cameras, sensors, and offensive weaponry, including internal rotating missile pods that popped out of its underside when needed. When coupled with the versatile CV-22, its autonomous midair refueling and retrieval capabilities made it a highly effective tool for reconnaissance, targeting, and close air support. But it was its advanced jamming and phantom-signal-generation equipment that Kenny was counting on to provide cover for their escape.

"On my go, drop to one hundred feet and maintain two hundred knots."

"Ready," Cal reported.

"Three, two, one—go."

Kenny hit the run program key. He switched radio frequencies so he could monitor the response from Mexican air traffic control. Up until now, the airwaves had been filled with nothing but angry threats.

"US aircraft about to enter Mexican airspace, this is your final warn—" The distraught Mexican air defense controller stopped midsentence.

Kenny grinned.

It would appear to anyone tracking them on radar that the Osprey had suddenly reversed its course, compliments of his software program and the drones' powerful jammers.

"Uh…sorry, Control," Kenny announced on the international guard frequency reserved for emergency transmissions. "This is Osprey four-six-niner declaring an emergency. Two souls on board. We've had a major instrumentation failure and request immediate vectoring back to Miramar."

"Stand by, four-six-niner, squawk ident," the controller said. Relief was evident in his tone. Kenny waited as Cal complied to the request with a quick press of the IDENT button on the Osprey's transponder. There was a brief pause as the controller presumably confirmed what his screen was telling him.

Kenny entered a few quick keystrokes to engage a program that would distort his next transmission to make it sound as if their communication gear was failing. It was an overused trick practiced in the movies by military pilots when they chose to disobey an order, made far more believable by Kenny's software.

He spoke naturally into his headset, but the transmission broke into: "M—control—comm—fail—" Then static.

Switching to the internal comm, Kenny said, "Okay, Cal, squawk seventy-six hundred and we're good to go."

The controller would assume from the international distress code that they had lost communication. The phantom blip on their screens representing the Osprey would continue to track northward toward Miramar. The drones could maintain the charade from as far as six hundred miles away. The Mexicans would assume there was no longer a threat and pass the CV-22 over to Miramar control. Controllers on both sides of the border would breathe more easily.

In the meantime, the cloaked Osprey and its twin escorts slipped unnoticed into Mexican airspace.

Chapter 32

THE IMAGE OF SARAFINA'S PLEADING EYES BURNED INTO Tony's mind. He wanted to jump after her. He *needed* to jump.

But strong arms from above held him fast.

"It's too late, Sarge!" Becker shouted over the rumble. The rushing water was too much for the drain to handle and the cavern was filling up. "You've got to climb."

Tony resisted.

"We need you," Becker yelled. "Your family needs you."

Mel. The kids.

Tony buried his despair. The next wave was nearly upon him. He pushed to a higher ledge and kept climbing, ignoring Becker's eyes and the empty hole in his gut. The two men were at the top of the cavern in less than sixty seconds.

* * *

Becker opened his eyes to a stream of early morning sunlight slicing through the vent hole above him. Josh still slept, his head resting on Becker's lap and his small arm draped over Max's neck. Bradley lay beside them, gently snoring.

The air had warmed considerably. Becker's clothes were nearly dry. He heard the flow of the river beneath them. It spun like a whirlpool just beneath their perch. Much of the bat guano had been washed away, clearing the air of ammonia. It now smelled faintly of creosote.

Marshall lay curled in a ball on the adjoining shelf. He used the backpack as a pillow. Becker was glad to see that he'd finally drifted off. He'd cried hard last night, and Becker couldn't blame him. It was a damn shame and a tragic loss. Only a miracle could have saved Lacey and Sarafina.

Tony stood beside Marshall. He squinted against the sunlight. He used his hunting knife to chip away at the opening. His face and shoulders were covered with a thin layer of powdered limestone. Beads of sweat carved tracks through the stubble on his cheeks. A small pile of shale spread around his feet. He'd been at it all night without a rest and refused to speak.

Becker removed his plaid shirt and wadded it up under Josh's head. Easing out his leg from under him, he stood, arching his back to stretch his aching muscles. He moved alongside Tony.

"There was nothing you could do," he said softly, placing a hand on the man's shoulder.

Tony ignored him. He continued to strike the ruined blade into the rock.

Becker hesitated. His friend was hurting. That's why he'd given Tony his space throughout the night. But it was time to return to the present. When the others woke, they needed to see that Tony was still capable of leading them to safety.

He tightened his grip on Tony's shoulder.

"Sarge," he said. "I think I've figured a way out of here."

The rhythmic scrape of blade against rock skipped a beat, but then Becker felt the tension increase in Tony's muscles and the attacks on the stone returned with renewed force.

Becker held his ground, waiting.

Finally, with an angry grunt, Tony let go a powerful stroke that impaled the blade in the limestone. He released the quivering handle and turned to face the Aussie.

"Talk." He wiped his forearm across his brow. It left streaks of powder in its wake.

"First off," Becker said, kicking through the meager pile of shavings at Tony's feet. "Judging by the progress you made in the last few hours, I need to revise my estimate of how long it would take us to cut our way out of here. Instead of five or six days, it's likely to take five or six weeks."

Tony's eyes narrowed.

"Anyway," Becker continued, "what we need is help from the outside. After that, a few squeezes of strategically placed C-4 and we'd be outta here in a skip." He pointed his finger up the shaft. "All we have to do is signal for help."

"Yeah, I already thought of that," Tony said. "But we don't have the sat-phone." His jaw tightened. His voice was somber when he added, "And the emergency life-vest transponders were swept away."

"I know," Becker said, "but with a little aboriginal creativity, I'm pretty sure I can get a signal up through that vent that will be visible for ten miles in every direction."

Tony's glum expression didn't change in any obvious way, but Becker was certain he saw a flash of hope in his eyes.

* * *

"That's all of it," Marshall said. He dropped the small bag of metal shavings into Becker's palm.

"Well done," Becker said, examining the magnesium shavings from the small brick of fire starter he'd found in the emergency pack. He'd given Marshall the task of scraping it into fine particles with his knife. The assignment provided a temporary distraction from the pain of his loss.

None of them had spoken much since awakening. Thankfully, most of the combustible ammonia gas had dissipated from the air. So Becker had lit the Sterno and boiled a pot of water for coffee and hot chocolate. It was followed by a hearty breakfast of freeze-dried spaghetti and meatballs. Under the circumstances it was a feast, though the glum mood of the group had been little better than that of condemned criminals eating their final meal.

Marshall retreated to a corner of the shelf to sit beside Josh and Bradley. The boy held his knees to his chest, rocking back and forth. Max paced in front of him, his tail down. Every once in a while he nudged at Josh's hands with his nose. The boy didn't seem to notice. Bradley kept to himself, seemingly resigned to his fate.

Becker sprinkled a dash of the magnesium into the boiling mixture in front of him and stirred it. The concoction smelled of ammonia.

"Don't waste that stuff," Tony said. "I need it for the Bronx candle."

"Go easy, mate," Becker said, handing the bag to Tony. He was glad to see Tony focused on something productive. The reference to his New York roots was the first sign that he'd compartmentalized his grief. "I only used a splash. It'll add a dandy sparkle when it's ignited."

Becker had loved making smoke bombs as a kid. What young boy didn't? Six parts potassium nitrate—in this case bat guano—plus four parts sugar, mixed in boiling water until it thickens. After that you can form it into any shape that strikes your fancy. Light it with a match and it will produce a thick white smoke that'll fill an entire house in less than a couple of minutes. He'd learned that lesson the hard way.

It was ready. Using a spoon, he scooped the brown, claylike clump onto one of the empty foil packets from breakfast. It was roughly the size of a baseball. Becker guessed it would burn for three or four minutes, producing a rising trail of dense smoke that would stretch a hundred feet into the dry desert sky. Smoke signals.

"The American Indians got nothing on me," Becker said, admiring his work.

Of course, Becker thought, this entire plan hinged on the hope that Cal and Kenny had received Jake's distress calls. They must be on their way by now. And when they discovered that the safe house had been destroyed, they'd do a grid search for survivors. Cal knew about the underground river, so he'd follow that track first. When Becker heard their plane or truck overhead, he'd ignite the clay, they'd see the smoke, and Beck and his boys would get rescued. No worries, right? About as simple as controlling the 'roos in the rangelands...

He motioned to Tony. "The pot's all yours, Sarge."

He watched as Tony poured the remainder of the magnesium shavings into a pile on a flat rock. There were two similarly sized mounds beside it—one of matchstick heads and the other of gunpowder. They'd removed the powder from their pistol slugs. Tony placed two wax candles from the emergency kit into the empty pot and set it over the Sterno flame.

When the candles were fully melted, Tony extinguished the canned flame and scooped the remaining Sterno jelly into the wax, stirring it into a gooey paste. Becker watched with interest as Tony carefully added the magnesium, match heads, and most of the gunpowder into the mixture. He stuffed the concoction into an empty twelve-ounce water bottle, tamping it down with a spoon handle. When the bottle was nearly full, he added a layer of gunpowder to top it off. Through a hole in the cap, he inserted a twelve-inch fuse fashioned from a shoelace coated with a mixture of crushed gunpowder, wax, and superglue.

"Inner-city napalm," Tony said. He tightened the cap on the bottle and hefted the makeshift bomb. "We can use it as a nighttime signal. Light it, toss it up the shaft to the desert floor, and it'll blow with a spread of white-hot fire that'll stick to anything it touches. Should be visible for twenty miles." He fingered the shoelace that dangled from the cap. "The fuse oughtta take about three seconds."

"Peaches," Becker said, staring up the narrow vent. "As long as we can throw it at an angle that will keep it from dropping straight down on top of us."

Tony held the bottle over his shoulder and cocked his arm back as if he were going to throw a Hail Mary pass. "That's why *I'm* gonna do it."

Chapter 33

T HE RANCH IS GONE," KENNY SAID OVER THE RADIO. "Obliterated. No one could've survived that."

Cal studied the video image on the cockpit's display. Kenny was right—it didn't look good. There were bodies strewn outside the blast radius of the ranch, some in uniform and even more that looked like locals. From the close-up images transmitted from the drones, he could see that each of them had weapons.

"Hell of a firefight," Cal said.

When the camera had panned the last of the bodies, Kenny said, "They're all tangos. None from our team."

Cal heaved a sigh of relief. He knew from experience that Jake, Tony, and Becker weren't the easiest people to kill. They would've done whatever it took to protect the others. He hoped they'd all made it out of there safely.

"In his last message, Jake said that Tony and the others were making their way into the underground tunnels," he said. Though he'd never visited the safe house, Jake had provided him with a vivid description of the ranch when they'd shared a few beers at Sam's a month ago. The river running beneath the property ran all the way to the Gulf of California. "Expand the search grid."

"Already done."

* * *

Max lifted his nose from his paws, eyes alert. His head canted to one side. Beside him, Josh stilled his rocking for the first time since Sarafina and Lacey had disappeared. He aimed an ear toward the ceiling.

"I hear a motor," Josh said.

Tony rose and stared at the slit of pale blue sky eight feet above. He heard it—the indistinct echo of an engine. He kicked Becker's curled form. The Aussie woke with a start. His hand reached for the hunting knife strapped to his shin.

"Light the smoke," Tony said, straining to identify the faint sound. He couldn't tell if it was a plane or vehicle. In either case, the sound wasn't getting any louder, which meant it wasn't heading toward their position. "Hurry," he added.

Earlier, after the volatile clay mixture had cooled, Becker had fashioned the smoke bomb into the shape of an elongated pear. It had a flattened bottom and a pencil-thick point at its crown. It rested on the rock ledge beneath the vent. Becker struck one of the remaining matches against the rock.

"Stand clear," he said.

Tony backed away.

Becker touched the flame to the tip of the molded clay. It ignited like a butane torch.

"Whoa!" Tony said. The intense six-inch flame sparkled and hissed. It emitted a dense white smoke that reminded Tony of the exhaust from a space shuttle launch. He and Becker jumped to the next ledge to escape the billowing cloud.

"That's just the preshow, mate," Becker said with a grin. "Wait 'til you see what happens next."

The hungry flame ate through the slender finger at the top of the device and quickly spread to the thicker, lower part of the pear. The torch's intensity grew tenfold, blasting the thickening plume of smoke up through the vent like the exploding ash from a miniature volcano. It must be a sight to behold from above, Tony thought. The funnel of smoke had to stretch several hundred feet up into the air. Impossible to miss.

"Nice one, Beck," he said, patting the Aussie on the shoulder as they crouched against the cold rock. "Way...to...go."

Though the majority of the smoke drafted up the vent, the excess spread across the roof of the cavern like fast-moving fog. Tony, Becker, and Marshall covered their mouths with their sleeves to avoid the worst of the fumes. Bradley pulled his shirt partway over his head, leaning over to cover him and Josh. Max joined them and burrowed his head under the makeshift tent.

Chapter 34

Sonoran Desert, Mexico

JAKE ROSE TO HIS TOES ON THE WOODEN CHAIR. HE PRESSED his ear to the wall-mounted vent, straining to eavesdrop on the conversation in the nearby room. The knife-wielding jihadist was on the phone. Francesca had identified the terrorist as brother to a man named Carlo. Jake chilled when he recalled the bastard, who had taken pleasure in torturing Jake. Francesca and Sarafina had been next on his list when Jake killed him. From the tension in his brother's voice at the other end of the vent, it seemed he was talking to a superior, probably Battista.

"We had an unexpected encounter from some locals," the man said in Dari. Jake's enhanced brain had given him a remarkable ability with languages. He'd learned Dari when he was Battista's prisoner in Venice. Since then, he'd added a dozen new languages to his repertoire. The learning process had become a coping mechanism that soothed him and helped take his mind off the specter of the alien pyramid.

"They were *more* than farmers," the man was saying, a bit defensively. "Part of a local drug cartel, I suspect. Well armed and very angry. They attacked like crazed demons."

Jake took some satisfaction from that last comment. He was damn glad *he* hadn't had to face the drug lord and his pals after their little videoconference. At least that part of his ploy had worked, though it didn't seem to be doing him much good at the moment.

He winced with discomfort when his gut cramped again. He'd woken fifteen minutes earlier to violent waves of nausea that felt like food poisoning, but the hypodermic puncture on the inside of his elbow told him it was something else. His brain cataloged the myriad of possibilities and a shiver crept up the back of his neck. The nausea had eased up considerably, but every so often a sharp stomach cramp reminded him that all was not good.

He and Francesca were holed up in what looked like an abandoned office. She was asleep, curled up on a cot on the other side of the room. Her auburn hair spilled in a billow of curls onto the old mattress. The front flaps of her torn slacks were cinched together with Jake's shoelaces. *Under which his child's heart was beating...*

A tarnished brass coat rack completed the office's sparse appointments. It stood beside the room's only door, which was locked from the outside. The midday sun pushed its way through a grime-coated window. Jake saw the silhouettes of two guards outside. They stood by a jeep and appeared to have rifles slung over their shoulders. A truck was parked behind the jeep. Jake figured the rest of the men were inside.

From what he'd gathered, Battista's men were waiting for their cohorts to fly in and pick them up. He still had no clue what Battista wanted with him this time around. Was he planning to reconstitute his mind-enhanced army using Jake's brain as the catalyst? Or was it something worse? The man had gone to a lot of trouble to capture him again. If it was merely revenge he wanted, Jake would have been dead by now.

He continued to listen at the vent. His brain sorted through the incoming streams of data while another part of his mind searched for an escape solution.

"We lost five men," the faint voice reported. "We disabled all but one of their vehicles during the pursuit. The remaining truck backed off. I suspect they'll be hard on our trail as soon as they gather reinforcements."

No shit, Jake thought. The cartel's private army could swarm down on them at any moment.

After another pause, the man continued. "The American's friends escaped down an underground river. They couldn't have gone far. I sent a team to double back and track them. When they surface, we'll be waiting."

Jake's heart swelled with hope at the news. Had his friends really survived the explosion? If anyone could have kept them safe, it was Tony. But his battle-hardened buddy wasn't likely to suspect that the terrorists would continue to pursue them, since Jake had been captured. No, Tony would assume that Battista's men were long gone. Jake needed to warn them.

"The American and his woman are unconscious. Interestingly, she is pregnant." The man hesitated a moment before adding, "Muhammad took it upon himself to use her as a test case for the chemical."

What the—

Jake's breath left him. He pressed his ear into the vent cover.

"But sheikh—" the voice rose in protest.

Seconds stretched as Jake waited desperately to hear more.

When the man finally spoke again, there was a defiant edge in his tone. "He is a scientist, not a strategist," he said matter-of-factly. "Nevertheless, it is done. In less than ten hours, the chemical's effects will be irreversible and the fetus will expire."

Jake staggered backward. What the hell kind of chemical had they given her? His chest heaved as he tried to catch his breath. Another violent cramp twisted his stomach into a knot, doubling him over. Jake welcomed the distracting pain; it fueled his rage. *Before this is over,* he swore to himself, *they're going to pay.*

But first things first. The man had implied the chemical could be reversed. Jake needed to get Francesca to a hospital within the next ten hours.

She stirred. Jake moved to her side. He brushed a lock of hair from her forehead as her eyelids fluttered open.

"Hey there, sleepyhead," Jake said. He stroked her head with a calmness he didn't feel.

The smile on her face vanished before it was half-formed. Her body tensed. She seemed to look right through him and Jake knew her empathic gift had kicked into gear. He'd failed to bury his fear deeply enough to prevent her from feeling it, too.

"What's the m—?"

Jake cut her off with a finger to her lips. There was movement outside. It appeared as if one of the guards was leaving. Ignoring another cramp, Jake leaned forward and whispered in Francesca's ear. "Stay brave. We're getting out of here."

Chapter 35

Beneath the Sonoran Desert, Mexico

Tony couldn't believe their luck. Becker's signal had worked like a charm. The smoke had cleared. He heard the distinct rumble of a truck engine approaching their position.

There was a squeal of brakes and the motor shut down. Doors slammed shut. The five of them fidgeted beneath the opening. They stared up anxiously, even Max, whose tail tapped rapidly against Tony's leg.

A shadow passed above.

"Anybody down there?" a voice called out in heavily accented English.

Warning bells went off in Tony's head. He threw an index finger to his lips to silence his friends.

Everyone saw the gesture except Marshall, whose lips parted. "Y—"

Tony clamped his meaty palm across his friend's mouth. Marshall's eyes went wide with confusion.

"Dari accent," Tony hissed under his breath, wondering if the man above had heard Marshall. "Get back," he added. He nudged Marshall toward the far corner of the ledge. Bradley was already halfway there, Josh cradled in his arms, Max at his heels. He'd apparently sensed the danger at the same time as Tony.

"Bloody hell," Becker mumbled softly. He pressed against the rock, his M9 pistol gripped in both hands. He still had one magazine left.

"Battista's boys," Tony whispered.

Becker nodded.

"I—know—you're—down—there," the man above said, stretching out his words.

Everyone remained silent.

More shadows passed across the opening.

"You will answer," the man said after a moment. His voice was gruff. All pretense of friendliness had vanished. "Or you will die."

Tony and Becker exchanged glances. Should they remain silent and keep them guessing? Or should they try to negotiate a way out?

The decision was made for them when Max let out a low growl that became a loud bark.

"Aah," the voice above said with satisfaction. "Surely the dog did not create such a magnificent smoke signal all by himself. So, my stubborn American friends, are you ready to see daylight or shall we leave you to rot?"

Son of a bitch, Tony thought. They were out of options. If left underground, they would die. Up top, they might at least have a chance.

He edged closer to the vent. "Okay," he shouted. "Get us the hell out of here!"

The sound of bullets being racked into multiple chambers was unmistakable. Tony leaped to the side just as a fusillade of supersonic lead tore through the rock where he'd been standing. The reverberating cracks of assault rifles filled the cavern. Chips of rock stung Tony's legs. A ricocheting round buzzed so close to his face that he felt the heat from its vapor trail. He and Becker dove to the safety of the far side of the ledge beside the others.

Magazines emptied and the shooting stopped as quickly as it started. A cloud of dust and particulate matter drifted across the beam of sunlight that streamed from the vent.

"Go to hell!" Tony shouted.

"B—bad word," Josh's trembling voice mumbled into Bradley's chest.

Someone above barked a series of commands in Dari. The voice wasn't directed downward so Tony couldn't make out what had been said. It didn't make much difference; there wasn't a damn thing he could do about it. At least the assholes' bullets couldn't reach them.

A few minutes later, a liquid splashed down the vent. The fumes hit Tony's nose an instant later. His stomach twisted into a knot.

Gasoline.

"Jesus!" Marshall cried. "What the hell are we going to do now?"

The spill of gas from above stopped abruptly. There was another Dari command. This time Tony made out the shouted words. *Get the other cans!*

The first volume of gas had pooled beneath the vent. A few ounces had spilled into a furrow that twisted toward Tony and his friends. When they emptied two more cans down the vent...

Tony glanced over the ledge to the dark waters below. They could either jump, risking the vortex that had sucked Lacey and Sarafina away, or they could burn.

A familiar fight-or-flight sensation swelled through him. His mind was groping for a solution when his eyes fixed on the napalm bomb he'd made earlier.

Tony swept the plastic bottle into his hand and ran toward the vent. Becker was half a beat behind him, matches in hand.

"I like the way you think, Sarge," he said. "Let's give the bloody bastards a little surprise from Down Under, eh?"

"Damn straight." Tony cocked his arm over his shoulder, leaning backward as he pointed his free hand up the crevasse. The twelve-inch fuse dangled beneath the device.

"Careful, Beck," he said. Becker was about to strike the match against the rock wall. Tony motioned down at their feet. Both men stood in the shallow pool of gasoline.

"Righto, mate," Becker said. He cupped his hand around the match to prevent any errant sparks from hitting the ground.

"Wait!" Bradley shouted behind them. He dumped Josh into Marshall's lap and rose quickly to his feet. He pulled a knife from his pocket and moved toward the two men.

Tony froze. Becker's eyes narrowed.

"The fuse is too long," Bradley said. He stepped around the puddle of gas and grabbed the end of the shoelace. He sliced it with his blade so that only three inches remained. "This way it'll explode just over their heads."

Tony hiked an eyebrow, appraising the man. This was a side to their quiet companion he hadn't expected. "A teacher, huh?" he said.

"Yep," Bradley said. He lowered his voice so that Josh's sensitive ears couldn't eavesdrop. "But when I was a kid, I loved blowin' up shit."

Tony coiled his arm and nodded to Beck. "Light the match. But don't touch it to the fuse until my go."

Bradley stepped back and rejoined Marshall and Josh.

Becker scraped the match against the rock. It flared to life, creating a jack-o'-lantern glow to the inside of his cupped hands. He positioned the flame a few inches from the end of the fuse, waiting for Tony's signal.

Tony narrowed his focus on the opening above him.

Two shadows appeared.

"Now!"

The match hit the fuse with a hiss. Tony flung the bottle upward in a wobbling spiral. He and Becker sprinted from the opening.

The deafening blast aboveground sucked the air out of the cave for a fraction of a second. Just as fast, the overpressure from the bomb pushed down through the vent. The superheated air ignited the pool of gasoline with a powerful *whoop.*

Tony's ears popped as the eruption of intense heat bashed him from behind. It lifted him from his feet and slammed him chest-down into the floor of the ledge. His arms flew up to protect the back of his head and neck. A half beat later the searing flash was sucked back up the chimney. The pungent smell of singed hair filled his nostrils.

He and Becker pushed themselves to their hands and knees. They beat out the spits of flame that stuck to their clothing and scrambled to the far side of the ledge. The hair on top of Tony's hands and forearms had shrunk to hundreds of smoking curls. He winced when he rubbed the tender surface. The tiny bristles turned to ash, leaving a trail of reddened skin. Marshall watched wide-eyed from where he and Bradley had curled together to shield Josh and Max from the conflagration.

The inferno gulped down the pool of gas, leaping upward as it licked the petrol that clung to the walls of the vent. The spiraling bonfire cast a flickering amber glow across the cavern.

Screams of pain from above signaled that the ploy had worked, at least to some degree. But as the gasoline was consumed and the flames died down, angry shouts confirmed the worst.

"What now?" Marshall said, watching the dwindling fire.

"Sit tight," Tony said. He leaned over the ledge and peered down at the swirling water. *Pray that the assholes still alive don't have any explosives in their truck.*

Chapter 36

Sonoran Desert, Mexico

S OMETHING ABOUT MOVING THINGS WITH HIS MIND DIDN'T sit well with Jake. It wasn't just the blistering headache it gave him afterward, or even the temporary lightheadedness that swept over him. It was the fact that it seemed so damn unnatural for a human being to do such things...at least at this stage in man's evolution.

Battista's scientists had proclaimed that the MRI accident had caused Jake's brain to leap forward thousands of years on the evolutionary scale, giving him the ability to project his thoughts, speed up his reflexes, and even move small objects to some degree. While that might have been true, the declining condition of his heart was a grim testament to the fact that the rest of his body was still firmly stuck in the twenty-first century and unable to keep up.

Sure, his telekinesis had been pretty cool at first, and he had used it to good purpose at the roulette wheel in order to fund their assault on Battista's stronghold. The talent had even saved his life when the plan had gone bad and he'd fallen into Battista's hands. But it had also been the singular attribute that had triggered the alien obelisk and launched it into space. Just thinking about it made Jake's head swim. If, or *when*, the aliens returned, they would find that mankind's violent nature had flourished.

Hell, he thought, when they last visited, we were only killing each other one at a time with clubs. Now we've developed the ability to kill millions with the press of a button.

He studied the sole window in the room. The three-foot-square frame was hinged on the upper corners, designed to swing outward from the bottom when opened. Using his sleeve, he wiped a small circle in the grimy glass and peered outside. It looked like they were in a hangar at an abandoned airfield. Only one guard remained. He sat in the passenger seat of the jeep, an AK-47 in his lap. One foot dangled out the open door.

Jake wrapped both hands around the paint-encrusted swivel lock at the bottom of the window. He tightened his grip and twisted. The latch opened with a soft crunch.

He hesitated, thinking back to the confrontation with the terrorists in front of the ranch house. Despite his best efforts, he'd been unable to tap into his quick reflexes when he'd needed them most. Whether he liked it or not, his super abilities seemed further from reach with each passing day. Like a failing afterburner, they sputtered and coughed when he firewalled the throttle. He would depend on his mind, not his speed.

A quick glance over his shoulder confirmed that Francesca was in place. She listened at the door. She would alert him in case anyone approached. They exchanged a quick nod.

He blew out a long breath and focused on a small pile of debris beside the jeep. He wrapped his mind around an empty soda can. His heart rate jumped in response. Jake grimaced, but he ignored the risk, and when he felt the familiar flush of blood at his forehead, he gave a sharp tug with his mind. The can skittered across the dusty tarmac as if reeled in by a fishing line.

Instantly the guard became alert. He slid to his feet and panned the area with his assault rifle. His gaze narrowed on the red soda can as it settled to a stop. It was three strides away from the exterior wall. With a focused burst of mental energy, Jake jerked hard. The can jumped forward as if it had been kicked. It smacked into the aluminum siding and settled just beneath the window.

The guard's face paled. He glanced nervously from side to side and edged closer to the building. The muzzle of his weapon was directed at the can.

Fighting a momentary wave of dizziness, Jake ducked beneath the sill. The man's shadow grew larger on the window, shifting side to side as he approached. Jake coiled his muscles, ready to spring. He measured the terrorist's movements in his mind: *He'll stop just in front of the window, focused on the can. Then he'll nudge it with the toe of his boot...*

Jake rose and launched a vicious heel kick that struck the base of the steel window frame. It flew open in a rising arc that collided with the underside of the guard's nose. There was a crunch of broken cartilage. The man's eyes went wide and he fell backward like a toppled statue.

Jake dove through the opening and landed shoulder-first in the man's solar plexus. But the discharge of air from the guard's lungs wasn't followed by the expected fit of gagging and coughing. Instead, the man remained still. Jake suspected that the cartilage of his nose must have driven into his brain. He checked his pulse. Dead.

Jake pushed aside a momentary wave of guilt and jerked the rifle from the man's death grip. He swung the muzzle from left to right to clear the area. No shouts of alarm. No heads popped around a corner. He motioned Francesca through the window. "Hurry!" he said, extending his hand. "We're outta here."

Jake leaped into the driver's seat. Francesca climbed into the passenger seat. He reached for the key.

It was missing.

"Crap," he mumbled under his breath.

Chapter 37

Beneath the Sonoran Desert, Mexico

NO TIME TO THINK.

Like a pro diver, Lacey knifed headfirst into the turbulent water. Her loosened cave helmet tore from her head. She surfaced and locked onto the twirling beam of Sarafina's helmet lamp. It was still on the girl's head. She was just out of reach, caught in a swirling vortex. Her orange life jacket was losing its buoyancy battle against the massive volume of flushing water. A distant part of Lacey's mind recalled Sarafina's insistence on keeping the jacket snug around her. She'd said, "It feels like Daddy's hugging me." Everyone else had dumped theirs onto a pile.

Including Lacey.

She clawed through the water with powerful strokes, determined to save her seven-year-old friend. But before she completed her second scissor kick, the surge threw her into a violent spin. It sucked her toward the underwater chute at an alarming speed.

She spiraled downward, her flailing limbs unable to counter the force of the water.

A flash of orange. Sarafina's startled eyes. A tiny outstretched hand. Lacey reached for her, but the current rag-dolled her around and their fingertips only grazed. She swept past the child and spun into the four-foot-wide chute.

She was enveloped in pure darkness. No up. No down. Lacey tumbled through the water at the mercy of the roiling current. She crossed her arms over her face for protection, fighting with every ounce of her core strength to position her feet downstream. Her shoulder caromed off the side of the twisting tube. A sharp outcrop scraped along her thigh, ripping jeans and skin. A slice across an elbow. The pain was distant. Her lungs demanded fuel. Speed increased and the water texture changed. It softened and filled with a churning froth. She felt her body lift and drop repeatedly and a vague part of her mind imagined that the rushing flow must be passing over a series of boulders. Time stretched. Seconds became a lifetime.

The fire in her lungs consumed her thoughts and Lacey realized the end was near. Reluctantly, she released the tension in her limbs and relaxed into the ride. *Wasn't I supposed to be on the movie set today? The role would have been my big break.* She allowed herself to be caressed by the water. The final minutes of her life were upon her. *If only I could have saved Sarafina...*

She thought of Marshall, being wrapped in his arms, and settled into the embrace of the froth-filled current.

Froth-filled current...

Bubbles in the water...

With a start, Lacey realized that the ceiling height must exceed the water level. It was the only way that air could be introduced into the mix. Fighting the urge to inhale, she pressed the last ounce of her energy into her limbs, arms outstretched. She jackknifed blindly. First in one direction and then another.

Her hand broke the surface. She clawed after it with a final desperate kick.

Bursting through, she gasped in a huge lungful of cool, blessed air. She sucked in again and again, the joy of life spreading warmth through her body. Her mind cleared and she realized that the loud rumble in her ears was not coming from her thankful heart. It emanated from a growing disturbance just ahead.

Mist filled the air, and a half beat later she was weightless, falling.

Lacey tumbled down the short falls, hitting the water sideways in a huge splash that wrenched her neck to one side. A stab of pain shot down her spine and took away her breath. An instant later the rushing current regained its hold. She struggled to keep her head above water. A wide halo of sunlight speared the darkness a hundred yards ahead, revealing an expansive cavern split by the river. The upcoming passage was strewn with large boulders, over which water crashed in thundering rooster tails. The turbulent rapids swept her forward.

She kicked out, dodging the first boulder, then the second, twisting through the surge, arms and legs pumping. The river curved sharply. Plumes of water cascaded around her, spinning her around.

Her unprotected head smacked against a rock.

Everything went fuzzy. Just before the blackness overcame her, Lacey could have sworn she heard a high-pitched scream reverberate from the falls behind her.

Chapter 38

Sonoran Desert, Mexico

S TAY PUT," JAKE SAID TO FRANCESCA, STILL IN THE JEEP. "I'M
going for the keys!" He grabbed the AK and ran toward the
dead guard. He patted down the body. No joy.

The second guard.

The squeak of a hinge blasted a surge of adrenaline into Jake's
system. He spun toward the noise. Five paces away, a door swung
ajar. It stopped midway as the person on the other side got a last
word in with someone behind him. Jake launched himself into
the door. It slammed into the man and shoved him back into
the room. Jake yanked open the door and rushed inside, leading
with his weapon.

The soldier lay sprawled on his side, propped on one elbow.
His shocked face turned beet red as Jake trained the AK-47 at
his forehead. The man's eyes narrowed. Jake read his intentions
an instant before the soldier snapped his foot out in an attempt
to sweep Jake's legs. Jake dodged to one side and thrust the butt
of his rifle into the man's temple. The soldier rolled over with a
groan and lay still.

In the split second that passed, the second man in the room
hadn't moved a muscle. He stood frozen in shock, mouth agape,
a white-knuckled hand clutching a corked test tube half filled
with an amber liquid. Even though he wore the same uniform as

the rest of Battista's gang, it was apparent from his short stature and pudgy face that he was no soldier. His dark eyes were huge behind his bifocals.

Jake trained the assault rifle on his ample gut. "Not a sound," he whispered.

The man nodded vigorously. He raised his hands in the air. One still grasped the test tube.

Jake felt his blood boil as he took in the contents of the small room: a cot with a thin mattress spotted with blood stains, a suspended IV bag, an open doctor's bag, a clutter of medical equipment on a side table that included a flexible probe connected to a laptop.

He closed in on the man, jamming the muzzle of the rifle into the underside of his pockmarked chin. The doctor had to rise to the tip of his toes to keep from being impaled.

"What—the—hell—did—you—give—her?" Jake growled in Dari.

The doctor's face paled. His chin stretched upward to its limit. His gaze twitched toward the vial in his upraised hand. "I—I was only following orders," he rasped.

Voices from down the hallway reminded Jake that time was his enemy. He snatched the vial from the man's hand. "And the antidote?" Jake said.

The man's shaking fingers pointed at the leather satchel on the bed. "In my b—"

A sharp knee to the doctor's groin silenced the man and doubled him over. Jake grabbed the test tube from his clutches. Then he cracked the butt of the rifle into the back of the man's balding head. The doctor dropped to the floor like a wet rag.

Jake dumped the contents of the medical bag onto the bed. There were three vials. Each had a different label. He rolled them in gauze and stuffed them deep into the side pocket of his cargo pants.

The voices from the hall were close. Jake searched the fallen guard's pockets. A wave of relief washed over him when he pulled out the jeep's keys. As he turned to leave, he noticed a spiral notebook protruding from the doctor's rear pocket. He doubled back and picked it up, scanning the first page as he made for the exit.

What he read stopped him cold. He flipped to the next page, then the next, his mind absorbing and cataloging the notes and calculations. His breath quickened. He turned the pages with increasing speed. The doctor's notes provided the scientific basis for a population reduction stratagem of a scale so massive that the death toll from a thermonuclear war would pale by comparison. Its goal was nothing less than the total extinction of every American residing in the continental United States. All in the name of "the one true religion." *And it could actually work.*

Jake shoved aside the wave of despair that threatened to overwhelm him, and focused on the single flaw he saw in their plan—*a flaw by the name of Jake Bronson, who now knows what you're planning to do.*

He fanned through the pages, blinking his eyes in a mimic of a camera's shutter. It was his way of signaling his eidetic brain to commit the contents to memory. He returned the book to the doctor's pocket, taking care not to rouse him. When the man regained consciousness, it was important that he believed his notes had not been disturbed.

Jake jumped into the jeep. Francesca huddled low in the passenger seat. She blew out a sigh of relief at his return. "Look what I found," she said, holding out a cell phone.

"Yeah!" Jake said as he started the engine and put the vehicle into gear. "It's about time luck turned our way. Keep your head down!"

He slammed on the gas and jerked the wheel into a sharp U-turn. It kicked up bits of gravel that plinked against the building's aluminum siding. As they approached the panel truck, Jake laid the barrel of the AK-47 on the windowsill and squeezed the trigger. The sound of the automatic weapon was deafening. Bullet holes stitched a line across the truck's side panel. He adjusted his aim downward and the rear tires exploded.

By the time Battista's soldiers poured onto the tarmac, Jake and Francesca were well out of range.

Chapter 39

Beneath the Sonoran Desert, Mexico

WARMTH ON HER SKIN.
A gentle rocking.
A peaceful tune filled with hope...
Lacey's eyes fluttered open. She lay on her back. Her head was cradled in someone's lap. Sarafina's face hovered inches above, backlit by the sun. The soothing tune she was humming cut off and her lips broke into a wide smile.

"Lacey!" she said, leaning over to hug her. She pressed a cool cheek against Lacey's. It was a bit of a stretch for the girl since she was still wearing the life jacket.

"How on earth—"

"Thanks for coming to get me!" Sarafina said. Her small arms clung to Lacey's head as if it were her favorite doll. She rocked them back and forth. Lacey returned the hug with all the strength she could muster.

They were still underground. But the sun beat down on them from a hundred-foot-wide hole overhead. They were on a beach of polished pebbles on the outside curve of the fast-moving river. Lacey's heels were still in the water. Apparently, the little girl could only pull her so far.

"How'd you do it, honey?" Lacey asked. She pulled her feet from the water's edge and rose to a seated position. Her head

179

spun with the effort. She winced as she pressed her hand against the golf-ball-size lump on her forehead.

"Y-you were sort of stuck," Sarafina said. Her face scrunched up in an empathetic wince as Lacey probed her head wound. "Wrapped around a rock."

The tip of Sarafina's tongue peeked from the corner of her mouth as she pictured it in her mind.

"Kind of like this." She made a fist with one hand and cupped her other hand around it. She wiggled two of the outside fingers. "Your arms were wobbling through the water like a flag. When I banged into you, I grabbed your belt to keep us together. But then the water pushed us free." Her eyes glazed over for a beat. "After that, it dumped us here." She pointed to five other life vests strewn alongside the water. "Those, too."

"And then you pulled me out," Lacey said, amazed.

"Well…mostly," the little girl said, glancing at Lacey's soggy shoes. "You're heavy!"

Lacey grinned. "Oh, yeah?" she asked playfully. "Are you calling me fat?"

After a moment's hesitation, Sarafina picked up on the joke and giggled. Lacey threw her arms around her and pulled her close.

"My darling Sarafina," she said, blinking away tears. "You saved my life."

As they held each other, Lacey's gaze drifted to the distant blackness that enveloped the river's continuing path. Jake had told her that it stretched for dozens of miles. Much of it passed through underground chutes far more deadly than the one they'd just survived. A shiver spread from her spine and she thanked God that she and Sarafina were alive.

They were surrounded by sheer walls. The opening to the surface was fifty feet overhead. Lacey considered how they'd ever make it out. Then she noticed that the white emergency lights on each of the life vests were flashing. She smiled at the realization that Sarafina was already several steps ahead of her.

Chapter 40

Sonoran Desert, Mexico

JAKE SKIDDED THE VEHICLE INTO THE NEXT TURN. CLOUDS of dust spit from the tires. A quick check in the rearview mirror confirmed there were still no signs of pursuit. The fuel gauge read near empty, but refueling with the spare three-gallon gas can strapped in the back would have to wait. They were less than a mile from the airfield and Jake wanted to put as much distance as possible between him and the terrorists. He accelerated out of the turn onto the dirt fire road that climbed the foothills above the airfield. He pushed the vintage jeep to the max. Francesca braced herself beside him in the convertible. One hand pressed against the dash and the other gripped her hair back in a ponytail. The hot desert air felt good.

"How're you feeling?" Jake shouted over the whine of the engine as he downshifted into a hairpin curve.

"O—okay," she said. Her voice stammered in time with the jeep's bounce over a pothole. "Drive faster!"

"You got it," Jake said. She'd changed in the last two days, he thought. Her newfound strength suited her. He punched the gas on the next straightaway. Although it was unlikely the jihadists would find two spares to replace the tires he'd shredded, he wasn't about to take any chances. He'd broken off the main road toward the foothills at the first opportunity, taking advantage of the jeep's all-terrain abilities. The fuel gauge was in the red, so there was no way they could outlast anyone in a long-distance chase. The high ground would provide them with advance warning of a pursuit and at least give them a chance to set up a defensible position. It wasn't the best plan, especially since he had only a few rounds left in the AK's magazine. But it was a hell of lot better than waiting for the other shoe to drop with those assholes down below.

At this point, their ultimate hope of rescue revolved around the cell phone Francesca had found. There'd been no signal on the desert floor. Jake prayed that would change as they gained altitude. He also needed to give Francesca the antidote—

The thought froze in his head. His mind raced through the details of the pages he'd memorized from the doctor's journal and he realized his mistake: he'd taken the vial and a hypodermic needle, but the drug had to be administered slowly using an IV drip. Injecting it with a hypo would be fatal. He needed to get Francesca to a hospital.

Five minutes later, Jake pulled up at a natural overlook.

"Give me a second," he said, squeezing Francesca's thigh before stepping out of the jeep. He cupped his hands over his brow and scanned the valley below. The truck was still at the airfield. But his relief was cut short when he noticed the long trail of dust racing across the desert floor.

"What do you see?" Francesca asked.

"Trouble," he said, as he studied the fast-moving caravan. "Seven vehicles, heading for the airport. It's got to be the narcos. They're hauling ass with a vengeance."

Jake panned the valley floor. His gut tightened when he noticed the ribbon of haze hanging over the fire road and snaking up to their position. It was like a neon sign that read THEY WENT THATAWAY!

A thunderous roar overhead squeezed the air from Jake's lungs and nearly knocked him from his feet. He ducked as an aircraft popped over the ridge behind him. It was flying at full bore. Its hundred-foot wingspan passed just thirty feet overhead as it dove toward the airfield. Jake recognized it as a vintage DC-3. It didn't take a genius to figure out that the terrorists' ride had just arrived. And by the looks of things, the plane would land before the narcos got close enough to draw a bead on them.

Timing couldn't have been better for Battista's boys.

It couldn't have been worse for Jake and Francesca. If the fired-up narcos were denied their taste of blood at the airfield, it wouldn't take them long to spot the jeep's trail.

He rushed back to the vehicle and jumped in. "Try the phone again!"

Francesca flipped it open and powered it up.

"No bars."

"Keep it open," Jake said, pushing the jeep for all it was worth. The ridge was just ahead. The fuel gauge was solidly on Empty. He'd have to pull over soon to refuel from the spare gas can, but for now, it was balls to the wall.

The jeep leaped over the crest at top speed. It caught air before crunching back onto the road in a neck-wrenching lurch. A straightaway stretched out before them, surrounded by sagebrush-covered hills punctuated with cacti and rocky escarpments. Jake scanned the hilltops, hoping against hope for some sign of civilization.

"Signal?"

Francesca shook her head.

A flicker of reflected light in the cloudless sky caught Jake's attention. He caught the faint outline of a small fixed-wing aircraft. It was difficult to make out its lines. It appeared to be descending in their general direction.

Francesca followed his gaze.

"Another plane?" she asked.

"Too small," Jake said. He brought the jeep to a stop. "I think it's a drone."

"A what?"

"A remote-controlled surveillance aircraft." He tensed as the approaching craft dumped its nose in preparation for what appeared to be a classic strafing run directly toward them.

"Get out now!" he shouted.

They were out of the jeep in half a breath. He grabbed her hand and they dove for cover behind a jumble of boulders. Jake wrapped himself around her to shield her from the threat.

But there was no attack. Jake risked a peek over the rocks and saw the small aircraft bank into a gentle circle fifty feet overhead.

"I'll be damned." He pulled Francesca up beside him. This was no run-of-the-mill predator drone he was looking at. From the rudderless triangular shape, he recognized it immediately as one of Kenny's modified stealth drones. The plane wagged its wings in greeting.

"What is it?" Francesca asked.

"Cal got my message, that's what!" Jake said. He threw his arms around Francesca and spun her in a circle. She smiled and the world was a better place. "We may just make it out of here yet. Let me have the phone."

He accessed the phone's cell number and then waved the device over his head so that his buddies could see he had a phone. With the equipment they had on board, they could zoom in close enough to see whether or not he'd shaved this morning. The drone's wings wagged in acknowledgment. Jake then used his fingers to communicate the phone number, holding his hand sideways—in the universal pilot fashion—to indicate numbers six through ten.

The phone rang a moment later.

Chapter 41

Sonoran Desert, Mexico

FINE TIME FOR A PICNIC, PAL," CAL'S VOICE SAID THROUGH the cell phone.

"Man, am I ever glad to hear from you!" Jake said.

"Hey, Jake," Kenny's voice chimed in.

"Thanks for coming, guys," Jake said. "I know it couldn't have been easy getting the approvals."

"Uh...yeah," Cal said. "What's your SITREP?"

"We have to get Francesca to a hospital in the next few hours," Jake said. He felt her stiffen at the news. He hadn't told her about the chemical yet. "What's your ETA?"

"Fifteen minutes. The Falcon will keep you company until we get there."

"Negative," Jake said. "Tony and the rest are somewhere along the underground river. Battista's boys are tracking them as we speak. They need our help. Send the drone to sweep the area between the ranch and the Gulf. Then floorboard the Osprey and pick us up ASAP."

"Did you say Battista? I thought that bastard was dead!"

"Yeah, me too. He's back. Big time."

"Holy shit! I don't like the idea of leaving you without cover, buddy. Falcon Two is already gridding the river track—"

Jake weighed the risks. The narcos would be occupied at the airfield, at least for a short while. Even if they headed straight up the mountain, the Osprey would beat them here by at least five minutes.

"We don't need the cover, Cal. And if you don't find our friends soon, Battista's goons will." Jake hesitated when he heard a beep from the phone. The low-battery icon was flashing. "Just divert the drone. We'll be fine on our own until you catch up to us."

"Already done," Kenny interjected. The drone banked sharply away and disappeared over a ridge.

The phone beeped again. "I'm going to lose comm any second," Jake said. "We'll wait for you at the plateau just up the road. Beat feet, guys."

"Wilco, boss. See you in—"

The line went dead. Jake pocketed the phone and turned to Francesca.

"Hospital?" she said. Her voice quivered.

Jake gripped her shoulders. "It'll be okay. I promise."

"But I feel fine," she said. Her eyes narrowed in that familiar manner that told Jake she had opened her empathic senses to him. It was time she learned the truth.

"It's a chemical," Jake said.

Francesca's face paled. "What kind of chemical?"

Their attention was drawn to a large explosion that echoed up from the valley below. It was followed by the chatter of multiple assault rifles.

"Back in the jeep!" Jake shouted. He grabbed the AK and moved to the ridgeline. The DC-3 had landed. The lead terrorist and his men ran from cover and launched themselves up the extended staircase into the plane. They were attempting to make good their escape.

But the narcos weren't about to let them leave without a fight. Their vehicles were less than a quarter mile away from the airfield and fast closing the distance. There was a flash from the bed of a pickup truck, followed by a rope of smoke that arced toward the plane. A large explosion ripped through the tarmac fifty yards short of the hangar. A half beat later the sound from the blast reached Jake and Francesca's position, framed by the staccato cracks of automatic weapons.

The DC-3 began moving before the last of the terrorists had climbed aboard. As it picked up speed, another rocket-propelled grenade exploded in its wake. Two of the fleeing terrorists stumbled short of the plane's doorway.

Jake sighted through the AK's scope to get a better view. He watched the scene unfold. The two men were back on their feet. They abandoned their assault weapons and sprinted toward the retreating aircraft. The DC-3 turned onto the runway. Hands urged encouragement from its open doorway. Automatic fire from the vehicles increased. With the shortened range, Jake suspected some of the rounds would impact the aircraft. The plane leaped forward. The pilot had apparently abandoned any thoughts of waiting for the last of his passengers. The gap between the DC-3 and the last two terrorists widened. They waved their arms frantically.

The aircraft lifted off. The narcos' vehicles bolted onto the runway and surrounded the remaining soldiers. Though the two men still had their sidearms, they chose not to use them. Instead, the jihadists knelt on the tarmac. They faced east and bowed their heads in prayer.

The narcos exited their trucks and jeeps, rifles slung behind shoulders. There were nearly twenty men. They closed in on the two soldiers, and pulled machetes from side holsters. The gruesome chopping motions of the circle of men twisted Jake's gut and triggered a new bout of stomach cramps. He doubled over in pain. He'd hoped, wrongly, that the side effect had subsided for good.

Wiping the sheen of sweat that had formed on his brow, he straightened himself. The DC-3 climbed past their position a thousand feet overhead. The terrorists were safely away.

But I'm on to your plan, asshole. I'll be seeing you again soon.

He used the scope for a final look at the airfield. The narcos abandoned the carcasses. They were making their way back to their vehicles when Jake noticed two of them hesitate. One of them extended an arm in Jake's direction. The other cupped his hands to his eyes.

Jake ducked beneath the ridge. There was no way they could see him from that distance, could they? No, he thought, as he crouched out of sight. *We're fine.* And then he remembered the dust trail he'd left in the jeep. He risked a quick peek.

Three of the vehicles were headed his way. Dammit, Jake thought. Even though the Osprey would pick them up before the narcos made it halfway up the hills, he still didn't like the idea that they were on his tail. If those dudes caught up to them and recognized Jake as the man who'd originally taunted their leader…

He ran toward the jeep, hurdled into the driver's seat, and punched the gas. The wheels spit a cloud of dust and gravel as they bit into the earthen road.

* * *

Cal studied the shrub-covered landscape that stretched out before the aircraft, checking for signs of activity. Sure, the effort was likely futile since one of the drones had already cleared the area, but Cal wasn't about to sit around twiddling his thumbs while the computer-driven eyes in the sky did all the work. Old habits were hard to break.

He pushed the CV-22 to its maximum speed of 275 knots. They were headed toward the choppy mountain range that broke the horizon forty miles ahead. Jake and Francesca were up there and they needed his help.

"We should be over their position in ten minutes," he said, making a small course adjustment.

"Roger that." Kenny sat at the UAV console in the belly of the Osprey. "That cell phone Jake had must have lost battery, because I can't pull 'em up."

"Anything at all from the Falcons?"

"A few more trucks and cars, but no sign of Tony and the crew. They must still be underground. I wish like hell I'd equipped the birds with ground-penetrating radar..."

"Don't beat yourself up, kid. One step at a time. First we pick up Jake and Francesca, and then we'll double back and locate the others."

"I guess. It's just that—" He stopped for a beat, then said, "I've got something. Emergency beacon. Northeast. Diverting Falcon One for a closer look."

Cal felt his blood race.

"A second beacon!" Kenny reported. "And another, and... two, no...make that three more!"

"Distance?"

"Thirty miles, bearing zero-five-zero. It's on your screen now."

The blinking icon on Cal's heads-up display, the HUD, was identified as Tango-1. They could be overhead in five or six minutes, he thought. But it might or might not be their friends. And in the meantime, Francesca needed to get to a hospital.

"How long before the Falcon can get us a visual?" he said, maintaining his current course.

"One minute."

They pressed forward toward the mountains, getting farther and farther away from the source of the emergency signals. Cal's fingers seemed to itch at the controls. A growing part of him wanted to divert to the beacons.

"I need that visual, Kenny."

"Zooming," Kenny reported, drawing the word out as he focused on the screen. "It's a sinkhole. I can see the river...it's Sarafina! And Lacey's lying next to her. She looks injured."

Cal snapped the Osprey into a sharp bank to port. "It looks like Jake and Francesca are going to have to wait a bit longer," he said. He was glad they weren't in any immediate danger.

* * *

Jake scanned the sky. He expected to hear the distinctive sound of the Osprey's rotors any moment.

He and Francesca stood beside the jeep at the evac point. The dirt road had flattened on a plateau about the length of a football field, just wide enough to make it a suitable landing site for the Osprey. The terrain fell off sharply to one side of the expanse and a boulder-strewn incline rose from the other. A hundred yards ahead, the serpentine road disappeared around a bend before resuming its climb into the barren peaks of the mountain range.

She took his hand. "The drug they gave me," she said. "Tell me about it."

This was a conversation Jake had hoped to avoid until they'd made it to the hospital. He pulled the wrapped bundle of vials out of his pocket. "We're going to figure out which of these is the antidote. You'll be fine."

"Or else?"

Jake pocketed the vials, then gripped her shoulders to steady her. "Or else you will no longer be able to conceive," he said softly.

Her momentary bewilderment morphed into a look of horror. "What? Why?"

"Don't worry," he said. "I prom—"

"I don't want platitudes, Jake." She twisted from his grasp and placed her hands on her hips. "I want the facts, and I want them now."

Jake blew out a breath and gave her a quick summary of what he'd learned from the doctor's journal.

"*Dio mio,*" Francesca said. "These men are evil incarnate."

"And I'm going to stop them," Jake said firmly. "Whatever it takes."

Francesca's head canted slightly to one side, her familiar expression leaving little doubt that she knew he was holding back something.

"There is one more thing," he said. He felt his eyes moisten. "The baby…won't make it without the antidote."

All the breath went out of her.

Jake moved to embrace her, but she stepped away. "You listen to me, Jake Bronson," she said. "Nothing is going to happen to this baby. We won't allow it. *Capito?*"

Jake nodded. "You got that right," he said. He took her hands in his. "I'm sorry I got you into this mess."

"We got in this together," she said. "We will get out of it the same way. Besides, the plane should be here shortly, *si?*"

Jake checked his watch and the knot in his gut tightened. The Osprey should have been overhead two minutes before. It's not like Cal and Kenny to miss ETA by such a margin, not when they were so close in the first place.

He peered over the edge of the escarpment. Three vehicles bounced their way up the road, with a thick cloud of dust behind them. One was well ahead of the others—a large SUV with tinted windows. At its present pace it would reach their position in less than ten minutes.

"Time for plan B," he said, heading back to the jeep for the spare gas can. The vehicle had sputtered earlier as they'd made the crest. They'd be lucky if the remaining fumes were enough to restart the engine. He'd top it off so they could stay ahead of the narcos until the Osprey arrived.

The moment he unlatched the buckle securing the can, Jake knew there was a problem. The can rocked easily under his grasp. It was empty.

He grabbed the AK-47 from the jeep and rechecked the magazine. Five rounds. Not much to work with against three truckloads of very pissed-off cartel boys.

He glanced around. There was a large outcrop fifty feet up the rocky incline that abutted the road.

Francesca laid her hand on his arm. "What shall we do?"

A plan unfolded in his mind. It wasn't perfect, but it should at least protect Francesca. He took her hand. "Come with me."

Chapter 42

Beneath the Sonoran Desert, Mexico

TONY WATCHED STONE-FACED AS THE LAST OF THE FLAMES in the limestone chimney flickered out. The waiting was the worst part. He huddled with the others, wondering what the men up above would do next.

His thoughts were answered by an explosive retort of an assault rifle on full auto. High-velocity slugs hammered into the blackened rock beneath the vent, ricocheting around the cavern. Not very original, Tony thought grimly. But you've definitely got our attention.

"Infidel pigs!" a voice yelled down from above. "You killed my brother!"

Tony heard another man's shout of alarm. It seemed to be directed away from them. The voice was quickly drowned out by long bursts from multiple automatic weapons. This time none of the rounds made their way down the vent.

"There's a firefight up top!" he said.

Tony and Becker edged closer to the opening. There was a distant vibration, beyond the gunfire, growing in volume. Tony held his breath as he strained to make it out.

Becker recognized it a half second ahead of him. "Yeah!" he shouted with a fist pump. A wide grin lit up his weathered face and he slapped his friend on the shoulder.

The distinctive throb of the CV-22's heavy props was unmistakable.

"'Bout time," Tony said. A wave of relief washed over him. He pounded fist to palm. "Go get 'em, Cal."

There were frantic shouts from above as magazines were replaced. A moment later the staccato cracks of gunfire were renewed in a frenzy of long bursts. Then a smooth zipping sound tore through the air and Tony knew that the CV-22's five-barrel Gatling gun had let loose. The ground shook above them from the impact of 25mm rounds puckering the earth at thirty-six hundred rounds per minute. The rain of lead would shred anything in its path.

Return fire from the ground ceased abruptly. No one could have survived.

"Good riddance," Becker muttered.

"Damn straight," Tony said.

The pitch of the props changed and Tony could imagine the bird's twin nacelles shifting upward as the versatile plane switched from horizontal to vertical flight. Dust and debris washed across the opening of the vent.

The engines shut down.

Marshall, Bradley, and Josh joined Tony and Becker under the opening.

Rushing footsteps. Bits of gravel tumbled down the vent. A tiny head popped into view, framed by a cascade of long hair that drooped down.

"Josh!" Sarafina shouted from above. "Are you okay?"

Max's joyful barks filled the cavern.

* * *

For Jake's plan to succeed, he needed the narcos close.

He posed as if he'd been killed or knocked unconscious when the vehicle flipped. His cheek rested on the dirt road. His contorted body was half in and half out of the overturned jeep. The AK-47 rested in plain view on the road, well out of reach. Francesca was nowhere to be seen.

There was a faint rumble of an engine. Steadying his breathing, Jake focused on a point fifty yards ahead where the road disappeared over the ridgeline. The black SUV bounded onto the plateau. It skidded to a stop in a whirlwind of dust and flying pebbles. The doors flew open.

Three men leaped out brandishing weapons and angry snarls. There was a rush of conversation—too distant to discern—as someone issued orders from the car. Two of the narcos trained their weapons on the jeep. The third opened the rear hatch and retrieved a scoped rifle. Jake cringed as the man jammed home a magazine and steadied the rifle on the SUV's hood. It was undoubtedly aimed at his head.

Snapping his eyes closed, Jake remained still. The bullet would either come, or it wouldn't. But if his limp form appeared to offer no threat…

Seconds passed. He imagined the sniper's eyes studying him through the high-powered lens, the crosshairs shifting across his face. Jake tensed when he felt something crawl onto his outstretched hand. He fought the urge to twitch or swat it away. Instead, he concentrated on shallow breaths. He prayed that Francesca remained still.

She'd resisted his plan, knowing full well the deadly risk he was taking. But in the end, she'd agreed. She would remain hidden until the Osprey arrived.

No matter what happened to Jake.

He'd restarted the jeep and driven up the steepest part of the incline at an angle that would ensure a rollover. He'd jumped out at the last second and then staged himself in his current position.

The insect skittered onto his forearm. *Tarantula? Scorpion?*

The sound of additional vehicles penetrated Jake's thoughts. *The trailing pickups.*

Jake bit off a grimace as his carefully laid plan fell to pieces. He'd expected them to approach his prone form. That would have given him a chance to overcome them—especially if his enhanced reflexes didn't fail him like they did at the ranch. Then he and Francesca could have fled in their SUV. Instead, the wary narcos had hesitated, waiting for backup.

Truck doors opened. More voices. Even through closed eyes Jake could imagine a dozen men jumping out with weapons in hand. He had no clue how in the hell he was going to escape this predicament. A part of him was tempted to rush for the AK-47 and dive for cover in the deep culvert just behind him. But the sniper would nail him before he took his second step.

Finally, a shout. "Gringo!"

Tiny claws hesitated on the tingling skin of his arm. Jake held his breath.

"If you are alive," the voice said, "I suggest for your sake that you give us a sign."

The man issued a sharp order. Jake heard the loud retort of the rifle at the same instant he felt the burning splatter of sand and pebbles scorch his torso. The high-powered round ricocheted off the road just inches behind him.

He flinched. His eyes opened in time to see a scorpion scurry away in the sand.

Exclamations from several of the distant men confirmed that they noticed Jake's movement.

"The next bullet goes into your head," the man shouted. Jake was certain it was the same man he'd taunted on video. What was it again that he'd said to him? Insults about his family and manhood…

Oh, crap.

Jake rose slowly and took in the sight before him. Fifteen armed men. They moved forward.

Jake spotted a flicker of movement in the sky behind them.

* * *

196

"Uh, we've got a problem," Kenny said as he maneuvered the UAV in for a closer look at the evac site.

He and Tony were seated at the Falcon console in the main cabin of the CV-22. They were en route to Jake's position. The rest of the exhausted group rested in the seats behind them. Lacey lay on her back across three seats. She'd suffered a mild concussion. Marshall had placed a pillow under her head and stroked her hair. The children sat across from them, their feet pulled up beneath a shared blanket. Bradley and Max sat beside them. The dog perked up at the sound of Kenny's voice.

"Jake and Francesca have company," Kenny said. He switched the drone's sensor from thermal to visual. "A dozen or more tangos closing in."

"Dammit!" Tony said. He kept his voice low so as not to alert the others. "How long 'fore we're there?"

"ETA eight minutes," Kenny said.

"Hell, it's gonna be over in eight seconds," Tony whispered. "Use the drone. Blast 'em."

"I can't!" Kenny said in a hushed breath. He pointed to a lone figure huddled behind a large outcrop. "Francesca would be safe enough where she is here, but from our current launch angle, Jake's well inside the missile's blast radius."

"Doesn't the drone have a Gatling?"

"No ammo. The live-fire exercise we set up for at Miramar was missiles only."

"Well, shit, man!" Tony said, more loudly than he intended. "We gotta do something!"

Marshall moved in behind the two men. "What's going on?"

Kenny's finger quickly panned the screen. "Bad guys, here. Jake, here. Francesca up in the rocks, here." He tapped the keyboard and a transparent red oval representing a projected missile-blast radius appeared on the screen. Jake was inside the kill zone. "Can't use air-to-ground missiles. And without the surgical strike capabilities of the Gatling gun—"

"Hold on," Marshall interrupted. "What's Jake doing with his hands?"

Kenny used the thumb knob on the drone's joystick to zoom in on Jake's face and raised hands. It appeared as if Jake was staring directly at the drone, his lips mouthing something while his hands repeated a pilot signal—the type used to communicate with a wingman when flying under radio silence.

"You've got to be kidding," Kenny said. He keyed the mike on his headset and reported to Cal. "Are you seeing this, boss?"

Chapter 43

Sonoran Desert, Mexico

J AKE LIFTED HIS HANDS ABOVE HIS HEAD. A GLIMMER OF hope swelled within him as the tiny spec resolved itself into the manta-ray shape of one of Kenny's stealth drones.

On my go, he mouthed over and over as he watched the drone approach from behind the narcos. One hand repeated the subtle twin-fingers-forward hand signal that he knew Cal and Kenny would recognize.

The narcos approached in a line toward Jake. They were thirty paces away. They'd relaxed their weapons. The men were dressed in an assortment of mix-and-match gear that looked put together from an army surplus store. Most of them wore olive green fatigues but two were dressed in desert camo. They wore webbed belts with spare magazines and holsters…and tucked machetes. The blades looked dirty. Except for their leader, they were an ugly bunch, ideal candidates for a low-budget action flick, Jake thought. But the bullets in their weapons were real enough. And they looked angry.

Their leader walked casually in the center of the line. His men were careful not to outpace him. In contrast, he was dressed as if he were on his way to a business meeting with a group of oil tycoons. His steel-gray suit shimmered under the midday sun. He stopped when he was five paces away and stared at Jake from behind reflective sunglasses. Except for a brief twitch of his pencil-thin mustache, his expression was unreadable.

It's now or never, Jake thought, fighting down a surge of despair. He kept his eyes on the narcos. His index and middle fingers froze in the downward position of the signal.

The man removed a paisley scarf from his breast pocket and crouched to wipe the silver tips of his snakeskin boots. Satisfied, he rose to his feet. "So much dust," he said. His English was perfect.

Jake's lips moved double time. *On my go, on my go!*

The narco noticed. "Prayers will not help," he said. He removed his glasses, wrapped them in the scarf, and tucked them inside his suit. His dark eyes never left Jake's. He nodded and the men on either side of him moved forward.

Jake edged backward, stopping just before he reached the deep culvert that ran along the base of the rocky incline. The two men grabbed his arms and twisted them behind his back— just as the Falcon wagged its wings in acknowledgment.

Jake's chances for survival just moved from none to slim. He coiled his muscles.

* * *

"But it's suicide!" Marshall said from over Kenny's shoulder. "He's sacrificing himself for Francesca."

Kenny ignored the comment. He'd already argued the point over his headset with Cal. They'd both arrived at the same conclusion as Marshall. Still, they had no other choice but to trust their friend. If anyone could pull a rabbit out of a hat in this situation, it was Jake. They'd play their role according to his orders.

Behind Kenny, Tony stood shoulder to shoulder with Marshall, his eyes glued to the screen.

"It ain't over 'til it's over," Tony said, resigned to watch Jake's plan unfold.

Kenny flexed his fingers like a master pianist about to lay down an intense bit of Mozart. He wrapped one hand around the drone's custom joystick and the other on the console keyboard. Though the drone could be controlled from either device independently, he found it faster to use both in concert. He tapped a three-stroke command on the underside panel of the stick.

A computerized voice responded in his headset. "Missile system activated. Confirm weapons pop-out."

He repeated the command that would open the seamless door on the underside of the drone's fuselage and rotate the missile pod into firing position. The pod held four miniature missiles—two air-to-ground and two air-to-air.

"Pod in firing position," the computer voice said.

Kenny adjusted the reticle on the screen and locked the targeting computer on a point just behind the group of Mexicans spread out before Jake.

"Target lock. Confirm target lock."

The need to input the commands twice was a necessary safeguard against accidental release. He repeated the command.

"Target locked."

Kenny continued entering and confirming commands, both hands making smooth movements over the controls.

"Weapons hot."

"Mini-Maverick selected."

"Ready to fire."

Kenny was in his element. He concentrated on the screen's image, his finger on the trigger as he waited for Jake's signal. The mini-Maverick was a "fire-and-forget," air-to-ground missile that used a TV-imaging seeker for precision targeting. Though it employed a high-explosive, shape-charged warhead designed for use against tanks and other vehicles, in open terrain it would prove deadly for anyone within its blast radius. Jake was only twenty feet from the targeted impact point.

Jake winced as the men on either side of him wrenched his arms farther up his back, forcing him to rise to his toes before something snapped. The two drug soldiers seemed to be enjoying themselves. The rest of their gang had formed a semicircle in front of them, hungry to observe what was coming next.

Their leader stepped forward and stopped one pace away. Jake needed him closer.

"You spoke of my family," the man said.

His English hinted at an education that most of the men around him probably lacked. Jake wondered if he could reason with him.

"Listen, amigo," Jake said. He projected a calm air of sincerity. "I'm really sorry about what I said over the video screen. It was all an act, really. You and I, we're on the same team. Those terrorists you encountered down at the airport? They're the problem. I was just trying to—"

"Machete," the man said. He reached out his manicured hand to his side. One of his men handed him a long blade. It had a single edge that appeared finely honed. There were bloodstains on it.

"Okay, pal," Jake said. "Let's not get carried away."

"If your family was here," the drug lord said, "I would kill them first. Slowly." The man's tone indicated that the act was something he had conducted many times before.

A deadly calm came over Jake. He steadied himself for what he knew he must do. The culvert was directly behind him.

"I'm going to warn you only once," Jake said, projecting his own menace. He spoke in Spanish, one of several languages he'd mastered in the past few months. "Unless you leave this place immediately, you and your men will all die."

The leader's eyes narrowed for a fraction. Then his face closed like a fist. He stepped forward. The machete rose.

Jake glanced up. The Mexican noticed. His gaze shifted over his shoulder. Jake gave the pronounced nod to signal the missile launch. He continued the motion and head-butted the man with the fury of his own pent-up anger and frustration. But the Mexican's head was turned so the blow didn't have the intended effect. He staggered backward but kept his balance.

Jake rebounded from the impact. He used his reverse momentum to heave himself—and the two guards—backward into the three-foot-deep culvert.

Just before the horizon disappeared from view, Jake saw the flash at the bottom of the drone that indicated a missile launch. He allowed his body to go limp, making no attempt to struggle with the startled Mexicans who tumbled beside him. They rose quickly. Their hands reached for holstered weapons.

Jake was huddled at their feet. He closed his eyes, cupped his hands to his ears, and opened his mouth to protect against the overpressure from the explosion.

The superheated blast shook the ground and knocked the wind out of him. Sound disappeared from shocked eardrums. Debris rained down on him. When Jake opened his eyes, the air was filled with smoke. The two men who'd stood above him had been killed instantly. Their scorched bodies bent over the far wall of the culvert as if a mighty wind had folded them at the waist.

He pushed to his feet and crawled out of the culvert. The ground was splattered with a scarlet porridge that smelled of offal and burned meat. Flames danced from the charred remains of the narcos' bodies. The smoke cleared and Jake saw the drone racing toward him, its wings wagging sharply from side to side.

There was a flash of movement in his peripheral vision. Jake spun to see the drug lord step from the culvert. A layer of dust coated him from head to toe. He held a chrome-plated pistol pointed at Jake's chest.

"As I was saying," the man said through clenched teeth. "You should never have spoken of my family."

"And you, signore," Francesca said, startling both men, "should not be pointing a gun at the father of my child." She was ten paces away, walking toward them.

The man swiveled the pistol toward her.

Francesca stepped over a mangled body with the casual grace of a hiker traversing a log. She emanated a fierce sense of determination Jake had never witnessed in her before. But her presence made no sense, he thought. Jake wasn't close enough to the man for her distraction to do any good.

The Mexican glanced between the two of them. He must have sensed Jake's desperation because he swiveled the pistol back in his direction. The corners of his lips turned upward.

"What a pleasant sur—"

Twin gunshots blew him off his feet. He was dead before hitting the ground. Jake stared at Francesca in disbelief. Smoke trailed from the barrel of the pistol that had suddenly appeared in her hands. She'd taken a knee in a classic two-grip shooter's pose.

He moved toward her. She set the weapon on the ground and rose. She was steady on her feet. Jake wrapped her in his arms.

"I had to be close enough to be certain I wouldn't miss," she said softly. "My papa taught me that."

Jake had trouble forming words around his astonishment. "W—what?"

She pressed her body close. "Isn't it time I saved *you* for a change?"

Chapter 44

Above the Sonoran Desert

ABBAS CONFIRMED WITH THE PILOT THAT ALL WAS WELL. He and his men were en route to Los Angeles in the DC-3. Fifteen minutes had passed since their narrow escape from the airfield.

He exited the cramped cockpit and made his way toward the rear of the plane. Several of the men gave him acknowledging nods as he passed by. Iranian shock troops—a well-deserved moniker for the seasoned fighters. They'd performed well, Abbas thought, in spite of the unexpected arrival of the Mexican drug gang. Two of their team had been killed at the airfield, and the four who had been tracking the American's friends had failed to check in—also presumed dead. *Acceptable losses.* The dozen who remained were stoic. They were currently stationed in Venezuela near the sheikh's new headquarters, on loan to him in support of their cause.

Abbas was proud to serve with them. *True warriors of Allah.*

He turned his attention to the doctor who cowered in the last row of the compartment. A flush of anger swelled from within. They had some unfinished matters to discuss.

"You *gave* the American the antidote?" Abbas said. His hand shot out to grip the doctor's scrawny neck and lift him to his feet.

"He was going to kill me!" the doctor squealed.

"Then you should have died," Abbas growled. His thumb dug deeper against the man's throat. Any farther and the larynx would collapse.

The doctor gasped as he tried unsuccessfully to draw a breath under the pressure of Abbas's grip. His eyes bulged.

Abbas marveled at the doctor's unwillingness to fight back, even if doing so meant hastening the inevitable. The man's lack of backbone disgusted him. His presence on board the aircraft was an insult to the other soldiers. Still, according to the sheikh, he was needed. Reluctantly, Abbas released him. The doctor slumped into his seat, gulping in lungfuls of air.

"There was barely enough antidote to treat the woman," he said, his voice thin and raspy. He massaged his reddening neck. "Besides, he knows nothing of our plans."

"And that is the only reason you are still alive!" Abbas said.

The copilot emerged from the cockpit. "Sir!" he said. "The sheikh is on the radio."

* * *

Abbas sat in the copilot's seat and adjusted the headset. The pilot and copilot had removed theirs in order to protect the privacy of his conversation with the sheikh. Abbas turned his back on the two men. The crack of a smile found his lips as he spoke into the mouthpiece.

"The American has escaped."

"Excellent. Does he suspect anything?" Battista said on the other end of the line.

"Nothing," Abbas said.

"Well done."

"Thank you, my sheikh. But it is your plan that should be applauded. I am but your tool."

"A sharp tool, to be sure."

Abbas smiled at the rare compliment. "Fooling the American was no more difficult than training a camel to *koosh*."

The sheikh allowed himself a chuckle. "And now, our camel shall lead us to the final oasis."

Part III

Chapter 45

Doc Finnegan stood among the research scientists seated at the lower of the tiered rows of control consoles. The steel shroud remained locked around the centerpiece of the Obsidian Project. He flicked a switch on the board and the polarized viewing window transitioned from opaque to clear. The black pyramid within was flipped upside down on its axis, its tip supported in a specially constructed frame. The four-by-four top surface of the object shimmered under the shroud's lights. It was covered in a series of pictograms and unusual symbols whose meaning remained a mystery.

"What have you got, Timmy?" Doc asked.

The junior researcher adjusted a remote control toggle on his panel. Inside the chamber, a small robotic arm swiveled a camera over the top of the object. The image filled the large LED screen at Timmy's station.

As many times as Doc had studied the etched surface of the artifact, he still felt the familiar rush of excitement he'd experienced when he had first laid eyes on it.

A series of eight rectangular grayscale images ran along the outside perimeter of the obelisk's smooth square surface. They were amazingly realistic, finely etched, and resembling a tooled printing plate. The detail was impressive, reminiscent of laser-etched photos. The images depicted early man—fur-clothed, bearded *Homo sapiens* in various stages of horrific battle against one another, using rudimentary weapons made of stone, bone, and wood. Each scene was more violent than the last, a haunting view of the savagery of man's ancestors.

The final image in the sequence was different. It depicted three slender, hairless humanoid figures, their backs turned, standing on a rock ledge looking down on a tribe of early man. One of the humanoids had his hands held out before him, as though he were awaiting a gift from heaven. Hovering in the air in front of his hands was a small black pyramid. Spikes of black light shot from its peak and pierced the heads of the people below. Their hands pressed against their temples, their eyes wild and faces in agony.

The macabre images framed a twenty-four-inch-square section in the center of the top surface. The outline of a smaller square—about three inches wide—appeared to be more deeply etched into the center of the object. The space between this small untouched square and the larger one that surrounded it was divided into eleven trapezoidal sections. Each contained irregular shapes and patterns.

Timmy zoomed the camera so that the obtuse symbols filled the screen. "I've discovered a pattern," he said.

Doc felt a jolt of adrenaline at his words, especially coming from this young man.

At twenty-three years old, Timmy Bretzel was the youngest of Doc's scientific team. Wearing black jeans and a heavy-metal T-shirt, he had dark eyes that looked like he never got enough sleep. His black hair was short and spiky and one ear was riddled with piercings. Two empty cans of Monster Energy drink rested beside his console. Doc had brought him along from his last assignment because he was one of the most brilliant up-and-comers Doc had ever met. The kid had a love for anything other-worldly and a genius-level IQ that gave him a knack for looking at problems from unique perspectives.

"A pattern?" Doc said.

"Yeah. We've been looking at these things all wrong."

Timmy waved his hand in a circular motion around the screen, indicating the string of symbols. Each was embossed or engraved with various textures and vivid colors. One of them looked like a puffy cloud with random dots embedded around it. Another resembled a splotch of thick paint, its rough edges surrounding a series of arcing lines. All eleven appeared nonsensical, like random scribbles in a child's coloring book.

"They're not spatial like we first thought," Timmy continued. "Not intended to depict a place or a time." He straightened in his chair. "They're numerical."

He entered a command on his keyboard and various numbers were superimposed over each of the symbols on the monitor. The numbers ranged from single digits to one that had eleven digits.

Doc studied the smaller numbers in the sequence: 2-3-5-7-23-719. His mind skipped through a series of calculations. He mumbled as he moved from one number to the next. "Prime… prime…prime…"

"Exactly!" Timmy said, his enthusiasm growing. "They're all prime numbers. Even the larger ones. But there's more to it than that. Out of the eleven numbers, only eight of them are factorial primes."

Doc's eyes narrowed. He went over the definition in his mind as he considered it. A factorial is the product of an integer and all the integers below it. A factorial prime is a prime number that is one less or one more than a factorial…Yes, Timmy was correct. Doc pointed to three of the numbers.

"Right," Timmy said. "All but three of them. There's no way that's a coincidence."

It was hard to disagree with that statement, Doc thought. Everything about the artifact reeked of exacting purpose, right down to its dimensions. Their laser measuring instruments had confirmed that it was perfectly equilateral down to the nano-meter, or one billionth of a meter. Timmy was right—there must be a distinct reason for those three symbols being different. He tapped the stem of his pipe against his chin.

"All right," he said, the scientist within still skeptical. "How did you translate the symbols into numbers in the first place?"

"It sparked last night when I was channel surfing. I caught the end of a special on autism on the Discovery Channel. They were discussing synesthesia. I followed up with an all-nighter on the net."

"Explain."

"It's a neurological condition in which stimulation of one sensory or cognitive pathway leads to automatic, involuntary experiences in a second sensory or cognitive pathway."

"Go on," Doc said warily. He suspected he knew where this was headed.

"It's found in rare cases among people with autism or spectrum disorders. They see numbers differently than we do. Where we see a string of digits, their brains see distinct shapes, with defined textures, colors, and depths."

"Timmy, you're a lot of things, but a synesthete isn't among them." Warning bells sounded in his head.

"Well, no," Timmy said, shifting in his seat. "The truth is, I'm not the one who translated them. Uh…I got some outside help."

"Tim—!"

"Don't worry, Doc," Timmy said. "I didn't divulge any top-secret stuff to anyone. I just shared photos of the symbols with a really cool dude they talked about on the show. He doesn't have a clue where they came from."

"For Christ's sake, Timmy," Doc whispered. He leaned over so he wouldn't be overheard. "You could get yourself thrown into prison for a stunt like that!"

"Doc, Doc. You gotta chill," Timmy said. "Sometimes you gotta stretch the boundaries, you know? Be bold. We're here to change the world, right? Besides, it's what we needed to crack this baby."

Doc noticed Lieutenant Colonel Brown making his way toward them. He was moving fast.

Terrific.

Timmy continued, pointing a thumb at the approaching man. "So, do you want to me to keep working to solve the riddle here, or are you going to have Fester lock me up in a federal penitentiary with a bunch of pervs?"

Doc straightened to face Brown. Out of the corner of his mouth, he mumbled, "One of these days, Timmy…"

The lieutenant colonel had a backpack slung over one shoulder. It appeared heavy from the way the strap stretched the fabric of his camo utility uniform.

"I've got a little surprise for you, Doc," Brown said. He plopped the backpack on the desk beside Timmy's console. He unzipped the top, reached in with both hands, and removed a dull metal container about the size of a tackle box. There was a battery meter embedded in the top of the box. Its indicator wavered just above the red zone. The box's single thumb latch was unsecured.

Setting the box on the counter, Brown said, "One of our teams searched Bronson's apartment. He was long gone, but we found this hidden under a floorboard."

Doc was unable to curb his excitement. Ever since he'd learned that Jake Bronson was responsible for the launching of the duplicate artifact in the mountains of Afghanistan, even mention of the man's name got him going. "Have you opened it?"

"Oh, yeah," Brown said, his normally somber manner replaced by a Cheshire grin. "And you're not going to believe what's inside."

Like a poker player eagerly gathering his chips, Timmy pulled the box toward him and snapped open the latch.

"Hang on," Doc said. He slapped his palm on the lid. "We'd hardly be following scientific protocol if we simply examined it on your desk without setting up some proper controls."

"Doc," Timmy said. "It's time to be bold. Remember?"

The kid is right, Doc thought. *When did I become so damn conservative?*

With a tight-lipped nod, he lifted his hand and said, "Go for it."

As soon as the lid swung open, a beeping noise sounded from the speaker at an adjacent console.

"Doc," the technician at the station reported excitedly. "I've got some sort of signal coming from the shroud!"

Another scientist across the room shouted, "Same here! Harmonic waves of some sort."

Doc heard the words, but his mind shoved them aside for the moment. His awareness was captured by the three-inch black pyramid lying within a nest of electromagnets in the box.

"I'll be damned," he muttered. His mind raced through a myriad of possibilities, all of which revolved around the obvious conclusion that the mini-pyramid must have originated from the larger one launched into space. How had Bronson separated it from its mother? Why had he kept it in an electromagnetic cocoon? What was its purpose?

He slammed closed the lid of the box. "Colonel," he said, "I don't care how you do it, but you simply *must* find this Bronson character!"

Chapter 46

Puerto Peñasco, Mexico

Puerto Peñasco—also known as Rocky Point to the many American tourists who streamed in from Arizona and California—was a small municipality situated on the strip of land that joins the peninsula of Baja California with the rest of Mexico. Only a hundred miles from Arizona, its warm beaches and picturesque setting on the Gulf of California made it a haven for American retirees. In this second week of June, the town bustled with its annual influx of summer tourists.

Jake peeked through the blinds that covered the second-story window of the small hospital room. The panel truck that had brought them into the city was parked on the curb below. He caught a glimpse of Becker standing watch in the shadowed recess of a small shop across the street. The truck's owner stood beside him, smoking a cigarette.

The local man was uncle to one of the boys in Papa's former LA gang. It seemed the former gang leader's tentacles reached far and wide throughout Mexico, a fact that had led Jake to the Mexican narco-ranch safe house in the first place. Jake had called Papa as soon as Cal picked them up in the CV-22. Papa made a few quick calls and within minutes was back to Jake with a plan. An hour later, the CV-22 landed at a remote spot five miles outside Puerto Peñasco, where they met up with Papa's contact. Cal and Kenny stayed with the plane.

Marshall, Lacey, and Bradley kept the children occupied on the far side of the room. They'd cleaned up as best they could in the adjacent bathroom, exchanging their soggy clothes for an assortment of colorful T-shirts, slacks, and shorts that their driver had picked up for them at a local tourist shop. Lacey's forehead was properly bandaged and the flesh wound in Bradley's arm had been stitched up.

The relief they felt was reflected in the children's relaxed manner. Josh listened wide-mouthed as Sarafina gave an animated account of her plunge through the underground river. Even Max seemed lighter on his feet. His tail wagged as he moved from hand to hand for a scratch behind the ears or a pet along his back.

Tony brushed up beside Jake and squeezed his shoulder. "She's going to be okay, man," he said softly. "We got here with time to spare."

Jake turned to face his friend. "I pray to God you're right."

Francesca was lying in the next room, an IV drip inserted in her arm. An insistent nurse had ushered Jake from her side as she and the doctor conducted the more intimate portion of a physical exam. At first, the doctor had resisted using the drug Jake had taken from the airport hangar. By process of elimination, he'd quickly identified which of the three vials had the antidote, but he'd insisted that more tests were necessary before administering it. The fact that Jake's tattered and worn group—two children and a dog included—had filed in through a seldom-used maintenance door at the rear of the hospital hadn't done much to set the doctor's mind at ease. But a handful of cash and a peek at Tony's handgun had transformed his attitude. The doctor had barked a quick series of orders and the nurse escorted the group to the treatment area of the small but clean hospital.

Jake prayed they'd gotten here in time. Would the drug save their unborn child? Would Francesca be able to conceive again?

When his wife and daughter died over a year ago, Jake had spiraled into a deep depression. It lowered his defenses to a point where the cancer he'd fought off a decade ago had been able to find its way in again. If it hadn't been for the freak accident in the MRI, he'd be dead by now. Even so, the loss of his family had remained an open wound. He'd found it impossible to imagine a time when the emptiness it left wouldn't overshadow everything. But Francesca had changed all that. She had given him hope. Now she carried their child.

"Why'd they do it, Jake?" Tony asked, his voice low to keep from being overheard by the children. "Why inject Francesca at all?"

"Based on what I gathered," Jake said, "I don't think it was a part of some master plan or anything like that. The bastard doctor acted on his own, probably overzealous in seeing if his drug worked. They knew she was pregnant."

"It still doesn't make sense to me. Why use an exotic drug? There are a lot of simpler ways to end a pregnancy."

Jake shuddered, remembering what he'd learned about the drug after reading the doctor's private notebook.

"There's a hell of a lot more to it than that," Jake said, speaking more loudly than he intended. "Ending a pregnancy is only a side effect of the drug. Its real purpose is far worse."

Lacey rose and approached the two men. Marshall was quick to follow, leaving Bradley to sit with the children.

"Say that again," Lacey said, her voice hushed.

The four huddled together. Jake blew out a breath as he prepared to give his friends the highlights of what he'd discovered. Even with his expanded mental capacity, he found it difficult to grasp the enormity of Battista's insidious plan.

"I'm guessing it's the brainchild of one of the two remaining implant subjects who made it out of the mountain," he began, then told them what he'd learned from the journal.

"One drop of undiluted serum is enough to infect an Olympic-size swimming pool of drinking water," he concluded.

"And if you drink it?" Lacey said.

"One sip is enough to render a woman infertile. Permanently."

Lacey gasped.

"Jesus," Marshall said. He wrapped his arm around her.

Tony's face narrowed to a fist. "What the hell are they planning to do with it?"

"I don't know. But whatever it is, it's happening in LA."

Tony took out the sat-phone and pressed REDIAL. Another busy tone. He clipped the phone to his belt.

"We'll stop 'em," Lacey said. Her eyes were daggers.

"We need to contact Homeland Security," Marshall said, reaching for the phone.

Jake stayed his hand. "Not so fast. It's not as simple as that. First of all, what would we say? We don't know where in Los Angeles the terrorists are based, or how and when they intend to insert the compound into the water system. And Homeland is not going to believe some anonymous tipster over the phone. We sure as hell can't identify ourselves, can we? Like it or not, we're all fugitives. Hell, after our guns-blazing escape at the Torrance airport, not to mention the theft of a fully-armed CV-22 by Cal and Kenny, we've probably made it to the top of the government's Most Wanted list."

"But we didn't do anything wrong!" Marshall said.

"Sure," Tony grumbled. "And after two or three years of confinement and heavy interrogation, they might actually believe you."

"Turning ourselves in isn't an option," Jake said firmly. He thought about Francesca in the other room and he imagined thousands—make that millions—of other women going through the same agony if Battista's plan succeeded. They couldn't allow that to happen.

He studied his friends. As much as he'd like to safeguard them from what was to come, he knew he couldn't do it alone.

"We're going to have to deal with Battista on our own," he said. "Once and for all."

A hush fell over the group as the enormity of Jake's words kicked in. Even the children, who had been chatting nonstop until now, quieted as if they sensed the tension in the room.

Tony was the first to break the silence. "We can't stick around here much longer."

"Yeah, I know," Jake said, encouraged by his buddy's matter-of-fact acceptance of the situation. "We need a place to hole up and strategize."

"It should be close to the target area," Tony added. The soldier in him had resurfaced.

"Someplace no one would think to look," Lacey said.

Marshall sighed. "With a solid computer system and high-speed Internet."

"And access to more manpower," Tony said.

Jake sensed Francesca's presence an instant before her hands wrapped around his waist from behind. "It must be safe for the children," she said. "And for God's sake, make sure there's plenty of bottled water."

Jake turned to face her. A wave of relief washed over him as he caught her smile. "The baby's okay," she said, folding herself into his arms.

"You heard everything?" he asked her.

"I heard enough. The man is the devil incarnate."

Jake felt her anger. He knew she was sickened by the ease with which Battista had drawn her into his web of lies at the Institute for Advanced Brain Studies in Venice. It had nearly cost her life. And Sarafina's as well.

A knuckle rap on the open door interrupted them. The doctor walked in with Francesca's chart. "You're cleared to go. I suggest you take it easy the next few days." He turned and appraised Jake. "I understand you've been suffering from some severe abdominal cramping."

Jake tensed. After all the health issues he'd been through, being poked and prodded by a doctor was at the absolute bottom of his list of favorite things. The abdominal attacks had lessened in frequency. The last one had been a couple hours earlier on the Osprey. But he admitted to himself that it had hurt something fierce. A part of him worried that the next attack would be even worse. Maybe the doctor could give him something.

The man continued, "A quick scan will allow us to identify the root of the problem. We have an MRI in the basement—"

Jake spun around the doctor and ushered him toward the door so fast that the poor man nearly toppled over.

"B—but—"

"Out you go, Doc," Jake said, shaking off a shudder at the mention of an MRI. The terror of what had happened the last time he'd been in one was branded in his memory. "Thanks for the offer, but we're out of time."

The doctor shook his head and left the room.

Fighting back a grimace from an ironically timed spasm, Jake was confronted by expressions of concern from his friends. Francesca appeared particularly worried and the crinkle on Sarafina's brow told him she was close to tears. He reached over and picked her up. Her arms clung to his neck with a fierceness that matched her fear.

"Don't worry, sweetie. I'm okay."

"But I can tell that it's hurting you, Papa," she said in Italian, reverting to her native tongue. Her spectral disorder had not only given her a masterful ability with music, it had also opened her up to a telepathic connection with Jake. The link was usually limited to those moments when Jake intentionally projected his thoughts. But occasionally, especially when he was in a highly emotional state, she was able to tap into him on her own. Coupled with Francesca's empathic ability, this often put the pair two steps ahead of him. In time he'd learned how to shield his inner feelings from them, but it required a conscious effort.

He steeled himself. "It's just a little tummy ache, that's all."

"Are you sure?" Sarafina sniffled. She buried her head in the crook of his neck.

"Of course I am," Jake said, hating the lie even as it left his lips. He projected a calming aura around her as he addressed the others.

"Well, what are we waiting for? We've got work to do."

Francesca captured his gaze. Her expression told him that the conversation about his health was anything but over as far as she was concerned. But she'd apparently decided this wasn't the time because she said, "He's right. We really must leave."

Tony was the last one Jake ushered through the door. His friend pulled the sat-phone from his belt and pressed REDIAL.

Chapter 47

Big Bear, California

WHAT THE HELL DO YOU MEAN, I'M NOT *ALLOWED* TO COME home?" Tony's wife, Melissa, shouted into the phone.

"Mel, please—"

"Don't you dare 'Mel-please' me," she said. "The last I heard from you was a voice mail telling me to sit tight, and that we couldn't make contact with any friends until you picked us up. No explanation. No reason. It freaked me out. So I waited. And waited. Do you have any idea how hard it is to keep our kids from contacting their friends? I must have tried to call you back a hundred times, but your damn phone is shut off."

"I know—"

"I'm not finished!" she yelled. "I'm sitting here at my mom's house with the kids, making up excuses for why their dad's not here, checking the front window every time I hear a car drive by, hoping it's you."

She fought a swell of emotion. Melissa hated crying around her husband. It put him into gotta-fix-it mode and she didn't need that right now.

Peering through the open kitchen window, she soaked in the peaceful landscape that surrounded her mom's lakeside cabin. The property was cocooned within a forest of hundred-year-old pines that stretched out of view above her. Their branches swayed gently in the cool breeze, distributing their scent. In the distance, the late afternoon sun glimmered off the rippled surface of the lake.

Her mother-in-law, on a forced but happy sabbatical from her writing due to their visit, sat with the kids at the picnic table on the wooden deck, sipping lemonade. Andrea sat beside her, her soft blond curls bouncing to the music that presumably streamed into the earphones attached to her iPhone. She flipped a page in a dog-eared *Cosmopolitan* magazine, her constant companion. *Lord, she's already a teenager. God help us.*

Across from them, Tyler—the spitting image of his father, right down to the stocky build, crew cut, and Yankees cap—had his head buried in the Call of Duty game on the PSP—PlayStation Portable. Nine years old, teaming up with his friends online to save the world one game at a time.

Imagining her children's lives without their father had twisted Melissa inside out.

She couldn't hold it in any longer.

"I—I was scared, dammit." She stifled a sob. "I thought something terrible had happened to you."

"I'm so sorry, honey," Tony said. The tenderness in his voice massaged her nerves. "If there had been any way on God's earth for me to contact you, believe me, I would have."

She did believe him. The big lug had always been good that way. Hidden beneath that hunky exterior and tough-guy persona was the most caring man she'd ever met. Being the wife of a soldier, and later a cop, was anything but easy. But if she had to do it all over again, she wouldn't change a thing.

"You're sure you're okay?" she said.

"Yeah. But listen to me, we're in the middle of something. It's…as heavy as it gets."

She tensed. "What do you mean…'we'?"

"All of us. Me, Jake, Marsh, and the girls. And others." There was a slight pause before he added. "Our family, too."

The words took the breath out of her. Short of giving her any gruesome details of his work, he'd always been honest with her, telling her all that he could without breaching security protocols. His suggesting that she and the kids might be in danger made the hairs on the back of her neck bristle.

He told her everything. By the time he finished describing the unbelievable events of the past couple days, she was shaken to the core.

"I heard on the news about the car chase and shootings in Torrance," she said breathlessly. "I figured it was just a gang-banger deal. I had no idea you were involved."

"Oh, we're involved all right," Tony said. "That's why it's so important for you and the kids to stay where you are. I need to know you're safe. Still no phone calls. No contact with friends. Got it?"

"Uh-huh," she said hesitantly, fearing what was coming next. "B—but…what about you?"

"We're gonna stop them, Mel. We're the only ones who can."

She knew he was going to say that. And she also knew from experience that nothing positive would come from her objecting. That's who he was, and as much as it hurt, she was damn proud of him for it.

Now she had to do her part. She steeled herself. "You said that a couple of Papa's boys have been watching over us?"

"Yeah. And the fact that you haven't noticed is a good sign that they know what they're doing."

"Well, give 'em a damn call and tell 'em to get their asses in the house. It's almost supper time."

"Will do," he said. There was a hint of relief in his voice.

"And Tony," she said softly. "If anything happens to you, I'm gonna kill you."

"Yeah, I figured. Love you, too."

Chapter 48

BATTISTA WINCED AS HE MASSAGED THE MEDICATED GEL into the raw and blistered skin of his neck, a ritual he now performed with the same regularity as his daily prayers. The infection from the shrapnel wound had been managed with strong antibiotics, but the grisly damage to his skin and underlying musculature would never heal on its own. His doctor had said it could be corrected with several complex surgeries.

Standing bare-chested in the small bathroom that adjoined the upstairs office in the warehouse, he considered his visage in the mirror. As usual, his eyes seemed unable to focus on anything but the damage. Everything else faded to a blur as his mind struggled with the severity of the wound. It was the same, he knew, for anyone who gazed upon him when he was not wearing his silk neck wrap. It looked as if a hungry shark had taken a chunk from his neck and lower jaw.

With a sigh, he turned his head to the opposite side, hiding the wound. The olive-skinned face that looked back at him was distinguished. The Van Dyke beard was neatly trimmed, his salon-styled dark hair combed back from his high brow. Touches of gray lent texture to his sideburns and accented the sharp planes of a bold face. He stood taller and expanded his muscled chest, admiring the textured rhinoceros handle of the

227

saifani jambiya slung at his side in its belt holster. He was proud of his heritage, his education, and his training. It had all led him to this glorious point.

There was a soft rap on the door.

"Kadir would like to speak with you," Abbas said.

"V—." Battista choked back a dry rasp from his damaged vocal cords. After clearing his throat, he said, "Very well. I'll be out in a moment."

Picking up a new bandage and the neck wrap, he turned his head and reexamined the wound. The numbing gel glistened, highlighting the pocks and tears of his skin. An ugly sight, he thought. But it was also an affirmation, a constant reminder that the blessings of Allah had been with him in that cave, defending him from the grenade deposited in his lap by the American. Allah's grace had kept him alive for a greater purpose, one that had ballooned exponentially in importance in light of the revelation from the alien artifact. To fail meant nothing less than the total annihilation of the human species. Now, more than ever, all who lived in this world must embrace the one true religion. Whatever the cost. And Sheikh Abdul Modham Abdali, the last in a thousand-year line of revered chieftains to his Afghan tribe, would deliver the fatal strike that would end America's reign and rally Muslims around the world to their cause.

He tucked the end of the paisley neck wrap into the collar of his white dress shirt and donned a tailored sports coat. Yes, he thought, I have every reason to want the American dead. He paused to imagine the satisfaction he would feel when he witnessed the insolent man's anguish as his loved ones were tortured and killed before him, helpless to prevent it, knowing that his own slow and painful death would follow.

Soon, he thought. But not until every ounce of usefulness is squeezed from his miserable existence.

Battista and Abbas pushed through the swinging door to Kadir's freestanding lab, situated within the large clean room on the ground floor of the warehouse. About the size of a three-car garage, the congested space had been designed as an LCD-assembly area by the former tenants. It held a small desk on one wall, flanked on either side by long open-front cabinets, all of which were empty except one. It held neatly organized blocks of plastic explosives and an assortment of colored wiring, timers, and detonators.

The center of the room was occupied by two counters. One supported a collection of beakers and mixing equipment. They surrounded an aquarium-size glass enclosure with rubber-fitted gloves protruding from one side for safe handling of the toxic materials contained within. A dozen or more portable breathing devices rested beside it—plastic nose-shaped cups with elastic head straps, and attached tubing connected to cigar-size pressurized canisters.

Battista picked one up and examined it. The devices would be needed soon. "They are charged?"

Kadir nodded. "They will allow you to move within the target premises without being affected by the gas."

If Allah wills it, Battista thought. The success of their tertiary mission—one that could prove more important than the distribution of the infertility chemical in Los Angeles—was wholly dependent on the ability of these devices.

"You are certain they will work?"

A flash of annoyance creased Kadir's brow, but it vanished as soon as it appeared, as if the doctor had suddenly remembered who he was talking to. "Yes, my sheikh. I've tested them several times. Once the gas is released into the facility, anyone in contact with it will lose consciousness immediately. However, the antidote delivered by the breather will neutralize the agent before it enters your lungs, so you and your men will be unaffected."

Battista nodded, satisfied. He stepped to the second counter where a small autoclave—used for laminating various substrates together under high temps and vacuum—occupied a third of the space. There was a sewing machine beside it, surrounded by loose remnants of thin neoprene rubber. A bare mannequin stood nearby.

"The vests are ready?" Battista said.

Kadir smiled. "Oh, yes."

"You appear satisfied."

"Because they are perfect, if I do say so myself."

A bold statement, thought Battista. Six months ago the man would have been chastised for such brashness. Not anymore. Not since the brain implant. If he said it was perfect, then it was.

"The kill radius?"

"Micro shrapnel from the blast will decimate anything within one hundred feet."

"And the nerve agent?"

"Simultaneously with the detonation, the modified VX will be dispersed in such a fine mist as to be virtually undetectable. I would expect it to spread to an area at least double the blast radius before settling to the ground. The viscous oil will not dissipate on its own. It will adhere tenaciously to anything it touches. Anyone coming in primary contact with the odorless chemical—emergency personnel, cleanup crews, and the like— will be dead within hours." His eyes seemed to get glassy as his brain pulled up a description of the effects of the compound. He spared them the details and said, "Paralysis of all the muscles in the body causes death by asphyxiation."

Abbas shifted uneasily. He crossed his arms as if to ensure that he didn't accidentally touch anything he wasn't supposed to.

Even the toughest soldier knew his limitations, thought Battista.

"That should suit our purpose nicely," he said, contemplating their deployment. Properly positioned at key points around Los Angeles, the three volunteers who ultimately donned and detonated the vests would provide the ideal distraction. They would strike terror into the heart of the decadent city, diverting police and emergency personnel while the rest of the team completed their primary mission.

"What about the bulk issue?"

"Resolved. The vests are virtually undetectable. In fact," Kadir said with a smug expression, "I'm wearing one now. Can you tell?"

Battista cocked an eyebrow. He was indeed surprised. And pleased. Over a white T-shirt, the doctor appeared to be wearing nothing but a thin button-down shirt, the sleeves rolled halfway up his forearm in the casual Western manner. He could easily pass as a thirty-year-old soccer dad ready to escort his children to an amusement park. The brain implant had allowed Kadir to tap into an entirely new level of creative genius. It gave Battista comfort. The team would succeed here under the doctor's guidance. And that would free him and Abbas to complete their mission—with the American's unwitting help.

Battista patted Kadir on the shoulder. "You've done well. Very well. We shall strike tomorrow."

* * *

It didn't take a brain implant to be a genius strategist, thought Battista. It was second nature to him. After all, he'd been at it his entire adult life. Like a master chess player, he was always a dozen moves ahead of his opponent. He knew how to shift plans quickly, use deception to distract and manipulate, and stay in charge of the ultimate outcome.

Mastering the art of the sacrificial pawn.

He paced back and forth behind the desk in the upstairs office. Abbas occupied the desk chair, his attention on the computer. Kadir was downstairs, directing the team in its final preparations.

Battista considered his next move. He was unnerved that the American had already crossed the border into California. He'd expected Bronson to rejoin his friends and remain in Mexico, especially with the authorities on his tail. His presence in the vicinity was troubling.

Pushing back his concern, he asked, "Where is he now?"

Abbas manipulated the keyboard, superimposing a GPS tracking signal onto the Google map.

"He just pulled into a rest stop off the 5 Freeway, midway between San Diego and Los Angeles."

"They'll be back in LA soon," Battista said as he mentally debated his next move. "Perhaps it's just as well. It will be easier to pick him up. As soon as they've reached their final destination, let the agency know."

"Another anonymous tip from Afghanistan? There will be questions."

"It matters not. Just tell them where he is and hang up. They'll follow up in any case. They want him badly."

As do I. But not yet. First he needed an insurance policy against the American's ultimate cooperation, not to mention leverage against the man's irritating group of friends. It was important that they not give in to the temptation of involving the authorities.

"Progress at the lake?" Battista asked.

"Now that we have the make, model, and license of their vehicle, it's only a matter of time."

Chapter 49

South Central Los Angeles, California

THIS IS CRAZY!" MARSHALL SAID FROM THE SEAT BEHIND Jake and Francesca. "We—"

"Hey!" Jake said, cutting him off. He stared him down and pointed to the back of the ten-passenger minivan. Sarafina, Josh, and Max were there, oblivious to any danger, their faces pasted to the windows. Bradley seemed to share their wonder at the passing scenery.

Francesca snuggled up closer to Jake, propping her head against his shoulder and wrapping her hands around his arm. The past couple of days had taken a serious emotional toll on her. She needed a soft bed and about twelve hours of uninterrupted sleep. But then, who didn't?

Marshall leaned forward and lowered his voice. "Sorry. But, hell, we won't last five minutes in this neighborhood!"

Seated next to him, Lacey whispered, "My dad always told me that if I ever had car problems on the Harbor Freeway south of LA, I should just pull over and call nine-one-one. Under no circumstances was I to ever exit into the residential areas."

Jake understood their fears. South Central was home to some of the toughest gangs in the country. He'd flown over it hundreds of times, but he'd never seen it up close and personal. After the violent stories he'd seen on the local news, he'd half-expected it to be reminiscent of a war zone, with homes in a sorry state of disrepair, and groups of serious-looking gangbangers lurking around every corner just waiting for someone to encroach on their territory.

Instead, the van drove through a neighborhood of compact, reasonably well-kept homes. Kids, mostly Hispanic, walked along the sidewalk on their way home from school while others played in their front yards. Some of the younger ones were under the watchful gaze of presumed mothers or grandmothers.

Sure, some of the homes had fenced-in front yards that protected little more than tattered lawn furniture, and security grates over windows were commonplace. But in spite of the tension Jake suspected was hidden behind closed doors, he also felt a sense of hope. The streets were unlittered, and well-tended flower gardens accented many of the homes. All in all, the area wasn't nearly as bad as he'd imagined. People lived here, struggled here, got married, had children, celebrated holidays. The circumstances here might be a lot more difficult than in the middle-class neighborhoods he'd grown up in as a military brat, but Jake suspected that underneath it all, the residents here wanted the same things as families everywhere: safety for their loved ones, food on the table, and an opportunity to participate in the American dream.

The van slowed as a group of boys paused their street soccer game to allow them to pass. Their small caravan included lead and tail vehicles. Becker and Snake rode in the car behind Jake, and three of Papa's well-armed compadres led the way. They'd met up with Jake south of the border bearing fake IDs for everyone. The trail of vehicles captured more than a few wary looks from the neighborhood residents.

Max let out an eager yip. His nose was pressed against the rear window, and his tail whipped back and forth as one of the boys bounced the soccer ball from one knee to the other.

"Lighten up, Marsh," Jake said. "We're in good hands."

"Got that right, holmes," Papa said from the driver's seat. "No one's going to mess with you while you're on my turf," the former gang boss added.

In the passenger seat up front, Tony grunted, stone-faced. His trained eyes panned their surroundings with military precision. He cradled an MP5 assault rifle in his lap.

"I sure as hell hope not," Marshall replied. "I will admit that it's a hell of a lot better than being trapped in an underground river with terrorists up above just dying to blow you to bits."

"Roger that," Jake said.

* * *

Jake hadn't spent this much time in the bathroom since he'd suffered through the agony of chemotherapy ten years ago. At least back then, he'd known what was causing his stomach to churn. This time around, it was anybody's guess. He'd drunk some of the local water while being held captive in Mexico, so hopefully it was simply a bout of Montezuma's revenge. But who the hell knows? Whatever it was, it was unnerving. The cramps had settled into a pattern, hitting him every couple of hours like clockwork.

He was in Papa's family home, their temporary safe house. The reflection that stared back at him from the bathroom mirror looked haggard. His bloodshot eyes reminded him of the mornings after a *cucaracha* day in pilot training, when the west Texas winds threw up a sandstorm that grounded the planes and sent the squadron of young pilots into party mode at the officers' club. But he'd developed a knack for bouncing back easily enough then, and he needed to do so again now. Quickly. After all, he and his team needed to do nothing less than prevent a maniac from destroying millions of lives.

But before he could wrap his mind around that problem, there was one last thing Jake needed to do. Otherwise, he'd never find the strength to face the enormity of the task that lay before him. Closing his eyes, he filled his mind with thoughts of Francesca, breathing her into his consciousness: the way her eyes sparkled when she looked at him, the sprinkle of freckles across her petite nose, the natural pout of her soft lips, her fragrance…

Ever since that first night in Venice long ago—that *amazing* night—he'd bottled up his feelings for her, not knowing what future, if any, lay in store for him. He'd convinced himself that keeping a distance between them would keep her safe.

Instead, here she was, right in the thick of it.

Carrying our baby.

She deserved so much more.

Jake splashed water on his face, ran his fingers through his unruly hair, and left the room to find her.

* * *

Francesca stirred at the sound of the door opening. She'd been napping on one of the beds in Papa's children's room. It was neatly split into a boy's and girl's side for the six-year-old fraternal twins. With the youngsters at day care, it was the only space in the home not crowded with people. Thankfully, the two-car garage of the modest suburban home had been converted into what Papa referred to as his "man cave." Most of their group had spilled onto the soft couches and overstuffed chairs normally reserved for Papa and his buddies.

Francesca's eyes fluttered open to find Jake framed in the doorway. The sight of him made her heart smile. He looked a mess, but a wonderful mess. His cargo pants drooped over soiled white sneakers, and the long-sleeved black T-shirt he'd borrowed from Papa fit snugly across his broad chest. The sleeves were rolled halfway up his tan forearms. As usual, his wavy hair needed a trim. For that matter, he could also use a shave, though she admitted to herself that she kind of liked the rugged edge it gave him.

If only they'd met under different circumstances, she thought. What a life that could have been! The image shattered when she thought of the mortal danger that had followed him to California. Would that end if he and his friends could find a way to stop her former mentor? Could she take that chance now that she was pregnant?

He closed the door and joined her on the edge of the bed. The springs squeaked under the added weight. He appeared tired, but there was also a sense of purpose to the set of his jaw. The intensity of his gaze set her nerves on alert. She opened her empathic senses to him and was immediately disappointed—but not surprised—to find his emotions shielded. It bothered her that he'd learned to do that; he was one of the few who could. She wished he hadn't found it necessary.

She recalled the depth of the unguarded feelings that had emanated from him on the day they'd first met in the Redondo Beach Library. At the time, she'd been overwhelmed by the connection. The attraction she'd felt for the man was unlike anything she'd experienced before. And it wasn't just a physical draw, though she felt that as well. It was something far different. There was a unique emotional quality about Jake that was indefinable. She'd tried to shrug it off, especially in light of his rude manner at the time. But it had been no use. The bond had been forged. Could she find the strength to break it now? Did she have any choice?

"Feeling a little better?" he asked. His tone felt a bit too casual.

"Much." She sat up and propped her back against the headboard. It was hand-painted with a wreath of colorful flowers. She wore a white cotton beach dress that she'd borrowed from Papa's wife, Carmen. The scoop neck was more revealing than she would have liked, so she adjusted the straps self-consciously, guarding herself against whatever was coming.

"It's amazing what a few hours of sleep can do," she said.

He nodded absently, as if he were trying to find the right words. After a moment he said, "I love you, Francesca…more than you could ever know."

The words tore at her heart. She checked herself.

"Ever since that night in Venice…" His eyes softened, and his voice trailed off as they silently shared the memory.

"You've been there for me," he continued. "Unconditionally. Right down to uprooting yourself from your home and family to come to California."

He waited a beat. She squeezed his hand.

"That meant the world to me. It still does. But…"

Her stomach twisted.

"I haven't been honest with you." He shook his head. "Hell, I haven't been completely honest with *anyone* since I launched that damn Armageddon magnet into space."

"It wasn't your fault."

"Yeah, I keep telling myself that. But it doesn't do much good. Regardless, the time for secrets is over."

"Secrets?"

His lips tightened. He nodded sheepishly.

"The thing is," he said, "the entire obelisk didn't make it into space. A small part of it—a pyramid about the size of a baseball—was left behind. I took it."

This conversation had taken a confusing twist. Francesca folded up her knees to her chest, linking her hands around them. "What about it?"

"Okay, here's the deal. That miniature pyramid—I call it the mini—has a sort of life of its own. When I first triggered the object, it created a link with my brain. In the blink of an eye, it exchanged a mass of information with me. That's how I learned its purpose. At first I thought it was just a scanning device, a way for the object to determine whether or not man's mental abilities had breached the threshold they'd established."

"So you kept the…mini?"

"I didn't just keep it. I never let it out of my sight." He hesitated. "The link got stronger every day. It strengthened my abilities beyond what they were after the MRI accident. I couldn't take in data fast enough. My brain gorged on it. The library, the web, TV, you name it. I wasn't satisfied unless I was streaming info into my head. I learned four new languages in less than a week."

She recalled the time. He'd vanished from his friends' lives. Everyone had been worried, especially her.

"After a couple weeks, I stopped sleeping altogether. My brain wouldn't slow down enough to let me doze off. The only thing that seemed to distract me was running full bore on the beach. I'd do it late at night so no one would notice, because with the mini in my pocket, even a racehorse would have trouble keeping up."

The news alarmed her. "That's not natural."

"At the time, a small part of me suspected as much. But it was like a drug. The more I got, the more I wanted. Nothing could stop me."

"But something did. You came back to us."

"Yeah, that's because what goes up must come down. One day I simply…collapsed."

Francesca held her breath.

"My mind went blank," he said. "Like a hard-drive crash. It was three in the morning. One second I was sprinting and then… nothing. Two days later I woke up in a bed at Little Company of Mary hospital. They had me listed as a John Doe because I hadn't been carrying ID. The nurse told me I'd been in a coma. She said my heart stopped twice. When she rushed off to tell the doctor I was awake, I hightailed it out of there."

She felt her eyes moisten. He embraced her. It felt good. "I could have lost you," she whispered.

"I'm not going anywhere," he said. "Besides, I locked the mini away in my apartment. It's more than my body can handle.

Despite the fact that the MRI accident caused some sort of evolutionary leap in my brain structure, the rest of my body is still stuck in the twenty-first century."

He hesitated before adding, "According to the doctor I saw last week, it's taken a toll."

Francesca remembered the panic she'd felt when his heart had failed in the school yard. The memory sent a legion of spiders up her back. She squeezed him tighter. For a moment, the rest of the world faded away.

Finally, Jake pulled back. His eyes seemed to take in the room for the first time. She followed his gaze. The room was a study in the contrast between boys and girls. Two finely dressed dolls framed a row of children's books on the dresser beside the girl's bed. A sparkly hairbrush rested beside a small table mirror, a dish of multicolored barrettes at its side. Everything in its place, even the line of stuffed animals that stared up at Francesca from the base of the bed.

The other side of the room was a different matter. The dresser drawers were partially open, a sock hanging over one lip, the top surface all but invisible under an army of toy soldiers and action figures. A few of them had found their way to the floor. The Spider-Man bedspread was pulled back, revealing a homemade sock puppet that she imagined was the little boy's last holdout from his nursery days.

Jake's features softened as he took it all in. She felt him struggle with whatever it was he wanted to say next.

"So," he said, taking her hand. "We're going to have a baby."

"Yes," she replied tentatively. She searched his eyes.

"There's something I have to ask you," he said.

He blew out a breath.

And another.

Francesca tensed.

Time stretched.

Maintaining a grip on her hand, he shifted off the bed and onto one knee.

Dio mio!

Jake's shoulders dropped and the walls surrounding his soul crumbled. Francesca felt his warmth. She reveled in the rare glimpse of the man she'd fallen hopelessly in love with. A smile threatened to replace her open-mouthed look of shock. She knew she should stop him, but her voice failed her.

"Francesca," he began, "I don't know if I'll be alive tomorrow, or next year, or twenty years from now. But I do know that I don't want another minute to go by without—"

The bedroom door flew open and banged against its backstop. Marshall stood there, his face ashen. "Battista…" he said breathlessly. "He's on the friggin' house phone!"

Jake rushed out the door.

Francesca wept.

Chapter 50

J AKE RACED DOWN THE HALLWAY ON MARSHALL'S HEELS. "Dammit, Marsh. How in the hell did Battista get Papa's home phone number?"

"You got me, man. The dude has been one step ahead of us the whole time."

Skirting past the oversize table in the breakfast nook, they ran through the kitchen and past Carmen—Papa's stout wife— and her young niece, Ophelia. The two women wore colorful aprons, and from the steaming pots on the stove, it was apparent they were elbow-deep in prepping dinner. The aroma of refried beans and grilled chicken filled the air.

Carmen had a white-knuckled grip on the wooden spoon she used to stir the beans, never missing a beat in spite of the sudden excitement that invaded her home. This wasn't the first dance for the former gang leader's wife. She glanced over her shoulder as Jake rushed past. Her tight-lipped nod said it all. It was likely the same expression Papa received from her on similar occasions. It said, "Whatever it takes, jefe, get this threat away from our home."

Jake returned her nod.

He and Marshall entered the converted garage. A curved, soft-pillowed couch centered the room, facing an immense rear-projection TV. The bar that hugged the opposite wall was framed beneath mirrored shelves filled with at least two dozen different bottles of tequila. Papa had bragged about the collection many times, though Jake had never seen it in person. A ceiling fan turned overhead, softening the stale pall of cigar smoke that hung in the air. There was a round game table with six chairs in a corner of the room. From the two juice sipper packs on the table, it appeared as if Sarafina and Josh had been sitting there. Bradley must have escorted the children and Max from the room when Battista's call came in.

Tony, Becker, Marshall, and Lacey hovered around a furious-looking Papa at the far end of the room. The hardened Latino swiveled around his chair to face Jake. His back was to a cluttered desk. He wore a white muscle tee over jeans. The exposed olive skin on his shoulders and arms rippled with tattoos. His shaved head and angry expression reminded Jake of a bullmastiff poised for attack. He held a cordless phone in one hand, while his other palm covered the mouthpiece.

"The son of a *puto* called my home," he growled. "He'll only talk to you."

Jake maneuvered around the couch and accepted the phone from Papa's outstretched hand.

"You bastard," Jake said into the phone. He noticed that Francesca had followed him into the room.

"Now, now, Mr. Bronson," Battista's raspy voice said over the phone. "Is that any way to inaugurate our reunion?"

"What the hell do you want?" Jake said.

"No pleasantries at all? Shame on you. Don't you want to know how I'm doing? Do you feel no remorse? After all, the last time we saw each other, you dropped a grenade in my lap."

"A lot of good that did. Next time—and believe me, there *will* be a next time—I'll stick around until it's finished."

"Ha! Such drama. I'm sure you'll try, but not today. No, today you and your friends are going to do exactly as I say." Jake sensed the smile behind the voice.

"Go to hell."

"Let me ask you," Battista said calmly. "Is your friend Tony nearby?"

Jake's breath caught in his throat.

"Your silence speaks volumes. Put the phone on speaker. I want you both to hear this."

Jake muted the mouthpiece against his chest. He absorbed the anxious faces of his friends.

Locking eyes with Tony, he said, "Brace yourself. The bastard asked for you." Jake caught a rare flicker of fear behind his friend's eyes. "Everyone else, stay quiet."

He placed the phone on Papa's desk and pressed the SPEAKER button.

"You're on speaker."

"Excellent. There's someone here who would like to say hello."

There was a shuffling noise over the phone. A young voice said, "P—Pops?"

It was Tony's son, Tyler.

Tony's face drained of color. He picked up the phone, grasping it in both hands, as if by doing so he could pull his child closer to him. "Tyler?" he said. His voice trembled.

"Pops!" Tyler said, the fear in his voice palpable. "They came during dinner. A bunch of 'em. They shot Papa's friends and...I—I think they hurt Grams, too."

Tony's face shut down faster than a slammed door. The ferocity emanating from him seemed to squeeze the air out of the room. Beside him, Papa lurched to his feet, his eyes on fire.

"Tyler," Tony said, "are your sister and Mom okay?"

"Yeah, I guess. They're locked upstairs. Mom hit one of them with a frying pan and she wouldn't stop yelling at 'em so they tied a scarf around her mouth." The boy hesitated a moment before adding, "Pop...at least they let me keep my PSP and—"

He was cut off and Battista's voice sounded through the speaker. "I believe you've heard enough."

"You sick bastard," Jake said. "What the hell do you want?"

"What do I want?" Battista replied. "You mean besides the ultimate conversion or death of every infidel on the planet?"

"Yeah, asshole. Besides that."

"You'll find out soon enough," Battista said, his voice flat. "In the meantime, don't even think about contacting the authorities."

The line went dead.

Chapter 51

South Central Los Angeles, California

J AKE WATCHED AS PAPA PACED IN THE FAR CORNER OF THE room. A phone was pressed to his ear. He was in the process of rallying a small army of Southern California gang members around the news that two of their own had been shot. A team had already departed their turf in San Bernardino, en route to the Big Bear house to check for survivors and search for any clues of the identity or location of the kidnappers.

At the opposite end of the room, Jake, Tony, and the rest of the group were huddled around the game table. Bradley joined them. The children and Max watched TV in the adjoining family room.

Tony's chest heaved in and out like a blacksmith's bellows adding fuel to an already red-hot fire. Jake could only imagine his friend's pain.

"I'm going to rip him apart and beat him to death with his own limbs," Tony said between clenched teeth.

Francesca placed a hand on Tony's shoulder. "You'll bring them home safe," she said softly. "Just like when you rescued me from that cave in Afghanistan."

"Bloody right, mate," Becker said. "They can't be far. We know they're still with Battista and he's gotta be holed up at his local HQ."

"Somewhere in LA," Jake added. "So he can personally oversee their mission."

"Yes, but where?" Marshall asked. "That's the million-dollar question."

"Aren't you all forgetting something?" Lacey said. "What about the fact that the bastard knows exactly where we are? He called us on the house phone, for Christ's sake. How's that even possible?"

"A tracker," Marshall said. "It's the only way. And since we ditched all our cell phones, it must be planted in something else—watch, jewelry, clothing. It would be easy enough to ferret out if I could get my hands on the right equipment."

Papa had ended his phone conversation. He must have overhead Marshall's comment, because he walked over and placed a notepad and pen on the table in front of him. "Write down exactly what you need and I'll get it here in less than an hour."

"An hour?" Marshall said. "I'm talking about some high-end stuff."

"It don't matter, holmes," Papa said. "In a few minutes this place is going to be swarming with my friends. In addition to providing perimeter security that'll put Fort Knox to shame, my boys can scrounge better than a supply sergeant on the take. No questions asked. We're going to convert this cave to a war room."

"In that case," Marshall said, scribbling on the notepad, "add a signal jammer to the menu. I don't want any cell calls in or out of here without our okay."

"No problem."

Max barked from the next room. Bradley rose as if to leave but Marshall stopped him. "Hang on, Brad, I could use your help here."

Noticing the teacher's hesitation, Marshall held up the list. "There's too much to do, and too little time. It's all hands on deck."

"The children—"

"Dude, the kids are fine," Marshall said. He added another item to the list. "Sit down and let's get to it."

Bradley sat with a shrug. "What can I do?"

Francesca was still focused on Tony. "We know they've not been harmed," she said. "They even allowed your son to keep his game."

Marshall stopped writing. "Yeah, that's peculiar."

"Not really," Tony said, a faraway look in his eyes. "It woulda been simpler for them to manage him. Tyler throws a hell of a fit whenever we take his PSP away from him. He loves playing with his buddies online."

Marshall's head snapped around. "What kind of games?"

"Huh?"

"You said he plays online with his friends, right?" Marshall asked excitedly. He opened the laptop he'd borrowed from Papa. "Come on, LAPD, don't you get it? Your son is friggin' brilliant! I wondered why the heck he would mention his game while he was surrounded by a bunch of gun-toting terrorists. He should've been freakin' out. Instead, the little dude was sending us a message. What games does he like to play?"

"Call of Duty. It's his favorite."

Marshall smiled in instant recognition. His fingers became a blur on the keyboard. "Boom...head shot!" he said, recounting the familiar tag words from the popular first-person-shooter video game. "Maybe," he muttered to himself, his attention lost in a cyber world that he called home. "Just maybe..."

* * *

Jake pulled Papa aside. Under his breath he said, "Are you sure we can depend on the gang you've got coming?"

"No doubt," Papa said. "There ain't gonna be no peewees or wannabes. Just hard core. Their methods are...unacceptable—I can't deny it. It's why I got out. But they embrace family, loyalty, and protection of their neighborhood above everything. Battista's plan spits on them in the worst way possible."

The garage side door opened and Snake swept in with four tough-looking Hispanic men. Two of them were dressed in distinctive *cholo* style, with Pendleton shirts, Dickies pants, and belt buckles with monikers engraved in Old English that Jake assumed identified their gang affiliation. One of them had a colored headband wrapped around his shaved skull. The two who followed wore untucked gray T-shirts over cargo pants and military-style combat boots, looking more like marines on leave than gangbangers.

The first of the gang members pushed into the room as if he owned the place. His number two was on his heels, with an ivory-gripped automatic tucked under his belt. The stocky, crew-cut leader was in his twenties, but his cautious eyes, thick brow, heavy nose, and downturned lips gave him an angry face that made him look much older.

His eyes swept the room, scanning for threats, a practice he'd likely perfected years ago in order to survive the streets. Like an alpha dog establishing his role, he shot a don't-mess-with-me look at Jake's friends seated around the game table. Marshall, Lacey, and Bradley shrank under his glare. Becker appraised him. Tony rose to his feet, and returned the flat stare. Neither of them blinked. The uncomfortable moment was finally broken by a barely perceptible nod from the gangster. A beat later it was followed in kind by Tony.

Respect given and accepted.

"Glad you're here," Tony said. "We can use the help."

Jake sensed the wariness beneath his friend's words. As a SWAT team leader with the LAPD, forming an alliance with one of the toughest gangs in the state couldn't be easy for him.

"Papa's part of the family," the gang member said. "He calls, we come." He motioned to the guy behind him. "This is Paco. You can call me Street."

The two military types shouldered past the group and Jake immediately recognized one of them as Ripper, a member of Papa's fire team. Jake noticed the slight bulges under the calves of Ripper's pants, where he usually carried twin combat knives. The man with him was huge. Though Jake didn't know him, from the worried scowl and ham-fisted features, he suspected the man was related to Juice.

Jake exchanged a firm handshake with Ripper. "It's good to see you, man."

"*Chingao*, hombre," Ripper said with a restrained grimace that revealed part of a gold front tooth. The wiry soldier was half Mexican and half American Indian, with a broad face, wide eyes, and long black hair tied back in a ponytail. "What you got us into this time, jefe?"

"It's not good," Jake said. He flashed back to the stories he'd heard of Ripper's heroic actions during the gun battle with Battista's men in the Hindu Kush while Jake was being held captive inside the mountain. Ripper had carried the squad's light machine gun, and it had been red-hot by the time they made it to the LZ. Jake was glad Ripper had joined them. "Thanks for coming," he said.

"The bastards shot Juice, holmes," Ripper said with a shake of his head.

Jake felt a flush of anger. He pushed down another stomach cramp.

"This here's Freddie," Ripper said, motioning to the man beside him. "Juice's brother."

The blunt-faced giant with the shaved skull standing beside Ripper stiffened at the mention of his sibling. Jake guessed his height at six-seven. He had a barrel chest and thick arms sleeved with tattoos, the most prominent of which was a set of praying hands. The team at the house in Big Bear hadn't checked in yet, so the conditions of Juice and Romeo were still unknown.

"I hearda you," Freddie said in a low growl.

"Your brother's a good man."

The giant's flat stare rooted Jake for a beat. Finally, he nodded and extended a hand that engulfed Jake's. "He said the same thing 'bout you."

Chapter 52

South Central Los Angeles, California

THE BARRIO WAS ON FULL ALERT.

A dozen or more of Street's gangsters milled in and around Papa's house, armed to the teeth with a variety of weapons. Many more were positioned at key intersections leading to the house, ready to provide advance warning of any intrusions.

Jake steadied himself against the bar that fronted Papa's impressive tequila collection. He struggled to hide the discomfort he felt as another cramp squeezed his bowels. Tony stood beside him.

"Even with an army of gangsters," Tony said, "a full-out assault ain't gonna cut it."

Without a target location, Jake thought, putting an effective plan together was impossible. "Wherever it is, I'll have to get inside unnoticed," he said absently, thinking that his abilities would give him an advantage. "Once I figure out exactly where in their facility your family is being held, I'll give you the cue."

"Let's get somethin' straight right now, pal," Tony said. "Wherever these suckers are, I ain't about to be waitin' outside."

The strain of the situation had taken a serious toll on Tony. Jake worried about his friend's ability to stay on point with his family's life in the balance. But he also knew it was senseless to argue. Tony wasn't about to budge. "Okay, we go in together."

Lacey glided toward them from across the room. It reminded Jake of the simple days not so long ago when she was still waiting tables at Sam's bar and all he and his friends had to worry about was what brand of beer they ordered.

"You guys are the last two," she said, adjusting a dial on the twelve-inch security wand she held in one hand. Motioning to Tony, she said, "Hands up and spread 'em."

Papa had been true to his word. Not only had his contact provided a computer system and a state-of-the-art signal jammer that had made even Marshall whistle in appreciation, he'd also brought a short-range bug sensor that would identify any trans-mitters hidden in their clothing or belongings.

Tony spread-eagled and Lacey moved the wand slowly over his torso and limbs. She rose to her tiptoes in order to reach the area above his shoulders. "You're clean."

Jake was next. He had stepped back from the bar and raised his arms when Marshall's shout filled the room. "I got him!"

The room went electric. Everyone rushed to hover behind Marshall at his computer station. A Google map with a satellite view of the South Bay was displayed on the screen. A red dot flashed in the center of the screen.

"God, they're in Torrance!" Lacey said.

"Just two blocks from City Hall," Marshall confirmed.

"Smug bastards," Becker said.

Hiding in plain sight, thought Jake. Less than twenty minutes away.

"Get your team leaders in here," he said to Street. "It's time to put a plan together."

* * *

Even as his mind raced through the myriad tactical options available to them, Jake considered the unlikely gathering of people surrounding him in Papa's war room. Their hastily formed assault team included gangbangers, military contractors, LAPD SWAT, and even a demolition and specialized weapons expert from Down Under. In addition, they had a support team that included an actress, a cyber expert, a teaching assistant, and an empathic child psychologist who was pregnant with his child.

Under different circumstances, any of them could easily find themselves on opposite sides of violence. But today they'd allied against a common enemy—an enemy who not only held part of their own family hostage but also threatened the very fabric of American society. The enemy of my enemy is my friend, Jake thought, recounting the ancient Arab proverb. Is that the solution to uniting man as a species? Is that the truth that the human race must ultimately swallow in order to have any chance at all of defending itself against a global threat that only Jake and a few others knew was coming? Would people unite if they shared that knowledge, or would they decimate one another in panic?

The room went dead quiet as Papa hung up the phone.

Freddie and Tony stood shoulder to shoulder, two mountains threatening to crumble as they awaited the news.

"Your mama's fine," Papa said to Tony. "She's worried sick about Mel and the kids, and a little bruised up. But she'll pull through. Two of the guys will stick by her side until this thing is finished." He turned to Freddie. "Juice took one in the shoulder, but he's going to make it. He's gettin' patched up at the hospital."

The men blew out a shared breath. Tension spilled from their shoulders.

"Thank God," Francesca said.

Papa's eyes went moist as he turned to the rest of the group. "They got Romeo. Two in the chest."

There was an angry murmur among the bangers. Their leader, Street, didn't blink, but Jake noticed his jaw pulsate as Street bit back his fury.

"Listen up," Jake said. "Make no mistake. We're going to take down these bastards. Here's what we're—"

The side door flew open and one of Street's boys rushed in. "It's Five-O!" he shouted. "Four black SUVs headed this way fast."

Chapter 53

THE MEN DREW THEIR WEAPONS, RAMMED HOME AMMO magazines, and stationed themselves at the windows and doorways of Papa's home.

Jake peeked through a slit in the curtains. A breeze slipped through the open window. With a squeal of braking tires, four black SUVs with tinted windows and flashing dash-mounted emergency lights skidded to a stop outside. Doors flew open and dark-suited men with compact automatic weapons took up offensive positions facing the house. They had GOVERNMENT AGENTS written all over them, right down to the earpiece wires that disappeared under their collars. Jake had little doubt these men were after him. The events that had transpired in the mountains of Afghanistan had finally caught up to him, though for the life of him, he couldn't imagine how the hell they caught up with him here of all places.

A man with a crew cut and sharp military bearing stepped forward and confirmed Jake's fears. The man raised a bullhorn to his lips and said, "Jake Bronson!"

There was a sharp intake of breath from Francesca, standing beside him. She clutched at Jake's arm with the ferocity of a mother preventing her child from dipping his hand into boiling water.

He turned toward her. "I need you to remain calm. This is about me. Not you, or Sarafina, or our friends. Stay clear of the windows."

Her face was desperate with fear.

"Don't worry," he said, brushing her cheek with the palm of his hand.

"We know you're in there, Mr. Bronson! Don't force our hand."

Jake turned. But before he could respond, Papa opened the front door and stormed onto the sidewalk that bisected his front lawn. He was unarmed but Street and four of his bangers spread out in his wake, all gripping weapons. The man with the bull-horn ducked behind the fender of the car. The agents around him trained their weapons on Papa's group.

"Who in the hell do you think you are, *pendejo*?" Papa shouted, his five-foot-eight frame standing tall against the wall of weapons pointed at his head. He spit on the ground. "This is *my* turf. My home! And you threaten me? *Mi familia?*"

Setting the bullhorn on the hood of the car, the military man rose slowly. He palmed the air. "Calm down, sir. We're not here for you or your family. But this is a matter of national security. We know Mr. Bronson's inside, and one way or another, we're taking him with us."

"Again with the threats!" Papa shouted. "*Hijo de puta*, are you stupid or just anxious to die?"

The man's face reddened. "Enough! You're outmanned and outgunned and I'm ordering you to stand down immediately!"

Papa stood his ground. He crossed his arms, tilted his head to one side, and belted out a roar of laughter. Though Jake couldn't see Papa's face, he caught smiles coming from two of the bangers covering Papa's back.

"Outmanned? Outgunned?" Papa laughed again, harder this time, as if he couldn't contain himself. After a moment, he raised his hands palms up as if he were addressing a crowd of thousands. He shouted, "*Oye*, compadres. The gringo says we're outgunned!"

Suddenly, neighboring doors opened and heavily armed gangsters spilled onto the scene. More of them streamed in from behind bushes and backyards. Windows opened and weapons peeked out from between curtains. Bandanna-wrapped heads popped up in parked cars, their engines roaring to life as they lurched forward from either end of the street to corral the four SUVs.

Within seconds the government agents were hopelessly surrounded. They glanced to their stunned leader for direction. Their short-barreled weapons panned nervously from target to target as the crowd pressed in.

A tense silence enveloped the scene.

So many triggers.

So many fingers.

Papa was the first to speak. He'd stopped laughing.

"Okay, suckers," he said. "This is what we call a Mexican standoff, South Central–style. It's your move."

The military man's initial shocked expression slowly melted away. Jake stiffened when he realized the man still wasn't ready to throw in the towel. This wasn't his first rodeo. He had the composure of a seasoned combat soldier under orders—probably an officer. And it appeared as though his directive to take Jake into custody included an at-any-cost proviso. The man nodded to one of his men, who lifted a small handheld radio to his lips. He delivered a silent message and then nodded back at his boss.

The lead man turned to Papa. "I'm only going to say this once, so listen up." There was a faint throbbing of a helicopter in the distance. "In a few minutes, this neighborhood is going to be crawling with LAPD."

Jake noticed a flinch or two from the crowd of gangbangers, but none of them lowered their weapons. They weren't about to back down from a threat in the heart of their turf.

The military man continued, "If you want a bloodbath in the meantime, so be it. But we're not leaving without Jake Bronson in custody."

While Papa seemed to consider the man's words, Jake caught a subtle change in Street's stance. It seemed as if he were coiling for action. As the current gang leader, the mob would ultimately take their orders from him.

Jake had to stop him.

"Wait!" he shouted out the window. "I'm coming out!"

Francesca's eyes went wide with fright. Jake gave her a fierce hug and whispered, "I love you. Keep our baby safe. I'll be back. I promise."

He released her and moved toward the door where Tony, Marshall, and Lacey waited, each of them grim-faced.

"It's up to you, Tony. Save your family and stop that bastard, Battista. I'm sorry I can't go with you this time." He motioned outside. "But at least you've got plenty of muscle out there to help."

Tony nodded. His expression of determination was chilling.

"Marsh, keep Tony in check. Don't let him go off half-cocked."

"I'm on it."

Lacey set the security wand on the edge of a side table by the door. She rushed forward and gave Jake a hug. "Oh, Jake. Be careful."

Jake returned the embrace. Then, fighting down another stomach cramp, he swung open the door.

As he brushed past the side table, no one noticed the brief string of chirps that emanated from the security wand.

Chapter 54

Torrance, California

"THEY'VE GOT HIM," ABBAS REPORTED AS HE AND KADIR monitored the moving red dot on the computer screen. They were in the upstairs office of the warehouse. "From their speed it appears as though he's on a helicopter."

"Excellent," Battista said, gazing absently out the office's window. A light breeze rustled the trees that lined the street of the industrial park. Their shadows lengthened under the late afternoon sun. The parking lots beside the buildings had thinned out early as employees hurried home to start their weekend, oblivious to the storm of terror about to be unleashed upon them. By tomorrow afternoon they'd be huddled in fear around their television sets. The pieces on the chessboard were all in place. Nothing could stop them now.

"Get the ERT team ready to go," he ordered. "I want us in position by tomorrow morning."

"Finally!" Abbas said with a grin. He left to gather his men.

Battista joined Kadir at the desk. "You're in charge now."

"Thank you, my sheikh. It is an honor to serve."

Battista appreciated Kadir's humility. It had not often revealed itself since he'd received his implant. "I have every faith in you. Have you selected who shall go first?"

"All three are eager. But it was Omar who suggested it be done during the parade."

"Perfect." Battista appreciated the irony of the suggestion. The unusual name of the parade would take on new meaning after the attack. "Omar has earned the privilege."

Kadir unfolded a map of the Los Angeles area and spread it across the desk. Using a felt-tipped pen, he drew an X over a spot in the center of Orange County. "The parade commences at three. The timer on his detonator will be set for five minutes after."

Battista knew that once it was armed and locked in place, the suicide vest could not be removed—or the timer adjusted—without detonating the explosives. This ensured the device's success against the man's interception by authorities...or a change of heart.

"The other attacks will occur an hour later," Kadir added. "The country will be in a state of shock."

Battista nodded, satisfied. "You've done well. Months will pass before they begin to suspect what has really happened here."

By then, he thought, we will have duplicated the process across the country. He felt a brief urge to remain with Kadir and the men to see this part of the mission through. But he quickly brushed aside the thought. He had an even bigger priority to focus on, one that could change the world.

Chapter 55

Area 52

JAKE SAT BETWEEN TWO BURLY AGENTS ON THE REAR BENCH seat of the small military transport helicopter. Two more agents sat in the rear-facing seats across from him, a curtain drawn behind them, hiding the cockpit from view. The muted throb of the spinning blades overhead shook the cabin. The view out the porthole windows was practically nonexistent, but from the angle of the setting sun, he could tell they were traveling north by northeast.

He raised his plastic-cuffed wrists and checked his watch, updating the mental map he'd maintained of their likely position. They'd been in the air for about two and a half hours at a cruise speed of 180 to 190 knots. The man seated across from him was the leader of the team who took charge outside Papa's home.

"When's this joyride going to end?" Jake asked him. The man had ignored the barrage of questions so far, but Jake had a sense he was getting under his skin.

"Not soon enough," the man grumbled.

"What's the big secret? I'm going to find out where we're going sooner or later."

"Not from me." The man's voice wasn't nearly as commanding without the bullhorn.

"How about I guess and you tell me if I'm right?"

"You're a pain in the ass, Mr. Bronson."

"So I've been told."

"Why don't you just sit there and shut the hell up."

Jake shifted his shoulders in order to gain an inch or two of space from the two linebackers who bracketed him. "I'm thinking we're in northern Nevada, about two hundred miles south of the Idaho border."

The man's eyes twitched. *Definitely not a poker player.*

"Yeah, I thought so," Jake said. He knew the fuel capacity and range of this machine. Hell, from one of the nights he'd spent speed-loading data into his brain with the help of the mini, he knew the specs of virtually every aircraft in the military's arsenal. He'd caught a glimpse of the instrument panel when they'd first boarded the helicopter. The fuel gauge had been at 70 percent. "Assuming the pilot doesn't plan on dipping into his reserves, I figure we ought to be landing in the next ten minutes."

"You think you're something real special, don't you?"

"My mom thinks so."

The pitch of the overhead rotors shifted. The helicopter slowed. The copilot stuck his head through the curtain and said, "We'll be landing in five minutes, sir."

Jake smirked.

The man's glare was the last image Jake saw before one of the guards placed a hood over his head.

* * *

It was bad enough that the black hood blinded him. But the fact that the stifling fabric smelled of someone else's sweat just pissed him off. As he was escorted out of the helicopter, one of the guards said, "One more step."

There were two more steps.

Jake stumbled.

The guards chuckled.

"Bastards," Jake mumbled.

The guard gripping his left arm pushed him forward. "Shut up."

After thirty paces, the heat of the sun on the back of his neck suddenly disappeared. They'd moved indoors. The group's footsteps echoed off the walls, signaling that the space was large. As they continued forward, there was a deep motorized rumble that culminated in a resounding metallic thud, as if a massive door had been closed behind him. The air tasted familiar. It was earthy, moist.

A shiver slithered up his spine when he realized he was underground.

* * *

Claustrophobia had become a recurring companion ever since he'd been imprisoned in the crushing confines of a collapsible torture box during USAF pilot-training POW camp. Regulations restricted the use of the box to no more than an hour, but Jake had been intentionally left there overnight by a particularly nasty guard he'd outsmarted during training. Jake had flipped out. It wasn't one of his proudest moments, and he'd hoped to put it behind him. Then he'd nearly died in a cave-in during the assault on Battista's underground mountain complex. That had sent him over the edge. Ever since, the panic was quick to return whenever he found himself in cramped spaces.

He forced himself to control his breathing. Oddly, even though he was blinded under the hood, closing his eyes seemed to help. He thought of Francesca and Sarafina and took comfort in knowing they were safe. If only he could say the same for Tony's family.

The texture of the ground changed and he sensed the group bunch together as they came to a stop. Doors slid closed and the floor dropped. They were in an elevator. Descending. Fast.

Terrific.

After twelve long breaths, he figured they'd sunk fifty to sixty stories into the earth. He adjusted his jaw in order to equalize the growing pressure on his eardrums. The car slowed to a stop. The doors slid open and a cacophony of voices and conversations in the space in front of them suddenly came to a halt. Footsteps approached.

An angry voice ordered, "Take that thing off! The cuffs, too."

The guards obliged and Jake squinted at the sudden brightness. He massaged his chafed wrists and found himself standing before two men who couldn't have looked more different. The shorter one wore a camo utility uniform with a sewn-on name tag that read BROWN. Silver oak leaves on his lapels indicated a rank of lieutenant colonel. He was thickset, with a bald head that reflected the overhead lights. His ramrod bearing told Jake that he took his military rank way too seriously. The tight jaw and narrowed eyes weren't welcoming.

On the other hand, the bespectacled older man standing beside the lieutenant colonel was beaming. He reached out, clasped Jake's hand in both of his, and shook it vigorously. "Mr. Bronson, I'm so glad you're here! The name's Albert Finnegan, but please call me Doc."

Jake blinked back his surprise. He'd expected a prison cell. Instead he found himself in a cavernous underground research facility that reminded him of a NASA launch room. A score of scientists and techs turned from tiered rows of high-tech consoles to stare at him. Eagerness shone on their faces, as if they expected him to provide the ultimate answers to the mysteries of the universe. The older man was still shaking his hand. His enthusiastic expression was infectious, and Jake couldn't help but return the smile.

"Uh...thanks, Doc?" he said hesitantly, allowing himself to relax a bit. "I'm Jake."

Doc appeared to be in his early sixties. He had a warm face, and blue eyes that sparkled with curiosity. His partially gray hair curled loosely onto the bunched-up hood of his black sweat-shirt. The slogan that stretched across the front of the sweatshirt read E.T., CALL, DAMMIT! With that, Jake realized the people in this room knew that the massive explosion in the mountains of Afghanistan involved much more than a firefight with terrorists.

He fought the urge to tense at the revelation, because a bigger part of him was relieved. Had he finally encountered someone who could truly share the burden of what he'd learned from the alien obelisk? After all, it couldn't hurt to have the power of the US government and its top scientists focused on the problem. Of course, in the end, he suspected there wouldn't be a damn thing they could do about it.

"This is all sweet and tidy, Dr. Finnegan," Lieutenant Colonel Brown said as he signaled the men standing at Jake's back. They moved forward and resumed their escort position around him. "But Lieutenant Bronson needs to come with me for a lengthy debrief. He's got a lot of questions to answer."

"Hold on, Colonel." Doc stepped forward. "For every question you have, I have ten. No, make that a hundred." He took Jake's arm and pulled him away from the goon squad. "You'll get your turn. But not yet."

Brown hesitated. He obviously didn't appreciate having his orders countermanded—by a civilian, no less—and especially in front of his men. But it appeared to Jake as if these two had butted heads before, and Doc must have carried the bigger stick because the lieutenant colonel backed off.

"All right, Doc," he said. "You get him for now. But my team remains here to keep an eye on him. And tomorrow morning, he's mine."

Jake didn't like the sound of that, but it didn't worry him. By tomorrow he planned to be long gone.

* * *

"This is quite the setup, Doc," Jake said after Brown left. The guards had positioned themselves at each of the three exits in the large space.

Doc pulled a key that was suspended on a chain beneath his sweatshirt. "As they say back home, you ain't seen nothin' yet. Follow me."

They walked down the steps that bisected the tiered rows of consoles and computer stations that surrounded an unusual steel enclosure.

Nods and smiles greeted Jake, distracting him from a growing sense of unease regarding what might be hidden beneath the steel jar. A young technician who looked more like a punk rocker than a research assistant offered a high-five. Jake obliged and slapped the young man's hand.

"Dude!" the kid said, unable to hide his excitement. "I can't believe you're actually here. I gotta question for you."

Jake hiked an eyebrow. "Yeah, I figured."

"How'd you do it? How'd you snap that beer mug right out of the air?"

Jake felt his shoulders slump. The kid was referring to the YouTube video that had captured Jake's seemingly superhuman speed at Sam's bar. He dodged the question. "So, you're a DDP fan, huh?" he said, pointing to the kid's black T-shirt. It was emblazoned with a photo of the heavy-metal band Dublin Death Patrol.

"You know DDP?" The kid looked astonished.

Jake flashed on the article he'd glanced at, one of thousands that now resided in his mental library. "Sure. Chuck Billy, the vocalist from Testament, heads the bill. The boys all went to Dublin High School together in northern California. Their drummer, Danny Cunningham, is unstoppable."

Doc interrupted them. "Not now, Timmy. We've got work to do."

The tech ignored his boss. He broke into a huge smile and his fist shot into the air. "DDP for life!" he said, referring to the band's slogan. "You're the man, Jake Bronson!"

Jake couldn't help but like the kid.

Doc shook his head and mumbled something under his breath. He stepped forward and inserted his key into a slot at Timmy's console. That simple act seemed to galvanize everyone in the room. Several of them cast furtive glances at the steel shroud. Doc turned the key and nodded to the kid. "Enter the code."

Timmy tapped an alphanumeric string into the keyboard.

There was a hydraulic hiss, several clicks, and a brief whir of electronic gears. "Locks disengaged," Timmy reported. There was an edge of excitement in his voice. "Standing by."

"Dump the shield."

The kid keyed the entry. "Electromagnetic shield deactivated."

A deep thrumming pulse assaulted Jake's senses. Instinctively, his palms flew up to cover his ears. To no effect; the sound wasn't diminished. He felt it in his bones, as if he stood beside an immense turbine that shook the room. His senses were overwhelmed, not by the volume of the all-too-familiar sound, but by the memories it invoked. It was the same vibration that had drawn him into the sacred cavern of Battista's mountain fortress, a sound that only he had heard because of his enhanced brain, a sound that had ultimately led to the premature triggering of an alien device that could ultimately bring about the end of the human race.

Jake pressed his palms harder against his ears, his arms quivering from the effort, his body doubled over in denial, his jaw clenched tight as a vise.

He felt a hand on his shoulder. "What's wrong?" Doc said, his voice filled with concern. "Are you okay?"

Jake shook his head repeatedly and rose slowly. After a brief struggle between mind and body, he exiled the insistent hum to a corner of his mind and eased his hands from his ears. There was little choice but to accept the inevitable. The anger and frustration he felt must have been evident on his face because both Doc and Timmy seemed to edge backward when he looked up at them.

"You don't hear it, do you?" he said, already knowing the answer.

"Hear what?" Timmy said.

Jake blew out a huge sigh. "Never mind."

It made sense now, Jake thought. Why else was he here with a bunch of scientists rather than in prison? He knew what was hidden behind the curtain. Hell, he knew more about it than anyone alive. Or at least anyone from planet Earth. It wasn't a huge surprise that a second device had been found. The ancient visitors must have planted them all over the planet. He just never expected to confront one again.

His gaze went from the steel shroud to a point in the reinforced concrete ceiling thirty feet above it. A few wrong moves and the alien artifact would blast a hole clean through it—and the hundred feet of rock above it—like a hot poker through butter. In minutes it would be deep in space, on its way—

A thought suddenly occurred to him. What if this device could be used to send a different message, one that explained that the first one was triggered prematurely because of the anomaly of Jake's brain? Could he correct his mistake and delay mankind's extermination for a hundred years? Or a thousand?

"Let's get that thing open," he said. "We've got work to do."

Chapter 56

Area 52

TWENTY PAIRS OF EYES WATCHED IN HUSHED SILENCE AS A heavy-duty ceiling winch reeled in the thick suspension cables hooked to the top of the steel bell jar. The shroud lifted from the platform to reveal its contents. From the anxious looks on the faces around him, Jake suspected that only a few of the scientists and technicians had ever seen the obelisk up close and personal. Several of them stood up at their control consoles to get a better view.

Jake shook off an involuntary shudder as the inverted black pyramid came into view. Someone threw a switch, and spotlights flicked on to illuminate it from multiple angles. Its tip was cradled in a steel frame; its square top surface shimmered under the lights. He approached it on unsteady legs, with Doc and Timmy beside him.

"An exact duplicate," Jake said as he studied the pictograms and symbols on its surface. "What have you learned about it?"

"We found a pattern," Timmy said. He pointed at the area surrounding the three-inch square etched in its center. "In the symbols."

"Really?" Jake said, testing him. "So which three are wrong?" It was the same phrase Sarafina had used when she'd revealed that three of the eleven symbols emitted a harmonic tone that was inconsistent with the other eight.

Timmy hesitated only a second before identifying the three. "These are nonfactorial primes. The others aren't."

Jake hiked an eyebrow. A different approach to solving the same puzzle. Impressive. "What else?"

"Not a hell of a lot," Doc admitted. "It's impervious to virtually every scan we've attempted. Material unknown. Origin unknown. Surface hardness beyond our means to measure. The only thing we know for sure is that it emits a subtle type of radiation our instruments can't identify. But whatever it is, we discovered it could be shielded with electromagnetics—just as you did."

"Like I did?"

Doc motioned to one of the techs. He reached under his console and pulled out the tackle box from Jake's apartment.

Son of a bitch. The goons who had picked him up must have ransacked his place. Well, the joke's on you, boys, he thought, because you just provided me with my ticket out of here. He hid his satisfaction and said, "Anything else?"

"Not really," Doc said. "That's why we need your help."

Jake considered his options. He wanted to grab the mini—regardless of the physical risks associated with using it—and return to LA in order to help Tony find his family and stop Battista. But he couldn't leave yet. Not until he downloaded what he knew about the artifact to Doc and his team. In the end, he would need their help to discover a way to launch this alien rocket with an entirely new message: *Mankind is not a threat.*

He pointed to one of the pictograms that ran along the perimeter of the object's surface—the one depicting three humanoid figures facing off against a tribe of early man.

"It began twenty-five thousand years ago..."

Chapter 57

THE TRACTOR-TRAILER RIG KICKED UP A FLURRY OF DUST AS it pulled off the paved highway and onto the dirt road. The driver slowed, downshifting to maneuver the big truck around the next bend on the narrow road. The barren landscape offered little in the way of trees to shelter the vehicle, but after two more twists in the road, the rolling hills provided cover from the main highway. He pulled to a stop with a hiss of hydraulic brakes and cut the engine.

A blast of hot, dry air embraced him when he exited the air-conditioned cab. The midday sun blazed overhead. He closed his eyes in silent prayer and welcomed the memory it brought of his Afghan village. The hum of the trailer's generator broke the momentary spell, and he walked the trailer's sixty-foot length, stopping at a chest-high access panel near its end. He unlocked the panel door, took a quick glance to confirm that the area behind the trailer was clear, and depressed the green OPEN button centered in the panel.

There was a metallic click as an interior lock disengaged, followed by the electronic thrum of twin actuators that slowly opened the bottom-hinged door. The ramp completed its arc and settled to the ground. From within the shadows of the cargo space, the twin headlights of a HAZMERV, the Hazardous Materials Emergency Response Vehicle, stared out at him.

* * *

Battista squinted against the sudden daylight that swept in through the descending ramp of the trailer. He turned away from the brightness, swiveling in the HAZMERV's front passenger seat to study the eight-man team behind him, lined up on the bench seats. Each man was fully encapsulated in a yellow biohazard suit with a self-contained oxygen system. LED lights inside the suits illuminated their hard faces, giving them an otherworldly visage. Battista and Abbas, who was in the driver's seat, were dressed similarly, though they had not yet donned their masks.

"Frightening, aren't they?" Abbas said.

"There isn't a soldier alive who wouldn't shy away at the sight of them," Battista agreed.

He keyed the mike on his headset. "You may remove your hoods for now."

The men complied. Grateful nods followed.

The twenty-six-foot-long, bright-yellow HAZMAT vehicle they occupied was a mock-up of the emergency response trucks used under the authority of Homeland Security and operated by the military. This USAF version had been carefully outfitted with the appropriate emergency lights, and red-and-white striped HAZMAT placards and bumper markings that warned of the truck's grim purpose. The rack of antennas and the top-mounted satellite dish added to its authenticity. It was indistinguishable from the official vehicles currently stationed in the region. A matching fifteen-foot-long enclosed trailer was hooked to its tail end.

Battista checked his watch. It was 2:00 p.m. They should get the call any minute. He grinned as he imagined the agony that Bronson should be feeling about now.

Chapter 58

Area 52

"THEIR TECHNOLOGY IS BASED ON TELEKINETIC PROPULSION," Jake said, standing at the lectern. The audience of scientists and techs leaned forward in their seats. Fingers hesitated over laptops and tablets. They were in a meeting room down the hall from the main cavern. In spite of the fact that Jake had been transferring information to them for nearly four hours, there wasn't a bored expression in the room. Doc sat in the front row with his sleeves rolled up and an unlit pipe jutting from his mouth. Timmy was beside him.

Jake glanced at the large flat-screen suspended from the ceiling in the front corner of the room. Normally used for video presentations or slide shows, it was currently connected to a camera mounted in the main cavern. The alien artifact shone on the screen. Jake shook his head in dismay and continued his lecture.

"Einstein taught us that every mass has energy, and vice versa," he said. It felt good to share extraordinary events and information with men and women who wanted nothing more than to learn—without judgment. "The greater the mass, the greater the energy. And it can be tapped into telekinetically."

Pulling the mini from his pocket, he held it on his outstretched palm and focused his thoughts. The tiny pyramid rose and hovered above his hand. There was a collective gasp from the audience. Jake allowed the moment to last until he realized that the effort needed to maintain the hover seemed to increase exponentially with each beat. With a grunt, he released his hold and the mini dropped back into his palm.

Another bad sign, Jake thought. It had been so easy to perform that trick a couple months back. But now, even with the additional energy provided by the proximity of the mini, it was increasingly difficult. He realized his heart rate had suddenly doubled and he remembered the warnings from the doctor. *You have the heart of a ninety-year-old.*

Noticing a flash of concern on Doc's face, Jake pocketed the mini. It was time to wrap things up. He needed to get out of here and help Tony and the others.

"I suspect they discovered a way to mechanically duplicate telekinetic ability," he said. "That would allow them to tap into the mass and energy of planets and stars, using it to push or pull them in any direction. Sort of like slingshotting their crafts through space. Acceleration would be unlimited."

Timmy's eyes narrowed. "Well, that's not exactly correct," he said.

"How's that?"

"Einstein's theory of relativity. When an object is pushed in the direction of motion, it gains momentum and energy, but it can't move faster than the speed of light, no matter how much energy it absorbs. Its momentum and energy continue to increase, but its speed approaches a constant value—the speed of light."

"Well, I know that, but—"

"That's how we know they can't get back here for forty years," Timmy added.

"What?" It was Jake's turn to be surprised. "How'd you figure that?" His mind was already ten steps ahead of his mouth. There was only one way to solve that equation.

"Easy, it's a simple mathematical—"

"I can do the math, Timmy. But not without a destination."

The confused expressions from Doc, Timmy, and several of the others signaled the answer before Doc voiced it.

"I assumed you knew," Doc said. "We figured it out in the first week or so. Even though our telescopes weren't prepped like they are when we're monitoring a satellite launch, we still caught enough of a glimpse to establish a track. The object was on a direct course for the Gliese Red Dwarf star system and specifically to a planet we call Gliese 581g. It's one hundred nineteen trillion miles from Earth and smack in the center of the habitable zone. It's just enough distance from the parent star to allow oceans to form without boiling away or freezing, and that means it can sustain life. The track is too exact to dispute. That's where it's headed."

"Here, let me show you," Timmy interjected. His fingers danced and slid across the surface of his tablet. He rose and showed Jake the screen. It was a simple animation of an object being launched from Earth. It followed a trajectory into deep space and then bounced back to its point of origin. "Forty years, round-trip."

Relief swept over Jake. It was the best news he'd heard in a long time, other than the fact that Francesca carried his child—a child that now would have a chance at a real life. Mankind could make a lot of changes in forty years, if given the right motivation. And the people in this room could help make that happen.

Things were finally turning around—

The stomach cramp hit him like a hammer blow. It felt as if something had exploded in his colon. His legs gave out and he doubled over onto the floor. There was a sudden expanding pressure and his bowels evacuated with a huge rush of air. The odor was tainted, as if it were chemically laced. Jake rocked back and forth from the nauseating agony. He heard startled shouts, cries of pain, and the sound of chairs toppling over. There were several heavy thuds.

Just before passing out, Jake saw Doc, Timmy, and several others sprawled across the floor.

None of them moved.

Chapter 59

Area 52

T HE SITE WAS FIVE MILES OFF THE MAIN HIGHWAY AT THE end of a box canyon. It was a rolling landscape that was scarcely alive, save for the short-rooted tanglers that edged the old mining road bisecting the narrow defile. The last two hundred yards of the road were recently paved, and a gated concrete wall topped with triple strands of concertina wire protected the area within. The wall stretched from one end of the canyon to the other. A newly constructed guard shack stood outside the gate.

Other than the armed USAF military police at the shack, there was no apparent activity around the half-dozen drab structures that stood within the perimeter. Two military transport trucks and an open-air jeep were parked in a small lot. A helicopter was tied down nearby. The paved road disappeared into the face of the canyon, blocked by a forty-foot-wide by twenty-foot-high blast door embedded into the rock.

The magnified scene jiggled as the HAZMERV and its trailer bounced over a rut in the road leading to the gate. Battista lowered the binoculars. "Three guards." He placed one of Kadir's plastic breathers over his nose and tightened it in place with the elastic strap. Abbas did the same. The men in the rear were already wearing the devices.

Battista reached for the cylinder affixed to his belt and twisted the valve. The antidote flowed like a gentle breeze across his nostrils and left a metallic taste in his mouth. He donned his hazmat hood and activated the microphone linked to the rest of his team. "Sixty seconds."

The sound of magazines ramming home told him the men had heard him. Their AK-47u submachine guns were small enough to hide on shoulder slings beneath their bulky hazmat suits. Abbas brought the truck to a stop at the front gate.

The men stationed at the gate would either open the massive blast doors, or they would not, Battista thought. Either way, they would die. He tensed as one of the policemen, armed with an M4 carbine, hurried to the driver's window. The man looked nervous. Abbas lowered the window and the guard's eyes widened when he saw that the vehicle's occupants were in hazmat suits.

Abbas spoke before the guard offered a challenge. His voice was amplified through a small external speaker embedded on the front of his suit. All traces of his Middle Eastern accent had vanished. "What the hell are you doing out in the open without a mask, Sergeant?"

"W…what—"

"Goddamn it. Contamination could leak from the facility at any moment. Hang on!" Abbas turned his back and barked an order into the truck. "Three masks. NOW!" He extended his arm out the door and handed the sergeant a full-face M50 gas mask. "Stow that beret and put this on, soldier."

"Yes, sir!" The sergeant allowed his M4 to dangle from its harness and donned the mask in record time. At his signal, the two remaining guards hurried over and followed his lead.

"Anyone else aboveground?"

The sergeant's reply was muffled beneath his mask. The voice amplification feature had been disabled in the device. When he realized that Abbas couldn't hear him, he just shook his head.

Abbas motioned to the remaining two guards as they fumbled with their masks. "Get a move on!" he ordered. "There are people dying in there!"

One of the guards rushed to the shack and started entering data at a console. The other two stepped aside as the gate swung open and a row of columnar barricades disappeared into the ground. Abbas put the truck into gear and moved into the complex. The blast door was directly ahead of them. The massive steel wall split open at its center and swung slowly outward. The tunnel beyond disappeared into the mountain.

At long last, Battista thought. He pressed a small button hidden within the glove of his suit. A signal activated microdevices hidden within the masks given to the guards. It released a brief spray of the same pressurized gas that had been carried in by the American. The effect was instantaneous. The guards collapsed to the ground and remained still. A brief whiff of the compound—another of Kadir's brilliant creations—was intended to cause a loss of consciousness that lasted twelve hours. The gas would prove deadly if it wasn't allowed to dissipate.

"Leave their masks in place," Battista ordered two of the men in the back of the truck. They had already removed their hazmat suits to reveal underlying uniforms that matched those of the guards'. The two jumped out the rear doors and ran to the bodies.

"Vigilance!" Abbas added sharply over his headset. "Keep the tactical net open at all times and report anything unusual." Both soldiers nodded as they dragged the first of the bodies into a nearby building.

Abbas switched on the headlights and drove into the mountain.

* * *

Jake opened his eyes to discover the image of Gandalf the Grey staring back at him. He blinked away his disorientation and refocused. It was the engraving on Doc's meerschaum pipe. It must have skittered across the floor when he collapsed.

Ignoring the uncomfortable wetness in his trousers, he pushed himself to his feet and rushed to Doc's side. His pulse was steady; so was Timmy's. A couple of slaps to their faces didn't change a thing. They were out cold. But alive.

Thank God.

Bodies were strewn all over the room. A few of them were still seated, their torsos folded over the tables. Everyone had lost consciousness in a matter of seconds. The fuzziness in Jake's head cleared and his mind went into afterburner, fueled by rage. He removed his pants and found the small cylindrical device that had obviously been implanted in his colon.

Bastards.

He pulled off his T-shirt, moistened it with the contents of a water bottle, and wiped the blood and mess from his legs. Then he donned a pair of clean coveralls he found in a row of lockers at the back of the room. It all made sense now, he thought—his abduction by Battista's men in Mexico, the all-too-easy escape, the recurring cramps. He fingered the four-inch-long flexible cylinder that had been embedded inside him. In addition to the concentrated gas it had held, it apparently housed a GPS tracker of some sort. Tracking Jake had been child's play. They'd obviously delivered the intel to the Feds, and his gnawing gut already suspected why.

He dropped the cylinder to the floor and stomped on it. It was probably too late to do any good. He looked at his watch. The fact that the device had been activated over an hour earlier meant that the next phase of Battista's plan was already in progress.

As if on cue, movement on the large screen at the front of the room caught his attention. Several figures in hazmat suits entered the main cavern and made their way toward the pyramid. One by one they removed their flexible helmets. Jake saw red when he recognized Battista.

He hesitated. Charging into the fray was immensely tempting. He couldn't deny he felt a primal urge to deliver extreme violence—up close and personal. But what chance did he really have of prevailing? The men out there were armed to the teeth. He bit off his anger and came up with another plan.

He'd have to settle for getting one step ahead of the bastards.

* * *

Battista's hazmat team fanned out in the amphitheater-like room, pausing to check the bodies of the few people who had been stationed at the rows of computer consoles. The team had passed several guards and technicians in the passageways leading here. Each was as motionless as those in this room.

Kadir had once again outdone himself, Battista thought. The small volume of self-regenerating gas contained in the implanted device had performed exactly as he had said it would, expanding and reproducing exponentially to invade every corner of the complex. Only the aboveground guards had been spared. They had been quick to make the emergency call that Battista's team had intercepted.

Of course, the American would have been spared as well. The capsule had included a dose of antitoxin that limited the effects of the drug. Otherwise, the heavy concentration of toxin would have killed him instantly. In any case, the half life of the gas was only ten minutes; it had become inert long ago.

Battista removed his hazmat hood. Abbas and the rest of the team did the same. One of the men at the other end of the room called out, "No sign of the American."

Battista didn't acknowledge the comment. It didn't matter. Nothing mattered, at least not at the moment. The artifact that had become his obsession stood just thirty feet in front of him. It appeared to be an exact duplicate of the pyramid that his tribe had idolized for over a thousand years. His sources had been correct—it truly existed.

He felt a surge of pride. The Americans weren't the only ones with undercover assets embedded in key positions of foreign governments. And now the fruit of his carefully crafted plan was within his reach. He'd grab the device, find the American, and—

Urgent words over his headset cut through his thoughts. "I have a call from Aamir!" the guard at the front gate reported. Though cell service was nonexistent this far beneath the surface, the call could be transferred over their tactical network.

"Patch him through," Battista ordered.

He felt the blood drain from his face as he listened to the man's report. After several minutes, the connection was severed.

Battista forced himself to breathe. The fury coursing through his veins had short-circuited his autonomic nerve responses. His hand went to his neck and he rubbed and twisted the patch of blistering scars, welcoming the mind-clearing pain it caused, reminding him of the debt that Jake Bronson had yet to pay. *The damnable American and his friends...*

Abbas removed the switchblade from his pocket. His face was a mask of deadly determination. He'd heard the report as well. "He will wish he was never born," he growled.

"Wait," the sheikh ordered. "There is a better way." The imaginary chess pieces in his mind shifted as he formulated his next move. After a moment, he smiled. "We shall have them all. Every last one of them."

* * *

It was dead quiet in the room. The previous sounds of a motorized vehicle had faded nearly fifteen minutes earlier. It had sounded like a forklift. The Dari voices accompanying it were gone as well, though a few of them had at one point been just a few feet from his hiding space. Jake opened the door of the metal closet he'd been crouched in. His foot slipped when he stepped into an expanding pool of blood on the tiled floor. He caught himself and stared unbelievingly at the scene before him. The two dozen people who had been unconscious just a short while ago were all dead. Their throats had been slit.

Jake checked the first body. Then the second. It was no use. Rushing to the bank of lockers, he yanked the first one open. Timmy's inert form spilled onto the floor. He was unconscious but still breathing. Jake opened the next locker and breathed a sigh of relief. Doc was all right as well. He'd stuffed them into the lockers just before he'd hidden himself. If there had been more time, he'd have done the same for the others. As it was, he'd barely made it into the closet before the first of Battista's men had entered the room.

He moved Doc and Timmy into more comfortable positions, muttering an apology for the terror he'd brought into their lives. Shaking his head in disgust, he hurried out of the room. He stopped short when he reached the main cavern. His heart caught in his throat. Even though he'd pretty much expected it, the sight hit him like a blow to the head.

The pyramid was gone.

Chapter 60

South Central Los Angeles, California

J EEZ, DUDE," MARSHALL SAID. "YOU'RE WALKING LIKE Herman Munster with those shoes."

"*His* boots woulda been a better fit." Tony had just returned to Papa's house from a rushed trip to the LAPD evidence room, where he'd picked up the black sneakers. They were heavier than he expected, and two sizes smaller than his feet. His toes curled painfully in their tips. He hoped like hell the shoes worked.

"We're ready to move out, Sarge," Papa said. Ripper and Snake stood beside him, armed to the hilt. Freddie towered behind them. Becker was outside, loading a little surprise of his own into a Tommy Taco food truck parked in the driveway. The team had emptied the contents of the truck and converted it to a mobile command vehicle. "Street and his boys already left. They should be on scene soon."

Papa must have noticed Tony's concern. "You can trust them, Sarge. They know how to keep a low profile. No one makes a move 'til you arrive."

"Okay, then," Tony said. "Let's mount up."

Lacey was the first to move toward the door.

"Whoa. Where d'ya think you're goin'?"

She rolled her eyes, opened the door, and kept walking.

"It's no use," Marshall said. "I've already been down that road with her. If I go, she goes."

"You're going too?" Tony said. "What the hell, Marsh? This ain't gonna be no picnic."

"Dude, of course I'm going." He handed Tony an inner-ear comm bud. "The rest of my gear's already hooked up in the truck. How the hell else are you going to coordinate this thing?"

Marshall had a point. Normally Tony would have a fully equipped SWAT tactical team backing him up in a hostage situation like this. But that wasn't an option here. The lives of his wife and kids depended on them keeping the authorities out of it. Hell, even if LAPD *was* involved, they'd never allow him to attempt the insane stunt he had planned.

He glanced toward the back of the room. Francesca, Bradley, and the children filed in from the kitchen. Max bounded in beside them, followed by three armed bangers. They would remain behind as guards.

They'll be safe.

He turned to Marshall. "All right," he said, inserting the device into his ear. "But you both stay in the truck, no matter what."

"No problem."

As they trailed Lacey outside, Tony went over the plan one last time in his head. So many things could go wrong.

He sure wished Jake was here to help.

* * *

"I still can't reach Tony's son," Marshall whispered to Lacey. He tapped the mouse pad on the laptop, preparing to send another Call of Duty game invite to the boy's user name. "Either they took his PSP away from him, or—"

"Don't think it," Lacey said. She glanced toward the front of the truck where Tony was huddled with Papa and Becker. "Keep trying."

It was stuffy inside the cramped truck. The leftover odor of refried beans thickened the air. Marshall sent another invite. He hoped they weren't too late.

He turned his attention to the large LCD screen mounted on the truck's interior sidewall. It depicted a live overhead view of the target area. The image was crystal clear, thanks to the Raven portable drone circling overhead, compliments of Papa's scrounger. It included a synchronized overlay from Google Maps so that he could easily identify street and business names.

Better yet was the fact every member of the team had one of the tiny ear buds. The device was both a comm unit and a GPS locator. He counted nearly two dozen flashing green dots on the LCD display. Each of the locators had a unique identification code that Marshall had logged into the system when he'd handed out the devices, so each dot included a text field beside it with the individual's name. Most of them were stationary, though a small group that included Street, Paco, P-Boy, and a few others was still fanning out in the thick copse of trees bordering the parking lot north of the target. Marshall activated the microphone on his headset. "Heads up, everybody. We're two minutes out."

Tony stepped over and surveyed the assault team's positions. He carried no weapons. His role in the plan required him to appear as unthreatening as possible, not an easy thing for the big man to pull off. He'd have to draw on the fear he felt for his family to complete his disguise. But for now, his face was granite, all business. He activated his comm unit and broadcast to the team. "Comm check."

Becker stood across from him. His hand went up to his ear as the message came across the tac-net. He nodded to Tony, as did Papa beside him.

"Five by five," reported Ripper. "Team One in position."

"Team Three locked 'n' loaded," Snake said.

After a short delay, Marshall said, "Team Two. Are you up?"

"Steady and ready, holmes," Street said. There was bloodlust in his voice. "It's time to waste 'em."

* * *

Tony let out a low growl at Street's tone. He shared a tense look with Becker.

Papa picked up on the exchange. "Don't worry, Sarge," he said. "Street will do his part just fine. He's getting his boys charged up, that's all. He'll wait for the signal, like the rest of 'em."

The sucker *better* wait, Tony thought. He was worried. Big time. This thing could go to hell in an instant. They had plenty of men, but only a few had the kind of experience necessary to pull this off.

Tony moved closer to the video screen and focused on the two-man sniper team positioned on a water tower two hundred yards northeast of the target. "Snake, whaddya see?"

"Three skylights. One propped open with an interior ladder leading rooftop. One sentry up top and another on a catwalk just beneath him. Neither one's on alert."

That's gonna change.

The target warehouse was in the far corner of an industrial park filled with light manufacturing and distribution facilities. It was Sunday, and the parking lots were empty. Traffic was non-existent. Situated down a private drive at the end of a cul-de-sac, the north side of the building backed up to a parking area lined with a thick copse of trees. That's where Street and some of his boys were positioned. Railroad tracks separated the northeast corner of the lot from the adjacent Chevron refinery and water tower, where Snake and his spotter monitored the rooftop of the warehouse through high-powered lenses.

Tony focused on the only building that was adjacent to the target warehouse. "Ripper, you set?" he asked.

"Waiting on your mark, Sarge," Ripper replied. He and six bangers were hidden inside the structure. During the assault, it would be their job to jump from their rooftop to the warehouse.

Tony felt their vehicle slow. On the screen, the taco truck rolled into view and came to a stop a half block from the target. Freddie's voice chimed in on the tac-net, "I'm right behind you, Sarge." His flashing dot emerged from an alley and took a cover position at the rear of the truck. He was tasked with protecting the command center once bullets started flying.

The last piece of the puzzle was in place.

Tony glanced at Lacey as he made his way to the rear of the truck. She nodded.

Time to go.

Chapter 61

FROM HIS PERCH ON THE INTERIOR BALCONY OUTSIDE HIS office, Kadir watched the beehive of activity on the ground floor as his team made the final preparations for their departure. Six men loaded two vans lined up by the rear exit. Kadir saw the shadows of others through the semitransparent windows of the clean room. They were prepping the charges that would start the fire. He'd made sure the fire would burn hot by adding a few chemical elements from his own mix. The structure would be reduced to ashes, and the remains of the woman and her children would be unidentifiable.

He was glad to be leaving this place. By tomorrow he'd be safely ensconced at the facility in Venezuela. He hoped the sheikh would permit his wife to visit him there.

He was proud of what they'd accomplished here, under the upturned nose of the Americans. Soon their lives would change. Soon they would share the fear that those in his homeland felt every day. Soon, they would be no more.

Down below, two men stood separate from the rest. Kadir watched as they unrolled their prayer blankets and knelt beside one another. They shared a unique kinship born of the final glorious task they had accepted.

Fools, he thought. Yes, they will serve a purpose. But they are fools nonetheless. It was one thing to dedicate oneself to a noble cause—he understood that—but his implant had opened his mind to many things. Now he believed that Allah's will was far better served by adding value in life rather than death. Still, their sacrifice would not be in vain. The specially constructed vests hung on a rack beside them—another of Kadir's wondrous achievements.

He checked his watch. Omar should be arriving at his target soon. Then it would begin.

"Someone approaches!" The shout went through the warehouse like a bolt of lightning. Men grabbed weapons. They ran to hidden cover positions at every exit in a well-practiced drill. Then silence.

Kadir hurried down the steps. The guard who'd issued the warning had flattened himself by the doorway leading to the front lobby. He motioned toward the building's front entrance.

Kadir nodded, waiting. A moment later a buzzer sounded. The sound sent a ripple up his spine. He remained still.

The buzzer sounded again, several times in short succession. It was followed by several sharp poundings on the glass door.

The visitor would soon wish he hadn't been so insistent, Kadir thought. He allowed the tension to melt from his face and made his way to the lobby.

* * *

Tony watched as a figure entered the lobby interior. He wore a white lab coat that hung loosely on his slight frame. His silver hair was combed back. He had a bulbous nose that supported Coke-bottle glasses magnifying his eyeballs. The man didn't look like much of threat, but there were others inside. Lots of them. The bastards had his family.

The man hesitated halfway to the door. His head cocked to one side. A beat later his eyes widened in recognition. He shouted something over his shoulder and three men with AK-47s rushed to join him. Tony raised his hands high above his head.

The door swung open and two of the guards pulled Tony into the lobby. They held him fast while the third man patted him down. Tony tensed as the man slid his hands expertly down his shins toward his shoes. "Nothing," the man said in Dari.

The leader seemed deep in thought. He studied Tony for a moment before striding past him to push through the door and step onto the sidewalk. He looked casually about. After a moment, the terrorist pushed back into the lobby and motioned outside to one of the guards. "There's a man with an ice cream cart. Make sure it's ice cream in that cart."

The guard stowed his weapon behind the front desk and left. The leader strode past Tony without giving him a glance. He motioned to the two remaining guards. "Bring him."

They shoved Tony down the hall and pushed him to his knees in the center of the warehouse. Nearly twenty armed men peeled from their hiding places to surround him. He shifted uneasily, making a point of facing the rear warehouse door. Half the bad guys were between him and the door; the rest were spread behind him. His face was full of fear, more real than feigned. It helped to bury his fury. He noticed that Battista wasn't in the crowd. That worried him.

The first guard returned from his forage with the ice cream vendor. He carried a handful of popsicles. The leader nodded, satisfied. He turned to confront Tony.

"How did you find us?"

"Where's my fam—"

He was cut off by a backhand across the jaw. Tony tasted blood on his lip as he glared at the bulbous-eyed asshole.

"How—did—you—find—us?"

"Not until I—"

A rifle butt struck the back of Tony's head. It splayed him to the floor in a blaze of pain. He struggled to push himself back to his knees, shaking his head to clear it. "Listen up, you stupid son of a bitch," he said. "I ain't telling you a goddamn thing until I know my family is okay. Until then, you can kiss my ass and just wonder about the shit-storm that's gonna follow."

Another guard cocked his arm for the next blow, but the leader stayed his hand. "Wait."

Every plan has a choke point, Tony thought, and this was it. Success or failure depended upon what happened next. The leader glanced up. Tony followed his gaze to a guard standing on the balcony above.

The leader nodded to the guard. "Bring them out."

The man's words were barely out of his mouth when Tony shouted, "Second-floor balcony, center office!" He closed his eyes, lowered his hands to his ears, and clicked the heels of his shoes together.

Chapter 62

Torrance, California
Two minutes earlier

EASY NOW," BECKER SAID OVER THE COMM-NET. HE AND three of the bangers were crouched behind a hedge across the street from the target. It was his job to coordinate the assault. "They've taken the bait. Keep your heads down." The muzzle of his M4 assault rifle was hidden within the hedge. He watched through the magnified lens of the scope as two armed guards pulled Tony into the lobby.

A moment later a middle-aged man wearing a lab coat exited the building. He stopped five paces out and surveyed the area.

Becker turned his attention to Papa and the ice cream cart. "Keep moving," he whispered. "Take it nice and slow. You're just a weary guy trying to make a few bucks selling ice cream to the poor blokes who had to come in to work today."

Lab Coat watched for a moment, then returned inside.

Papa kept coming. He pushed his cart down the sidewalk that fronted the building. As he turned toward the parking area that skirted the west side of the structure, a guard pushed through the lobby door and walked toward him. Becker tensed. He centered the red dot of his scope on the man's head.

"Stay breezy. The tango's got no visible weapons."

Papa grunted in acknowledgment. The guard was behind him, approaching slowly. One hand reached in his pocket.

"You there!" the man shouted.

Papa stopped the cart and turned to face him, a hopeful expression on his face.

"*Sí*, senor? Ice cream?"

Becker was amazed at Papa's transformation. The leader of one of the toughest fire teams on the contract circuit—a soldier who had killed dozens in the performance of duty—looked about as threatening as a newborn puppy.

The guard's posture relaxed. He said something Becker couldn't quite make out. Papa nodded in reply. A smile brightened his face as he lifted the lid on the cart and pulled out a handful of popsicles. The other man handed over some bills, took the treats, and returned to the lobby.

"The *pendejo* didn't even leave a tip," Papa muttered. He rolled across the parking lot and along the edge of the building. Fifty yards later he positioned the cart in front of the warehouse roll-up door. Then he ran like hell.

"Stand by," Becker said. He flipped the safety cap off the remote detonator attached to his web belt and waited for Tony's signal.

* * *

Marshall held his breath. He and Lacey watched the scene unfold on the wall-mounted monitor. The high-def video stream from the overhead drone displayed everything in exacting detail. Marshall adjusted the mouse and tapped a key to center the image on the ice cream cart. Then he zoomed out so that the teams surrounding the warehouse were in view.

Any moment now.

Lacey sat beside him. Her hand gripped his forearm. She was a coiled spring.

A brief squawk on the comm-net preceded Tony's booming voice. "Second-floor balcony, center office!"

Marshall's skin twitched in anticipation. An instant later there was a muffled explosion inside the warehouse. It was followed two seconds later by a massive blast outside the warehouse door. It rocked the taco truck like a 6.0 aftershock. The C-4 that Becker had embedded within the cart had done its job. The expanding smoke from the blast obscured most of the scene on the monitor.

Only the green dots were visible now. They converged on the warehouse from all directions.

Chapter 63

THE REAR-VECTORED BLASTS FROM THE PLASTIC EXPLOSIVES molded into the bottom of Tony's sneakers jolted every bone in his body. He was thrust forward on his knees across the floor. His arms windmilled and his upper body torqued backward from the force. The leader leaped from his path and stared behind Tony. The shocked expression on his face was the first clue to the devastation wrought by the explosion.

The thick soles had been hollowed out and fashioned after the design of a claymore mine. A steel inner sole shielded his feet when the deadly payload of lead pellets blasted in a directed spray toward the enemy. From the sudden smell of blood and offal, he could tell the shoes had performed as advertised. Tony didn't need to look. He'd seen shredded flesh before.

The nine or ten terrorists in front of him recovered quickly. The sudden look of outrage on their leader's face echoed their intentions. Weapon muzzles shifted.

Tony sprawled forward, cupped his ears, and squeezed his eyes shut.

The second blast shook the entire building and sent a ripple of energy through the floor that knocked over crates and men. Tony opened his eyes to see streams of sunlight pouring through the bus-size hole ripped through the roll-up door. The terrorist leader scrambled away on hands and knees and clambered up the staircase.

Tony pushed himself to his feet and bounded after him, the shredded remains of the shoes flopping at his ankles. His bare feet slapped against the blood-slickened floor. The burns from the C-4 made it feel as though he were running across a hot skillet. Spasms of pain shot up his legs.

He shoved the sensation aside with a grunt and took the steps two at a time. Half seconds mattered. The guard who had been posted on the balcony was gone. He and his boss had ducked into the open doorway leading to his family. Racing forward, Tony caught a glimpse of a man above the skylight aiming his assault rifle in Tony's direction. He jinked to one side, expecting the burn of hot lead. Instead there was a shatter of glass. The guard plunged through the skylight, a quarter-size hole in his temple.

Snake.

Men shouted from below. A blister of automatic gunfire ripped a pattern in the wall just behind Tony. He charged like a bull toward a cape and rushed through the open door.

He slid to a stop in the carpeted office.

"You're too late," the terrorist leader sneered, lifting his hand from the desktop keyboard.

The man stood with his back to the tinted window. Tony barely noticed him. His gaze was on the expressions of horror on the faces of his trussed-up family on the couch—and the muzzle of the AK-47 thrust deep into his wife's left breast. The huge guard holding the weapon towered over the trio. His steely expression was a challenge. He stood three paces away.

Too far.

The gunfire below intensified. Becker and the rest of them would be charging hard. Footfalls on the roof told him that Ripper's team had spanned the rooftops and would be pouring through the skylight at any moment. But none of that mattered.

In fact, if even one of them popped a head through the door, his wife would die.

Tony's muscles tightened into steel cables. He measured the distance to the man holding the gun. Then he slowly peeled his gaze from his pleading family and focused on the terrorist leader. "You're—gonna—die—slow," he growled.

"Perhaps," the man said. "But I won't be the only one." He casually removed his glasses and folded them into the breast pocket of his lab coat. It was as if he were no longer interested in seeing what was about to happen. His expression softened; he'd accepted the inevitable.

Reaching forward, he swiveled the desktop monitor around so Tony could see it. The video image was an interior shot of a lab or assembly area. A wheeled cart in the center of the room supported a dozen bricks of plastic explosives. They were bundled around a high-pressure canister the size of a scuba tank. An organized jumble of wires surrounded the device. They led into a black box with an illuminated digital timer.

The clock was ticking.

Forty-five...forty-four...

"Beck," Tony said without hesitation. "Explosives. Chemical ordinance. Ground-floor clean room. Forty seconds and counting."

The gunfire beneath them intensified. A shadow of concern flashed across the face of the man behind the desk. The man would be dead already, Tony thought, if the reflective coating on the large picture window behind him hadn't made it impossible for Snake to see into the room.

But any second now...

The shatter of window glass was followed by the heels of Ripper's boots. He swung into the office, sighted down the barrel of his MP5, and opened up on full auto. The terrorist leader was blown off his feet. His body twitched and jerked and then stilled.

Tony was already on the move. He bowled into the startled guard, swatted his rifle to one side, and landed an uppercut to the man's chin that made him topple backward. But the guard was no stranger to violence. He converted his fall to a tumble and rose with a curved dagger in one hand. His eyes calculated the shortest path to Tony's wife. The muted screams of Tony's gagged children spurred him on.

Ignoring the knife, Tony freight-trained forward and tackled the man. The guard was a mass of hard muscle. They fell away from the children and landed hard on the floor. Wind blew from the guard's lungs. But Tony's bear-hug tackle had failed to contain the knife. It slashed across his back. Tony roared from the pain, but he refused to let go. He poured every ounce of his strength into his arms. His face was buried in the crook of the man's thick neck and he welcomed the stench of him as he tightened his grip. Bones snapped, but still, another savage burn flashed dangerously close to Tony's kidney. Pain watered his eyes and Tony felt the first chill of fear. His grip loosened. He sensed the guard's arm cock back for a final thrust.

The guard's head snapped backward, and his body went limp. His blood-smeared knife dropped to the carpet. One of Ripper's combat knives was plunged to the hilt through his right eye. Ripper had thrown it from the opposite end of the room. He rushed forward and untied Tony's family. Tony pushed himself up, wincing from his wounds. His back burned, and felt wet with blood.

"Pops!" Tyler shouted after he ripped the tape from his lips. He rushed to help his dad.

"I'm okay," Tony said breathlessly. "Help your mom and sister. We gotta get outta here fast!"

He glanced over at the LCD monitor. Only fifteen seconds left. They ran out the door. The gunfire downstairs had stopped, but the relative silence was interrupted by the deep-throated roar of an engine, followed by a squeal of tires.

Chapter 64

Torrance, California

A BLISTER OF BULLETS SHREDDED THROUGH THE SHEETROCK above Becker's head. He ducked behind a forklift and returned fire. "Stay low! Pick your shots," he shouted to the two bangers behind him. The third was already down, a pool of blood spreading beneath his limp form. These kids are stupid-brave, he thought. With a little field training, they'd be right as rain, but right now the buggers were in way over their head. They crouched behind a row of fifty-gallon drums, and nodded to Becker as they rammed new magazines into their P90 submachine guns.

The terrorists had split into two groups. Half had holed up behind a pile of crates, directing its fire at Becker and his bangers. The other half focused its assault weapons on Papa and Street's crew, who approached from outside the roll-up door. The tangos had AK-47s and they knew how to use them.

But something else had Becker worried. He slid the muzzle of his rifle in the slot between the back of the forklift seat and its fuel tank, and sighted through the scope. There, suspended from coat hooks on a wall behind the vans, were two strange-looking vests. He focused the lens and confirmed the worst.

Wires hidden in the folds.

"Mind your targets," he said into the comm-net. "Suicide vests on the back wall could blow us all to hell." A chance detonation would kill indiscriminately, he thought. But for now the terrorists were trapped, good and sure. No place to go. As soon as Ripper's blokes drop in from the catwalk—

"Beck," Tony's voice was urgent over the comm-net. "Explosives. Chemical ordinance. Ground-floor clean room. Forty seconds and counting."

Becker's blood chilled. From the bangers' worried expressions, he knew they'd heard it, too.

"You've got to cover me, mates," he told them. "Give 'em the full tank, righto?"

Their eyes went wild. Toothy grins followed.

Becker set down his rifle and coiled into a crouch. The clean room occupied a space thirty feet away, midway between him and the enemy. But its semitransparent acrylic walls provided zero protection against a 7.62 slug from an AK.

Becker gave the signal. The two bangers popped their P90s over the top of the drums and opened up on full auto. The weapons sounded like twin chainsaws, spewing nine hundred rounds per minute at the tangos. Heads disappeared behind cover.

Becker bolted across the warehouse. He slid to a stop at the clean room door like a baseball player sliding into base. Staying low, he pushed through two sets of swinging doors and entered the room. Rows of waist-high cabinets and countertops on the opposite wall shielded his silhouette from view.

The positive-air filtration system was shut down, so it was warm in the space. But the deadly cargo on the cart in front of him made his skin tighten as if he'd just stepped into a freezer. There was enough C-4 in the room to obliterate the building and kill anyone standing within a hundred yards of its perimeter. And the chemical canister amid the explosives...

Bloody hell.

Outside, additional gunfire erupted from directly overhead. That would be Ripper's boys joining the fray. AK-47 fire answered in force. Men shouted. Some screamed in pain.

Becker crab-walked to the cart. The LED timer beside the apparatus read twenty-five seconds.

Twenty-four...twenty-three...

He studied the device from every angle. One hand traced the mass of wires. The other slipped his hunting knife from its holster. Five precious beats passed. Then ten. His breathing slowed. The gunfire around him disappeared from his consciousness. He identified two—make that three—separate booby traps.

He'd need more time...

A tremor shook his hand when he realized it was no use. He hadn't trembled since his aboriginal grandfather taught him how to dance with a fierce snake on his first walkabout. He shook his head. There was nothing he could do. Running was senseless.

The roar of an engine and a squeal of tires yanked his attention up. That's when he noticed the thin veil of frosted mist emanating from a tank in the corner of the room.

* * *

Tommy's Taco Truck

Lacey paced liked a caged leopard. "I can't believe I'm stuck in a taco truck right now!"

"Jeez, Lace," Marshall said as he shifted the joystick to change the angle of the overhead image. "You don't want to be anywhere near that place. It ain't a movie set."

The crackle of gunfire outside the van provided a grisly sound track to the images streaming on the screen. The smoke had cleared. Muzzle flashes jumped from the interior shadows of the warehouse door. Tracer rounds arced inward from the tree line in response. There were bodies on the pavement. One of them raised an arm as if asking for help.

"That's it," Lacey said. She grabbed a military-grade crossbow from the shelf and made for the door.

"What are going to do with that?!"

"I don't know yet. But I sure as hell can't sit here—"

Jake's voice crackled through a loudspeaker at the front of the truck. "Marsh, you there?"

Lacey gasped.

Marshall switched frequencies on his console. Jake's voice had come in over the truck's built-in dispatch radio. "Sweet mother, Jake! Where the hell are you?"

"I'm on the way, pal. Coming in high and hot."

"High and hot?"

"Stolen chopper. Five minutes out. Status?"

Lacey slid her cheek beside Marshall's to get to the microphone. "It's a war zone down here," she said.

"Tony's family?"

"They're alive, but we don't know if Tony—"

"Wait!" Marshall shouted. He flipped a switch and patched in the tail end of a message from the comm-net:

"Chemical ordinance. Ground-floor clean room. Forty seconds and counting."

"Goddamn it!" Jake shouted.

"Look there!" Lacey pointed at the screen as a white van shot out of the warehouse.

"Crap!" Marshall shouted. "A van's breaking away. No, make that two vans. Moving fast!"

"Marsh, I won't get there in time. You gotta keep track of those vans!"

"I'm on it," Lacey said, a plan already forming in her mind. With a roll of duct tape in one hand and the crossbow in the other, she launched herself out the rear door.

Chapter 65

Torrance, California

SEVEN SECONDS.

Becker shoved the bomb cart next to the frost-laden tank labeled LIQUID NITROGEN in the corner of the clean room. Using his vest as a makeshift glove, he twisted open the valve at the top of the tank. There was a brief hiss and the attached coil of high-pressure cryogenic hose jumped to attention as it filled with the liquid refrigerant.

Becker grabbed the discharge wand. With a silent prayer, he squeezed the trigger, spraying the minus-320-degrees-farenheit liquid on the bomb. He started at the timing device and moved down the leads to the bricks of C-4. Metal and wire frosted over. A spiderweb of cracks and ice crystals formed on the plastic explosives. One of the zip ties cinching the C-4 to the chemical canister broke into hundreds of tiny pieces. Then another. The cracks and snaps sounded like someone wadding up a sheet of cellophane. The LED timer stopped at three seconds—just before the lens clouded over. Becker held his breath. His insides felt as cold as the refrigerant.

Two seconds...one...zero...

A moment later he felt a grin twitch at the corners of his mouth.

The brief moment of hope vanished when he noticed the remnant of a label on the central canister: O-Ethyl-Methylphosphonothioate.

Holy Mother!

Silhouettes passed outside the walls and he knew that Tony and his family had made it downstairs. Safe...as long as the device didn't warm up faster than he hoped. He dropped the wand and used his knife to snap the remaining zip ties to free the cylinder of gas from its nest of explosives. He grabbed it.

As he made for the door, he noticed six chemical storage cylinders. The polyethylene tanks appeared full, neatly arranged beside a mixing vat and an assortment of raw chemicals and lab equipment. The infertility chemical, he thought. He felt a surge of relief. They'd arrived in time. The explosion would obliterate Battista's plan.

He bounded out the door.

"Clear out fast!" he shouted over the comm-net. "I bought us a few seconds but that's all."

The gunfire outside had died down. Both vans were gone. Becker raced after Tony and his family through the smoking roll-up door. On the way out, his gut wrenched tighter than an Australian *willy-willy* when he noticed that both suicide vests were missing.

* * *

Using the back of the truck as cover, Lacey stopped to cock the heavy bow. She lowered the tip to the ground, placed her foot in the stirrup, and pulled back with both hands, just as her brother had taught her. It wouldn't budge. She regripped and tried again, straining from the effort. Nothing.

"It ain't safe out here, *chica*."

Lacey jumped. The mountain that was Freddie had appeared out of nowhere. It was his job to cover the truck.

"I gotta stop a van," she said, relieved to see him.

He arched a brow. "With that?"

"No time for chitchat." She unclipped a bolt from the quiver and handed him the bow. "Just cock it for me and keep up."

She sprinted down the side alley. The echo of Freddie's footfalls faded behind her. There weren't many men who could keep up with her, running or otherwise. As she ran, she used the duct tape to modify the bolt. She slowed at the end of the last building in the row and peeked around the corner.

The first of the vans was a hundred yards away. It sped directly toward her along the tree line that bordered the north end of the industrial park. Gunfire erupted from the trees, the deep-throated crack of Papa's shotgun among them. She heard the solid plunks of lead puncturing steel. The van accelerated through the gauntlet. Lacey worried that it would pass her position before Freddie caught up with the crossbow.

As the van neared, a lone gunman stepped from the trees. He stopped in its path, twenty yards ahead of Lacey. It was Street. He held an Uzi in each hand and at the last possible moment, as the van bore down on him, he let loose on full auto. Twin lines of holes pockmarked the windshield.

The van didn't waver.

Neither did Street. He adjusted his aim downward. A shredded tire, the screech of metal on pavement, then the van lurched to one side, sparks flying, wheel catching on a cement parking block. The van launched into the air end over end.

Street belted out a defiant war cry. He skipped to one side, guns chattering in his hands as he emptied both magazines into the spiraling mass of metal.

Balls of steel, thought Lacey. She ducked behind the wall just as the van exploded in a fireball that singed the hair on her arms. Freddie caught up to her, breathless. He handed her the bow and took up a cover position behind her. She loaded the bolt.

"What's the plan?" he asked.

"Sh!" She held up a hand and cocked an ear. There was a distant squeal of tires, the throaty roar of a motor, a crescendo of additional gunfire. The second van, she thought. She checked around the corner but it was nowhere in sight.

"Ask Marshall which way the second van's heading."

Freddie complied, not thinking why she didn't ask herself. "West down the far alley. And that hombre is pissed. I'm supposed to bring you back to the truck."

"Yeah, right," Lacey said, already running. She flipped a middle finger over her head for the benefit of the Raven's camera. She sprinted west down the alley that paralleled the van's path. Eventually it would have to turn her way in order to get to the street that exited the park. Freddie fell behind.

She was thirty yards away from the next intersecting alleyway when the van raced across her path.

Shit!

Two beats later she slid into the intersection, dropped to one knee and sighted down the magnified scope of the bow. *I may not have the physical strength to cock this weapon, but I sure as hell can squeeze the trigger.*

Lacey adjusted her aim upward to compensate for the vehicle's acceleration. She let it fly. The modified steel bolt wobbled, but the force of the powerful crossbow was enough to true its flight. It embedded itself in one of the rear doors just before the van turned the corner and disappeared from view.

Chapter 66

THE CHOPPER WOULDN'T MOVE FAST ENOUGH. JAKE WAS FIVE minutes out, but his friends needed him now.

"The second van's getting away!" Marshall reported over the headset.

Dammit!

"Go after them, Marsh!"

"How am I supposed to do that? I'm in a friggin' taco truck!"

"Track 'em with the Raven."

"Don't you think I thought of that? I can't, man! We scrounged the bird but the control console didn't come with it. My transmitter has a max range of five hundred yards."

Once the van left the industrial park, it could head in a dozen different directions. One van, thousands of vehicles.

Becker's voice broke through. "We gotta stop that van, boss. It's carrying two suicide vests and I'm pretty sure they've got VX gas canisters on them."

The comm-net went silent. There wasn't a tough guy around whose blood didn't ice up at the mention of one of the deadliest biological weapons ever made. Jake's words caught in his throat. "V...X?"

"Or a derivative. I got part of a label. I'm holding a tank filled with the stuff."

Papa chimed in. "I got people running to their cars now but they parked so far away..." Jake's mind scoured a hundred possible solutions. Only one made sense—they needed to call in the cops, regardless of the jail time they'd face in the aftermath. Even then it could be too late to prevent the terrorists from finding a highly populated area.

"Wait a minute!" It was Lacey.

* * *

Five minutes later, Marshall and Becker were in the helicopter with Jake. "You've got to hand it to her," Jake said over the intercom. "She always comes through."

Marshall sat in the copilot's seat. "I can't believe it. Every time I think I've got her figured out, she pulls something like that."

"Quick thinking. Taping her earpiece to that arrow..." Jake said. He banked the copter northward.

Marshall's laptop was plugged into the instrument panel via USB. He shifted it to one side to shield the screen from the passing glare of the sun. "They're headed north on Prairie."

"Not many remote locations on that route," Jake said.

"All we need is a short stretch," Becker said from the backseat. He wound another length of duct tape—sticky side out—around an athletic sock that had two baseball-size bulges in it. A shoestring dangled from one end of the bundle. "Give me a hundred yards' clearance from any civilians and I'll take care of the rest."

"There's a golf course a mile ahead," Marshall said. "But the on-ramp to the 405 Freeway is this side of it."

"We can't let 'em on the freeway," Becker warned.

"Roger that," Jake said. He clicked the TRANSMIT button. "Papa, how close are you?"

The former gang leader was in one of three chase cars filled with very angry bangers. "Three blocks back, jefe. We'll be on them in thirty seconds."

"It's going to be close," Marshall said.

"You need to block the freeway and keep them heading straight ahead," Jake said. "We'll backstop them after that."

"Understood."

"Don't get too damn close, Papa. If those suckers flip the switch…"

He left the rest unsaid. This was nuts, Jake thought. So many things could go wrong. But if they could tie up this final loose end, they'd be home free. Sort of.

He watched the scene unfold through the windscreen. The van had stopped at the on-ramp intersection, its left turn signal flashing as it waited for a break in oncoming traffic. The chase cars had closed to within a few car lengths but intervening traffic separated them from the van.

"They're about to turn onto the ramp!" Jake warned.

He heard Papa's growl over the comm-net. His El Camino jumped across the double line into a snarl of oncoming traffic. Cars swerved out of his way. Jake saw an angry fist pop out of a window and he could imagine the blare of horns. A panel truck displaced a fire hydrant and a sudden geyser arched halfway across the boulevard.

The terrorists must have noticed the commotion behind them. The van jerked forward and braked twice as it attempted to nose through traffic. A bus skidded to a stop and the van broke through. But just before it made the on-ramp, Papa's El Camino broadsided it more efficiently than a border collie herding sheep. The ramp was blocked and the van's nose was redirected back toward Prairie. With no other options, it raced ahead, leaving a trail of tire smoke in its wake.

Time to go to work.

Jake pushed the nose forward and dumped altitude as he flew past the van. The sudden negative Gs caused the laptop to float for an instant above Marshall's legs. He clutched it to his chest, his eyes wide.

"Dude!"

Jake ignored him. This wasn't his Pitts and—natural stick or not—it took every ounce of his concentration to work the unfamiliar controls. When the chopper reached a point just beyond the service entrance to the golf course, Jake spun it on its axis right over the pavement. It hovered face-to-face with the oncoming van.

They were close enough that Jake was able to see more than fear on the driver's face. The man's eyes narrowed and his white-fisted grip on the wheel didn't waver. His passenger's hands waved back and forth. He seemed to be yelling at the driver as he motioned toward an open service gate to his right. The two remaining chase vehicles approached from behind.

At the last possible moment, the van swerved to its right and onto the service road.

Jake followed, keeping the van just under the chopper's nose. The service road skirted a fairway. A golfer waved his club at them as they raced past.

"You're up, Beck," Jake said.

The side door slid open and wind rushed into the helicopter. Becker had one hand gripped around a safety strap as he leaned out the door with his bundle.

"Get me ten feet ahead of the bastards!" Becker shouted into the headset.

Jake complied. The van disappeared beneath the windscreen and Jake shifted the attack angle so he could still maintain visual contact. The aircraft crabbed forward just ahead of the van.

"Closer!" Beck shouted.

Jake nursed the chopper lower. His eyes darted in a triangular pattern from the van to his instruments to the copse of trees dead ahead.

"Four seconds, Beck."

"I need five!"

Trees grew in the windshield.

"Two—one!"

Jake waited an extra half second before yanking back on the cyclic. The heavy blades bit into the air and the chopper swept up over the trees. There was a brief gut-wrenching jerk as the landing skid trimmed a branch on the way past. *Too close.* He banked into a steep climbing turn and glanced out the open doorway at the receding van. Becker's special delivery package was stuck just aft of center on top of the cargo area.

"Boom," muttered Becker. He held the shoelace in his free hand. Two grenade clips dangled from its end.

A beat later a massive explosion lifted the speeding van into the air and toppled it onto its side within a mushrooming fireball. All the windows had blown outward from the blast. No one inside could have survived. Several golfers sprinted toward the explosion, but they stopped and ran in the opposite direction when the two chase cars swept in with automatic weapons firing into the air to keep them from harm's way.

"Call it in," Jake transmitted.

"Already done," Tony reported. He'd been listening in from the command vehicle. "Police, fire, and hazmat will be on scene in two minutes. Clear out and meet us at LZ."

Jake turned toward the emergency helipad at the west end of Zamperini Field.

Things were finally going their way.

* * *

Seated at the command console in the taco truck, Tony signed off with Torrance PD before they could back-trace the 9-1-1 call. There was no advantage to broadcasting their involvement in today's events. A firefight and building explosion in an industrial park? Bodies everywhere? Followed by suicide bombers at a golf course? Christ, he and his friends would be tied up in the court system for years. Jobs lost. Lives ruined. So they'd gathered their

THE ENEMY OF MY ENEMY

three dead comrades—bangers who until now Tony could not have imagined he'd call friends—and split the scene before the cops arrived.

He propped his heels on a corner of the console. It was good to have his regular shoes on again. His feet still hurt like hell. His wife placed a hand on his shoulder and Tony allowed himself to relax for the first time in days. They exchanged a glance and a lifetime of feelings passed between them.

"Took you long enough to get here," she said in a thick New York accent.

"I was kinda busy."

"You're always busy."

"I heard you went down fighting."

She grinned. "Never mess with a Brooklyn mom when she has a frying pan handy."

"It was cool, Pops," Tyler said. He didn't look up from his PSP console. "Smacked him right upside the head."

"It wasn't cool, you idiot!" His sister, Andrea, elbowed him in the side. Her eyes were red and puffy.

"Hey! I'm playing a game here!"

"Cut the crap. Both of you," Melissa said.

Andrea crossed her arms with a sniffle. Tyler was lost in his game. "Boom. Head shot!" he muttered.

The truck pulled to a stop and Lacey called out from the driver's seat. "We're at the helipad. Chopper's coming in."

Tony rose, anxious to talk to Jake about what had happened between him and the Feds.

Chapter 67

THIS IS DISCREET?" FRANCESCA ASKED AS JAKE PULLED OUT the high-backed bar stool for her.

"As good a place as any," Jake said. Another set of emergency sirens faded in the distance. "We've taken care of Battista's local crew. The cops and fire department are cleaning up the mess."

"You're sure?" Marshall said. A waitress placed a bag of chips and salsa on the table.

Jake considered his answer. He still hadn't told his friends everything that had happened at Area 52. *So many dead*…and more were killed today at the warehouse and golf course. Death followed him. The faceless man with the sickle was angry that he'd been cheated by Jake's unexpected recovery. In the meantime, he lurked in the shadows with growing impatience, snatching life from those around Jake. Who would be next? Marshall? *Francesca…*

Sensing his concern, Francesca took his hand in hers and placed her head on his shoulder. It felt good.

"Yeah, I'm sure," Jake replied. Battista had gone to a lot of trouble to steal the artifact from the top-secret government installation, he thought. And he kicked up a massive hornet's nest in the process. He wouldn't stick around and get stung.

"I seriously doubt that the authorities are cruising the Redondo Beach Pier on the off chance of finding us," Jake added.

"And what the hell—after everything that's happened in the last few days, I think we've earned a Sunday afternoon at Naja's."

"Cheers to that, mate," Becker said, holding up a half-finished beer.

Tony, Marshall, and Lacey raised their mugs and chimed in. "Hear! Hear!"

Francesca lifted her water glass and gave a soft-spoken "*Salute.*"

Tony's wife scowled at her husband from a nearby table. She had one of those just-wait-'til-we-get-home expressions that made Tony twitch and Jake smile. Her mug was empty but her hands were full. She sat with Andrea, Tyler, Josh, and Sarafina amid an assortment of appetizers and sodas. Max sat attentively at Josh's side, tail wagging as he sniffed the air in anticipation of the next handout. Bradley had just returned from the bathroom to join their table. The teacher had found his rhythm through all that had happened. Like everyone else, he seemed at ease for the first time in days. He slid over his untouched beer and traded it for Melissa's empty glass. It brought a rare smile to her face.

She'd almost lost her life, Jake thought. Her children, too, if it hadn't been for Papa and Street and his boys. The gang was probably sharing shots of tequila at its hangout in South Central. They wanted nothing to do with the cops, so it was back to business as usual for them. But their participation had taught Jake a lesson he wouldn't soon forget. Turf and family trumped historical divides.

Could the human race do the same thing?

The rest of them were gathered around bistro tables at Naja's Place, one of the most popular hangouts at the pier. The hole-in-the-wall featured simple food, live music, and over eighty taps with one of the best selections of beer in the South Bay. A row of fishing boats was moored twenty feet from the open-air entrance. The boats swayed in the gentle ocean breeze. The aroma of fish and steamed crabs drifted in from a nearby restaurant, mingling with the scent of fries and onion rings from the kids' table. A dozen wall-mounted monitors streamed various sporting events.

"It's time to spill it, pal," Tony said. "I wanna hear about Area 52."

Jake hiked an eyebrow and motioned toward the kids' table. Though the other children remained intent on their food, Josh had tilted his sensitive ears in Jake's direction.

Tony understood. "Yeah...okay. At least give us the highlights reel."

Now was as good a time as any, Jake thought. "Here's the short version—there was another artifact. Battista took it."

"Holy sh—!"

Lacy elbowed Marshall in the ribs. Getting the point, he leaned forward and whispered, "You're kidding!"

"Wish I was."

"*Bastardo,*" Francesca said, pushing away her glass.

"We gotta find him," Tony said.

"Bloody right," Becker added.

Marshall's stunned expression said it all. "Are you guys nuts? By now he's probably halfway around the world. And good riddance, too. We don't want to be anywhere near that sucker!"

"*Somebody*'s got to stop him," Lacey said.

"You, too?" Marshall said.

"Marshall's right...," Jake said.

"Finally," Marshall said. "Someone with some sense. You dudes better listen to Jake. He seems to be the only one with brains in this outfit."

"...about Battista being long gone," Jake continued. "We can't find him on our own. We're going to need help."

"Oh, crap."

"That's why we're turning ourselves in tomorrow."

"Double crap!"

"Are you sure that's a good idea, boss?" Becker said. "The authorities aren't going to take kindly to everything we've done.

And besides, I'm not one for tight spaces, if you know what I mean."

Jake knew exactly what he meant. The thought of being confined in a prison cell made his nerves twitch.

"What about Cal and Kenny?" Tony added. "They're holed up in Mexico with federal warrants waiting for 'em. Stealing that plane was no prank. If the government calls it treason..."

Jake had already gone over and over it in his mind. He was worried about their friends, too, including Papa and his boys. But the proverbial cat was out of the bag. And when Doc regained consciousness at the underground complex, he'd call upon the full resources of the US government to find the men responsible for the attack. If Jake didn't turn himself in, he would be on the top of their list. However, he couldn't force his friends to accept the same fate.

"I can keep you guys out of it," Jake said. "But—"

There was a collective gasp from patrons seated at the bar.

"My God!" someone shouted, pointing to one of the video screens.

Every one of the television monitors had shifted to a breaking news broadcast. After a few startled shouts, the crowd in the bar quieted. Everyone focused on the streaming video. The grainy, smoke-filled scene jerked and shifted as if it had been recorded with a cell phone camera. At first Jake thought it was a scene from the warehouse district. But when the camera panned to one side, his throat closed tight. He rose to his feet in shock. There wasn't a child in the country who didn't recognize that landmark. It was Matterhorn Mountain. *Disneyland.*

A woman screamed. A mug shattered on the concrete floor. Sarafina shouted, "Daddy!"

A man wearing a Tequila Jack baseball cap pointed a remote at one of the screens. The volume kicked up.

"...the suicide attack occurred just minutes ago during the Celebrate a Dream Come True parade. Many were killed, dozens injured." The announcer's voice broke. "Dear God, the children."

Jake had heard enough. He turned from the screen to face the shocked expressions of his friends and loved ones. One of the terrorists had slipped away. How many more were there? He lifted Sarafina to his chest. She shivered under his grasp. Francesca joined their embrace, biting back sobs.

Bradley had sprung to his feet and stood transfixed under one of the monitors. His face reddened with a fury that Jake hadn't seen before from him. "Not the children," Bradley muttered. Josh leaned against him, his face filled with fear. Max whimpered at the sudden tension in the room. He scuttled closer to his young charge.

Tony's family had gathered within his protective arms. "You're right, Jake. We need help."

"It's time," Becker agreed.

Marshall and Lacey nodded in unison. They had white-knuckled grips on each other's hands. They stood as if to lead everyone out. "We're ready," Marshall said.

"Not yet," Bradley said.

The group turned his way.

"We can't just waltz into a police department with the children in tow," the teaching assistant said. Noticing that he'd drawn the attention of a couple at a nearby table, he lowered his voice. "What are you thinking?"

Jake hesitated. Everyone turned to him for direction. But he was all out of answers. He shook his head, "I don't—"

"I have a plan," Bradley interrupted.

* * *

Twenty minutes later, Jake, Tony, Marshall, Lacey, Becker, and Bradley were seated around a table in a private room behind Naja's kitchen.

"Good thinking," Jake said.

There were nods around the table.

"The kids have no business being a part of this," Bradley said. "They're scared enough as it is."

"Mel and Francesca will watch over 'em good," Tony said. "My mom will help."

There'd been more than a few tears when Francesca and Mel had driven away with the children. They were on their way to a friend's house in nearby Palos Verdes. Francesca had resisted at first. So had Melissa, who'd thrown around more than a few colorful words at the prospect of leaving Tony again. But in the end they knew it was the only way.

"I wish you'd gone with them," Marshall said to Lacey.

"Right," she said. "Like that was going to happen."

"So how're we going to do this, boss?" Becker asked. The toe of his boot did a woodpecker tap on the floor. It was the first time Jake had ever sensed nervousness in the Aussie.

"I'll get to that in a minute," Jake said, turning to face Bradley. "Are you sure you want to be here? The rest of us don't have much choice in the matter, but you've been an innocent bystander. It'd be easy for us to keep your name out of it."

Bradley appeared as if he was trying to stave off a sneeze. He held up a finger, as if asking for a moment. He pulled an inhaler from his pocket and sucked a blast through his mouth. Jake hadn't realized the man was asthmatic.

"Whew, I needed that," Bradley said. He glanced at his watch and smiled. "Anyway, thanks for the offer. But believe it or not, there isn't a place in the world I'd rather be than right here." He leaned forward on the table and whispered, "Let me show you why."

Curious, the group edged closer. Bradley removed a pen from his pocket and held it between his outstretched hands.

Becker sensed the threat first and sprang forward.

Bradley dodged his grasp. With a twist of his fingers, he snapped the pen in half. There was a hiss of compressed air. Jake felt a sudden wave of dizziness. The table rushed up to meet his forehead, and the last thing he saw was Bradley's satisfied smile.

Part IV

Chapter 68

M UDDLED DREAMS. EYES CRUSTED. LIMBS HEAVY.

Jake sensed Sarafina's presence beside him and sighed. Her breath was like an ocean breeze on his cheek. He draped an arm around her.

"How touching."

The voice sliced through his fog and Jake's heart rate tripled. He opened his eyes and sat up.

Luciano Battista stared at him from outside the thick shafts of bamboo that formed the perimeter of his prison cell. He wore a lab coat over pressed trousers. Abbas stood beside the terrorist leader, dressed in military fatigues. He held a four-foot aluminum pole that had a rubberized handle and trigger on one end, and a gripping clamp on the other. It reminded Jake of the tool used by janitors to pick up debris from the floor.

Jake was on a soiled blanket on the earthen floor of an eight-foot-square cell. Sarafina was curled beside him. So was Francesca. Neither of them stirred from their drug-induced sleep.

His mind flashed and the puzzle pieces of recent events snapped into place.

Jake was disgusted with himself. Battista had bragged from the onset that the purpose of the implant subjects had been to help spies infiltrate America. There had been three subjects unaccounted for. The first had died during his attempt to kill Jake and blow up Francesca's school. The second had masterminded the activities at the warehouse and had been killed by Tony. And the third was Bradley, the mild-mannered teaching assistant who'd baited Jake and his friends into the trap that had brought them here. With everything that Jake's new brain allowed him to do, it had done nothing to help him sense the man's duplicity.

Jake rose to face Battista. "Bastard."

"That's it?" Battista said. His voice was raspy. "After everything we've been through, the best you can come up with is 'bastard'?"

"Go to hell."

Battista ignored the comment. He gestured to the expansive space behind him. "Welcome to your new home."

The enclosure was the size of a basketball court. Stout rough-hewn columns supported a rusted aluminum roof fifteen feet overhead. Cinder-block sidewalls ended short of the ceiling and Jake saw a canopy of vegetation through the insect screen that covered the open-air gap.

The air was sticky and humid. The sound of cicadas, birds, and rustling leaves surrounded the structure. A howler monkey whooped. There were another half-a-dozen bamboo cells like Jake's along either side of the space. Armed guards stood at attention at the two exits. A group of dark-skinned men huddled in a cell at the far end of the building. From their ragged clothes and weathered features, Jake figured them for locals. But it was the two cells opposite Jake that captured his attention. Marsh, Lacey, and Becker were in one cell; Tony, his family, and Josh in the other. Even Max lay sprawled beside them. They were all unconscious.

Jake felt a primal rage. His body shook. If not for the bamboo bars that separated them, Battista would already be dead, he thought. "You are going to pay," he growled.

"No, Mr. Bronson," Battista said. He rubbed the ugly wound on one side of his neck and lower jaw. "It is *you* who is going to pay." He motioned to Abbas.

Abbas used the toe of his boot to pop the lid from a two-foot-tall basket on the floor. Battista took a step back. Abbas dipped the tip of the handler tool into the basket. His focus on the task was absolute. There was a rustle of movement. Abbas snapped the probe downward. Once. Twice. On the third try, he breathed a tentative sigh. When he lifted the probe, it gripped a three-foot-long writhing snake.

"Bushmaster," Battista said, maintaining his distance. "Deadliest viper in the western hemisphere. This one is but a baby."

Abbas eased the suspended snake between the bamboo bars of Jake's cell. Jake edged backward, keeping himself between the viper and the girls.

"It's known for its aggressiveness..." Battista continued.

Abbas jerked forward the probe like a fencer with a foil. The snake struck at the air, its anger focused on Jake. Venom squirted from its fangs. It thrashed and coiled about, desperate to be free of the claw that gripped it.

"And its speed."

Battista nodded. Abbas released the trigger on the handler and the snake dropped to the floor.

Jake jumped, barely avoiding the lightning-fast strike at his foot. The snake rushed toward the next closest target—Sarafina's bare ankle.

Reflexes took over and time slowed.

The viper cocked its neck, mouth wide, fangs locked into strike position. Jake lunged, fingers outstretched. The snake started its forward strike, venom glistening, inches from Sarafina's skin. Jake snatched its neck. Cool reptilian texture within his grasp. A violent yank. The viper flew across the cell to smack against the bamboo bars. Its blood spattered on Abbas's astonished face.

The entire move had taken less than a second, but the effort caused Jake's heart to pound like a sledgehammer against the inside of his chest. It staggered him.

Battista's voice was steady. "We have many snakes, Mr. Bronson. We are surrounded by them." He motioned to Francesca and Sarafina. "You won't always be so close at hand. Do you understand?"

Jake was bent over like a runner after a marathon, hands braced on his thighs. He sucked in another lungful of air. He glanced at Sarafina's sleeping form and said a prayer of thanks. He was shocked—and grateful—that his reflexes had kicked into gear. If only for a moment.

"From this point forward, you will do exactly as I say. Without hesitation. Because if you make one false move, even if it's just a smart remark that rubs me the wrong way, I will see to it that your friends and loved ones taste such pain and anguish that even Dante would be shaken."

Chapter 69

J AKE SQUINTED AGAINST THE MORNING SUN. HE STILL WORE
the coveralls he'd taken from the lockers at Area 52. The fabric felt sticky against his skin. He massaged the muscle of his upper arm. It ached from the injection they'd given him. It was a counteragent to the gas that Bradley had administered. Battista wanted Jake awake. Francesca and the rest of them were still unconscious.

Two guards escorted him across the grounds of the large installation. The hopelessness of his situation sank in further with each step. The facility was in a half-mile-square clearing surrounded by a hundred-foot-tall wall of canopied trees. Mountainous terrain and rolling jungle stretched in every direction as far as Jake could see. Inside the tree line he counted a dozen structures and a beehive of soldiers. A wind sock and hangar in the distance signaled the presence of an airstrip. Nearby, a yellow bulldozer spun tracks as it felled an encroaching copse of underbrush. A golf cart traced a course along the perimeter, spewing a fog of insecticide. The sporadic crack of gunfire echoed from the opposite end of the camp. The lack of reaction from his guards told him the gunfire was expected.

A week earlier he'd been flying free and easy in his Pitts. Now he was at a terrorist training camp in the middle of a rain forest. Hell, he didn't even know what country he was in. He had no plan, no means of escape, and his heart was on the edge of failure. So why did a part of him feel at peace? Was it resignation? Or had his messed-up brain finally slipped over the edge into insanity?

Battista had finally won, right? He'd outsmarted Jake at every turn. And in an ultimate display of his superiority, he had imprisoned nearly everyone Jake cared about, including the children—

Jake stopped in his tracks; his mind went into afterburner. *And that,* he realized with a start, *was your ultimate bad move, Luciano Battista. You think you can control me because I have so much to lose. But the truth is, you will never allow any of them to live, will you? So, I now have* nothing *to lose. Saving the world, saving my friends, saving my life—all impossible because you placed me in a no-win situation.*

One of the guards prodded his back with an assault rifle. Jake accepted the nudge and moved forward. He walked taller. His mind drifted to the pleasure he would take in bringing Battista's world down around him. He imagined the look of shock on Battista's face when he realized that an American infidel could display a resolve that was second to none, even if it meant the sacrifice of his loved ones. He anticipated the satisfaction of crushing the man's scarred throat with his bare hands...

It was in that moment that Jake realized the ancient alien visitors had been right all along. Man's violent nature *was* instinctual. The argument was unassailable. When faced with his life being short-circuited by another, even Jake felt the call. *Violence begets violence,* he recited the biblical concept in his head. After a moment's thought he added his own twist: *but extermination leads to peace.*

The guards again urged him forward. Jake picked up the pace. The military called it MAD, mutual assured destruction, where the force used by opposing factions is great enough to ensure the total and irrevocable annihilation of both the attacker and the defender.

Jake examined his surroundings with a different eye.

Memorizing. Plotting. *Targeting.*

He noted the throaty hum from a pair of diesel generators as he and the guards approached the largest building on the site. Unlike the other structures, which appeared renovated from an old mining camp, this one was new. It resembled a double-wide hangar, with aluminum roof and sidewalls and a fresh coat of camouflage paint.

There was a wall-mounted keypad beside a security door. One of the guards entered a five-digit code and Jake was escorted inside. The cool blast of air conditioning was a welcome change. The cavernous space had been divided into two major work areas. The overhead lights on one side had been turned off, but a snapshot glance into the shadows was all it took for Jake to memorize everything he saw. The sight shook him at first. But only for a moment.

Perfect.

The guards urged him to the opposite side of the building. Battista, Abbas, and a dozen techs and scientists stood in a semicircle. They watched as he approached. Jake suppressed a flash of anger when he noticed Bradley beside the group. He wore a bandage across one cheek and the area surrounding it was red and swollen.

They studied Jake's approach. A few of the unfamiliar faces appeared eager to meet him. Others looked as if they would like nothing more than to slit his throat. Jake wasn't surprised to see the inverted alien pyramid on a raised dais behind them. The unusual vibration it emanated—one that only he could hear—had announced its presence the moment he'd woken in his cell. It was illuminated by an overhead rack of halogens and surrounded by tables supporting computers and analytical equipment. The equipment looked top-notch but the layout lacked the sophistication of what he'd seen at the underground facility in

Nevada. The mini from Area 52 that he'd stowed in his pocket was missing. But he sensed its presence in the room like an alcoholic smelled liquor in a bar. It could buy him the time—and *speed*—he needed.

For now, he would play along.

Chapter 70

BATTISTA MOTIONED TO THE PYRAMID. "IT'S AN EXACT DU-
plicate of the one from my home."

Jake shifted uneasily. The mention of Battista's Afghan home
was accompanied by more than a few glares from the men surrounding him. Scientists or not, they likely had friends and
relatives who had been killed as a result of Jake's assault on the
mountain stronghold. Until Jake could set his plan in motion, he
needed to pique their interest, establish his bona fides, and keep
them at ease. "I'll bet there're a lot more of them planted around
the planet, traps just waiting to be triggered."

"Assuming what you told us about the first one is the truth,"
Battista said.

"Oh, it's the truth all right," Jake said, grateful for the opening. "When the visitors arrived twenty-five thousand years ago,
they witnessed a simple but violent species. At the time we posed
no threat to anyone but ourselves. But the aliens surmised that
one day our brains might evolve to the point where we'd be able
to tap into the infinite power of the universe. When that happened, they wanted to know about it. Because then, we posed a
risk beyond the bounds of our planet, and they'd deal with it as
necessary."

A bespectacled scientist stepped forward. He was older than
the rest and his curiosity had temporarily blunted his contempt.
"Infinite power of the universe?"

"That's right," Jake said, pleased that the man had taken the bait. "Which means no need for power plants, nuclear reactors, solar collectors—you name it. Energy doesn't need to be produced mechanically." He made a sweeping motion with outstretched hands. "Because it's already all around us. It exists in every bit of mass, from the smallest subatomic particle to the largest star in the universe…"

Time to set the hook.

"And mankind has the ability to tap into it telekinetically."

Glares vanished. Curious glances were exchanged. Even Battista seemed intrigued.

"You can do this?" the scientist asked.

Jake nodded.

"Show me."

Jake motioned to the man's pocket protector. "Let me see your pen."

The scientist handed it to him. Jake supported it in his palm. The group edged closer. Clearing his mind, Jake braced himself for the headache that would follow. Using his mind this way had become more taxing with each attempt. He wrapped his thoughts around the pen and slowly lowered his hand.

The pen hovered. Gasps from the group. One man uttered a prayer in Dari.

The pen rose and even Jake marveled as he willed it to spin like a propeller. It was easier than he expected and he realized that the mini's proximity had already boosted his abilities. He felt strong. No headache. He imagined he could fling the pen with enough force to penetrate the aluminum roof. He fought the temptation—and the giddiness that came with it—and instead released his hold and allowed the pen to drop to the concrete. No fatigue. But his heart rate increased.

The lead scientist had taken it all in stride. He'd obviously been briefed about Jake's abilities. He pocketed his pen and said, "Can you explain the science behind it so that it can be duplicated mechanically?"

"Not entirely. But the answers reside in the object."

"And how do you know this?"

"Because I connected telepathically with the…other one. Before it took off."

The scientist glanced at Battista. He confirmed Jake's statement with a nod.

"And you can do this again?"

"I think so."

The scientist considered Jake for a moment. Then he stepped aside and motioned to the obelisk. "Then let us proceed."

Jake hesitated. "Not so fast," he said. He needed to hide his eagerness. "I want assurances."

Battista said, "What assurances?"

"The children—"

"Will all be killed if you don't do exactly as you're told," Battista said.

Bradley shifted uneasily.

"And if I do help?" Jake asked. "Won't they be killed anyway?"

Battista hesitated. Jake saw the man's wheels turning, weighing his response. *Carrot or stick?* It didn't matter either way. Jake's course was already set.

Battista scratched the wound on his neck. He seemed to draw a perverse pleasure from the discomfort it caused him, as if it fueled his resolve. "This is the last time you will receive a warning. You shall follow Farouk's instructions or Abbas will return to the cells and introduce one of the children to the hazards of the Venezuelan jungle."

Venezuela.

As if on cue, the hoot of a howler monkey drew Jake's thoughts to the thick overgrowth that seemed to stretch on forever beyond the camp. He'd read about it during one of his brain-gorging sessions. The jungles of the Venezuelan rain forest were known for the extreme dangers they posed to human trespassers.

Snakes weren't the only issue. It was filled with jaguars and crocs. Clouds of malarial insects targeted anything with warm blood. Waterways teemed with man-eating piranha, and it was said that the electric eels called *trembladores* could electrocute a man with 440 volts.

An outpost in Venezuela made sense. Jake had read that a growing number of Iran's paramilitary shock troops had been welcomed here by the anti-American government. Battista would have found a friendly ally here just as easily, especially if he'd shared his plans for attacks on their common adversary.

Jake and his friends were surrounded by men who hated Americans. They'd squeeze what they could out of him and discard their captives without a second thought. And the jungle made escape impossible.

All the more reason to continue on track.

Allowing his shoulders to slump in feigned resignation, he blew out a long breath and turned his attention to the scientist, Farouk. "Okay, let's get started."

Chapter 71

Marine Corps Air Station Miramar
San Diego, California

DOC STUDIED THE SCENE THROUGH THE ONE-WAY MIRROR. Former sergeant Pedro "Papa" Martinez was cuffed to a chair in the interrogation room. Lieutenant Colonel Brown stood red-faced in front of him.

"Up yours, *pendejo!*" Papa said. "I ain't telling you shit." He spat on Brown's polished shoes.

Doc grunted. The lieutenant colonel's demanding approach was all wrong. He muted the sound from the room and turned his attention to Timmy. "I need to do this my way."

The kid only nodded. He was slouched in a chair. His eyes were red, his expression lifeless, the boyish enthusiasm vanished. Doc could understand it; he felt the same way. Every one of their coworkers was dead at the hands of the men who had stolen the obelisk—the same men who had apparently kidnapped Jake and his friends.

"Is the video set up?"

Timmy looked up. His eyes were moist. "I—I can't look at it again, Doc."

"I know. You don't have to." Doc pointed to Papa on the other side of the glass. "But he needs to see it."

Timmy nodded. "It's ready to go next door."

Doc placed a hand on the young man's shoulder. "We're going to get through this, Timmy. Don't give up on me, okay? I'll bring Martinez into the fold. Don't worry about that. But in the meantime, I need you back in the control room to see what you can learn from the satellites."

Timmy rubbed his nose with his sleeve and stood. "I can do that."

"If anyone can, it's you," Doc said, and he meant it.

Homeland Security had circled the wagons in the aftermath of what had happened at Area 52. The full resources of the US government were now at Doc's disposal. But all that stood for nothing unless they could figure out where Jake had been taken. He hoped like hell that the man in the next room could lead the way.

Doc keyed the microphone beside the one-way mirror. "Bring him next door, Colonel. There's something I want him to see."

* * *

"*Madre de Dios*," Papa whispered.

Doc paused the video. The image froze on the sneering face of a man wearing a blood-splattered hazmat suit. He wore no hood and his hands were gloveless. Blood dripped from the knife he'd wielded to slit the throats of the two dozen unconscious men who had been sprawled around in the room.

"Do you know this man?"

Papa shook his head.

"There's more," Doc said. He clicked the remote to jump to the next bookmark and hit Play. Bodies lay motionless on the floor in front of a row of lockers. A wardrobe door slowly opened. A man stepped out, slipped on a pool of blood. Jake. Papa stiffened at the sight of him. On the screen Jake rushed to open a nearby locker. He pulled out a body, propped it up, and checked for a pulse. A nod, then another locker, another unconscious body. The limp form was Doc.

"You were there," Papa said.

"Jake saved our lives by stuffing us into those lockers."

Papa nodded. "He would've saved the rest, too. If he could."

"I believe that."

An exchanged look.

"You were in Afghanistan with him, weren't you?" Doc asked. "You know all about the pyramid."

The comment struck a chord; Doc saw it in Papa's face. But the man remained silent.

Doc's tone softened. "I don't know everything you've done, either in Afghanistan with Mr. Bronson or back here in the last few days. I know lives were taken. And even though the men who died may have had it coming, it was not sanctioned by a governmental authority. Some would call that murder..."

Instead of cowering, Papa sat taller in his chair, as if proud of what he had done.

"...but not me," Doc continued. "After everything I learned from Jake about what happened—Battista, the kidnapping, and even about the obelisk—I would name you a loyal friend. I believe you did what was necessary to correct a wrong and prevent the slaughter of hundreds, if not thousands, of innocent Americans."

Papa's expression softened. Doc sensed he was getting through. The man wanted to help Jake—that was obvious. But the former gang leader had to be worried about the ramifications of admitting his involvement.

Doc added, "I can promise you—"

"I don't need your promises," Papa interrupted. "Jake saved your life. That tells me you're okay. And if you're saying that I can help save Jake and our friends, then I believe you." He held up his cuffed wrists. "So let's get off these cuffs and get to work. And when this is all over, if you need to lock me up for the things I've done, then so be it."

Doc liked this man. He nodded to one of the guards to remove the cuffs. Doc extended a hand. Papa rose and clasped it in his own.

"I'm proud to know you, son," Doc said. "Friends call me Doc. And before you interrupt again, let me finish what I was saying." He looked Papa squarely in the eyes. "I can promise you one thing. You help us now and I'll lever the full force of the government to see that you and your friends are granted immunity."

Papa smiled. "Hell, Doc. You don't have to feed me that crap. I'm already on board. Besides, you and I both know you don't have the authority to back that up."

A commanding voice boomed over the loudspeaker. "You're right, Sergeant Martinez. Dr. Finnegan doesn't have that authority. But I do."

Doc couldn't help but grin at the astonished look on Papa's face. There weren't many people in the country who wouldn't recognize the voice of the president of the United States.

Fifteen minutes later, they were in a briefing room with Lieutenant Colonel Brown and a dozen other military types. A couple hard-edged team leaders sat across from Doc. One represented SEAL Team 1 and the other was from the CIA's Special Operations Group (SOG). Even though Doc was in charge of the group, he admitted to himself those two made him a bit nervous.

Papa, on the other hand, seemed right at home as he answered another question from the SOG leader. "That's right. One of the vans got past us. Two dudes wearing kill vests. Jake and Beck took 'em out at the golf course."

An angry-looking suit from Homeland Security interrupted. "And in the aftermath more than a dozen emergency personnel died from the VX oil that was dispersed, goddamn it."

"We couldn't have known that the vests were laced," Papa reminded him. "In any case, the death toll could have been ten times as many if we'd let 'em get to the freeway."

"What about the hundred twenty-seven dead at Disneyland! Apparently that killer got past you, too, didn't he? You should've called it in. But no, you and your glory-seeking friends had to go all vigilante on us. You're going to pay for that!"

The mention of Disneyland brought a flash of sadness to the sergeant's face. But his expression hardened just as quickly. The soldier ignored the suit's outburst as he would a barking dog chained to a post. He directed his attention to the team leaders and said, "We split up afterward. Jake and the rest of them went to the beach bar."

The angry suit stood up and pointed a finger at Papa. "You listen—"

"Sit down and shut the hell up!" Doc ordered. "We need to keep our eye on the ball here, understood?"

The suit's face turned beet red, but he knew better than to mess with the president's man. He sat down.

"How do you know there aren't more of them out there waiting to blow themselves up?" Doc asked.

Papa grimaced. "Can't know that for sure, Doc. But according to Tony's son, he saw three vests when they allowed him to use the bathroom. They're all accounted for."

Doc nodded. Then he directed his attention to a large wall-mounted display. Timmy's image filled the screen. He was seated at a computer console in the control room. "Any luck on a location?" Doc asked.

"Still nothing," Timmy said. "We're backtracking the sat-logs, but there are literally tens of thousands of permutations and possibilities. They obviously had the escape route set up months in advance. They would've switched vehicles several times in underground garages. Were they in one large vehicle or several smaller ones? Did they stick together or split up? If we proceed under the assumption that they left the country, was it by plane, car, or boat? We're checking them all, looking for patterns that will connect the dots. In the end we'll find them, but without something more to go on, it could take days."

Doc felt his gut tighten.

The SOG leader asked, "How many hostages?"

Papa answered, "Including the four children—eleven. Three of the adults are women. Oh, and then there's Max, too."

"Max?" Doc said.

"Yeah, Josh's dog."

"Wait a minute," Timmy interrupted. He sounded excited. "Josh is the blind kid, right?"

"Yeah, so?"

"God, please," Timmy said, leaning into the camera so that his face filled the screen. "Tell me Max is a guide dog."

"Well, sure, but—"

"That's it!" Timmy shouted. "I'll be right back!"

The video image went black.

"What the hell was that all about?" the SOG leader said.

Doc couldn't contain his smile. "That, gentlemen, is genius at work. Gather your teams."

Chapter 72

Venezuelan rain forest

JAKE'S BODY REACTED TO THE PROXIMITY OF THE MINI. Weariness vanished. His mind embraced a clarity of purpose.

The upside-down pyramid was cradled within a metal framework in front of him. Its black square surface shimmered under the spotlights. He ran his hands across the images etched into the perimeter. They were cool to the touch. He marveled at the details in the images of early man's bloodthirstiness—exactly the same as on the obelisk from the cavern in Afghanistan. This is what the otherworldly visitors saw, he thought. It was also what they feared. But why not deal with us then and eliminate the risk? He suspected that destroying Earth's inhabitants would have been child's play for them. He'd wrestled with the question repeatedly, always arriving at the same conclusion:

Hope.

Hope that man would embrace the sanctity of life and overcome his violent tendencies. It was a hope that Jake no longer shared. He glanced toward the darkened side of the warehouse and shook his head. *Sorry, E.T., it ain't gonna happen.*

"What are you waiting for?" Battista's voice interrupted his thoughts. The man stood several paces back from the device.

Good question. "Don't rush me. I don't want to launch the damn thing."

Battista backed up a step. He'd been incapacitated during the previous launch. It had almost cost him his life.

Jake had been studying the device for hours, trying to unlock its secrets. He returned his attention to the group of irregular shapes that formed a circle around the center of the surface. Unlike the etched perimeter images, these shapes were embossed with various textures and vivid colors. To most people, the shapes looked nonsensical, like a child's renderings of clouds, or snow-men, or a seemingly random scatter of raised dots and smooth indentations. But to Jake's synesthetic brain, the texture, color, and shape of each pattern represented a distinct prime number.

He laid a hand on one of the shapes and the device responded with a shift in the harmonic vibration he felt in his head. No one else in the room sensed it. Each shape emanated a different tone. In Afghanistan he discovered that three of the shapes were math-ematically and harmonically distinct from the remaining eight. Activating two of them with his hands and the third with his telekinetic ability had triggered the device. It had momentarily paralyzed him while it scanned his brain to confirm the existence of his advanced abilities. Then it had launched itself into space with its false message. Back in Area 52, he'd secretly hoped to find a way to embed this one with a different message.

"It's like a keyboard on a computer," he said. "One sequence of keys will launch it. There has to be another that will allow us to access its hard drive."

"How can you be certain?"

"When the first one scanned me, there was a moment when information flowed in both directions. That's how I learned its purpose. I felt...an intelligence. It's artificial, like a learning com-puter, and the technology is way beyond our capabilities. But to my way of thinking, it's still just a machine. That means there's got to be a way to interface with it."

* * *

Battista considered the American's words. He couldn't shake the feeling that the man was hiding something. He seemed oddly energized, even hyper. Yet he'd made no progress whatsoever with the machine. Battista's sense of achievement at manipulating the American had been replaced with a gnawing sense of unease. He'd learned long ago to trust his senses in such circumstances. There was no room for complacency in his life. Too much was at stake. Yes, he wanted to master the secrets of the object, but not at the risk of his other plans. He'd give Bronson one final opportunity.

"You have until tomorrow at noon," he said. "Solve it by then or you and your friends will be of no further use to me."

The American remained silent. He returned his attention to the device.

Battista turned and made his way toward the door at the opposite end of the warehouse. Abbas and Bradley were at his side.

"You may eliminate the prisoners tomorrow," he said.

"All of them?" Abbas asked with an eagerness that Battista understood, but didn't appreciate.

"Yes."

Bradley faltered, but said nothing.

It prompted Battista to reconsider. He thought of the twelve-year-old boy, Ahmed, who had been the only friend his dead son had ever known. Besides Bradley, Ahmed was the only implant subject still alive. He'd been taken into custody following his failed attempt to martyr himself in Afghanistan, and was being held in an American mental institution. That was a situation Battista would deal with soon.

"On second thought, allow the girl to live," he said, recalling how close the two children had been when they'd lived together at the institute. "She may yet prove useful."

"Yes, sheikh," Abbas said.

As the trio continued toward the exit, Battista glanced at the darkened area of the warehouse. Prior to his arrival in the camp, it was being used to design and assemble small-yield nuclear weapons. The joint Iranian-Venezuelan plan had been simple: Iran provided the enriched materials and expertise. Venezuela provided the secure location, ancillary equipment, and personnel. The suitcase-size weapons would be smuggled into the United States amid the thousands of illegal Mexicans who crossed the border each month. Position them in major cities and detonate them simultaneously—a glorious stroke that would cripple the American economy and permanently scar its inhabitants.

Battista had thought it a bold plan, but there was a glaring downside. What the Americans lacked in spiritual values, they more than made up for in resilience and technological resources. The risk of discovery was high, and retaliation would be unforgiving and decisive. So when the Iranian and Venezuelan leaders learned of Battista's more subtle, *permanent* approach, they put their plans on hold. Whatever Battista needed, they would provide. By the time the Americans discovered what had been done to them, it would be too late to do anything to stop it. In time, their entire population would simply cease to exist.

The bombs need never be used.

Chapter 73

I T WAS THREE IN THE MORNING WHEN THE GUARDS ESCORTED Jake out of the research area. Each step took him farther from the rejuvenating effects of the mini. The day's mental efforts with the obelisk hadn't borne fruit. And it had taken a serious toll on his system. By the time he reached his cell, an intense weariness had overtaken him.

The guards shoved him into the empty cell. He stumbled to the floor. They secured the thick bamboo gate with a chain and padlock and then relieved the guards posted at either exit.

"Daddy!" Sarafina shouted from across the space. She rushed to the wall of her cell. "I knew you'd come back!" Francesca stirred beside her. They'd been moved from his cell to join the rest of his friends. There was a hushed murmur as one by one they rose to their feet. Max barked a greeting.

"Silence!" one of the guards ordered. He unslung his assault rifle and brought it to the ready position.

Everyone quieted. A few of the local prisoners at the far end of the makeshift prison stirred.

Jake pushed himself to his feet. Francesca drew Sarafina to her side, and her penetrating gaze never left him. He felt her presence in his mind and it soothed him.

Though it required more mental energy than he could spare, he queried her thoughts. *You okay?*

She nodded. So did Sarafina.

Jake had to steady himself against the bamboo bars. He'd nearly lost consciousness from the simple thought transmission. He'd felt a tightness in his chest. His body was failing him. Francesca's troubled expression told him she'd noticed. He straightened himself and offered her a reassuring smile. Then he turned his attention to the rest of the group.

They'd lined up behind the bamboo bars of their cells. Marshall and Lacey holding hands, with Becker standing beside them. Mel and her children were pressed up against Tony, while Josh held on to Max. Beneath their worn and tired exterior, Jake sensed an undercurrent of readiness, like a football team lined up for the kickoff. Even the kids seemed a part of it. Josh knelt to keep Max quiet. The rest of them watched Jake intently. It was as if they were waiting for him to drop the first domino that would lead to their escape.

He wondered if they'd really been sleeping at all, especially Tony and Becker. The two former soldiers would've dreamed up any number of contingency plans, waiting for the right moment or opportunity. In spite of their circumstances, they appeared hopeful. Jake wasn't about to take that from them. A part of him was glad they were separated and unable to speak. He'd rather not lie to them in the final hours of their lives.

Tony shifted slightly and motioned toward his daughter, Andrea. She'd edged backward between him and Mel so that her hands were out of the guards' view. Her fingers flashed three separate signals. After a brief pause, she repeated the motion. Jake recognized them as sign language, but he had no idea what each of the symbols represented. Andrea shifted her gaze toward Jake's hands and repeated the process. He got the hint, and mimicked the motion. She nodded and transmitted three new symbols. Jake understood. She was teaching him the alphabet in sign. He motioned for her to continue. She started with the first three symbols—A, B, C—and kept going. He memorized them easily.

As she finished, one of the guards approached and motioned them back from the bars. He mumbled something in Spanish that Jake couldn't make out. While his back was turned, Jake flashed a quick message to Andrea. "*I got it.*"

Andrea nodded to Tony. She and the rest of them moved deeper into the cells and sat down. Jake did the same, making sure he was outside the guard's sight line.

And so they communicated. Jake signed and Andrea whispered a translation to her father and the others. He told them about the soldiers, Battista, and the obelisk. He fueled their hope by hinting that he had a plan, but that it depended on finding time alone with the obelisk.

"Beck says he can help with that," she signed.

That got Jake's attention. He signed, "How?"

"Be patient. He—"

The lights went out.

* * *

Starlight spilled through the screened gap between the aluminum roof and the cinder-block wall. Jake could make out the silhouette of one of the guards pacing the rows of cells. The buzz of cicadas and other jungle insects seemed to increase in volume in the still space. Someone snored in a distant cell.

Jake wondered what Becker had up his sleeve. The Aussie was the most resourceful man Jake had ever met, a Down Under MacGyver. But what the hell could he do in this situation? The last sign Jake had received from Andrea was "be patient." Not the easiest thing to do under the circumstances. But what choice did he have? He wrapped himself in the blanket and pretended to sleep.

Thirty minutes later the muezzin's call to prayer sounded over loudspeakers throughout the camp. This would be *fajr*, he thought, recalling the lessons he'd first learned from Battista's pupil, Ahmed. The predawn prayer. Which meant sunrise was an hour or two away. The door at the far end of the building opened and a shaft of moonlight cut through the darkness. The guards stepped outside and closed the door behind them. Each had a prayer rug under his arm.

Footsteps and a shadow outside his cell. "Good to see ya, mate," Becker whispered. He crouched down, fiddled with the padlock, and was in Jake's cell in less than ten seconds.

"Jesus, Beck. How'd you get a key?"

"There are always keys around, Jake. A man just has to know where to look." He held up two twisted bobby pins. "Got these beauts from Melissa's hair." Becker took the blanket from Jake's shoulder and wrapped himself in it. "They've bundled some clothes across the way to make it appear as if I'm still in my cell. Now I'll play you so you can do what you gotta do. Get moving. Lock me in when you leave."

Jake didn't hesitate. Fueled by a surge of adrenaline, he secured the padlock and rushed out the exit.

Keeping to the shadows, he made his way toward the central building. Other than the muezzin's call over the loudspeakers, the camp was relatively quiet. A couple jeeps patrolled the distant perimeter, more to discourage wildlife than anything else, Jake guessed. The distant roar of a jungle cat sent a primordial chill up his spine and seemed to confirm his analysis.

Jake reached the secure door just as prayers ended. He punched in the security code, slipped inside, and headed straight for the pyramid. The mini was on the counter where he'd left it. He grabbed it, welcoming its cool touch, savoring the surge of energy and clarity that infused him. Fatigue vanished. His senses sharpened. It was as if *life* in its purest state coursed through his veins, regenerating his organs, his bones, his muscles. He sucked in a huge breath of air. He'd never felt better.

Time to go to work.

Forty minutes later, the tactical nuke was nearly complete. His hands moved with the precision of a watchmaker—at blurring speed. He tightened the series of machine screws around the spherical beryllium pusher shell that surrounded the plutonium-239 isotope. He knew the effort was taking a toll on his heart, but so what?

He was surprised how easy it was to build a version of the most devastating weapon ever made. What was once held as one of the world's most secure secrets was now available to anyone with Internet access. Jake had memorized every detail of the process several weeks earlier. Of course, he could also recite virtually every recipe from *The Joy of Cooking* by Irma Rombauer. At the time he actually thought he might be able to use that knowledge to impress Francesca. Instead, he was assembling the nuke that would kill her—and anything else within a two-mile radius.

Everything was in place. His mind traced each facet of the device, double-checking the wiring and assembly against the schematics from his memory. Confident with the results, he flipped open the panel to reveal the timing mechanism. His hand hesitated over the ten-key pad.

Jake was ready to die. He'd been ready for months. But the woman he loved? His unborn child? His friends? They weren't prepared. One moment, here; the next, nothing.

If only he'd remained hidden following his escape from Battista's mountain. But no, he'd been weak. He used the alien threat as an excuse to justify seeking help from his friends. Now they would die because of it.

Damn. Was he really going to do it? Wasn't there something, anything, he could do to help them escape? He'd been through it over and over again. It wasn't that the solution eluded him; there simply *wasn't* a solution.

He glanced at the obelisk at the other end of the warehouse. Earlier he'd hoped that linking with it might help. He'd tried one combination after another with the symbols, hoping to find the sequence that would gain him access to the device. It was no use. Nothing had worked. He knew how to launch it, but that was the *last* thing he wanted to do.

No, he was out of options. They would all die here, one way or another. Better that it be swift and painless.

Jake set the timer for ninety minutes and left the building.

* * *

He was ten paces from the prison structure when distant gunfire erupted from one of the patrolling jeeps. Tracer rounds arced into the trees. Sirens sounded over the loudspeakers. Lights came on, doors flew open, and armed men stormed out of nearby barracks. They sprinted toward the gunfire. Jake ducked into the shadows behind the cell blocks. Any hopes of slipping back into his cell unnoticed had vanished. And when he got caught, Becker would pay the price.

There was a barked order and one of the soldiers split from the main force and ran in Jake's direction. He flattened himself against the wall and willed the jihadist to look the other way. Instead, Jake's rushed entry into the man's thoughts drew startled eyes in his direction. The muzzle of the soldier's assault rifle swiveled. A short warning burst peppered the dirt at Jake's side. Bits of gravel bit into his shins. A door swung open and the two prison guards rushed out, weapons raised. Jake tensed. With the mini in his pocket, he thought he could take all three of them, but he wasn't certain. He didn't want to die out here. Alone. He needed to see Francesca and Sarafina one final time. He dropped to his knees, threw both hands over his head, and begged for mercy.

"Don't shoot!" He shouted as loudly as he could so that Becker would hear him inside the cell block. "Please!"

The soldiers rushed forward. One trained his weapon at Jake's head. The other searched him. He pulled the mini from

Jake's pocket and it felt as if the oxygen had been sucked from the air. The man tucked the device into a compartment on his utility belt. Jake's body gave in to the stress of the accelerated pace he'd forced upon it over the past day. He sagged to the dirt, his heart pounding against his rib cage. His gasps for air seemed in vain. The other guard kicked his legs.

"Up!" he ordered.

Jake pressed his palms to the dirt and pushed. But before he was halfway up, his strength gave out. His cheek hit the earth with a dull thud.

The guards grabbed him under both arms and dragged him to his cell. The third soldier stood guard outside the building.

Jake was dazed, but still conscious. He exhaled a sigh of relief when he saw that Becker was back in his cell with Marshall and Lacey. The door to Jake's cell was wide open.

"How did he get out?" one of the guards whispered in Dari. There was fear in his voice.

"By Allah, I do not know!" the other guard said. They dumped Jake into the cell. "I thought he was sleeping."

The first guard hefted the padlock as if to examine it. Jake sat up. "Next time, lock the door, dumb shit," he mumbled, hoping to prevent an inspection that might reveal that the lock had been picked.

The man turned on him and kicked him in the stomach. Jake rolled away. The guard struck again. His steel-toed boot dug into Jake's kidney. White-hot flame radiated from his lower back. A wave of nausea brought him close to puking. A shout from the guard stationed at the door interrupted the beating.

"They're bringing in another prisoner!" the guard reported.

The two guards standing over Jake exchanged worried glances. "The sheikh will surely follow," one of them said. "He need not know that this one almost escaped."

"Agreed!"

They rushed to relock the cell gate. A moment later a group of soldiers entered with a bedraggled Hispanic in tow. He was filthy and unshaven. Even from ten paces away, the aroma of sewage emanated from the man. The group neared Jake's cell, and what he saw jolted him like a live electric current. Papa Martinez offered Jake a sly wink as he was dragged past the cell. He puckered his lips and whistled the first bars of a song that any red-blooded American patriot would know. Jake started whispering the lyrics to the tune before he even realized he was doing it.

From the halls of Montezuma...

The butt of a rifle stifled Papa's whistle, but not Jake's excitement. The looks of shock from his friends across the corridor told him that they got the message as well. *The cavalry has arrived.* Jake sensed the swell of hope that radiated from the group. They believed the end of their ordeal was close at hand.

They had no idea how right they were.

Chapter 74

Venezuelan rain forest

TWENTY MINUTES LATER, THE SUN WAS UP. THE CALL TO prayers had passed. Sounds of activity outside. Vehicular movement. An officer issuing orders. The footfall of trotting soldiers. The normal sounds of a military encampment coming awake. Jake's internal clock told him he had less than thirty minutes to disable the bomb. He was still dog tired, running on adrenaline. But he wasn't dead yet.

Papa had used tactical hand signals with Becker to fill them in about the plan. The rest of them had coordinated with sign language. Everyone was ready. Jake gave the nod.

A moment later Lacey let out an Oscar-winning, bloodcurdling scream. She collapsed to the floor of her cell, writhing and shaking in a violent seizure. The guards rushed to the cell, uncertain what to do. Marshall and Becker crouched to calm her. A flailing hand smacked Becker in the nose and he staggered backward. Lacey rolled to one side. Her blouse was unclasped and a tanned breast spilled out. Marshall reached to cover her up when she abruptly rose to her knees, doubled over, and retched. Marshall's surprise was genuine and Jake knew what was coming next from his weak-stomached buddy. He vomited beside her.

The scene riveted the guards. Neither noticed the flurry of activity in Papa's cell at the end of the building. He'd removed the worn length of rope holding up his tattered pants. A twist of his wrists and the cord split into four lengths. He affixed three to the hinges of the cell gate and twisted the fourth around the padlock. A whisper to the other men in his cell and they moved to the back wall. Then he pressed a finger to one ear and muttered something to whoever was listening at the other end of his inner-ear comm unit. When he got the response he was waiting for, he shouted at the guards.

"*Oye, pendejos!* What's up over there?"

His use of English had an immediate impact. The guards spun and made their way toward Papa's cell. By the time they were halfway there, Becker was already crouched by the padlock of his cell.

"I asked you a question, *hijos de la gran putísima*," Papa sneered. His finger was still pressed to his ear.

The guards drew closer. Jake tensed for the final countdown. The first guard drew abreast of the gate. Papa uttered an order over the comm-net. A rash of distant gunfire sounded outside. The guards froze. The first one noticed the cord, and shouted, "*Moazeb bash!*"

Too late. Papa had already turned his back and transmitted the signal to the miniature detonators embedded in each length of det-cord. The muffled explosion ripped the bamboo gate from its hinges. The blast lifted the first guard off his feet in a spray of skin-shredding bamboo slivers. The second guard stumbled backward but maintained his footing. Jake watched in horror as the jihadist raised his assault rifle. The scene slowed in his mind. The muzzle rising. Flashes of fire from the barrel. Papa moving to shield the cowering prisoners behind him. Bullets stitching a line in the floor. Becker launched in the air, leading with the heel of his boot...

The full force of Becker's 190-pound charge struck the guard at the base of the head, snapping his neck and propelling him forward. The rifle went flying. The man was dead before he hit the ground. For a moment, the echo of gunfire was the only sound. It was replaced an instant later by Francesca's scream.

Papa lay still on the floor. Smoke drifted upward from a line of holes running up his back. The former gang leader was dead.

* * *

The rattle of gunfire woke Battista. He sprang to his feet.

The door to his private room flew open and Abbas rushed in. "We are being attacked!"

"Of course we are, you fool!" Battista growled as he pulled on his camouflage trousers. "Get out there and do something about it!" Abbas raced out the door, shouting orders. Battista cinched the laces on his boots, threw on his shirt, and pushed out the door.

A jeep and two Humvees kicked up clouds of dust as they sped east toward the attack. Abbas led the charge in the jeep. Two others were with him. One of them manned the .50-cal machine gun mounted in the rear. Three dozen soldiers raced after them on foot. More of them poured out of nearby barracks and followed.

The scene startled him. It was a disconcerting feeling for the master strategist. This was a move he had not anticipated. Rather than rushing into the fray, however, he analyzed the situation. His forces were under attack. The camp operated under the full authority of the government. Their only enemies were local tribes, and they didn't carry automatic weapons. Rage rose from his core as the inevitable truth hit him. *Americans!* They were the only ones with the technology and gall to launch an operation deep in the heart of a sovereign nation. They must have arrived by air.

He pulled the comm unit from his belt and issued an order to one of his commanders. "Deploy your SAM teams. They will have air support."

Battista's eyes narrowed on the dust trail left by the vehicles and the mass of soldiers running toward the threat at the eastern perimeter...

By Allah! he thought with a start. He switched frequencies. "Abbas!" he shouted into the mouthpiece. "It is a feint. The prisoners!"

Chapter 75

BECKER PEEKED OUT THE DOOR OF THE PRISON STRUCTURE. "All clear," he whispered to the stack of people behind him. He pointed the AK-47 at a point in the distant tree line. "That's our exit. Don't stop running until you're well into the jungle. Someone should be there to lead us to the planes."

Jake was at the back of the group, gripping an AK. He and Becker had taken the weapons from the two dead guards—Beck because he knew how to use it, and Jake because he was too weak to carry either of the smaller children. Tony was near the front of the line, Papa's body slung over his shoulder.

No man left behind.

Melissa, Andrea, and Tyler were beside him. Andrea seemed close to hyperventilating. Tyler had a gleam of excitement in his eyes. Marshall held Josh. Max pranced in place at his side. His tail beat rapidly against Marshall's pant leg. Sarafina had latched onto Lacey's chest. Francesca stood beside her. She turned and leaned to one side to look past the heads of the six locals who stood in front of Jake. Their eyes met and a world of emotions passed between them. He saw the muscles of her jaw pulse. She was determined to make it out with their baby. It was his job to cover their back.

If only I had the mini, Jake thought. The third guard had left with it after his capture. There was no telling where it was now.

He'd pulled Tony and Becker aside earlier and told them about the nuke. Their initial shock had been quickly replaced with steely determination. They had twenty-five minutes before the bomb went off. They needed to get in the air ASAP.

"Now!" Becker ordered. He brought the assault rifle to shoulder-ready position and pushed through the door. The rest of the group followed on his heels. By the time Jake exited, Becker and Tony were already twenty paces ahead and moving fast. Jake struggled to keep pace. Adrenaline was his friend, but it wouldn't last long. His heart rate doubled. He ignored it and swiveled the rifle from side to side and behind, looking for threats.

In the distance, a line of vehicles and men sped in the opposite direction, lured by the decoy fire from Papa's allies. But a single set of wandering eyes could change that in a beat. The lead jeep in the pack opened fire on the tree line with its .50-cal. Even from two hundred yards away, the rumble of the high-grain rounds found its way to Jake's bones.

Tyler's shout returned Jake's attention to the front. "Come on, Jake!" The nine-year-old boy was a natural athlete, MVP of his soccer team since age six. The kid was fast. He'd noticed that Jake was falling behind and returned to urge him on. His pop's son in more than just looks, Jake thought. "You can do it!" Tyler said, running backward beside him. "Keep your eyes forward and I'll watch your six."

Jake didn't argue. He pushed ahead.

"Lever down one notch," Tyler added.

"Huh?"

Tyler pointed to the assault rifle. "You've got the safety on. Flip the lever down one notch for full auto!"

"Christ," Jake muttered. He adjusted the lever and looked at Tony's son with a newfound respect.

Tyler grinned. "Call of Duty. Best game ever!"

They were a hundred yards from the jungle when the boy shouted, "They're turning!"

Jake swiveled and took a knee. "Keep running," he yelled between heaves of breath. The kid sprinted to join his family.

The lead jeep was two hundred yards away and closing fast. It was headed on a cut-off course toward the tree line. The gunner opened fire and time slowed. Dirt exploded among his friends. They scattered. Two of the locals were blown off their feet. Tony went down and Papa's body tumbled from his shoulders. Max leaped into the air with a startled yelp. A trail of tracer rounds punched its way toward Lacey, Marshall, and the children. Francesca screamed.

Jake pressed the stock of the AK to his cheek and squeezed the trigger. The gun chattered in his unsteady hands. He raked the sight picture through the jeep's path. One of the rounds must have hit pay dirt because the vehicle veered suddenly and headed straight for him. The .50-cal continued to fire. Pocks of exploding dirt closed in on him. Jake's AK clicked on an empty magazine. The jeep kept coming. A cry of rage burst from his throat.

He dodged to one side and shouted to his friends, "Run!" He'd never make it to the tree line in time, but with a few more seconds, they could. Jake rose to his feet. He was too weak to sprint, but none of that mattered. He shouted in defiance and charged the oncoming vehicle.

The gunner adjusted his aim.

In the stretched instant when Jake realized that death was coming, a single wonderful thought infused his mind.

Love...

Francesca and Sarafina were safe. The rest of his friends, too. And suddenly Jake knew that everything was as it should be. He embraced the peacefulness of the moment, splaying his arms in the air to welcome the round that would end it all.

The jeep swerved violently to one side thirty yards away. It nearly toppled over in a cloud of dust. The gunner was thrown from the rear as the jeep lurched to a stop. The driver and front passenger were in a fierce struggle. The gunner pushed to his feet and moved toward them. One of his legs dragged limply behind him. He drew a sidearm.

Jake shifted positions to place the jeep between him and the gunner. That's when he recognized the two men still in the vehicle—Bradley and Abbas. Teeth bared, knives slashed, and a trail of blood arced in the air. Jake stumbled forward, breathing hard. Bradley had just saved his life.

Jake was unsure what he could do in his weakened state, but he sure as hell wasn't going to sit by and watch. He moved toward the two fighting men. He felt a surge of renewed vigor that he assumed was fueled by the last drops of adrenaline in his system. The men continued grappling. The passenger door at Bradley's back sprang open. Abbas kicked and Bradley spilled onto the dirt. Blood darkened the front of his shirt. His eyes met Jake's.

Abbas shouted to the approaching gunner, "Kill the American!"

Jake's mind cleared. Everything happened at once.

The gunner rounded the vehicle.

Abbas cocked an elbow. His throwing knife dripped with blood.

Bradley pulled something from his pocket and tossed it.

Abbas loosed the knife. Jake dove forward and grabbed the mini from the air. Time slowed. Jake's limbs and muscles came alive. Abbas's blade tumbled end over end, tiny droplets of blood spinning from its tip. He snatched it from the air and snapped his wrist in a powerful side throw that would have looked like a blur to Battista's right-hand man. With a loud thunk, the blade buried itself to the hilt in Abbas's forehead. His wide-eyed stare remained frozen as he toppled to the ground.

A beat later Jake's shoulder drove into the gunner's gut. The shocked terrorist flew backward. The pistol spiraled from his hand. He grunted in pain as his injured leg twisted beneath him. Jake retrieved the pistol, turned, and shot the man twice in the chest. There was no hesitation. Jake had long since stopped wondering whether killing was a justified means to an end. Hell, not long from now every living thing in a two-mile radius would be dead at his hand.

He rushed to Bradley's side. The teaching assistant's face was pale, his breathing labored. A bloody hand pressed against a wound in his gut.

"I'm sorry, Jake."

"Shut up," Jake said. He removed his shirt and wadded it up.

"Th—they were going to kill Josh."

Jake handed him the shirt. "Press this against the wound. How bad is it?"

Bradley grimaced.

The sounds of gunfire from across the camp changed in pitch. The feint from Papa's allies had played itself out. Battista's forces were headed this way.

Bradley shook his head. "L—leave me."

"No way," Jake pulled the man to his feet. Bradley groaned in pain. Jake hefted him into the jeep's passenger seat. He ran around to the other side, yanked out Abbas's body, and slid behind the wheel.

* * *

The path through the trees was barely wide enough to accommodate the jeep. Jake leaned closer to the windshield to avoid getting whipped by low-hanging vines. "Keep your heads down!" he warned.

Tony ducked. He sat in the passenger seat beside him. He and Becker had waited at the tree line for Jake. Bradley was slouched in the backseat with Becker.

"There's a clearing half a click ahead," Becker yelled. "The rest of them should be there by now."

"Christ, Tony," Jake shouted, as he pushed the jeep to its limits down the trail. "I thought you were a goner."

"Yeah, me, too. The slug hit Papa's body and knocked me on my ass. Even in death, that tough Mexican saved my life."

Heavy gunfire flared behind them. Bullets ripped through the foliage. The jeep hit a straightaway and Jake floored it. In the trees ahead, a pair of SEALs waved them forward. The heavy throb of a CV-22's rotors filled the air. Its silhouette buzzed toward them above the canopy. Jake caught a brief glimpse of the gunship as it passed overhead. The underside bristled with weapons. Twin rockets leaped from its wing-mounted pods and Jake heard the chainsaw buzz of its Gatling gun. Explosions shook the ground behind them. Battista's men would be scattering.

"Hoorah!" shouted Tony.

They sped past the SEALs and broke into a clearing. A second Osprey was nestled amid an expansive stand of tall grass. The wash from its rotors whipped the grass into a frenzy of swirls that emanated outward like waves in a storm. Birds scattered from the surrounding trees. The ramp was down. Marshall leaned out and waved them forward. More explosions in the distance behind them. The gunship was buying them the time they needed. They had twenty minutes to clear the area before the nuke went off. Plenty of time, Jake thought. Battista would never threaten his friends again.

Ashes to ashes.

The jeep skidded to a stop. Tony jumped out and gave Becker a hand with Bradley. The two men lifted him out of the vehicle. Bradley winced in pain.

"Hurry," Jake ordered. "Get him inside." He turned to Marshall. Lacey stood beside him on the ramp. "Morphine!" he shouted.

"No!" Bradley said as they carried him up the ramp.

"Whaddya mean, no?" Tony said.

"N—not yet." Bradley's words were forced. He stared at Jake. "There's something I must…"

Jake leaned closer.

"The sheikh…" Bradley said. His eyes were glassy and his words were separated by labored breaths. "Chemical…in the water…LA."

The mention of the infertility drug set Jake on edge. "Save your breath, Brad. I know you're sorry. In the end you changed your mind. That's what matters. In any case, we stopped it. All six bottles are toast."

Bradley shook his head. He struggled to gather enough air to form his words. He tried to say something but the words wouldn't come. His breathing slowed.

Jake tried to comfort him. He whispered in his ear. "You saved us. You saved the children. Allah will forgive you. And the sheikh will never harm anyone again. In another few minutes, this jungle is going to blow sky high."

Bradley grabbed Jake's lapel. His eyes were pinched in pain. He coughed blood. "Seven bottles," he gurgled.

Jake's blood froze. The teacher took two wheezing breaths and his lips formed around his final words. "H—hidden…helicopter." His body sagged.

The words cut into Jake's core. There was still one more canister—and Battista had an exit plan. He snapped around his head and gazed at his friends and loved ones. His fingers caressed the mini in his pocket. His mind raced. The two SEALs who had provided rear cover ran toward the ramp.

No choice.

Jake rose and took Francesca in his arms. His walls had collapsed. She knew what was happening. He entered her thoughts.

All my love…

All my life…

He kissed her and said, "Take care of our child."

Francesca's sobs electrified the group.

"What's going on?" Sarafina said, her eyes brimming with tears.

Jake crouched to her level and she swarmed into his arms. "Don't go, Daddy!"

"My darling child, my heart has been yours since the day we met in Venice. A sweeter soul than yours doesn't exist. You need to be strong. For yourself. For Francesca. And…for your baby brother." He ushered her into Francesca's waiting embrace.

"Brother?" Sarafina sniffled.

Francesca's lips opened in surprise.

"Yes," Jake said. "It's a boy. Don't ask me how I know; I just do. And he's special, Francesca. Soon you'll sense it, too. He might even be the harbinger of a *new* human race. Better, smarter, stronger. Protect him."

The SEALs stormed up the ramp. Cal shouted from the cockpit. "We're outta here!"

Jake stepped to the edge of the ramp.

Becker and Tony moved to his side. "Whatever you're doin', I'm goin' with ya."

"Don't you dare!" Melissa shouted from the forward area. Tyler, Andrea, and Josh were strapped down beside her on the inward-facing seats. Max was curled beside Josh. The four surviving locals cowered across from them.

"What the hell's going on, Jake?" Marshall said. He started to unbuckle his safety belt. Lacey was already on her feet.

"I gotta go, pal."

Marshall rose. "Screw that, dude!"

"Bad word!" Josh yelled.

Max barked.

"Everybody stop!" Jake shouted.

The engines revved. The rotors picked up speed. He raised his voice over the noise.

"Listen to me. All of you." He snapped the assault rifle from Tony's grasp before his friend even saw him move. "Live your lives! Count each day as a blessing. Don't worry about alien visitors. They probably don't even exist anymore. And even if they did, the soonest they could arrive is forty years from now. In that time, mankind can change. We've seen it. Gang members working hand in hand with cops and ordinary people like you and me." He motioned to Bradley's body. "A devout terrorist changing sides because of the innocence of children. *That* is man's nature, too. In the end, that part of us *will* prevail."

The CV-22 began to rise. "See that the world takes a lesson from what we've done. We can accomplish anything if we stick together. And Battista will be no more. That's my parting gift to all of you. Instead of death, I offer you life!"

He leaped into the air.

By the time Becker and Tony peered over the edge, Jake was racing toward the jungle in the jeep.

Chapter 76

Venezuelan rain forest

JAKE DREW ENERGY FROM THE MINI, INFUSING EVERY FIBER of his being with its unnatural fuel. He felt exhilarated. Nothing could stop him from doing what must be done. Nothing but death, he corrected himself. But he'd fought it off before and he could do it for a few more minutes. Then he'd welcome it. It was his time. His heart was in its last throes anyway. And his friends were safe.

The jeep burst through the trees and headed toward the center of the compound. Bodies littered the ground. Three vehicles smoldered dead in their tracks. The gunship was overhead. Cal must have ordered it to hold back and cover Jake.

Dammit. Get the hell out of here!

The aircraft's nose swiveled from side to side, looking for new targets. Its missile pods were empty, but the Gatling was still a threat. Battista's forces had either melted into the jungle or retreated to the shelter of the buildings.

Jake floored it. The gunship followed. Its shadow sped alongside the jeep.

Battista was somewhere in the compound. He wouldn't risk taking off with the gunship in the vicinity. And there's no way he'd leave without the obelisk. Jake steered toward the main structure.

In the distance, a group of soldiers popped out from around a barrack. Two of them held bulky objects over their shoulders. Twin flashes—

Jake spun the wheel. The jeep fishtailed in protest, kicking clouds of dirt from its wheels. The surface-to-air missiles weren't intended for him. Their contrails painted a straight line toward the gunship, which was directly overhead. At such a short range, they couldn't miss.

Jake stomped on the gas. The missiles impacted the aircraft with a thunderous explosion. The fireball singed the hair on Jake's head. The jeep surged forward, and debris rained down around him. One of the Osprey's thirty-eight-foot-long rotors cartwheeled across his path. Jake veered to the right and barely avoided it. He steered a course that would put the main structure between him and the terrorist fire team.

That's when he caught sight of Cal's CV-22. It was headed away from the compound, and climbing toward the mountains. If he could see it, so could the fire team. Jake turned back toward the terrorists. Even from two hundred yards away, he could see they were reloading the bulky weapons.

His eyes darted back and forth between attacker and target. The jeep flew across the dirt. Fifty—sixty—seventy miles per hour, bouncing over ruts and swales. The loaders completed their task and stepped back. The shooters swiveled their aim.

Jake couldn't stop them in time. His mind screamed for a solution. Flashes of light. Twin contrails. A flood of panic swelled from his gut.

"No!" He slammed on the brakes.

The missiles arced in tandem as the CV-22 veered hard to one side. Streams of infrared-sensitive chaff scattered in its trail as Cal tried to decoy the missiles. But the projectiles couldn't be fooled. They didn't waver. Which meant—

Jake returned his focus to the shooters. Time rushed past him. His brain was already ten steps ahead of his body's reaction.

The missiles were laser-guided. The shooters needed to maintain their aim through impact. He flashed on the image from the obelisk with the humanoid figures, where the mini hovered above them and shot beams of energy into the heads of the tribesmen.

It all happened in the same beat: he jumped from the jeep, held the mini before him, aimed at the shooters, imagined the vulnerable textures of their brains. The mini warmed and pencil-thin beams of pure energy shot from it.

The shooters collapsed. So did the three soldiers beside them.

A sharp pain in Jake's skull. The mini tumbled from his hands. He pressed his palms against his temples and dropped to his knees. Through pinched eyes he saw the missiles corkscrew into the jungle and explode harmlessly beneath the canopy.

The CV-22 disappeared beyond the horizon.

Then nothing.

Chapter 77

A WAVE OF COOL AIR BROUGHT JAKE BACK TO HIS SENSES. HE was indoors.

Battista's gravelly voice ordered, "Over here."

Jake tensed. The guards on either side of him felt it and tightened their grip. Each had one of his arms draped across a shoulder.

As they dragged him across the floor, he felt the bulge of the mini in one of the men's pockets. It gouged into Jake's side with each step. He welcomed its proximity.

They were in the main research building. A group of soldiers hammered nails into the crate they were building around the cradled obelisk. The top was still open.

Jake had been unconscious for a minute or two, but his internal clock had kept ticking. A glance toward the opposite end of the building confirmed that the bomb-assembly area was undisturbed.

Twelve minutes and counting...

Jake found his legs and used them to walk the last few paces to where Battista waited. The guards adjusted their hold. They twisted his arms behind his back and escorted him forward.

"Quite impressive, Mr. Bronson," Battista said. "You never cease to amaze me."

"You ain't seen nothing yet, asshole."

"Arrogant to the end. And vulgar. Like the rest of your countrymen."

"We just call 'em like we see 'em. And what I see is a bitter old fart with illusions of grandeur."

Battista's neck muscles twitched beneath his scar.

Jake pushed harder. "You think you're quite the master strategist, don't you? But in the end, you've been beaten silly by a bunch of Americans whose only claim to fame is their willingness to stand up for their friends."

Battista's face flushed, but he didn't take the bait. "A familiar situation we find ourselves in, wouldn't you say?"

Jake couldn't disagree. He flashed on their confrontation in the sacred cavern. The similarities were unnerving: he was surrounded by Battista's soldiers, an alien obelisk nearby, his friends heading home in the CV-22. He shrugged. "Whatever."

"Except this time, my primary mission has already been accomplished. Whatever happens from this point forward cannot change that." His expression was smug.

Jake didn't want to reveal that he knew about the seventh canister. The best way to learn of its location was to let the man brag about it. "Yes," Jake said tentatively. "You murdered women, children, and families while they laughed and cheered during a parade at an amusement park. You must be so proud. Such a fierce warrior."

The words brought a smile to the terrorist's face. "You Americans are so predictable. Because we embrace the past, you think we are out of touch with the present. We honor our faith in traditional ways and you call us backward. We reject your modern technologies and you think us simpleminded."

Keep talking, you son of a bitch.

Battista continued, "But it is you whose judgment is clouded by the rhetoric of a corrupt government, weakened by your materialistic obsessions, stifled by your never-ending desire for more, and blinded by your righteous insistence on forcing your superficial values on others. The rest of the world sees you for what you are—an infection of decadence and faithlessness that threatens the fabric of our world. It must be dealt with by aggressive treatment. That you cannot see it for yourself is mystifying. It is also inexcusable. It is time to put an end to you. Once and for all."

Jake feigned a puzzled expression.

"Aah," Battista sighed. "I see your confusion. A part of you has realized you're not quite as smart as you thought you were. Yes, your actions have created some difficulty for me, but nothing that cannot be easily dealt with. I lost a few pawns, even a rook or two. But the match is still mine, Mr. Bronson."

Nine minutes to go.

Jake's nerves were on edge. Time was his enemy. He needed to discover the location of the final canister. Or, God forbid, the target it had been used against. He fought to maintain his composure. Battista's need to gloat was his only hope.

"The deadliest blow is the one your opponent never sees coming," Battista said. "Feint to the left, strike from the right, yes?"

"Disneyland was a feint?"

Battista's chuckle was contemptuous. "It's exactly the kind of attack you would expect from a backward people, isn't it? All eyes turned to the horrifying event, making it so much easier for us to plant the seed that will lead to your annihilation. Today, the water supply of Los Angeles. Tomorrow, every major city in America."

"Poison in the water? That's your grand plan?"

"Not poison. In fact, it's nontoxic. Your high-tech, water-processing screeners will never notice it. It seems only fitting that the so-called harmless chemical is a by-product from the manufacture of rubber and plastics—essential underpinnings to your technologically dependent society. And it's thanks to you that its true usefulness was revealed."

"Thanks to me?"

Seven minutes.

"The analysis of your brain allowed us to perfect the implants. The chemical was discovered by one of the recipients. You never met him. He was killed by your friends in Torrance, but not until after he uncovered its secret. You see, it has a very unique property." He smiled in anticipation of his next words. "Once ingested, it attaches itself to the ovarian follicles in women, rendering them infertile."

Jake's anger was real. "You bastard."

Battista beamed with delight.

"Interestingly," he added with the nonchalance of a professor speaking to a group of students, "it's being used quite effectively in Asia to control the rodent populations. We merely modified it for a more deserving demographic. By the time your scientists realize what has happened, it will be too late. The damage is irreversible. Your government will want to strike back. But against whom? You can't kill an ideology. You will scream and shout, but the end result will be the same. No more children will be born, your population will age, and America will be no more." Battista's chest swelled.

"Too bad for you we blew up your supply."

A cloud passed across Battista's face. It disappeared just as quickly. "You caused a minor delay. That is all. In any case, enough of the chemical remained for us to prove our point with our allies. Six hundred thousand residents around Silver Lake will provide a good start, wouldn't you say?"

Silver Lake!

Time to move. Jake shifted his weight and the two guards tightened their grip. He used the opportunity to lean into the guard who had pocketed the mini. Jake felt a surge of energy.

Battista noticed. A pistol appeared in his hand, aimed at Jake's heart.

Jake ignored it. He stomped on an instep, twisted free, yanked the mini from the pocket of one guard and a curved knife from the waistband of the other. More guards rushed forward. Then everything seemed to slow down. Sound deepened.

Jake dodged to one side. The pistol went off. Once. Twice. Like the boom of a bass drum. *Missed.* Jake spun and then he was among them. Eyes wide, teeth bared. The knife slashed. A throat. A spray of blood. A step forward. A plunge and twist through an artery. He ducked and smashed the mini into a man's temple. He was a killing machine. Hands reached toward him. Severed fingers tumbled away. Blood everywhere. More men. Weapons unholstered. Jake's mind calculated angles, prioritized threats, and commanded his body to respond. He ducked, slashed, kicked, and rolled through them. Bones snapped, throats crushed, eyes pierced. Nothing could stop him—

There was a sudden staccato of automatic gunfire. Screams. Gasps. Death cries. Wounds blossomed. Men toppled around him in a twist of limbs and blood. Multiple exit wounds through a man's back splattered gore on Jake's face.

Then there was a white-hot fire in his shoulder and Jake was lifted off his feet. He crashed into the open crate that encased the obelisk. The mini flew from his numb fingers and tumbled across the floor. The abrupt disconnect stopped him cold. His heart was an out-of-control jackhammer. Battista stood three paces away, his face contorted in rage. The assault rifle in his hands was at waist level. It leaked smoke from its barrel. More soldiers rushed toward them from the far exit.

Not going to make it.

Battista lifted the rifle to firing position. He sighted down the barrel with deadly intent, aiming at Jake's head. He squeezed the trigger.

Click.

The gun jammed.

Half a breath and Jake's body would collapse on its own. There was a single desperate move still available to him. He sprang to his feet, spun around, and placed his hands on top of the obelisk.

Chapter 78

Venezuelan rain forest

SIX *MINUTES.*

Jake placed his hands on two of the textured glyphs circling the center of the inverted pyramid. The instant he touched it, he felt the familiar surge of energy. It was accompanied by a harmonic resonance that bounced off the walls. Battista was suddenly beside him, grappling desperately at Jake's hands, knowing what he was up to. Jake held his ground, took a deep breath, and focused his mind on a third symbol.

Push.

All three symbols gave way like keys on a computer. The device responded immediately, just as its twin had when he had accidentally triggered it in Afghanistan. Jake felt a pulse coming from deep within the obelisk, like the hum of an immense turbine.

Battista was beside him. His hands tightened reflexively around Jake's wrist. From the terrorist's surprised expression, Jake knew he felt the vibrations, too. Guards rushed forward. The muzzle of an AK-47 poked into Jake's side.

"Wait!" Battista ordered. He didn't want to break the link with the object. Jake understood; the sensation was mesmerizing. The guards backed away.

The obelisk warmed to Jake's touch, and one by one, the etched images and symbols on its surface vanished, sucked into its inky blackness as if they had never existed. The small square in its center was the only remaining blemish in the polished surface. It shifted upward, protruding from the device.

Battista maintained his grip on Jake's wrists. He leaned forward for a closer look. The object rose upward, revealing itself to be another upside-down pyramid—a duplicate mini. Jake had hoped to reach out for it and run like hell. He couldn't do that with Battista so close at hand.

The mini rose until it was several inches above the table, hovering at eye level. Gasps from the men around Jake filled the room. Several of them stepped backward. Battista gazed at it, his eyes filled with wonder.

The tiny pyramid righted itself and spun slowly on its axis. Jake caught faint glimpses of geometric symbols and numbers appearing randomly across its surface, only to fade away with each spin. He'd seen it before; it reminded him of the Magic 8 Ball he had when he was a kid. A distant part of his mind wondered if Battista could pull the same memory from his twisted childhood.

The mini spun faster, its edges blurring like a hypnotist's charm. Jake allowed himself to be pulled in by its allure. He knew what was coming. This time Battista would learn the truth for himself. Which was fine with Jake. As long as the terrorist leader was occupied, none of the guards were likely to plug Jake full of holes.

His scalp tingled and his hair lifted from static electricity. Jake braced himself.

A dark beam of light shot from the tip of the pyramid into Jake's forehead. Battista's, too.

Their heads whipped backward from the contact. To Jake it felt like his head was being overfilled with air, ready to burst. The black beam probed every corner of his brain; a flash of numbers, data, and images invaded his mind. He relaxed into it, comforted by the knowledge that Battista would be terrified by the experience. The man might be a master strategist, but his brain hadn't been prepped by a freak accident in an MRI. Jake drifted in a black void of streaming information. It felt as if every neuron in his brain fired simultaneously in response to the massive exchange of data between him and the pyramid.

Suddenly, an additional presence joined in the exchange. Not from the pyramid. From...*above*! Its existence froze the marrow in Jake's bones. Battista gasped. His hands twitched around Jake's wrists, trying to pull away. The object wouldn't allow it. Rivulets of blood leaked from Battista's bulging eyes.

It all happened in a brief instant of time, and over just as fast. The link broke, Battista sagged to the floor, and Jake snapped the mini from the air.

Time stretched. The guards moved forward with underwater slowness. Jake staggered backward. The moment he broke contact with the primary obelisk, it triggered the chain reaction that he knew would follow. A heavy throbbing emanated from deep inside. The ground shook. Keyboards and pens danced on desktops. A high-pitched vibration echoed through the building and assaulted Jake's nervous system. The mini grew warm in his palm as it counteracted the effect. The men surrounding him weren't so lucky. They stood frozen in place by the oscillating sound. The rapid rise and fall of their chests was the only sign they were alive. Their eyes were filled with fear. After what he'd just discovered, Jake shared the emotion tenfold.

The pyramid rose out of the floor, hovering as its miniature offspring had before. It righted itself and began to spin, picking up speed with each rotation. Jake shuffled backward. The obelisk spun faster, its visage blurred to a black void in the center of the space. A mini tornado of dust and sand from the floor swirled into a vortex beneath it. The warbling vibration reverberated off the walls and rose even higher in pitch.

There was a crackling buzz, and a laser column of blinding light burst from the top of the spinning mass. It burned through the ceiling and into the sky. Jake raised his hand against the intense brightness. He squeezed his eyes closed. There was a deafening whoop and a rush of wind that popped his ears.

The ground stopped shaking and the room fell silent.

Jake opened his eyes. Dust and debris flittered within a column of sunlight that spilled through a perfectly smooth circle in the ceiling. The obelisk was on its way back to its makers.

Panic took over. Jake spun to leave. He startled when Battista latched onto his ankle. The terrorist leader had been spared the paralysis from the obelisk, but it had nevertheless taken a serious toll. The sheikh's brain hadn't been able to handle it. The capillaries in his eyes had burst, and blood stained his cheeks. He appeared close to death. His grip weakened.

"I—I saw it," he muttered. "Everything you said was true. The end. It's coming."

A shiver squeezed Jake's spine. *Much sooner than we thought,* he realized.

"Allah, forgive me," Battista muttered. His breaths were ragged. He looked up at Jake. Beneath the reddened eyes, the bloody face, and the horrible scar, a sudden awareness washed over the man. Jake pushed past his hatred, and for the first time ever, it felt as if the two men connected as human beings. "I doubt even you can save us," Battista rasped. His voice grew faint. Jake drew closer. Battista's damaged brain allowed him one final breath. "Ahmed...please protect him."

The sheikh folded to the floor. The guards stirred.

Four minutes.

Jake sprinted for the rear exit.

The tree line was four hundred yards away. No human had ever broken the three-minute mile, but to get beyond the two-mile blast radius, Jake had to do it in two minutes.

Twice.

Through a jungle.

Jake poured it on. He burst across the field, sucking energy from the mini. The burning pain from the bullet in his shoulder didn't slow him. He flashed on the six hundred thousand people who drank water from the Silver Lake Reservoir. Lives depended on speed.

He raced through the compound and onto the grass perimeter. He pushed hard past the smoking remains of the CV-22 gunship.

Jake was twenty paces from the trees when his heart gave out. He grabbed his chest, lost his footing, and tumbled forward. The momentum from his speed caused him to roll over and over. A bone in his leg snapped; he barely noticed it. The searing pain in his chest filled his senses. He drew in a breath, but oxygen no longer existed. He clung desperately to consciousness, unwilling to accept that his final moments had finally caught up with him. Images flashed across his mind. He thought of his mom, his sister, and the anguish that his passing would cause. Of Marsh, Tony, Lacey, and the others. Of darling Sarafina.

The measure of a man's life can be weighed by the love of those he leaves behind.

Finally, he thought of Francesca. He embraced the tenderness of her smile, the warmth of her spirit, and the hope of the child she carried.

Jake rolled onto his back. He squinted against the brightness of the sun. His hands clutched at his chest. Failure engulfed him. His heart faltered. It beat once, twice...

Gripping pain.

The sky darkened. He felt the odd sense of spinning within a tornado. Dust swirled around him.

Then blackness.

Chapter 79

Above the Venezuelan rain forest

FRANCESCA COULDN'T BELIEVE IT WAS HAPPENING AGAIN.
The aircraft hugged the canopy of the rain forest. Every passing second increased the distance between her and the man she loved.

"There's no turning back," she said. She clutched Sarafina to her chest. The child's small frame shivered.

"No," Tony agreed. He sat beside her and wrapped an arm around her. "Jake knew that when he jumped. He did it for you. For all of us."

She nodded.

"He was the only one who could stop Battista," Marshall said. He and Lacey sat across from them.

Lacey leaned forward and placed a hand on Francesca's knee. "Don't give up hope. Jake has gotten out of tighter fixes than this, remember?"

Francesca caught a fleeting glance between Tony and Marshall. They knew better. So did she. She'd overheard them whispering about the bomb, something they obviously hadn't mentioned to Lacey yet. Francesca faced the truth: Jake had no chance of leaving the jungle alive. Her hand went to her belly. She leaned her head against Tony's shoulder and stared at nothing.

* * *

Tony wrapped his arms around Francesca and Sarafina. Melissa did the same with their own children. She nodded to her husband.

A glance from Becker told Tony the Aussie shared the silent sentiment. Josh's head rested on Becker's lap, with Max curled beside him. Across from Tony, Marshall whispered something to Lacey. Her eyes went wide and she sagged into his embrace. Her shoulders shook. Marshall's eyes glistened.

Tony blew out a long breath. He glanced out the porthole as a twin CV-22 pulled up in wing formation beside them. It had taken a while for the plane to catch up. It held the team that had provided the diversion at the opposite end of the camp. The third Osprey—a gunship—had been shot down. Kenny's experimental drones flew high overhead, cloaking them from Venezuelan radar.

They were headed away from the camp—and his closest friend—at top speed. They needed to be as far away as possible when the nuke went off. He checked his watch.

Thirty seconds.

In a blaze of glory, thought Tony. You wanted to make a difference before you died, Jake? Well, you sure as hell did that, pal.

Chapter 80

USA Today: WASHINGTON (AP)—*The source of the nuclear explosion in the Venezuelan rain forest remains a mystery. The Venezuelan government continues to block efforts by the international community to inspect the site, blaming American clandestine forces for the unprovoked attack. The president of Iran was quick to register his support.*

Redondo Beach, California
Two weeks later

IT WAS MIDAFTERNOON ON A TUESDAY. THERE WERE FEWER than a dozen people at Naja's waterfront bar. A marine layer shrouded the sky.

Tony watched as Lacey weaved through the tables, a pitcher of beer balanced easily on a tray over her shoulder. The server was on a break, so she'd handled it herself. It rekindled memories of Sam's bar—where it had all begun.

"Just like old times," Marshall said when she placed the pitcher on the table. Then his face clouded over. "Well...not really."

Lacey filled his empty mug and motioned questioningly at Tony.

"Bud?" he asked.

"Longboard Lager," she said. "Jake's favorite."

Tony nodded and held out his mug. So did Becker, Cal, and Kenny. She filled them.

Becker tipped his mug at the pilots. "Thanks for being there, mates," he said.

They clinked glasses. "Anytime," Cal said.

"We'd never have found you if it weren't for Max," Kenny said.

Josh's guide dog truly lived up to his purpose. The GPS chip embedded under his skin led the rescue team right to their doorstep.

Francesca had both hands wrapped around a wineglass. It was still full. She and Sarafina were leaving tomorrow, returning to her home in Venice. It was safe now that Battista was gone. When they'd first returned from the jungle, the man Jake referred to as Doc had insisted that she undergo a battery of tests. He hadn't provided much of an explanation as to why. It had something to do with his concern over the drug she'd received in Mexico. Better safe than sorry. In any case, they'd given her—and her unborn child—a clean bill of health.

It had been a difficult week for all of them. In the end, it was Doc's intervention that got them off the hook. The man had some serious connections. Of course, they'd had a lot of explaining to do. After the debriefing, they'd been forced to sign strict nondisclosure agreements. The terms were simple: Reveal the truth, go to prison.

Afterward, a lot of lies had been thrown at the press, sprinkled with enough truth to make them plausible. Doc had also used his influence to pay a debt owed to Papa. The former soldier was given a military burial with full honors and benefits. In addition to a nomination for a posthumous medal and folded American flag, his wife, Carmen, had been granted a full pension. That had been a nice touch, Tony thought. And well deserved.

Jake's service had been more subdued. No body. No ashes. No fanfare. Just the way he would have liked it.

Tony held his mug in the air. "To the best man I've ever known," he said. "To Jake!"

The others clinked their mugs and glasses against his. "To Jake."

Epilogue

FOX News: LOS ANGELES (AP)—*Health officials discounted the recent rumors regarding contaminates in the Los Angeles water supply as a publicity hoax by a Mexican bottled water company. Its products have been banned in the States, and the local water has been declared safe to drink.*

Area 52

THE WORLD WAS IN FOG. AN EVER-CHANGING KALEIDOSCOPE of memories flashed across Jake's consciousness. He grasped at one. It slipped away, replaced by another, and then another. His limbs were lead. His fingers, toes, and eyelids wouldn't respond to his commands. Was he paralyzed? Or was this death? If so, the priests had been right after all. There was a hell.

He felt detached sensations of pain radiating from his left shoulder and right leg. There was tightness in his chest. Signs of life. He wondered if he should welcome them or shove them aside.

"How's he doing?" someone said.

The voice was familiar. The swirl of images in Jake's mind settled on that of a man holding a meerschaum pipe.

Doc...

Jake tried to speak, but his lips wouldn't move. His mind cried out. He needed to tell Doc what he'd learned from the obelisk.

"Vitals are steady," another voice said. "I've noticed a slight increase in brain activity."

"According to the medical team, that's to be expected," Doc said. "Residual activity can continue for quite a while in cases like this."

"So there's really no hope?"

"Not unless you believe in miracles, son. But don't blame yourself. You did an outstanding job of keeping his body alive when you picked him up. And we gave him a new heart because we owed him that much. But a body—a brain—can only take so much."

The hell with that! Jake shouted in his mind. *I'm right here, dammit.*

"You sure he didn't say anything else when you found him?" Doc asked.

"Sorry, sir," the man replied. "After we defibbed him, he was only conscious for a few minutes. He told us about the chemical at the Silver Lake Reservoir and that the antidote had been injected into Ms. Fellini. It was nonsensical mumbles after that, right up until he went comatose."

Jake remembered. He'd awakened in a CV-22. A medic had revived him.

"Just mumbles?" Doc asked. "Nothing specific?"

"Well, there *was* one thing," the medic said. "But I'm sure it was nothing."

"Spit it out, son." Doc sounded anxious. "What did he say?"

"He kept repeating, 'They're here, they're here...'"

Author's Note

I HOPE YOU ENJOYED READING *THE ENEMY OF MY ENEMY* AS much as I did writing it. If so, it would be great if you left a comment on the Amazon Customer Reviews page. I'd love to hear from you!

Are you ready to find out what happens next to Jake and his friends? *Beyond Judgment, Brainrush 3* is now available. You can read the first chapter at the end of this book. Or, if you're reading this on your Kindle, visit the detail page on Amazon.com.

Happy reading,
Richard Bard

Acknowledgments

’D LIKE TO RECOGNIZE ALL OF THE WONDERFUL PEOPLE ON THE Thomas & Mercer team. To the folks on the Author Relations & Marketing teams, especially Jacque and Danielle, to those on the editing team, no less than five of which had a hand in fine-tuning Jake's story, and especially to senior editor Alan Turkus, whose enthusiasm for the Brainrush series brought me into the fold—a heartfelt and sincere thanks for all that you've done. It's an honor to work with you.

Writing is done in solitude. But a good story is created with the support of many. I offer my sincere gratitude to:

My family and friends, whose encouragement kept me motivated. Thanks, Mom, for always insisting that I can do anything I set my mind to.

To the "Feel the Rush" team—my daughter, Danielle, and her boyfriend, David, who manage the promotions, newsletters, and so much more. I could never have done it without you.

To the accomplished team of instructors at UCLA Extension Writers' Program, including Lisa Cron, Linda Palmer, and Claire Carmichael. Your insight transformed me from a "wannabe" to a "maybe" author. Special thanks to instructor and *USA Today* best-selling author Rebecca Forster, who steered me to the best writing-hole coffee shop at the beach and has since become my favorite sounding board.

To my editor, Elyse Dinh-McCrillis. The depth of your research and attention to detail never cease to amaze me. Editing is a mysterious and crucial art that only a few can master. Now I know why you are known as the "Edit Ninja."

To my agent, Scott Miller, and the entire team at Trident Media Group. Thanks for taking a chance with a new kid on the block. The best is yet to come.

I'm also thankful for the active imaginations of all the readers who enjoyed Jake's first adventure. Writing is a collaborative effort. I create the weave, but you fill in the blanks. You paint the scenes with your mind and bring the characters to life. And it's your willingness to suspend disbelief that breathes life into the story. Thank you very much for your many encouraging e-mails and reviews. They mean the world to this new author.

And finally, to my amazing wife, Milan. It's all meaningless without you. All my love, all my life…

Beyond Judgment
Brainrush 3

Chapter 1: Haunting Eyes

Le Focette, Marina di Pietrasanta, Italy

HE HAD NO PAST. BUT THE FUTURE HELD PROMISE.

The woman seated across from him was in her late twenties. An American tourist who'd blushed when they'd met. Her Italian was broken. Her alluring curves and inviting smile had inspired him. A sip from her cappuccino left a thin line of foam on her upper lip. It disappeared behind a slow lick of her tongue. Her eyes never left his.

They sat at an outdoor café and *ristorante* in *Le Focette,* a quiet Tuscan enclave situated a block from the beach resorts of the Mediterranean Sea. It was a warm and sunny afternoon. A salty breeze stirred the thick canopy of trees overhead. A dislodged pine nut bounced from a *Cinzano* umbrella beside their table and skittered to the ground. He picked it up. He wore an open linen shirt, casual slacks, and a three-day stubble. His skin was tan.

"They used to serve these at the outdoor cinema down the street," he said in Italian. Her expression told him she hadn't understood. He brushed off the nut and popped it in his mouth. "Mmmm...*buono!*" he said.

Her eyes widened. He winked. She smiled.

"*Bella,*" he said. His hand padded the air as a signal to hold the pose. The pastel stick in his other hand moved swiftly across the canvas. She blushed. It was his turn to smile. He wondered if she would be the one.

The café was filling up for lunch. A group of local teens crowded around their customary tables not far from his corner. Two of the boys strummed guitars. The rest chatted with an infectious effervescence. A middle-aged couple sat nearby. German, he thought, judging from their stiff demeanor. That would change after they'd been in the area a few more days. The magic would set in: The easy pace. The food. The friendly smiles. Impossible to resist.

He switched sticks, working a blend of colors into her luminescent eyes. There was eagerness in her stare. It stirred him. His movements were automatic. His brain orchestrated a talent that he'd discovered when he'd awakened four months ago. The doctor who cared for him told him his name was Lorenzo Ferrari. Everyone called him Renzo.

His mind wandered but his strokes didn't falter. The closer the portrait was to completion, the faster the pastel stick moved. As if it had a life of its own. The doctor had told him what little he knew. Renzo had been wheeled in by an anxious, young American man. Renzo had been unconscious. His skin hung loose on his 180-centimeter frame. His muscles had atrophied. Money had changed hands, a room in a local *pensione* had been leased, and the doctor had accepted the assignment of restoring the patient's health. The American had left in a rush, leaving final instructions for Renzo in a sealed envelope.

The hiss of the *latte* steamer brought his attention back to the sketch. When he took in the final image his shoulders slumped. The portrait was perfect in every detail—except for the eyes. They belonged to someone else. Instead of sky blue like the girl's seated across from him, they were liquid chocolate, filigreed with rings of gold dust. They were penetrating. The girl sat forward. "Is it ready?" she asked in broken Italian.

"No," he said, flipping his art tablet closed.

She frowned.

"I must apologize," he said. "I'm having an off day." He pushed his chair back as if to leave.

"Wait," she said softly. Her hands reached out and cupped one of his. Her touch was tender. Her gaze was an invitation. "I go with you?"

Renzo faltered. How long had it been? Longer than he could remember—like everything else. She was beautiful. And his *pensione* was only a block away. All he had to do was ignore the feelings of guilt. His free hand absently patted the pocket of his slacks. The wrinkled envelope from the American was there—his only link to the past. The hastily-scrolled message had been brief:

Trust no one. Lives hinge on your ability to remain anonymous.

Surely, this young woman posed no risk, he thought. He was torn.

The decision was made for him when he noticed two men stop short on the opposite side of the street. One of them stared his way. The other had a hand to his ear. He seemed to be speaking to himself. They were dressed in casual clothes. But Renzo's artist's gaze narrowed at the incongruence of the matching pair of rubber-soled shoes and dark glasses. The hand dropped from the man's ear and a whisper was exchanged. They started toward him.

A buried instinct set off alarms in Renzo's head. He rose. His chair toppled, the girl yelped, and the tablet fell from his lap. The pages fanned on the way down and a corner of his mind saw the same pair of brown eyes staring back at him from each portrait.

They all shouted the same command in his mind:

Run!

He shouldered through the woody hedge beside the table. Brambles caught on his shirt. He pushed through, shredding his skin. Angry shouts behind him. A girl's scream. Rapid footfalls. He raced down the tree-studded lane, thankful for the snug fit of his running shoes. He headed inland. Past villas, the old church, and the rows of stone counters that had supported the fish market for a hundred years. The *pineta* was four blocks ahead. They'd never track him through the myriad of paths in the forty-acre forest. He filled his lungs with the pine-scented air and dashed toward it. He knew the men behind him wouldn't be able to keep up. He'd yet to meet anyone that could. Sure, Renzo had memory issues, but his physical rehabilitation had revealed that he had remarkable endurance—thanks to a heart that the doctor had proclaimed a miracle of science. According to him it had been formerly owned by a seventeen-year old female athlete.

He wondered at his instinctual decision to flee the café. He didn't doubt the validity of the command generated by his subconscious. But he wished he could pull up the memories that prompted it. Perhaps it was the assuredness of the movements from the two men. Even behind their dark glasses, he'd sensed the spark of recognition in their expressions.

Lives hinge on your ability to remain anonymous.

He hungered for answers, but only questions were served: Who were they? What did they want with him? Did they know where he lived?

Renzo was a block from the pineta when a car careened from a side street to block his path. Doors opened. Three men exited. They had the same feel as the two behind him. They held silenced weapons. The flush of adrenaline triggered a doubling of his heart rate, fueling his muscles. He jinked to the right between two villas. Bullets hammered into the limestone walls behind him—and the question of what they wanted was answered.

Chips pelted his trousers. A ricocheted round spun past his ear with a hornet's buzz. Terror filled his gut. He leapt a stone wall and wound a serpentine trail through gates and yards and streets. The solitude of the woodland was no longer an option. But maybe the anonymity of a crowd would provide an escape. The beach was dead ahead.

He twisted through traffic across the four-lane coastal road. Cars skidded, scooters dodged and motorists shouted. Renzo ignored them. He sped across a gravel parking lot, through a busy open-air *trattoria*, past a row of private cabanas and showers, and onto the sand. There was no sign of his pursuers.

Each section of white-sand beach was privately owned, passed down one generation to the next, demarked by the color and style of the umbrellas and lounge chairs that extended in neat rows to the water. It was packed with tourists, in large part because of the influx of college students visiting during Spring break. Renzo kicked off his shoes, removed his torn shirt, and plopped himself in their midst. He was shaken. He dug his hands and feet into the warm sand, searching in vain for the familiar calm that the act usually brought. Two bikini-clad girls offered an approving stare. He was accustomed to the attention, more for his tan physique than his crooked smile. He forced a wink. They giggled. He blew out a breath and sank deeper into the sand. He needed time to think.

"*Ciao*, Renzo!" a man shouted.

He recognized the voice before he turned around. It was the *bagnino*, Paolo, responsible for this stretch of beach. The fifty-year-old, pot-bellied lifeguard was a bronze fixture who always had a kind word. Unfortunately, he also loved to hear the sound of his own voice. Once he started talking, it was impossible to get him to stop. He waved as he approached.

"Another run today?" the man asked in his booming voice.

Tourists turned their way. Paolo appreciated an audience.

"It's a wonderful day!" the lifeguard proclaimed, his arms outstretched as if to soak in the sun.

So much for blending in, Renzo thought. He rose and glanced nervously about. A man with dark glasses and familiar rubber-soled shoes stared back at him from the trattoria. His hand was to an ear. His lips moved urgently.

Renzo took off. The bagnino shouted behind him, "Renzo, you forgot your shoes, your shirt!"

He hit the wet sand that was his daily running track and poured on speed. One familiar resort after another passed in a blur. His plan was simple. He wouldn't stop running until he came abreast of the police station in Forte dei Marmi. Renzo needed help. After four months in hiding, remaining anonymous was no longer an option.

He was nearly there when he saw the girl from the café. She blocked his path. So did the two men that gripped either of her arms. The girl tried to act natural, but her fear was palpable. She was a hostage, not an accomplice. The men's deportment left no doubt of the deadly consequences of noncooperation. A big part of him screamed to keep running. To put the two men and the girl that he had only just met behind him. But he could not. Amnesia or not, a man's character doesn't change. He stopped.

The men were all business. They had crew cuts and chiseled features. The taller one appeared in charge. He removed his glasses. He had angry dark eyes and a boxer's crooked nose. Through tight lips he said, "You for the girl." The words were English. Renzo didn't understand.

"*Cosa?*" he said.

The man's eyes narrowed. He seemed surprised. He switched to Italian. "We trade you for the girl," he said. His Italian was good, but Renzo caught the trace of a German accent.

The girl's expression pleaded.

"Let her go first," Renzo said.

The man stiffened, as if unaccustomed to conditional surrenders. He scanned his surroundings with military precision. "We make the exchange in the parking lot."

Where it will be easy to stuff us into a car and kill us later with no fanfare, Renzo thought. No thanks. He considered his options, grateful that the physical trainer hired by the doctor had included martial arts in his regimen. The movements had seemed natural to him. He remembered wondering if his muscles held memories that his brain could not.

Renzo pointed to a ping-pong table by the showers. It was still in view of the crowded beach but only a step or two from the walkway leading to the parking area. "We walk together to that point," he said. "Then she goes free."

The second man nodded to the first and they escorted the girl up the beach. Renzo followed, recalling the key weakness that his trainer had identified in his fighting skills. *No killer instinct*, he'd said. *Stick to running.*

That was his plan.

The walkway between the beach and the parking lot was lined on either side by rows of cabanas. The first two were bathroom stalls. The men turned to face him. Their grips tightened on the girl's arm. She winced. The leader inched up the hem of his polo shirt to reveal the pistol tucked at his waist. "Any tricks and she dies," he said.

The girl's breathing quickened. Renzo nodded. He readied himself. The leader motioned to his subordinate.

The man shoved the girl into the first stall. "Not a sound," he growled as he closed the door behind her. Her soft whimper was filled with relief. Renzo could imagine her huddled into a ball beside the toilet, watching their shadows through the slats in the door. Both men turned to face him.

"Let's go," the leader said.

The girl was safe for the moment, Renzo thought. The sooner he and the two men turned the corner into the parking lot, the sooner she could slip away. He allowed himself to be taken. Each man grabbed an arm.

They stopped when they reached the graveled lot. The leader's gaze panned the area. The black BMW that had blocked Renzo's path earlier was parked by the entrance. Its motor idled. The driver nodded. His hand went to the dash and the sedan's trunk popped open.

My coffin, Renzo realized with a start. There was no one else around. They would kill him here and dump him later. The men tightened their grip and walked him forward. But instead of responding with tension, Renzo relaxed his muscles—as he'd been taught. The subconscious reaction of the men holding him was instinctual. They relaxed as well.

He sagged, allowing his dead weight to pull at the men's grip. They held on with angry grunts and yanked upward. In the same instant Renzo combined his force with theirs by springing into a back flip. Grips gave way. Renzo turned to run. But instead of freedom, he found himself staring down the barrel of a silenced weapon. It was wielded by a third man who had followed them down the walkway. A wisp of smoke leaked from the muzzle—and Renzo knew that the girl was dead.

"*Bastardo,*" he gasped. The other two spun him around.

"You're fast," the leader said. He pressed his own pistol against Renzo's chest. "But experience trumps speed every t—"

He cut off when the horn sounded from the waiting sedan. A van filled with bobbing heads drove into the lot. It was followed by a man on a scooter. Guns disappeared. A door slid open on the van and a family of six piled out. Two of the youngest children jumped up and down with enthusiasm. The leader patted Jake on the back as if they were old pals. He whispered, "They will die unless you get in the car." Renzo could barely breathe past the rage he felt over the death of the girl. But he didn't doubt the truth of the man's words. He allowed himself to be ushered toward the sedan.

The scooter idled under the shadows of a tree. The rider wore an oversized helmet that looked odd above the shorts and polo that revealed thin arms and bony knees. The tinted helmet visor hid his face. His head tilted to one side as if he was taking in the scene. Renzo willed him to leave for his own safety. The man didn't budge.

The two thugs walked on either side of Renzo. The one that had killed the girl moved ahead of them. He opened the rear passenger door, motioning for Renzo to get in. But Renzo's attention was still on the scooter driver. It appeared as though the man stared directly at him from behind his visor. His helmeted head shook slowly from side to side as if warning him not to enter the car. But a firm hand on Renzo's lower back reminded him that he had little choice. He glanced over his shoulder. The family had gathered their beach bags. They were walking toward the sand. The kids ran ahead.

The sudden whine of the scooter sent a shock of tension through the men surrounding him. The bike raced toward them. The rider had flipped up his visor. His teeth were bared, his eyes narrowed, and he held a dark object in an outstretched hand. The German's reached for their guns.

Renzo cried out, "Noooo!" The young rescuer didn't stand a chance. Renzo stomped the instep of the man to his left. The German folded to one knee with a surprised grunt. Ducking to avoid the leader's fist, Renzo countered with an upper cut that smashed his nose. Cartilage cracked. Blood flowed. He turned to face the third man when out of the corner of his eye he saw his would-be rescuer fling the object. An instant later there were twin spits from within the car. The helmeted rider was thrown backwards to the gravel.

The object arced toward Renzo in a wobbling spiral. It looked like a small pyramid.

He felt a tingling sensation in his forehead.

About the Author

RICHARD BARD WAS BORN in Munich, Germany to American parents, and joined the US Air Force like his father. But when he was diagnosed with cancer and learned he had only months to live, he left the service. He earned a management degree from the University of Notre Dame and ultimately ran three successful companies involving advanced security products used by US embassies and governments worldwide. Now a full-time writer, he lives in Redondo Beach, California, with his wife, and remains in excellent health.